COLLARED

Imprisoned by Artificial Intelligence

MICHAEL EDGAR MARTIN

This is a work of fiction. Names, characters, and events are the products of the author's imagination. Any resemblance to actual persons, living or dead, or actual events is purely coincidental.

Cover design by Scott Stortz

ISBN 978-1-953058-39-3

Published by Butler Books
www.butlerbooks.com

In memory of my father and mother,
whose life stories were more fascinating
than any story I could imagine.

1

"Why doesn't that asshole just pass me?" Walter mumbled as he glanced at the screen in the middle of the dashboard, which showed a beat-up, faded green pickup truck behind them. "He's been following us since we got off the freeway, and he keeps getting closer. I don't like it."

"Give it some more juice and see if he keeps up," Ted, the guard riding with him, suggested without showing any particular concern.

Their armored truck kicked up dust as it rumbled along at 45 mph on the nearly deserted eastbound road toward the Arizona-New California State Prison, commonly known as the State Line Prison because it was just on the New California side of the boundary between the two states. The road was flat and perfectly straight for miles, as one would expect in the middle of the desert the two states shared.

Inside the truck cab were a uniformed driver and a guard, both employees of London Tower, a private prison system contracted jointly by Arizona and New California to incarcerate individuals found guilty of a felony in either state. The State Line Prison was the first in a planned series of high-tech institutions that London Tower promised would be more cost-efficient.

In the back was a single prisoner whom they were transferring from the San Diego county jail to the State Line Prison.

"Okay, let's see what happens." Walter gradually increased the pressure on the accelerator. With an increasingly louder whine, the motor began working harder as their speed increased: 50, 55, 60, 65 mph. Walter had to focus on the road to keep the truck from veering onto the narrow and hardly visible soft shoulder. Both his hands gripped the steering wheel firmly. But his expression was more of anger than of fear.

"He's still right behind us. Guy looks like he's singing," Ted noted coolly.

Suddenly Walter jerked the steering wheel to the left, but he failed to miss a pothole momentarily obscured by blowing sand. Taking his foot off the accelerator and tapping the brake to maintain control, he quickly dropped to 50 mph. Ted took his eyes off the screen as he bounced in his seat and his shoulder hit the truck door.

"Whew, that was a big one!" Ted shouted in pleasured excitement, as if on a roller coaster.

Of course, potholes on this road weren't a big surprise. The road was in a poor state of repair; repairs of desolate roads simply weren't a high priority for the New California Highway Department.

"Looks like our green friend hit it too . . . and he's turning onto a gravel road," Walter said with a sigh as he brought the truck's speed back to the 45 mph limit.

"So this is your final run out here, huh, Walter?" Ted turned to his left and eyed the man in the driver's seat, who now had drops of glistening perspiration on his forehead. Ted had a menacing appearance, made all the more so by a two-day growth of coarse black facial hair. Too much time munching on chips while planted in front of a big-screen TV, along with a job that seldom required walking more than 50 yards at a time, had produced a belly that hung over his belt and made it difficult for him to draw out his Taser. With just one prisoner in the back of the truck, it was unlikely he would have to use it today anyway.

"Yup, unless there's another inmate we have to transport out here in the next week. With the slowdown in business, that don't seem likely."

"I hear that, Walter. Not sure if crime is going down, if they're not as successful in arresting the punks, or if the judges are just getting lax in sentencing people to serious time."

"Probably some of all three, plus the big hole in the state budget. This prison is supposed to save money compared to the old ones, but it still can't be cheap." Walter pulled an oil-stained handkerchief from his pocket and wiped the back of his neck. "They don't want to put guys in prison unless they're in the news and the public will be PO'd if they're back on the street."

Walter kept looking from side to side and glancing in the rearview center screen, still wary of someone following or about to pull out in front. If there were ever a place for an old-style Western ambush, this was certainly it.

"You know, Ted," Walter said, "we're kinda lucky this prison is out in the desert. Otherwise we might have lost our jobs some time ago."

"How do you figure?" Ted cocked his head and stared at Walter.

"In the city and on major roads, there's lots of traffic. Self-driving works just fine in avoiding accidents there. But if some bad guy is going to try to spring a prisoner en route to a prison, he's not likely to try it in the city or on a major highway."

"Too many potential witnesses and cops," Ted said.

"Right. If you wanted to bust out a prisoner or rob an armored car, where would you do it? Probably in some lonely, out-of-the-way place."

"You mean like this road. We've only seen that one pickup in the past couple of miles." Ted paused and thought for a moment. "I still don't understand why we'd be out of a job."

"Well, just think about it," Walter said. "That guy was following us, and I gave it some more juice. We were doing 20 over the limit. Do you think self-driving would do that? Or suppose some car pulls out right now and blocks the road. What would I do?"

"Don't slow down; get around him as best you could." Seemed to Ted like a simple question with an obvious answer.

"Even if we clipped his fender?"

"Sure. You don't want to stop out here. A little damage to the truck is a fair price to pay to avoid getting shot."

Walter nodded. "But those tech guys designed the self-driving gizmo to avoid accidents. So if we had the truck in self-driving mode, it would automatically jam on the brakes and come to a stop to avoid a bent fender or anyone getting hurt. And the ambushers would have an easy time busting out the guy in the back. Those tech guys just haven't figured out a way for self-driving to know the difference between a real accident to be avoided and an 'accident' that's being staged."

"Or to outrun some singing idiot who's tailgating us," Ted

said. "I see what you mean. So London Tower needs us to manually drive this lonely stretch. I never thought of that. I always thought you wanted to drive because you're better at missing the potholes."

"Thanks, but I'm not sure about that," Walter replied as the truck bounced over some broken asphalt. "Ted, I'm guessing it won't be long until they do figure out a way for self-driving to make that decision, and when they do, they won't need any drivers and might not need any guards either. So I'm glad they're offering early retirement to some of us now."

"Which retirement package did you take?" Ted asked, hoping that London Tower would make him a similar offer before long.

"I'm taking the 54 weeks at half wages. The wife was thinking that 112 weeks at quarter wages was better, but the way things are going, you don't know what's going to be happening a year from now. Two years from now? Anyone's guess. So I thought, better to get the money sooner."

"Yeah, that makes sense."

"So who do we have in the back?" Walter asked, shifting the conversation back to the job at hand. "Just another geek who thought he could get away with robbing a bank from the outside?" He chuckled. "You know, I can always spot a cyber thief in a truckload of convicts. He's the wimp. All you have to do is bark at him and he'll cower in a corner."

"Not this guy; I don't think he's the computer whiz bank robber type." Ted made eye contact with Walter to let him know he wasn't just making conversation. "He seems pretty cocky and not likely to back down from a fight, at least that's the impression he gave me when they transferred him from the jail to the back of this mobile sweatbox. I wouldn't let your guard down, Walt. Besides, he can't be more than 25, and he's in good shape. He could probably beat your brains in, even wearing those shackles."

"Okay, I'll keep that in mind. I don't want to cash my first early retirement check from a hospital bed."

They drove on for a couple more miles and then turned left onto the entrance road to the prison. Unlike traditional prisons, this one had no guard shack at the gate. Walter simply slipped his and Ted's ID cards into the reader. The first barrier came down and a computerized voice told them to drive up onto the blue pad and turn off all electronics on the truck. They did so and waited for almost two minutes as the truck was scanned.

Walter and Ted had no idea what the scanner was checking. In fact, very few people outside of an elite group of London Tower programmers and administrators knew what it scanned.

A pleasant chime indicated the scan was complete, the barrier came down, and the computer voice said they should now drive the 300 yards up to the building entrance and park on the green pad.

The prison structure had no windows visible from the road. Constructed of concrete, it was a single story with the exception of the second-floor administrative and control offices in the center of the structure. This second floor had some windows, with awnings that could be rolled out. On the roof were solar panels at least 12 feet high that rotated and angled automatically to capture the direct rays of the sun. Someone who didn't know the building's purpose might have assumed that it was a warehouse and that they were looking at the back of it.

There was no landscaping to speak of, just some crushed

rock along the base of the wall. Here and there, scraggly desert weeds were poking through, trying to make this their home.

Ted knew the routine, and before Walter had brought the truck to a full stop on the green pad, he was already opening his door. A prison guard was standing at the back of the truck. Both he and Ted put their cards in the reader and then pressed the button reading **UNLOCK**. The back door to the truck opened.

Blinded by the sun that was directly in line with the opening door, the prisoner, Mykola Steinman, tried to shield his eyes with his hands, but the shackles wouldn't let him raise his arms any higher than his shoulders. The best he could do was bend over and look at the ground.

The guard gave Ted an electronic receipt for the prisoner. Ted and Walter's day was done, with the exception of the 165-mile drive back to the company transport depot. It would be a few more mind-numbing hours for Ted and Walter, but at least without a prisoner in back, Walter could put it in self-driving mode and wait to get there. They departed, leaving a plume of desert dust behind.

Both Mykola and the guard were anxious to get out of the searing afternoon heat. It was a short walk to the inmate induction room, and the cool concrete floor inside provided instant relief to Mykola's feet, covered in only canvas shoes. The thin shoes were another way to discourage any prisoner from even thinking about escape, Mykola surmised.

As they walked in, the door behind them closed. The latches and deadbolts moving into locked positions produced clicks and ringing metal sounds Mykola knew he'd always remember. "Welcome to your new home," he muttered to himself sarcastically.

The room was perhaps 30 feet square. A uniformed officer, likely considered obese by contemporary standards yet tanned and well-muscled, sat behind a slightly elevated desk. On the desk were two computer monitors, one facing the officer and the other facing the chair on which Mykola was told to sit. Behind that chair were two rows of benches, probably for those times when more than one inmate was being brought in.

Still in shackles, Mykola sat down on the chair, and the guard who had brought him in stepped back.

Without looking up, the officer stated in a flat, bored tone, "You are Mykola Steinman, and you have been sentenced to seven years, to be served in this facility operated by London Tower under contract with the departments of correction of Arizona and New California. Please note the information as I read it and it appears onscreen."

As he spoke, a form appeared on the monitor and information about Mykola began to fill it in. Most of the information was similar to that entered for a new patient in a medical practice. It seemed rather pointless to Mykola to go through this information; it was all in the state's database already. He simply nodded as the information appeared on the screen.

The officer could sense that Mykola didn't much care what was on the screen. He abruptly stopped talking and pushed his dark glasses up on his nose. The sudden quiet in the room made Mykola look up at the officer.

"Hey, I'm only going to tell you this once: pay attention!" the officer said. "If there's anything wrong here, this is your only time to offer a correction."

"Well, there is one mistake . . . someone extended the length of my sentence. It's just one year, not seven years."

In the past couple of months Mykola had gone through several of these administrative procedures. To his mind, each served only to remind him of the injustice he was being forced to suffer. A bit of sarcasm was his only available method of rebellion.

"Hey, Bill, this pretty boy thinks he's clever," the officer said to the guard behind Mykola. Then, slowly leaning forward with squinted eyes focused on Mykola, he continued, "Well, it'd be easy enough for me to add a one in front of that seven, and while someone might find that change a few years from now, there's no guarantee. Since London is paid on the basis of inmate years, we don't have much incentive to find such mistakes in the records, now, do we?"

The guard behind Mykola smirked. He had heard this line from the induction officer before, but it never ceased to give him pleasure to hear it and to see an inmate's face lose all color.

"Per our contract, we have to allow you contact with people outside this facility." The officer paused, and Mykola looked up at him to confirm he was paying attention. "Accordingly, you can email up to five different people and have one hour of videoconference visits each month. I'll need the names of those five people, and we'll set up the connections. That may take a week or two."

This was a surprise to Mykola. He had heard this new prison was different from others, but he hadn't given it much thought since he'd never thought he'd actually be living here.

Mykola thought for a moment and decided that his lawyer, younger sister, father, and business partner were the ones with whom he wanted to stay in contact. He couldn't think of a fifth person he was really close to, so he just added a woman he had dated a few times before he was arrested four months earlier.

The names and email addresses were displayed on the screen, and Mykola confirmed them by tapping on their respective checkboxes.

"You gotta select the relationship," the officer said. "It's on the right side of the screen."

Mykola looked again and saw a drop-down list next to each name: ATTORNEY, BUSINESS ASSOCIATE, FAMILY MEMBER, FRIEND, HEALTH CARE PROFESSIONAL, OTHER. Again there was the temptation to test the rules, to touch OTHER for each of them. He thought about it for an instant but realized that this was all automated and he couldn't annoy a computer. The officer looking down at him certainly didn't care. Mykola pressed the appropriate relationship for each of his contacts.

"One more thing. I guess this is new; I haven't seen it before. What is your preferred language? You don't have an accent, so I assume it's English."

"That works," Mykola replied, though at the moment he couldn't figure out why this would have to be entered into the system.

"Okay, now sign on the screen."

Not wanting to worsen an already subordinate position, Mykola held back the urge to make a snide comment and signed the screen with his finger. The shackle chain on his wrists clanked.

Almost as if that signature were connected to the second door in the room, the door opened and a prison inmate entered. Mykola and the officer both turned to look at him, and the officer made the introduction with a pointed finger.

"This is Sly, and he's going to be your tour guide. He's going to explain all the rules, and you'll want to pay close attention. Failure to do so could be quite unpleasant."

The glee in "quite unpleasant" made Mykola's heart start to pound.

With that, the guard who had brought Mykola in came up behind him and told him to stand and move to a red square on the floor of the other half of the room. The guard then removed the shackles from Mykola's arms, though the leg shackles remained in place.

The shackles had rubbed his wrists raw and Mykola was relieved to have them removed, but now he wondered what came next. At least he could finally stand up straight and flex his wrists without pain.

"Take off your shirt," said the guard standing behind him.

The inmate tour guide who was now standing near the desk didn't seem at all surprised, so Mykola figured this was part of the routine. He did as he was told.

Mykola stiffened and arched his back as he felt the guard standing behind him put his hands on Mykola's bare shoulders. "Hold still, I'm going to put a collar on you," the guard said in a gruff, demanding tone. Before Mykola could respond, a polished steel ring was put around his neck, and he heard a click as it was fastened in the back. The cold metal sent a shiver down his spine despite the sweat still rolling off his chest.

Instinctively he reached up to feel the collar that was about as high as the collar on a dress shirt but as thick as a heavy turtleneck sweater. He turned his head slightly to the left and right. Then, dropping his chin, he saw that the collar had semicircular extensions that rested on his collarbone and touched his shoulder blades. This would make it virtually impossible to turn the collar around when it was fastened.

Next the guard called out the seven-digit letter and number

combination engraved on the collar, and Mykola could see the officer typing it into the computer.

"Alpha-two-six-two-four-zero-one," the officer repeated to confirm.

That done, Mykola heard another click that tightened the collar a bit more. He thought it would strangle him, but the tightening stopped as soon as the collar was firmly around his neck. Though the collar wasn't entirely comfortable, it was still much better than the shackles.

The inmate tour guide, seeing Mykola's distress, said, "Don't worry; in a few days you'll forget you have it on." He pulled down on the neck of his yellow shirt to show that he was wearing one too.

Now that the collar was on, the guard removed Mykola's leg shackles. "Okay, you can put your shirt back on," he said. Then, pointing to the tour-guide inmate: "He's all yours."

"Call me Sly," the inmate said to Mykola. "My mother gave me this name because she wanted me to grow up and be an action hero like one of the old-time actors she always admired."

Like his namesake, Sly stood about five-eight, but unlike the actor, he only weighed maybe a buck-fifty. He wasn't handsome, nor was he ugly. He had the type of face that could best be described as average.

"As you can see, it didn't work out that way for me," Sly said in a matter-of-fact way. "I imagine this address isn't what your folks had in mind for you either."

Mykola didn't know how to respond to this strange introduction, but seeing that Sly expected some sort of response from him, he simply said, "Nice to meet you too," doing his best not to sound sarcastic.

They walked out the inside door into a long hallway, and Sly closed the door behind them. The predominant color of the hallway was white: a glossy bright white that was hard on the eyes. White was the color of the walls, the ceiling, and every door. The navy gray floor was the only contrast. One would have thought there'd be smudges and handprints on the walls, but there were none. The white was pure, as if it had been painted on earlier that day. Other than a sign here and there, there was nothing on the walls to interrupt the monotony of white.

2

"I'm doing five for stealing a car and then crashing it when I tried to override the self-driving function and take it off road," Sly explained rather proudly as they walked out the door and into the facility. "How 'bout you?"

"Nothing so exciting. I got seven years for assaulting a retired cop in a parking lot after I had an argument with him in a bar," Mykola said with a note of irritation.

"Wow, sounds pretty exciting to me," Sly said in almost a whisper. Shifting his gaze up at Mykola and eyeing his lean, muscular build, he assumed the cop had gotten the worst of it.

"Yeah, it probably would have been exciting if I'd been there. Even though we had an argument in the bar, I was long gone and nowhere near the parking lot during the assault." Mykola glanced at Sly to see if he was listening. Mykola had told his story many times, and he'd become accustomed to people ignoring him. "They convicted me using footage from their security cam and facial recognition software. Hell, they keep that bar so dark it's a wonder they can distinguish the men from the women."

Sly was tempted to say that many of the other inmates had similar stories of innocence, but he recognized that continuing this conversation would probably just agitate Mykola even more. "Sorry to hear that," he said simply. "Okay, let's do the tour."

Sly began walking slowly down the mysteriously empty and quiet hallway. It seemed he was being vigilant about something, but there wasn't anyone else in the hallway or any other sound.

They'd taken a few steps when Mykola stopped and turned to face Sly with an expression of cautious mistrust. "Hey, before we do, why are you the one who is doing the tour rather than a guard?"

"Hmmm. You don't have the foggiest notion of how this prison works, do you?"

"It's a prison. There are people who wish they were somewhere else and other people who make sure they don't get their wish. Seems like an easy concept to understand," Mykola replied.

Sly didn't appreciate Mykola's condescending tone, but he assumed it was simply first-day bravado.

"Sure, it's a prison," he said, "but London Tower is in it to make money, and so they work with the state guys to reduce costs. One of the ways they do that is to use tech to replace the guards or at least most of them. They also recruit some inmates to do stuff the guards in other prisons do. That's why I have a yellow shirt; it signifies that I do some of those jobs."

Mykola took a half step back, as if Sly had just told him he had a contagious disease. "So you're a guard in an inmate's uniform? That can't sit too well with the other inmates."

Sly could see the mistrust still in Mykola's eyes, and he responded in a soft, empathetic tone. "That's what I thought too, but since us guys wearing the yellow shirts don't get to go home after a shift, we're careful not to use what limited say-so we have unless we have to. If you're constantly getting hostile with other inmates, you lose your yellow shirt."

"Hmmpf. Okay, besides getting a stylish yellow shirt and maybe some respect from inmates, is there any other incentive to do guard work?" Mykola asked. "Doesn't seem like that would be enough to get you to go from a lawbreaker to a law enforcer."

"That's easy. They also got a system of points us inmates can earn that are considered when we apply for parole. See, I'm up for parole in six months, and I earn points for doing a good job as a tour guide for new inmates."

"But how do they know you're doing a good job of giving me the tour?" Mykola asked, beginning to realize that he'd have to change his expectations of what prison life would be like.

Sly gave a "let's go" motion with his left hand, and they continued walking down the hall. He pointed with his index finger. "See that piece of round glass in the ceiling? That's a camera, or maybe a couple of them, and you'll see them all over. They watch everything that's going on."

"Sort of like that security cam in the bar," Mykola said.

"Sure, but this is what they call 'real-time,' and it's real smart. Some of the guys who understand the tech lots better than me say it was adapted from self-driving cars. The cameras look for things like guys putting things in their mouths, scuffles between prisoners, and even guys making a fist."

"Sort of ironic, isn't it? You got pinched for stealing a self-driving car, and now self-driving tech is keeping you in prison," Mykola pointed out with a wry smile.

"Funny. Let's go in here," Sly said, opening the door to what appeared to be a linen storeroom. On the table were three pairs of gray pants and three shirts with "A262401" in bold black letters outlined in reflective orange on both the front and back of the shirts and down the outside of the legs of the pants.

"Boxers or briefs? Take your pick from that shelf behind you." Sly gestured to shelves piled high with underwear, arranged by size. "And then put on a uniform. One of the guys will take the rest and put them in your cell."

Mykola did so. The pants and shirt fit fairly well. The pants had an elastic waistband: no belt or drawstring. The shirt was a pullover with loose-fitting half-length sleeves. Neither garment had pockets.

"Socks?" Mykola asked as he was taking off his shoes.

"Oh yeah, those are on the bottom shelf."

"A wonderful selection of colors and styles, I must say. So very fashionable," Mykola commented. Sly didn't pick up the cynical tone in Mykola's voice. What could he be talking about? Everything was prison gray and indistinguishable except for size and, in the case of the shirt and pants, the prisoner's ID number.

"Okay, now listen up," Sly said, looking Mykola straight in the eye. "I'm gonna tell you maybe the most important thing about surviving in this place: everyone's uniform is their own. You don't wear someone else's uniform for any reason, and you don't let anyone else wear yours."

The earnestness in Sly's voice got Mykola's attention.

"If you're caught wearing someone else's numbered uniform, you'll probably have another year added to your sentence or at the least be denied parole, even if you're not eligible for another five years. Usually they also nab the guy who the uniform really belongs to."

Mykola thought for a moment and then asked, "Nobody wants a longer sentence, but what does that have to do with surviving in here?"

"That's where the collar comes in." Sly paused dramatically, as if he were about to offer up the big reveal. "Your collar is what they use to keep you on the straight and narrow. It's got three shock levels. Level 1 is for minor stuff like not being at your assigned post on time. Most of the time the big computer makes the decision that you screwed up and triggers a jolt, but any guard or staff member can also click a button that sends you a jolt, like if they think you're not paying attention to what they're saying. You'll probably get a jolt or two in the first week. It feels like a hard slap in the face and at the same time like someone stepping on your fingers and toes. No fun for sure, but you'll live."

Mykola nodded and absentmindedly fingered his collar.

"Now, Level 2 is serious, and if you get a 2, you'll remember it. It gives you a jolt of juice that lasts longer and makes you feel the pain of your muscles cramping up. You can't move, and you'll think you're paralyzed. I've only seen a few guys get a Level 2, and it wasn't pretty. You could get a 2 for stuff like taking a steel utensil out of the kitchen or fighting with another inmate. There's a full list in the handbook; you'll want to read it."

"Sounds like torture. Does a guy recover?" Mykola tried to imagine what it might feel like. A strange and eerie sense of being under the control of someone or something he couldn't see or touch came over him.

"Of course they recover." Sly thought this was a rather naive question, but he felt obligated to provide a complete explanation.

"It wouldn't look good for the Tower if they didn't. Most are carted off to the infirmary and stay there for a few hours. No permanent injury, usually, though one guy I know who got a 2 don't seem to be right in the head now."

"Should I even ask about Level 3?" Mykola inquired half seriously, trying to hide his apprehension.

"Whether you ask or not, I've gotta tell you." Sly looked at Mykola and waited until he made eye contact. "The handbook says Level 3 is used when deadly force seems to be the only choice, like an inmate attacking a guard in the chow hall. Everyone assumes it's deadly, but it hasn't ever been used as far as I know."

"You mean it's sort of like wearing an electric chair around your neck and just waiting for someone to flip the switch?" Mykola asked in all seriousness.

"No, I don't think it's that powerful. But a guard told me that if you have a weak heart or some other medical condition, it could be deadly. I think they just put in words like 'deadly force' to discourage anyone from testing it. I sure ain't gonna test it; Level 2 is scary enough."

Mykola tried to shift his collar just to make sure it hadn't gotten any tighter around his neck. "Okay, all this makes sense, but I still don't understand what the number on my shirt and pants has to do with surviving here."

"Their system can identify most violations, but it isn't perfect," Sly explained. "I've been here pretty much since this place opened, so I know they've had some problems with it. Originally the system was all automatic, but it could either miss someone breaking the rules or 'see' a rule break that wasn't really there. Sometimes guys would get a jolt and have no idea of what they'd done wrong, and other times they'd get away with something."

Sly sensed he was slowly gaining Mykola's respect, and he enjoyed being on center stage.

"After about three months, they changed it. Now Level 2 and 3 jolts can only be delivered by a guard or someone in the control room. At least that's what they expect us to believe."

The importance of the numbered uniforms was becoming clear to Mykola. "So if someone else wore my uniform, I could get a jolt, maybe even a life-threatening Level 3, for something they did wrong."

"You got it," Sly said with a smile. "You don't want to take the blame for someone else's screwup, especially if they're screwing up big-time."

With Mykola now in his numbered uniform, the two men continued the tour.

"We're going to have to pick up the pace," Sly said. "Dinner is at 6:00 in the chow hall, and we have to be in there by then. Otherwise—"

"We catch a jolt." Mykola threw up his hands as if catching a ball.

They spent a few minutes in each of the many large rooms of the prison, including some that had never been thought of in older prisons. There was a learning lab where inmates could take online courses and even learn another language. They could also read novels and nonfiction for enjoyment. There was a huge workshop in which inmates were producing several different types of products, some of which were unrecognizable components of larger products and systems. There was an infirmary and of course a kitchen and laundry.

In the center of the building was the "big room," a lounge where inmates could relax when they weren't at an assigned station in the prison and it was too hot to be outside. It had a number of park benches bolted to the floor and positioned along what could be considered a winding, irregularly shaped walking path. Unlike typical park benches, however, these weren't green. They were the same glossy white as the walls and most every other fixture in the prison. Water fountains were set along the side walls. And while other rooms and hallways had 12-foot ceilings, the big room had a 24-foot ceiling.

"See that up there?" Sly pointed to a glass panel along one wall and near the top of the room. "That's the control room. There's a couple of guards up there looking at a ton of screens to see what's going on all over the prison. If you ever see it, you'll think it's part of a spaceship control room. I tell you, there's no privacy here, not even in the showers or the crappers."

"The monitors are linked to the cameras in the ceiling." Mykola could see six camera bubbles on the walls and ceilings with just a quick look.

"I'm not sure of this," Sly said, "but I heard that the cameras also record and that the recording is kept for at least one day."

"Bottom line: I shouldn't do anything that violates any of the rules," Mykola said. "If I do, I'm going to get caught."

"Now you're catching on," Sly said enthusiastically. He felt like a grade school teacher who had heard a student accurately recite a multiplication table for the first time.

In each room Sly introduced Mykola to a couple of the other inmates he knew, but there were far too many names to remember. Each inmate had on his numbered uniform, and while they all seemed to be immersed in their tasks, Mykola sensed a simmering tension amidst the sea of stainless steel collars. The prison was like a planned company town of times past, built to be efficient and providing most all the services and functions necessary to discourage anyone from ever leaving. Of course, in the prison, leaving wasn't discouraged; it was forbidden.

As Sly turned his head to talk to one of the other inmates, Mykola noticed a guard, a slightly built older man in a blue uniform, standing near a door looking down at a computer tablet. Mykola was walking toward him with the intention of asking him a question about the showers when suddenly he felt a jolt of electricity extend down from his shoulders to the tips of his fingers and toes. His limbs were suddenly frozen; for perhaps five seconds, Mykola couldn't move. It wasn't particularly painful, but it frightened Mykola as he quickly thought through the jolt levels Sly had explained earlier. As soon as he could move again, he instinctively put his hand to his chest to see if his heart had stopped.

With that jolt of electricity, a short, high-pitched alarm had gone off, and all the inmates and the guard in the room turned to look at Mykola.

As Sly heard the sound, he quickly turned around. "Man, I'm really sorry," he said with palpable sincerity. "I should have told you that you can't get within two arms' lengths of a guard, otherwise you'll get a Level 1. It's automatic, and it'll happen again in 30 seconds if you're still close to the guard."

Letting out the breath he realized he'd been holding since he felt the jolt, Mykola quickly stepped farther back from the guard.

The other inmates continued on with their work, and the guard continued to read from the computer pad in his hands.

Mykola shook his arms, trying to shake off the tingling in his fingers.

"That explains it," he said. "I thought that guard we saw earlier was just a mean son of a bitch and that's why the inmates were hugging the wall as he was walking."

"Some of the guards are mean sons of bitches," Sly said. "If a guard has it in for one of us inmates, you might see him casually walk up to him from the back so that when he gets within six feet, the inmate gets a jolt. There aren't many guards, but when one of them walks into a room, you'll ordinarily hear a bunch of guys yell out 'Guard!' so other inmates won't accidentally get too close to him."

"So this collar not only delivers the pain, it also tracks where everyone is?" Mykola asked.

"Yup. It's something like an old GPS system, but since we're all confined to this establishment, it uses what I think they call 'transponders.' They're on poles at the four corners of the property. I don't understand it, but that's what one of the tech guys told me.

"Speaking of those poles, we need to go outside. I messed up by not telling you about the six-foot circle around the guards; I certainly don't want to mess up about the yard."

3

Sly and Mykola walked down a couple of long hallways. Mykola now had a better idea of how big this prison was. When he had arrived hours earlier, he'd only seen one side of the facility, and that only briefly.

When they finally pushed open the unlocked door and went outside, Mykola was in for another surprise: there were no walls and only an unimposing fence about 200 yards away. Again there were no guards.

"You can stop thinking what you're thinking right now," Sly said in a serious tone. "You aren't going to just walk away from this place. Let's go out to that berm and I'll tell you why."

They walked quickly and gingerly on hard-packed desert sand and clay out to the berm about 150 yards from the door. The late afternoon sun had heated the desert surface to the point where it was painful to stand in one place.

The berm was about one foot higher than the surrounding ground and was covered in a four-foot-wide strip of crushed limestone. Sly had Mykola turn and walk parallel to the berm a few feet from it. He explained that this was sort of like the warning track in a baseball stadium. It warned you that you were getting close to the 'wall.' In this case, it was a virtual wall.

"If you step on the berm, you'll get a Level 1 shock," Sly explained. "That's a friendly reminder not to go any farther. If by chance or stupid determination you make it over the berm, you'll get a Level 2 shock. If you're still on your feet and go a bit further yet, you'll get a Level 3. Remember, Level 3 could be a killer. We don't know the exact place where Level 2 ends and Level 3 begins: no one has been dumb enough to try it."

"What about that fence over there?" Mykola asked, pointing to the four-foot-high wire netting that was another 30 to 40 yards away.

"That's just to keep the civilians out, though I'm not sure why anyone would come all the way out to this hellhole to begin with."

Beyond the fence was simply barren desert with shimmering heat waves coming off a road Mykola could not see.

"Last thing," Sly said. "All jolt levels out here on the perimeter are automatic. The system controls it, so you can't even bribe the guard in the control room to look the other way for the half minute it would take to sprint out of here."

Mykola brought his hand to his forehead to shade his eyes from the setting sun and stared at the nearby mountains. If he didn't turn around, he could imagine himself exploring the desert. Sly tapped him on the shoulder and brought him back to reality: he was in a prison, and while it was modern and progressive, it was as confining as any other.

"Tell you what: We got a late start, and it's almost time for dinner. There's a booklet in your cell that explains all the rules and should answer most of your questions." Sly paused, eyed Mykola, and wondered for a moment before he asked the humiliating question. "You can read, right?"

"Of course I can read. What makes you think I can't?" Mykola was caught off guard by the question and had to resist the impulse to display his offense.

"Sorry, but I had to ask. Lots of guys come in here and they can't read and are embarrassed to admit it. On the outside they always had someone who could read the directions on prescriptions and anything else important. In here, guys don't admit they can't read, and that gets them into trouble."

"You mean the only way they find out about the rules is by breaking them and getting a shocking education?"

"Uh-huh. Or sometimes inmates will get a sense that a new inmate can't read and they'll take advantage of him."

"So what's the alternative if you can't read?"

"It's pretty simple. In the communications room, there are scanners. You put a printed instruction card, the rules booklet, or whatever on the scanner, press the green button, and it reads it out loud to you. It'll even translate into another language. If a new inmate admits he can't read, I demonstrate the scanner to him.

"But you can read. Read the rules tonight and take the test tomorrow. The test isn't hard; they just want to make sure you understand the rules. When you pass the test, that makes me look good too."

"What if I don't pass it?" Mykola asked, more out of curiosity than concern.

"Well, you get three tries, and I don't think anyone has failed it all three times. So I don't really know," Sly replied.

Bunch of bureaucracy just like everywhere else, Mykola thought.

Sly took Mykola to the chow hall. They, along with many other inmates, were there before the 6:00 deadline. Even if you weren't hungry, Sly explained, you had to be there at your assigned time. For some it was 5:15, for some 6:00, and for others 6:45. You also had to be finished and out before the next "shift" arrived.

When they were just inside the hall, Sly stopped. He lifted his head and took in a deep breath through his nostrils. "Hmmm . . . I think they got lima beans in the trough. Can you smell 'em? I love lima beans."

Mykola let out a sigh of disgust. "In the trough? Are they just slopping the hogs?"

"Hey, it's just an expression!" Sly said. "There's big plastic trays and bins on the serving line, and you can eat as much as you want of whatever is out there. That's one nice thing about being in here: you never have to worry about going hungry."

Sly was surprised at himself. He was actually defending what he realized was his home.

"Sorry," Mykola said. "I didn't mean anything by it. I guess I just have to learn some of the terms used here."

Sly was a nice enough guy, and Mykola knew it would be good to have some friends here. It wasn't as if he could just move to another neighborhood.

The chow hall was a huge room. In the center were aluminum bench tables, the kind you'd see in a public park, but these were bolted to the floor. Each of the 50 tables seated six inmates, but Mykola noticed that with few exceptions, there were only four inmates at each table. If you were going to sit in the center seat, you'd want to be among friends.

Around the perimeter of the room were another 50 four-seat square tables, again bolted to the floor. The seats were round and had no backs, making them easy to slide onto, but they were small and perfectly flat. Short inmates had to slide to the forward edge of the seat to be able to get near their trays, while the biggest inmates looked like they were stuck on a pole, their buttocks covering the seat and hanging over the back and side edges.

Sly and Mykola sat at a table with one other inmate, who barely acknowledged them as they sat down. In turn, they talked as if he weren't there. Before he'd finished half of what was on his tray, the other inmate picked it up, carried it to the garbage bin, and dumped it.

"See that?" Sly jerked his head toward the inmate who had just emptied his tray. "The system sees that, and while he doesn't get a jolt for wasting food, it'll be recorded and someday he's gonna wonder why he's always assigned to dirty jobs like cleaning the crappers."

"Why doesn't someone just tell him he shouldn't waste food?" Mykola asked.

"Somebody probably did, but there are some guys here who don't listen to good advice. They just don't seem to care."

Dinner was a bland combination of vegetables and some sort of soy meat that was supposed to taste like beef. Of course, few people really knew the taste of beef, since the beef tax had been levied a few years earlier, tripling the price. The soy meat, like everything else served, could be cut and eaten with a fork: a plastic one. There were no knives in the chow hall and none in the kitchen either. Most of the food that came into the prison was either preportioned or precut. Bulk food like lima beans came in cans or big plastic pouches. Not too appetizing, Mykola thought, but Sly enjoyed it and got a second helping.

In the brief period that they'd been together, Mykola had already seen that Sly was the type of inmate who was a good fit for this prison: someone who liked order and didn't mind following rules. In addition, Sly obviously felt safe here. He wasn't muscular or intimidating and probably couldn't defend himself if assailed by another inmate, but in here he didn't have to worry about that. The collars would keep even the most vicious, depraved, and unpredictable inmates in line. Mykola smiled at Sly, who was shoveling food into his mouth, drops of sauce landing on his yellow shirt.

Mykola didn't eat much, but he made it a point to eat everything he'd put on his tray. He had a feeling of déjà vu: the whole experience made him feel like he was eating lunch back in high school and would have to be in class afterward.

Conversations at the tables also reminded him of high school, with a mix of gossip and sports. Serious discussions of world events were not to be heard. Mykola found out later that was by design. By and large, little news was available to the inmates. Studies had shown that an endless stream of news on controversial topics resulted in anxiety and aggressive behavior, and London Tower was doing everything they could to maintain tranquility in the prison. What news the inmates did receive was through email and perhaps word of mouth from the guards and staff members.

During dinner, Sly explained to Mykola that after dinner he

could go anywhere he wanted as long as he was in his assigned cell by 8:00. His cell would be easy to find: his inmate number and signs in the halls would make it like finding a gate in an airport.

·

Mykola found his cell with lots of time to spare. His cellmate was already there.

"Hey, I'm Mykola," he said in an upbeat tone as he walked into the cell.

His cellmate, resting on one of the narrow bunks bolted to the wall, responded with "Alex," barely making eye contact with Mykola.

Alex looked to be about 55 years of age. Like Mykola, he was over six feet tall and kept himself in good shape. His hair was graying, and deep lines around his eyes, mouth, and neck gave him a weathered, leathery appearance. He was a bit intimidating, even to Mykola.

Alex returned to reading his dog-eared paperback. This cool reaction wasn't what Mykola had expected, and for a moment he didn't know what to do. Then, seeing that his other two uniforms had been placed on his bunk, he moved them over and sat down.

Alex was still reading, and now Mykola pulled his legs up onto the bunk, clasped his hands behind his head, and fell back on the thin pillow, which let out a puff of air. The bunk sagged in the middle and the blanket on which he reclined was coarse, feeling like the bristles of a scrub brush on any exposed skin. It wasn't comfortable, and the metal collar that now pressed into his shoulders and neck made it even less so.

Still, lying down caused Mykola to realize how tired he was. He hadn't done much of anything that day, but the day had been a long series of new experiences, and it had been stressful. His aloof cellmate was the capper.

Alex kept reading for a couple of minutes, until it appeared he'd gotten to the end of a chapter. Setting the book down, he looked over at Mykola and studied him for a moment.

"After four months they decide to give me another cellmate," he said. "Too bad; I was getting real comfortable with all the extra space." He checked the number on Mykola's shirt to confirm that Mykola hadn't wandered into the wrong cell, but no luck: it was one higher than his own.

"Well, you might as well get it over with and tell me about yourself," Alex continued with a distinct tone of resignation.

Mykola didn't care for the tone of Alex's voice. Without looking over at him, Mykola responded with facts about himself in a sort of verbal résumé format.

Alex replied with a condensed version of that. "I'm in for six to twelve on national healthcare fraud. I'm a psychiatrist, and I overbilled on my patients. It worked out fine until I accidentally billed for a guy who was killed in a construction accident. I figured he just didn't want to come in for his regular appointments; I never guessed he had a good excuse."

Mykola couldn't help but grin just a bit. That dry comment made Alex's appearance and cool demeanor a bit less menacing.

"Six to twelve for an overbilling? I'm doing less than that for supposedly beating the crap out of an ex-cop."

"You'd think that. Of course, when they found one fraudulent billing, they went looking for more and found 23 that stretched back a few years. Somehow they also found out about the side business I had in recreational pharmaceuticals. So here we are.

"I hope you like to read, 'cause I'm not into mindless chit-chat or listening to your personal problems and complaints," Alex continued. "That's too much like my old job."

Alex looked at Mykola with a mixture of imploring and demanding.

"Well," Mykola said, "I'm not much for reading." Then, noticing the chessboard and pieces on the shelf with Alex's uniforms, he added, "But I do like to play chess."

Alex looked up at the chess set too, trying to judge whether his new cellmate was joking, being sarcastic, or being sincere and honest. He had assumed that his new young cellmate was part of the distracted generation: those people who couldn't or wouldn't pay attention to anything for more than five minutes.

"You any good?" Alex asked. He now sat up and put his bare feet on the cool concrete floor.

"Let's play and you'll find out," Mykola responded.

The ice had cracked, but their first game would have to wait. Almost simultaneously a three-tone ring sounded down the corridor.

"That's the 60-second warning," Alex explained, "and when you hear it, you'd better be in your cell if you value your health."

Moments later the cell door slowly slid shut and a latch clicked into place.

"Time to take off these damn collars," Alex said. There was an almost inaudible click, and Mykola's collar loosened to the point where he could get two fingers under it. Mykola looked perplexed.

"Stand up," Alex said.

He walked over and flipped the latch on Mykola's collar so that Mykola could remove it. He then reached behind his own neck and flipped the latch on his.

"You sure as hell can't sleep with these things on, but I doubt that's why they remove them," he said. "Word has it that they put them on a charging system overnight, check to see if they're damaged, and upgrade the firmware if needed. Put yours on this tray." He pointed to a tray built into the cell bars.

Mykola slipped off his collar and put it on the tray. Reaching up, he put both hands on his neck, rolled his shoulders, and gave himself a vigorous massage. "Damn, that feels better."

A few minutes later, a guard came by with a cart and placed both collars on it.

Mykola sat on his bunk and surveyed his new home. The walls were painted with the same glossy white paint as the rest of the prison, and immediately Mykola wondered if he'd be able to sleep in this bright environment. In the center of the nine-foot ceiling was a recessed light fixture that cast an even light over all corners of the cell, a light so blindingly intense that it was hard to lie on the bunk and look up. Perhaps Alex was using the paperback as an eyeshade while he was reading it.

The light would remain on until 9:00.

Between the two bunks was a three-tier shelf where Mykola put his uniforms after making sure they had the correct numbers printed on them. At the foot of one bunk was a commode and at the foot of the other was a small sink. Both looked to be of the minimalist water usage design recently required by most states.

There was no privacy whatsoever, and now Mykola understood why Alex was disappointed to have a new cellmate.

4

The next morning at 7:00, a loud, pulsating, but not unpleasant tone came on the loudspeaker and lasted for 30 seconds. It sounded like the type of wake-up alarm most people had at home, but this one had no snooze button and the 30-second duration assured that the inmates couldn't fall asleep once again.

Alex alerted Mykola with a motion of his arms that looked as if he were trying to levitate Mykola out of his bunk. "We've got 30 minutes to get ourselves into the hall for breakfast."

Noise from outside the cell made it clear that other cellmates were also getting up and out. Periodically the distinct sound of a gate rolling on its tracks and locking into the open position was heard, but the gate to Alex and Mykola's cell was still closed. The collars were back on the small shelf built into the bars. Alex picked up one, checked the number on it to make sure it was his, put it around his neck, and closed the latch.

"C'mon and hurry up; the gate won't open until we both have our collars on," Alex said to Mykola, clearly irritated with having to educate his new cellmate on the basics. Moments after Mykola had his on, having fumbled with a latch he couldn't see, the collars on both inmates tightened until they put the slightest amount of pressure on their necks. The steel gate to the cell moved with agonizing deliberateness to the right and stopped. It would remain open all day.

"Wait. Before you go, check your assignment," Alex said, pointing to a small screen on the outside and just above the cell door. On the screen were photos of Alex and Mykola, along with some text next to each photo.

"If you can't read, just press your face"—Alex glanced at Mykola to see if he understood—"on the screen, and it'll read it out loud for you."

Mykola hadn't given any thought to what he was expected to do that day, and seeing his schedule on the screen relieved him of that concern. He ignored Alex's arrogant 'face on the screen' remark.

"What's 'industrial workshop'?" he asked, reading off the screen.

"Most inmates start off in the industrial workshop. You'll be given some tests to measure your knowledge on various topics, your ability to learn, and your manual dexterity. From the results of those tests, you'll be assigned a job."

"What's that 'ABC' business at the bottom of the screen?"

"Sly didn't explain that to you? The guy is really slipping. If he doesn't shape up pretty soon, he'll lose his yellow shirt.

"Everyone's number has a letter prefix. Yours is *A* and mine's *C*. Meals and such are scheduled by your letter; they can't get everyone into the chow hall at the same time. So today we're both scheduled for breakfast at the same time, but we have different lunch and dinner times. They don't change often; maybe once every three or four months. Sometimes you'll see that a movie is available to one group or another after supper."

Mykola continued to look at the screen and check his mealtimes. Alex stood there with one hand on his hip and the other motioning to say, "Let's go."

Mykola saw on the screen that Alex was to go to the infirmary. "Wait—you sick?"

"No, that's where I work. I've had enough general medical training that I can be a glorified nurse in the infirmary. They have a doctor on call by teleconference if there's anything serious. It's pretty easy; most of what I do is hand out aspirin and tell guys to drink lots of fluids. You know, the universal cure. C'mon, we've got to go."

Alex and Mykola joined the other inmates in the corridor moving toward the chow hall. Mykola found it to be a strange procession. He expected to hear some greetings and banter typical of men going to work, but there was none. A few comments about "another day" and "better not be beans for breakfast," but that was it.

Mykola also noticed that in some cells the inmates were still lying on their bunks, though they had collars on and the gates were open.

Alex noticed Mykola's puzzlement. "Some guys are always last to chow. You'll probably see them later during free time, back in their cells and just lying on their bunks. The cell gates are open all day."

Breakfast was as bland as the previous night's dinner. The only thing with any texture to it was the toast, but that was as tasteless as the yellow congealed mounds Mykola assumed were eggs. Alex and Mykola sat at the same table, but there was no further discussion. Mykola found himself having to consciously think about swallowing the small portions of food he took from the trough. In ten minutes they were done, going in separate directions to their assignments.

Mykola reported to the industrial workshop. As Alex had explained, he was given a series of tests, not by guards but by other inmates wearing yellow shirts just like Sly's.

Mykola had assumed that the demeanor of these yellow-shirts would be similar to Sly's: pleasant, helpful, almost like a big brother. That wasn't the case. These yellow-shirts took their higher rank in the prison hierarchy much more seriously, and "grays" were expected to respond to their directions as if they were guards. There was no friendly banter; just robotic instructions and blank expressions.

Though the yellow-shirts had no enforcement authority, all they had to do was point to an inmate with both arms fully outstretched and the intelligence system would note it and send a signal to the control room. There one of the officers would execute a Level 1 jolt, usually without bothering to determine the source of the yellow-gray conflict. Gray-shirted inmates quickly learned to treat the yellow-shirts with more respect than they had earned.

The first test was a 10-question multiple choice test on prison rules, the one Sly had told him about. It wasn't challenging; Mykola looked it over and was pretty sure he could have aced it even if he'd been given it in the truck on the way here. But he decided not to. He had not yet been in the prison for 24 hours, but he'd already started to feel like a piston in an old automobile engine, ready to go into motion at the command of some other part of the engine and ultimately controlled by a faceless driver. It wasn't right, and for a moment he thought he'd answer all the questions intentionally wrong in the spirit of rebellion. What could they do?

No, he thought, that would be too obvious. Even if he couldn't read, random selection meant he'd likely get two or three right. Mykola had no idea how long he'd be with the yellow-shirt that day; bringing the man's ire upon himself wouldn't be a smart move.

So Mykola decided to answer five questions correctly and five incorrectly, picking the most obvious wrong choices. No need to hurry, he figured. Changing his answers a couple of times to feign confusion and lack of confidence in the right answer, he took 10 minutes to complete the test he knew he could have done in two minutes.

The yellow-shirt walking slowly and impatiently back and forth behind him convinced him that this bit of rebellion shouldn't go on any further. Mykola touched the DONE button and then the YES button in response to ARE YOU SURE? With the yellow-shirt standing directly behind him and looking over his shoulder, the test was instantly scored, and YOU PASSED came up in big, bold, golden letters on the screen.

"Congratulations, let's move on," Mykola heard from the sullen yellow-shirt. For the first time in days, he felt like laughing out loud. The test was a formality, probably required by contract between the departments of corrections and London Tower. YOU PASSED was like the certificates of participation they used to award kids for playing some team sport. It didn't mean anything, but everyone thought it was important. Of course, participation in the prison wasn't voluntary, and violation of rules could have painful consequences whether or not you passed the test.

The other tests were much more challenging but measured mental acuity rather than knowledge of anything specific. All were done on a touch screen, including the final few, which measured fine motor skills and reflexes. On these tests Mykola did his best, in part because he found them interesting but also because he hoped he'd be assigned a job that wouldn't become boring after a couple of hours.

Mykola thought about what Sly had asked about his reading ability. He'd obviously been right to ask. Each test had a "talking voice" icon, and if you pressed it, it would read the words on the screen, highlighting them in yellow as it went along.

The industrial workshop floor was bigger than a football field, with inmates working at a variety of machines, some individually and others in short production lines. In one corner was a glass-enclosed room in which inmates were working on computers. Mykola was assigned there, to his surprise; he had no computer skills beyond those of any typical person on the street.

The yellow-shirt led him to a small booth with a computer monitor mounted on the wall. Mykola's job, as the yellow-shirt explained, was to listen to a brief description of an individual and watch a short video showing that individual, sometimes alone and sometimes interacting with someone else. Then the system would ask Mykola to answer a series of questions about him. Seemed simple enough, and Mykola put on the headphones with a microphone attached.

The first video was a demonstration of the process. At the end, the system verbally asked open-ended questions: "How is Danny feeling right now?" and "What will Danny do now?" A text box appeared onscreen, and whatever Mykola said in response to the question appeared in the box. However, there were limits as to how long the response could be. Short, to-the-point responses fit in the text box, but rambling, thinking-out-loud comments didn't. In addition, if the computer couldn't understand what was being said, the response would be erased and the respondent would have to start over.

Mykola had to go through the demonstration exercise twice to show he understood the process. He assumed there was some limit as to how many times one could go through the demonstration process before the system would shut down and a yellow-shirt would escort you to some easier assignment.

Mykola understood now what was expected of him, and he treated it like a game. He thought carefully about what he said in response to each question and got a sense of satisfaction when his first response to a question was accepted. Once he thought he'd test the logic of the system and entered a response that was the opposite of what he felt. The system processed his response, and "Are you sure this is what you think?" came up onscreen and through his headphones. Mykola said no and changed his response.

It didn't take more than 15 minutes for Mykola to forget he was talking to a machine; the voice sounded human and even had tonal inflections to emphasize key words. Mykola watched 10 videos, each of a different character and in a different setting.

This wasn't what Mykola had expected to be doing in prison. It certainly didn't seem like punishment. If anything, it was engaging, something like trying to predict what would happen next in a movie mystery.

Finally he was shown a series of photos of similar-looking individuals and asked to select the ones he thought were most trustworthy, most compassionate, most intelligent, or any of a number of human attributes. Two to four people were presented simultaneously onscreen for five to ten seconds, and Mykola simply had to touch the screen to make his selection. If he made no selection in the allotted time, the next group of images would appear with a different question.

How can anyone judge a person's trustworthiness or intelligence just from a photo? Mykola asked himself. He suspected this was a test of his biases, since some photo blocks had all men or women of the same race while other photo blocks were of men and women of all races and age groups.

This exercise went on for about 20 minutes and then the screen went blank. A red light came on above the booth, and moments later the yellow-shirt was back.

"That's the end of playing video games," he said. "Now it's time for some real work."

"Can you tell me what this was all about?" Mykola asked as they walked out of the room.

"Nope. I have no idea. I just bring guys in here, tell them enough to get started, and then it's all between you and the machine."

"Will I be doing this again?" Mykola asked, not sure whether he was hoping for a yes or no answer.

"Don't know that either, but most new guys are assigned to this for the first five to ten days here. One guy was assigned to these video games for 22 days straight, though."

"22 days? Was that reward or punishment?" Mykola joked.

"You'd have to ask the guy; maybe it was both." The yellow-shirt's response was far too serious for Mykola's whimsical question.

For the balance of that first shift, Mykola was assigned to a small machine that printed custom graphics on T-shirts. He put a shirt on the screener, pressed a button, waited, then lifted the printed shirt and put it in a box. The shift went by quickly for Mykola. It was the government-required six-hour workday, with 45 minutes for lunch; by 2:45 he was done and on his own until dinner.

⊙

"How was your first day?" Alex asked Mykola when they were both in the cell getting ready for gate closure.

"Sort of amazing, to be honest. Air-conditioned, and nobody standing behind me with a baton; I almost forgot I was in prison."

"That's a good attitude, but I doubt that'll be your attitude in six months," Alex responded. "This place eats away at your sense of self bit by bit, and one day you'll find you don't know who you are. You'll question your life's purpose and even if you *are* alive."

The tone of Alex's voice reminded Mykola of the judge pronouncing his prison sentence.

"Alex, aren't you being overly dramatic? I mean, the guys I've met so far seem to be well adjusted. Sure, there are a few guys who seem to be a couple of tacos short of a family pack, but that's probably what got them in here to begin with."

"Think so? This prison has been open for just four years, and

I already see inmates coming to the infirmary with self-inflicted cuts or doing things they know will result in Level 2 jolts. Their eyes are glazed over, their shoulders slumped, and they have trouble just expressing their thoughts. Like you, lots of guys come in here and get the impression that this will be easy time, only to find out later—when it might be too late—that time seems to have come to a standstill. The multisensory outside world is gone, and an unengaged brain starts creating its own reality. You feel a pounding in your skull as if your brain is trying to break through, and I'm not sure that's entirely an analogy."

Alex paused. He could see in Mykola's expression that Mykola wasn't ready to completely believe what he was describing, but the smile on Mykola's face was gone.

With a more jovial voice Alex continued, "With that uplifting insight for you to ponder, let's play some chess."

The first game lasted 15 minutes, and Alex won. Most of that time was spent with Mykola deciding on his next move; Alex's moves were almost instinctive. Still, Alex enjoyed the game and thought that in time Mykola would become a more challenging opponent.

"By the way, what did you do today?" Alex asked as he was putting the chess pieces back in the box.

"I started by answering some questions about videos I watched. For the most part I found it interesting."

"You know what that's for, don't you?" Alex smiled.

"I assume it's used to measure whether I could and would pay attention to what I was doing," Mykola replied hesitantly, shifting his weight from one side to the other as he sat on his bunk.

Alex responded with a knee-slapping laugh that Mykola

immediately found offensive. Then, seeing Mykola's scowl and understanding he'd affronted him, Alex continued in an almost apologetic tone, "No, I suspect you were helping to develop that final and most challenging part of an AI system."

"AI?"

"Artificial intelligence. It's so ubiquitous that we've come to expect it in most everything we interact with."

"Can't argue with that," Mykola said, nodding. "I've been on the phone talking to customer service lots of times, figuring I'm talking to a machine, only to find out it's an actual human when they say something stupid or cough."

"Right. Computers can do most anything a man can do and they'll do it better, faster, and cheaper. Even in here. AI practically runs this place. The one thing it can't do is make decisions when there are conflicting and changing priorities.

"It's like you and me deciding to play chess tonight, but tomorrow we decide not to because I've got something on my mind. AI can decide how to do something most efficiently and react to any roadblocks, but unless priorities are programmed into it, it can't decide what to do now and what can wait."

"I guess that makes sense." Mykola was listening intently to Alex's explanation.

"The other thing AI doesn't yet have is a theory of mind," Alex continued.

"Theory of mind? Now you're really getting into stuff that's beyond this furniture maker's comprehension."

"No, not really," Alex said. "It's a pretty simple concept, one that we apply and take for granted. In fact, you're applying theory of mind right now. Theory of mind is having an idea of what someone else is thinking.

"For instance, I don't know exactly how I've come to this conclusion, but right now I believe you might be thinking that I consider myself smarter than you."

"I suppose that notion did cross my mind," Mykola said. "But what do you mean when you say you don't know how you came to that conclusion?"

"It could be lots of things, Mykola. It could be the tone of your voice, the questions you ask, your posture, your facial expressions. Hell, it probably has something to do with me as well. I like to think I'm the smartest guy in the room, and I probably say and do things subconsciously to support that self-image and then assume you've gotten that impression."

Mykola sat quietly on his bunk waiting for Alex to continue explaining his thoughts. It appeared that Alex was talking to himself as much as he was talking to Mykola.

"You know, we humans are remarkably complicated. That ability to sort of 'step outside ourselves' and see what we're thinking, and to make judgments about what others are thinking, is uniquely human. In a more general way, we call it consciousness. AI doesn't have that ability, at least not yet."

"So you think that's what I was doing? Helping develop AI consciousness?"

"I can't be sure," Alex said. "Perhaps you're right: perhaps those exercises you went through really were measuring your ability to pay attention and notice things."

"Whatever. It was more stimulating than making T-shirts." Mykola looked down at his own prison shirt. "Alex, let me ask you something. You obviously know things about this place that aren't written down in that booklet."

As he said the words, Mykola recognized that Alex's theory

of his mind was right. Furthermore, he was employing his own theory of Alex's mind by prefacing his question with a compliment. In turn, it was no surprise that Alex now had that look of enhanced self-esteem that comes with being asked for an expert opinion.

"What happens if we don't put on the collars in the morning? Do we just sit here in this cell until we get hungry enough to put them on?" Mykola asked as he leaned forward with his hands clasped.

"You'd better have a damn good reason for not putting it on, like having suffered a stroke during the night. In about 15 minutes you'd see two red-shirts come into the cell . . ."

"Red-shirts? I've seen a few guys wearing red shirts, but Sly didn't tell me what they signified."

"Hmm, Sly forget to tell you that too? A few more orientations like yours and he'll be back to wearing a gray shirt." Alex paused. "Red-shirts are inmates who have been designated as enforcers. They're the guys the guards call on whenever some inmate needs 'physical encouragement' to do the right thing . . . like put on the collar. They'll put the collar on you even if you say you're so sick you can't stand up. Then they'll drag you down to the infirmary."

"Doesn't sound so bad," Mykola snorted.

"There's more," Alex continued. "If the guards then decide you were faking it or your explanation just doesn't cut it, you're sent to detention."

"Detention? What is this, high school?"

"You wish. I was sent to detention for a week shortly after I got here. I was like you, thinking I was tough enough to handle anything they could throw at me. I wanted to prove to myself and every inmate around me that I was someone you didn't want to mess with.

"Detention is the 'humane' version of the old solitary confinement. You're put in a room that has about 20 cells in it, just like this one but smaller, with only one bunk. You wear your collar just like you do here: on during the day and off at night after the cell gate closes. Here's the kicker: you're with a bunch of other guys, but you can't talk to them. If you do—"

"Let me guess: a jolt. I'm quickly learning there's a jolt for just about everything," Mykola interjected.

Sly hadn't shown him the detention room, and perhaps that was intended. Perhaps the prison authorities thought it was better to get compliance to the rules by the constant threat of a jolt rather than by threatening inmates with a punishment widely used in the 19th and 20th centuries. That 1990s program Mykola had read about, "Scared Straight," hadn't worked; showing new inmates the detention room probably didn't reduce violations either.

"Right," Alex was saying. "And they add another day to your detention time. It might not sound so bad not getting to talk to the other guys, but there are no books, no videos, nothing! There's nothing to help you pass the time. There are no windows, and the light has a bluish cast to it so that everything has a monotone color. You're basically living in an old-fashioned black and white TV screen."

Alex was getting visibly agitated as he described his experience.

"That's also where I found out that the collars have microphones built in. So be careful what you say, even if you're just talking to yourself. I can't be sure, but my guess is that the system uses voice recognition and tabulates words like "kill," "meth," and any other slang term associated with violence, drug use, or theft. I wouldn't even be telling you this if we still had our collars on."

For Mykola, this was all becoming a confusing mix of cutting-edge corrections science and out-of-date techniques. Just as he was beginning to think he understood how the prison operated, Alex threw in something else, like detention and microphones in collars. He'd need some quiet time to think about this.

As if he required a prompt to do just that, the lights in the cell went out. It was 9:00, and the only light in the cell came from the faint LED night-lights in the corridor.

5

Mykola had been in the prison for two weeks and had fallen into a routine. Other than the Level 1 jolt he'd gotten on his first day, it had been a painless couple of weeks. "Numbing" might be a better description.

With his shift in the lab complete, he thought it would be good for him to connect with the outside world through the prison messaging system. In his induction, he'd been told he'd be able to use the system in 10 days. Certainly it had to be ready by now. There was no mention of the messaging system in the handbook, but Mykola was fairly confident it couldn't be much different from the text and video systems everyone grew up with and used daily.

The communications room was at the end of a long corridor, rather out of the way and perhaps an afterthought in the design. Or perhaps London Tower wanted to make the system available but not encourage its use. A small sign above the door identified the room. There was no lock or other security, but Mykola looked up at the ceiling and saw the imbedded glass hemisphere which housed the system cameras. There was no anonymity here.

Opening the door, he expected to see a number of terminals lined up against the wall or on a center table. Instead there were individual terminals spread throughout the room, each about eight feet from the next, in eight rows and five deep. Around each of them a red square had been painted on the floor, creating what looked like streets going around city blocks. At the very back of the room were eight dedicated video communications terminals, identified by a crude handwritten sign taped to the wall.

Surprisingly, only nine of the email terminals were in use. Mykola had assumed this would be a popular place for inmates to spend their discretionary time; he'd planned to wait for a seat and terminal to become available.

Walking toward one of the inmates typing a message, Mykola stopped short as the inmate looked up at him and growled, "Hey, what the hell do you think you're doing? Don't you see the red line?"

Mykola took a step back and now stood on the "street" between the terminals.

"Sorry," he said. "It's my first time here. I was wondering if you'd explain how to send and receive emails."

"Just go sit down at one of the empty terminals. You'll figure it out." The inmate returned to reading the message on the screen.

Not sure what the red lines on the floor signified but unwilling to tempt another confrontation with an inmate, Mykola walked down the "streets" to the last row and sat on the stool before a terminal. As he did, the screen came alive:

WELCOME MYKOLA STEINMAN—PRESS TO CONTINUE

It's the collar, Mykola said to himself. The system knew his exact location, and when he was within the red square around a terminal, it assumed he was going to use that terminal. Now the sign he'd seen at the entrance, "One Inmate per Terminal," made more sense. It also explained why the other inmate had been mad at Mykola for crossing over into his space: probably the system would lock up if two inmates were in the same space.

Mykola touched the screen. There were five new messages, all from the system administrator. All but one were titled with a phrase that began with "Approved" and the name of one of the people Mykola had identified during the induction process as email contacts.

The exception was the woman he had dated a few times before his arrest. That one began with "Not Approved." Mykola touched that message to open it. It simply said, "Janice Weathers has declined to accept electronic communication from you. Janice Weathers has been removed from your address book."

The wonders—or is it the horrors—of technology, Mykola thought. He hadn't established a long-term relationship with Janice, but he'd thought they had potential. With just a touch of the screen, she'd ended it without as much as a "Hope you're well" or a "Best of luck in your new home." It would have been nice to read anything she might send, just to imagine her sitting in front of the monitor and sipping a cup of the herbal tea she enjoyed. So much for that harmless fantasy.

A WRITE NEW MESSAGE button was at the bottom of the screen, and when he touched it, the four other people he had identified during induction came up. He could select one or more, and that opened the title line and message field.

At the top of the screen were two countdown measures: time began at 30 minutes and word count began at 500.

The first and only message he was going to send today was to his attorney.

There was no physical keyboard attached to the monitor. Mykola sat before the screen and looked for a button that would bring up an onscreen keyboard. There was no button to press for one. Mykola jabbed at the message field a couple of times, thinking that would bring up a keyboard. Instead a message in all red caps appeared onscreen:

SPEAK CLEARLY TO ENTER YOUR MESSAGE. WHEN DONE, PRESS SEND.

Voice to text. This wasn't new technology, but Mykola hadn't used it before. He moved closer to what looked like a microphone at the bottom of the screen and began speaking. The words appeared onscreen as he spoke, but when he read the message, it wasn't clear and to the point. He paused. Then, taking a chance that the system could distinguish his text from commands, he said firmly, "Start over." He waited a few seconds. All the text onscreen disappeared. He began again, this time choosing his words carefully.

> Roberta—
> As I think you know, I'm now in the Arizona-New California State Prison. We need to talk. I want to find out how my appeal is coming along and what I can do. I can do one hour of videoconferencing per month, and I'm available every day from 2:45 to 5:00 p.m. Give me a day and time and I'll call you. Make it soon!
> Thanks,
> Mykola Steinman

Satisfied, he touched the **SEND** button on the screen. It then occurred to him that he didn't know he'd be available every day from 2:45 to 5:00. That was the open time he'd had every day since he'd gotten here, but there was no way to know when his schedule, displayed each morning on the screen outside his cell, would change. Too late now; he could only hope his discretionary time wouldn't change, at least for the next few days.

The timer still showed 19 minutes, so Mykola figured he'd wait and see if he got a response. There was nothing else to do. Four minutes later a button on the screen appeared: **NEW MESSAGE RECEIVED**. Mykola touched it and two more buttons appeared: **READ** and **LISTEN**, with open book and human ear icons underneath the terms. Mykola shook his head; obviously Sly was right about the lack of literacy among the inmates. Mykola was curious as to what sort of voice would read the message, but he thought better of it. This wasn't the time to go exploring. He pressed **READ**.

Mykola—

Yes, I had been told you were transferred to the prison. I hope you're starting to make the adjustment. I know it isn't easy. I can do a videoconference with you next Tuesday at 3:30. I don't think we'll use anywhere close to the full hour. I just don't have much to tell you that you don't already know, but I assure you we're looking at all the possible grounds for appeal.

See and talk then,
Roberta

Mykola had hoped for a more optimistic response from his

attorney, but since he'd had to initiate contact with her, that probably wasn't realistic.

He leaned back in the chair and played back the trial in his mind. Roberta had kept reminding him that they didn't have to prove his innocence; it was the state's responsibility to prove his guilt. That was a good mindset; Mykola didn't have a solid alibi, so innocence was difficult to prove. Yet had the jury, despite the judge's instructions, seen the lack of a strong alibi as increasing the weight of evidence supporting a guilty verdict? Roberta and Mykola couldn't know exactly how the jurors had come to their decision, and perhaps the jurors themselves didn't know.

Mykola lost track of time, and the countdown timer on the screen started flashing and beeping as it went under one minute. No cause for concern, however; Mykola didn't need to write, read, or listen to anything else. When the timer showed 0:00, another message came up: YOUR SESSION HAS ENDED. EFFECTIVE JUNE 2, VISUAL TEXT OPTION WILL BE DISABLED. 'LISTEN' WILL BE THE ONLY OPTION.

⊙

The following Tuesday, Mykola got to the communications room 30 minutes before he was scheduled to videoconference with his attorney. Though several of the video terminals had not been in use on his first visit, he wanted to be sure that was not the exception, that he'd be able to contact Roberta at their prearranged time.

Only two of the eight terminals were in use, but the first available one Mykola checked had a piece of yellow tape across the cracked screen. Mykola guessed that an inmate had let his fist convey his anger at whomever he was talking to.

"That had to be a Level 2 violation. I hope it was worth it," he mumbled to himself.

Unlike the email terminals, the video terminals had curtains to the left and right so that only the person sitting directly in front of the screen could see what was on it. In addition, they were placed so that the inmate had his back against the wall. Nobody could stand behind him and see what was on the screen. It was a nice concession to the desire for privacy, but Mykola knew the system was recording and reviewing both the prisoner's voice and the voices and images coming in from the outside.

It was still a few minutes before 3:30, and Mykola's curiosity had to be satisfied: what was the reason for the curtains and the terminals' placement along the wall? A yellow-shirt had just gotten up from an email terminal and was walking toward the door.

"Excuse me," Mykola said. "It's my first time here, and I was wondering if you could answer a question for me."

"I'm no techie, but okay, I'll try." The inmate, with deep lines in his face and a stooped posture that made him look like he belonged in a retirement home, was obviously pleased to engage in any sort of conversation where he might be able to help someone. Probably that was especially the case with a request coming from an inmate young enough to be his grandson and whose tone of voice reflected respect and humility.

"Why do the video terminals have curtains, and why are they placed in the opposite direction of the email terminals?"

"Well, that I can answer. They're positioned like that so nobody can stand behind the inmate using the screen without it locking up and going blank. Plus, whoever is on the other end of the call can't see the inmates walking by. They said it was done to maintain privacy, at least that's the official explanation. The real reason?" A mischievous grin appeared. "When they first set this up about two years ago, the video terminals were still along the wall, but they were turned around just like the email terminals. Inmates had their backs to the door and wouldn't see a guard or red-shirt come in. Problem was, anyone standing outside the square"—he pointed to the red squares on the floor around each terminal—"could see what was on the screen."

The yellow-shirt cleared his throat. "It took about a day and half for inmates to figure out this could be used as a community peep show. Sometimes a guy's wife or girlfriend would show a little skin or maybe even lots of skin. If they set it up in advance, some of the guys would charge others for a standing position just outside the red box.

"That lasted about two weeks. Even the guards were making it a point to stop by and linger when there was rumor of a 'show.' The warden found out and shut down the video terminals until the curtains could be put up and the terminals repositioned."

"Mass communications at the most primitive level! That's really funny." Mykola laughed, and it felt good. The tension that had built in anticipation of the video call with his attorney eased for the moment. "Thanks. I've got to talk to my attorney. I'm sure she'll be dressed in proper office attire, but I certainly wouldn't mind if she wasn't."

Mykola sat down at one of the terminals and, using a process similar to the one on the email terminals, made the connection with Roberta. Headphones were available, and since this was a conference with his attorney rather than a talk with a friend or family member, he chose to use them.

"Hi, how are you?" Roberta was sitting at her desk, wearing, as expected, a conservative business suit and an eggshell-colored blouse buttoned up to her neck. Makeup that highlighted her dark green eyes, small jade earrings swinging from her ears as she moved her head, and a crown of raven-black hair that glistened in the light coming in from the window behind her added a distinct note of individuality to her professional image.

To her right, on the corner of her desk, was something Mykola had not seen since he'd been in prison: flowers. Surrounded by baby's breath, peonies, dahlias, gladiolas, and asters were arranged in a chorus of color in a large crystal vase. Mykola couldn't help but stare at the flowers. These were living colors, colors he'd almost forgotten existed outside the drab grays and harsh whites throughout the prison.

"Mykola, are you there?"

"Yes, yes, I'm sorry. I was enraptured by that vase of flowers. A gift from a friend?"

"No, I have a weekly standing order with a florist down the street to send a bouquet of flowers of his choosing. When I see them on my desk in the morning, the day has started right. I think they help me stay positive. It's kind of silly, I know."

"No, not silly at all," Mykola replied.

Roberta was about five years older than Mykola, and he'd always considered her attractive, but necessarily, she'd always been professional in her demeanor. That hint of a smile, coupled with the flowers on her desk, suggested that there was another side to Roberta.

"So, going back to the original question . . . how are you?" she asked.

"I'm fine, all things considered. I'd like to tell you all about the prison experience, but we have limited time and you probably have a full schedule. So let's get down to business."

"Agreed." Her smile disappeared. "Before we begin, you need to understand how this videoconference works from a legal perspective. I'm supposed to read you this 500-word official document filled with legal terms, but I'm just going to explain it to you in my own words. It's not that complicated."

Mykola nodded. "I appreciate that."

"Fine. Mykola, we can both treat this videoconference like a personal face-to-face conference we're having in my office. The same rules of attorney-client privilege apply. There is one exception, and it is significant. Two years ago the New California legislature passed a law that requires the prison to record all attorney-client videos. Those video files are then kept in storage; nobody in the prison or law enforcement system sees them."

"If no one sees them, what's the point of recording and retaining them?" Mykola interjected.

"I'm getting to that. The only exception is if there is evidence of something illegal going on, perhaps bribery of an official, distribution of contraband, or witness tampering. That evidence has to be outside of the video, but if such evidence is presented, a judge has the right to view prison videos of the attorney and client and then decide if both the prosecution and the defense should also be allowed to see them.

"So talk freely, but be careful of what you say. Even a joke about selling drugs in prison might come back to haunt you years from now."

"I've got nothing to hide, but I promise to keep my tongue under control. Thanks."

Roberta continued. "We're looking at several avenues for

your appeal, but unfortunately, there's not much there. We haven't found any judicial errors, conflicts of interest, or personal relationships that might convince an appeals court to issue a ruling for a new trial. We've talked to jurors, and there's no indication of any outside influence by either the prosecution or friends of Mack Beranger, the guy you allegedly assaulted."

Roberta looked directly at Mykola for a reaction.

This was basically what he'd been told in the days following the jury verdict. Three months had now passed. Mykola tried to suppress his frustration, but his voice went up a couple of decibels. He wasn't shouting, but he wanted to make himself heard and, more importantly, understood.

"Look, Roberta, you know the law, and I've relied on you since day one. I think you've worked diligently on my behalf—"

"As I do for all my clients," Roberta responded before Mykola could shift to a "but."

"Right. The problem I see is that you're using your knowledge of the law to have me sprung on a technicality. But I didn't beat Beranger at all, much less with a bat, and quite honestly, now I'm not entirely sure you believe that. I don't want to have my sentence overturned with a footnote explanation."

"I didn't intend to aggravate you, Mykola. I'm sorry, and yes, I do believe you. The problem is that the time to argue the facts has passed. Unless there's some dramatic new evidence we couldn't possibly have known before now, your best hope and my professional advice is to continue to focus on possible procedural errors in the trial." Roberta was now sitting up perfectly straight with her hands folded on her desk, wearing her serious courtroom face.

"By dramatic new evidence, you mean my evil twin brother,

separated at birth, walking into the district attorney's office and confessing?" Mykola asked sarcastically but without accusation.

"That would do it, but it isn't going to happen in the next seven years." Roberta immediately hoped she hadn't rekindled Mykola's anger by mentioning the length of his sentence.

"I'm sorry, you're right," Mykola said in a calm, controlled manner. "What's next? Or *is* there even a next?"

"I'm not giving up. I'm going to look into possible perjury on the part of some of the prosecution's witnesses, including Beranger. It would have to be a significant and intentional misstatement, but it is a possibility."

"Okay, thanks. We'd better cut this off now so I'll have some time if we need to talk again."

"I think we're done for today anyway, but don't worry about the videoconference time, Mykola. If we need more time, I'll just make a call to the bureau and get it. As long as you're consulting with your attorney, you should be allowed all the time you need."

"Okay, bye." Mykola touched the button to end the call. The screen went back to black, with PRESS TO CONTINUE the only text on it.

6

Mykola walked by the trough and loaded his tray with a multicolored assortment of food, most of which was fresh, for a pleasant change. Water was his beverage choice, and it came out of a dispenser with some sort of filter attached. Nobody was sure whether the filter actually did anything, but at least it gave the impression of clean water. Mykola held the plastic glass up to the light and was pleased to see the water didn't have anything floating, swirling, or swimming in it.

"Hey, come on and sit over here," Sly called out, motioning to Mykola. Mykola smiled, walked over to Sly's table, and sat down. He hadn't made many friends at the prison, and Sly was one of the few men he'd encountered who always seemed to be upbeat. Lunch with him would surely be one of mindless chatter and a couple of jokes: a nice bit of mental relaxation.

"Thanks. I didn't know you had lunch on the same shift as I do," Mykola observed.

"Actually—it's Mike, right?" Sly had forgotten Mykola's name, but he didn't seem particularly embarrassed.

"Close, but it's 'ME-ko-la,'" Mykola said. "Of course, anything short of 'Hey, you' or 'Michele' would probably be okay."

Sly grinned. "Sorry . . . Mykola." He said the name slowly to get the pronunciation correct and help him remember. "Actually, I can eat lunch on any shift I want. It's one of the benefits of being a yellow-shirt."

"That so? How many yellow-shirts are there?"

"Don't know exactly, but I guess about fifty." Sly carefully and deliberately pushed some off-color beans to the side of his plate.

"I take it you like being a yellow-shirt?" Mykola asked.

"Well, yeah. There's some problems once in a while, and I don't like all the assignments I get, but for the most part I seem to get more respect here than I ever did on the outside."

"I think you're earning that respect. You certainly made my first day here a lot easier than I expected. And I thank you for that."

Sly beamed. "I know coming here can be pretty scary, even for tough guys. So I try my best to take some of the edge off when I do the tour and explain stuff."

Mykola ate his salad, which included a leafy vegetable he thought was spinach, cut-up tomatoes, and a crunchy vegetable that was either celery or bok choy.

"Speaking of explaining stuff, can you explain something else to me?" he asked.

Sly looked up and nodded, somewhat relieved that Mykola's facial expression didn't appear fearful or intense.

"I've met a bunch of the inmates here, and though I wouldn't call any of them friends, I'm starting to notice that some are pretty wired up and look like they'd jump if you just touched them on the shoulder. At the same time, they seem to be fighting their collars and all the systems in here that control them."

"Fighting their collars? You mean like trying to get them off?" Sly asked, confused.

"No, not physically fighting the collar but mentally battling it, like a kid who thinks his mother is being unfair to him when she wants him to clean up his room, wash his hands before supper, and go to bed at his bedtime. Sly, you are one of the few inmates here who doesn't seem to be fighting his collar. Why is that?"

Mykola could see that Sly was taken aback by his question, and it came out in Sly's snarling response. "You mean you think I *like* this collar? I hate this collar just as much as the next guy. I'm looking forward to the day I take it off for good."

"Sly, I'm sorry. I didn't mean to suggest that. It's just that I've seen more smiles on your face than I have on any ten other inmates combined. Heck, you even smile when you think about lima beans. How do you maintain that upbeat attitude? If you have a secret for not letting this joint get you down, I want to know."

This was a personal question, the type Sly seldom was asked. Most all the questions he answered every day were about procedures, and his answers were either right or wrong. Here was someone asking him about what was going on in his mind, and he quickly realized he hadn't even asked himself why he felt as he did. Mykola was right; he didn't like his collar, but he wasn't fighting it 16 hours each day.

"I'm not really sure . . ." Sly looked away from Mykola for a moment to compose himself. "Maybe it's because we're all pretty much equal in here. I'm not the best-educated guy or the smartest, and I certainly don't have a bunch of money in the bank. But in here I eat just as well as the guys with letters after their names, and my cell is no worse than the cell of the guy who used to live in a mansion."

"That makes sense, but how do you get past not having choices about what's for lunch and when you have to go back home to your cell?" Mykola watched intently as Sly chewed and swallowed a forkful of beans.

"That's a little easier to answer. Before I was sent here, I know I had even fewer choices. I'm not proud of it, but I made some mistakes even before I got caught stealing that car."

Mykola recalled Alex telling him that Sly had a history of making bad decisions including shoplifting, public inebriation, resisting arrest, and indecent exposure. Stealing the car had been only the final poor decision that had landed him here.

"I couldn't find a job, and everyone who I thought was my friend didn't want me around," Sly said. "So it wasn't so much a decision of *what* I was going to eat but *if* I was going to eat. I didn't have a home, and no matter where I woke up, I pretty much figured that by the end of the day I'd have to find another place to sleep."

"Sounds like you've had a tough life. I can see that having three squares and a cell you can call yours, at least for the time being, is a step up."

"I don't know if it's a step up, Mykola. I stole a car and got caught." Sly didn't want Mykola or anyone else to think being in prison was fortuitous for him. "I guess I wound up trading my freedom for a meal and a mattress. If there was anything I learned on the outside, it was that you have to accept the situation you're in and deal with it as best you can. Wishing and dreaming things are different isn't going to help; it'll only make it worse. Each day you're gonna wake up and find out your dream didn't come true."

"And being a yellow-shirt probably earns you respect, even from the guys who have more money and a better education," Mykola said with a smile.

"Well, yeah, there's that too, now that you mention it." Sly cocked his head, puffed up his chest, and posed like a statue of a Civil War general on his horse. He held the pose for just a moment until he and Mykola burst out laughing.

"So, about being a yellow-shirt. How did you become one?" Mykola asked.

"You want to get a yellow shirt?"

"No, just curious. I've run into a couple guys in the lab who are plenty smart, and they seem like they should be wearing yellow shirts. They always seem to have the answers to my questions."

"I guess I was just lucky. Some yellow-shirt got three jolts in three months and lost his shirt. They put up a sign for a replacement. I figured I didn't have anything to lose, so I was first in line. I don't cause any problems in here, and I figure that's why they gave it to me."

"So you can lose your yellow shirt if you break any rules?"

"That's it. Sometimes you break a rule and don't even know it until you get the jolt, but if it happens too often, you're back to a gray shirt."

Mykola started to lean back, remembering just in time that there was no back on the stool. "That explains it."

"Explains what?"

"My cellmate is a doctor, and he's usually assigned to the infirmary. You'd think he'd be a yellow-shirt."

"Maybe he doesn't want to be or he's wired too tight. Or maybe he's gotten more than a couple of jolts."

"You certainly have a good sense about people, Sly. I haven't asked him, but I suspect you're right about him being wired too tight and getting more than his share of jolts. I'm cautious about what I say to him."

Sly found a few more beans that weren't up to his standards while Mykola finished his salad and bit into a fresh apple.

"Nice surprise, having apples in the trough," he said. The crunch and sweet juice brought him back to his childhood for an instant, to when his mother would pick out a big and unblemished red apple and give it to him as a reward for helping her around the house.

"Must be some kind of mistake," Sly observed. "We get applesauce once in a while, but I can't remember the last time I saw a real red apple."

"Speaking of red"—Mykola held up the apple and motioned to a nearby table—"you ever think of becoming a red-shirt?"

"Me? I'm much too small, and besides, those guys are just mean. You never see them sitting with gray- and yellow-shirts. You'd have a good chance of getting a red shirt, though, if you wanted one."

"Well, I'd first have to get some tattoos, and I'm really not into pain," Mykola said.

Both Sly and Mykola laughed and then became instantly quiet when one of the three red-shirts turned and glared at them.

"So, how did your video call with your attorney go today?"

Alex had met up with Mykola outside, under the shade of

a roof overhang that extended several feet from the building. Along the wall other inmates were congregating in pairs or in small groups, and some simply stood alone. The temperature was in the mid-90s, and it was decidedly more comfortable inside. Yet being outside and seeing the expanse of desert was therapeutic. The subtle variations in the color of the sand, the tumbleweeds rolling and bouncing with every gust of wind, and the silhouette of mountains against a cloudless blue sky were a wonderful contrast to the monotone prison interior. Inmates could imagine themselves on their front porches, talking to neighbors who had stopped by. A cold beer from an ice chest would have completed the illusion, but that was not to be.

"Pretty much as I expected, and I didn't expect much." Mykola leaned back against the concrete block wall and felt the imperfections in the cement joints pressing into his shoulder blades. "She said they're exploring avenues of appeal but aren't making much progress."

"I'm sorry to hear that. I don't want to dash your hopes, but successful appeals are very rare, and I doubt that small-time law firms put much effort into pursuing them."

"Especially with nobodies like me . . ."

"I didn't want to say that, but you're right. If you were a celebrity of some sort and reporters were clamoring for updates, they'd probably be working harder just for the publicity."

"Damn thing is that I didn't do it." Mykola's head was down, and he stared at a crack in the concrete at his feet.

Alex could feel himself once again becoming the psychiatrist he'd studied so long to become. In the brief time Mykola had been his cellmate, Alex had become more sensitive to his moods and involuntarily read between the lines of his comments about everything from his childhood upbringing to his disputes with his partner in the furniture repair and refinishing business they had started.

Alex had resisted the urge to provide any counseling. Mykola was a fellow inmate and was becoming a friend, and Alex wanted that to be the relationship. A doctor-patient type of relationship would change that, and Mykola might even resent any attempts Alex might make to help him.

If nothing else, Alex understood that Mykola was proud, confident, and self-reliant. He was a man who would accept responsibility for his actions and do so without complaint. Alex had not seen this state of helplessness and acquiescence in him since he'd arrived at the prison. Maybe he really was innocent of the crime that had landed him here. Perhaps Alex could talk to him about it—as a friend.

"You know, you never did tell me exactly what landed you in this desert resort. You already know about my . . . let's call them 'billing errors and unlicensed herbal remedies.'"

Mykola looked up and saw a grin slowly developing on Alex's face.

"It's pretty simple," Mykola said. "I was at this bar that I go to occasionally after we close the shop for the day. I'd go there for a beer or two, basically to wait out the afternoon traffic. The Jam Session is an old, run-down bar that never kept up with the times. The customers are mostly older working guys who like to talk about sports and reminisce about the good times they had with their wives and old girlfriends."

"A dive bar."

"Yeah, I guess you could call it that. The beer is cheap, and the lights are so low you can't see the dirt pressed into the hardwood floor or the cracks in the vinyl barstools.

"So, I'm there talking to a pretty gal, Gina, who loves hockey, and I'm about to ask her to go to a game with me when this guy taps me on the shoulder. I recognize him; a guy who goes by the name of Mack. Obviously a regular, because he's there every time I come in. You couldn't miss him, because he was always talking over everyone else."

"I've known a couple of guys like that; don't want to be within ten yards of them."

"Anyway, he starts accusing me of hitting on his wife. I don't know what the hell he's talking about. Besides this gal Gina, there are only a couple of other women in the bar. Then he tells me his wife has been to our shop and talked to me about building some furniture. Supposedly I'd been leading her on with comments about good wood and applying shellac."

"Wood, varnish, and shellac are your business," Alex said.

"Exactly. I figured out the woman he was talking about, a Botox brunette about 40 years old who had come into the shop several times with a project but never made a commitment to have the work done. I'd finally given her an inflated price, figuring that would end the visits and discussions. She'd surprised the hell out of me by saying, 'Okay, when can you come by and take the measurements for the bookcase?' Then she gave me a 25 percent deposit in cash."

"You think she was coming on to you?"

"No doubt about that, but she definitely wasn't my type. Anyway, I go to her house a couple days later to do the measurements and get her to pick out the type of wood and stain to match the rest of the furniture. The bookcase she wants me to build is a big one, but the damn thing is, I look around and there's not a book to be seen."

Alex was now pressing his lips together, doing all he could to avoid laughing. Mykola noticed.

"That's okay, go ahead and laugh, because this part of the story is pretty funny. Oh, I forgot to mention that when I got there she had just come inside from what she said was a dip in their pool. So she's got a beach towel wrapped around her shoulders, and she's wearing a bikini that couldn't have been made with more than one square foot of material, in my professional estimation."

Alex could sense that telling his story was helping Mykola deal with the disappointment of the discussion with his lawyer. Just having someone listen, as Alex had learned long ago in his psychiatric practice, was all the therapy some people needed.

"Go on," he said. "Did you get more measurements than you came for?"

"I got the measurements I needed, and while I was tempted to get a few more, I didn't. This woman was manipulative, and I didn't want to have anything to do with her. Still, I agreed to build the bookcase, and a couple of weeks later I delivered it and attached it to the wall. I must have been there about an hour. This time she was wearing a bathrobe, acting like this was perfectly normal attire at 11:00 in the morning."

"Did she ever mention a husband?"

"No, and I didn't know this guy Mack was her husband until that night in the bar. I figure he saw my truck parked outside and tracked me down. The fact that we liked to go to the same bar was a coincidence, I suppose.

"So anyway, me and Mack are getting into it, and with his

loud voice, several of the other patrons hear us. By this time Gina, the gal I was talking to, has gotten up and left. I'm getting angry, and I figure the best way to end this is to just walk out. I'm going out the door, turn to look back at Mack, and he's boasting to his friends how he 'laid down the law.'"

Mykola's smile was gone. His muscles tightened and his hands curled into fists as he spoke. "I drive home. It's about an hour, maybe a little more because of construction. Two days later I get a knock on the door and I'm arrested for aggravated assault."

"Assault of who? Mack?"

"Yeah. Turns out Mack is an ex-cop turned security guard. Someone had bashed him in the back with a two-by-four or baseball bat, and I was the one who supposedly did it."

"I'm confused. What reason would you have for assaulting him?"

"I don't know, other than settling the score after the verbal scuffle and put-down in the bar. That's what the prosecution argued."

"Any witnesses? Did he see who hit him?" Alex was now listening to Mykola as if he were telling a whodunit story.

"No, this happened in the parking lot about an hour after I left. It was already dark, and the guy who hit him sneaked up on him just as he was getting into his car. No one saw it, but a security camera caught the assault. With the shadows and darkness it wasn't immediately clear who was carrying the club, but the guy was my height and weight and looked to be my age."

"Doesn't sound like enough to convict anyone."

"That's what I thought, but then they ran the camera footage through a facial recognition software program the police use,

and it identified me as the attacker. They showed the video
footage in court and then a single enlarged frame from the video
that *appeared* to show my face. Jurors looked at that single
frame and at me, and that was all it took. Hell, when I saw that
image I thought I might have forgotten what I did that night."

"You couldn't prove you were at home? The tracking systems
on cars are active whenever they're in motion. They would have
shown your car slowing for the construction traffic and then
being shut down in your garage, all with regular time stamps."

"My car doesn't have that technology. It's a '98 Z06 I restored, and they didn't have tracking tech back then."

"So you couldn't prove you were home, and you'd had an
argument with Mack a few hours before, and then the security
video . . ." Alex summarized.

"Yes. But I didn't do it."

Alex couldn't be sure Mykola was telling the whole story,
but the unwavering tone in "But I didn't do it" was enough to
convince him Mykola wasn't the one who had swung the bat.

"There are enough guys in here who deserve to be here,
including me, and I can see they're having a tough time of it.
It must be much harder if you don't deserve it. I'm sorry you're
here," Alex said.

The sincerity came through, and for Mykola, just having
someone who believed him was a surprising change. Alex had
become a friend, someone he could trust.

7

"By my count, we've played 30 games and you've beaten me 27 times," Mykola said deferentially.

"True, but the games are lasting longer and you've won two of the past seven. I'm starting to really think about every move," Alex said with the hope of encouraging Mykola to continue playing.

Alex liked how the chess games took his mind off everything else and helped him to put things in perspective. Sure it would be nice to be playing at home and following up with a cognac nightcap, but this was pretty close to the same experience, and for that he was thankful.

"How did you learn to play?" Mykola asked as he moved his bishop across the board, taking Alex's pawn and setting it aside.

"Learned when I was a kid, but then I didn't play for about 20 years. Then one summer, when the kids were about eight and sixteen, my wife and I decided we were going to take a one-week, no-electronics vacation. You know how it is: everyone is on a phone or a pad or sitting in front of a screen. Or, the worst, playing an online game with people they will never meet. We wanted to get away from all that, spend some good family time together.

"So I rented a small house up the coast about a mile from the beach. Sarah and Allen were all excited about it until I told them there would be no electronics. Nothing. Except my cell for emergencies."

"I don't have any kids, but I imagine that was distressing for them," Mykola said.

"You know it," Alex said. "Of course my son Allen, the consummate negotiator, said that if we were going back in time, there couldn't be any microwaved or prepackaged food. Everything had to be made from scratch."

"He had you there." Mykola snickered.

"But that was okay. I really wanted us to be a family, not just four people sharing a house. Spending time in the kitchen, preparing meals, could also bring us closer together. With Sarah in high school, she was already spending more time away from home than at home, and Allen was too often alone in his room welded to his video games."

Alex stopped and suddenly had a faraway look in his eyes as he rested his chin on his clasped hands. It was only a moment, and he shook his head as if to regain his focus.

"So, anyway, we went up there. During the day we'd go to the beach or hike up the hills. In the evenings we read books or played board games. There were some silly games, and everyone enjoyed them, but they were the kind that you play once and then they're boring. That was the warm-up."

Alex was now speaking excitedly, with hand gestures to emphasize key points, and Mykola listened intently.

"Then I brought out the chessboard . . . and they surprised me by not protesting having to learn what they called 'an old-guys game.' They learned to play in one evening and actually enjoyed it. Still, it didn't measure up to the action of a video game."

"So that was just a one-night chess event?" Mykola asked, somewhat disappointed that the story apparently had come to an end.

"Oh, no. I was ready for that, and the next night I brought out a chess clock and we all played speed chess. Allen got so hyped up, he had a hard time falling asleep.

"Then, for the longest time after we came back from that vacation, we set aside a couple of hours after Sunday dinner to play chess. Allen and Sarah are exceedingly competitive, and I found that I really had to concentrate to beat either of them."

This was the first time Alex had talked about his family, and Mykola could sense that just reflecting back on those times was emotional for him. A display of weakness was something Alex just didn't do. To avoid any further uneasiness Mykola asked, "So, what are they doing now?"

Alex looked up and brought himself back to the present.

"Sarah works for ZG Manufacturing in their digital security department. ZG is a recent start-up that makes high-tech and biologic products in zero gravity. I don't really understand it. She's part of a team responsible for protecting all the company's computers on the ground and in space from hackers, both home-grown and foreign agencies. Want to hear something funny? You can't tell anyone . . ."

"Of course. Who could I tell?"

"Well, Sarah got her master's in digital security online, just like everyone does these days. She was getting straight *A*'s throughout the three-year program, but on the final project she got a *B*. Gee, was she pissed!

"So what did she do? She hacked into the college's computer system, the one designed by the professor who conducted the course, and changed her final project grade to an *A*. No one ever found out," Alex said with obvious pride.

"Now, Allen is taking a somewhat different route. He's still in high school but is already working on a gig basis with a business consulting company that is teaching managers game theory to improve their strategic decisions."

"Wait, you lost me there. What's game theory?" Mykola asked. "Is that some sort of computer programming process?"

Mykola was getting more comfortable admitting to Alex that his knowledge of technology and science was limited. Alex, in turn, appreciated Mykola's honesty and self-confidence; he'd encountered so many people who were loath to admit they didn't understand something until they were forced to apply it. Mykola was a pleasant exception.

"Game theory? In its simplest form it's easy to understand and apply, but it does get increasingly complex, and I won't pretend I understand it well enough to explain the multifaceted aspects to you. Ever heard of the prisoner's dilemma?"

"Sure, I've heard of it, but never thinking I'd be in a prison, I didn't have any interest in it," Mykola said with a cynical tone.

"Actually, it's just a model of the outcomes when two people make individual decisions that affect each other. Let's say two guys have been arrested for robbing a convenience store. The cops don't have enough evidence to convict either one, and so they try to get one or the other to testify against his partner. In exchange, reduced prison terms are offered. Neither of the robbers knows if the other will testify against him. Are you with me?"

"I think so. Each has a choice to testify against the other or remain quiet and proclaim his innocence, but they don't know what the other will say," Mykola offered. "Logically, they should both proclaim their innocence. That's what I'd do."

"Right, pretty simple. But let's say the cops can get them on a lesser charge, like carrying an unlawful weapon. The cops tell each of them there are three possible outcomes. If neither testifies, both will be charged with the lesser offense and serve two years. If only one agrees to testify against the other, the one testifying gets no prison time, but the other guy, if he's not willing to testify against his partner, gets a ten-year prison term. If they both testify, they both get six-year terms." Alex paused to see if Mykola understood. "Do you see the dilemma?"

"If you testify against the other guy, you get either no sentence or a six-year term, depending on what the other guy says. If you don't testify, you get a two-year term or a ten-year term, again depending on what the other guy decides to do. Tough choice; I can see that," Mykola responded.

"Right. And that dilemma applies to a lot of decisions we make when other people's decisions affect the outcome for themselves and for us. It applies to decisions on everything from what to bring to a potluck dinner to declaring war. It gets a lot more complicated, but that's the basis of game theory."

"Something to think about, isn't it?" Mykola rubbed the back of his neck and felt the cold steel of his collar. "Of course, not everyone is just out to get the best for themselves. Some people look for a better outcome for others or the fairest outcome for all."

"Most definitely, Mykola. The point is that many decisions we make are not made in isolation. We have to understand the payouts not only for ourselves but for others. When we know that, we can better judge what someone else is going to do and make our decision accordingly."

"That may be good advice for the analytical types, but I have to rely on my gut feel. Most of the time that's all I've got," Mykola mused.

"So, going back to Allen's work. This consulting company creates business games based on game theory. It's a way for executives to practice what they learn in their seminars. In the games, however, they play against people they haven't met, and Allen is one of those people. It's done online, so they don't know he's just a high school kid. Like I said, Allen is extremely competitive. He's learned the game theory models the company teaches, and often as not, he'll beat the mid-level managers he's playing against."

"Whew, a couple of geniuses in your family!" Mykola exclaimed.

"I'm pretty proud of them. Sarah is highly respected at ZG. She's got a knack for making the right, unemotional decision. Also, if she says she's going to do something, you can count on it getting done no matter how challenging it is. She believes in herself, but she doesn't have an inflated sense of self-importance or a need to feed her ego. She listens to people and finds something of value in everyone, no matter their position, education, or failings in a prior life. I hope one of these days she makes me a grandfather; I have no doubt she'll be as talented and creative as a parent as she is at digital security."

"Allen doesn't sound like a sloth either." Mykola was envious of his cellmate.

"He is the little wizard. He's about a half foot shorter than Sarah, but in terms of intelligence he's about a half foot taller." Alex paused, and Mykola could see in Alex's expression that there was more to Allen's story and Alex was trying to decide if he should share it.

"And . . . ?" Mykola leaned forward and looked directly at Alex.

"Well, as you can understand, we don't get into a lot of deep talks these days, either through email or video. Hard to do that when you know somebody's listening in. Mostly these days it's just 'I'm fine, how about you?' kind of chatter. So I don't know if Allen has grown out of this. But he was always pushing himself to impress other people. He loved to surprise people with his ability to solve problems and do what people thought couldn't be done, whether the challenge was mental or physical.

"Once, when he was ten years old, he somehow got his bike into a department store and rode it down the escalator, to the amazement of his friends and the consternation of a store clerk."

Mykola couldn't help but laugh. "Whew, he sounds like a handful!"

"He just keeps pushing himself. So far he's been lucky and hasn't hurt himself or anyone else. I hope Sarah can be the steadying influence on him now that I'm not there." Alex sighed and slowly shook his head.

"What about their mother?"

"Mykola, that's a whole other story, a story I might tell you some other time. Let's call it a night."

⊙

"You've got mail," Alex bellowed the following morning, trying to imitate the AOL voice made famous in his youth.

On the tray with their collars were two pieces of paper, one addressed to Alex and the other to Mykola.

"What the hell are you talking about? Somebody wrote me a letter?" Mykola asked, hopefully, but figuring Alex was teasing him.

"Yes. It is a letter from His Highness, the warden."

"What has gotten into you? You're acting really strange, in a warped sort of way." Mykola was waiting for the punch line, as if Alex were doing a stand-up comedy routine and he was the object of the joke.

"It's the monthly points report."

Mykola looked puzzled, even a bit suspicious.

Dropping the drama in his voice, Alex asked, "Didn't Sly tell you about the points system during your introduction?"

"He mentioned earning points, but I thought it was just a colloquialism for getting in good with guards and staff here."

"It's much more than that. Your actions in this place can earn or cost you actual points." Alex handed Mykola his copy of the report. "You earn points for the work you do in the industrial lab and lose points for infractions that get you a jolt."

"And I should be concerned about how many points I have because . . . ?"

"Because the points can be exchanged for days at the end of your sentence. Every 500 points shortens your time here by one day."

"Wow, I've been here less than a month and I've already earned 5,650 points. I should be walking out the front door before dinner."

"Look closely, Mykola," Alex said, pointing to the sheet. "You got 5,000 points on day one. They give you that to get you on board with the program. On a typical day you'll earn 10 to 20 points, but if you get a Level 1 jolt you'll lose 1,000 points, and a Level 2 will pretty much wipe out your balance."

"You mean it's like the frequent flyer programs some of the airlines had years ago?" Mykola asked with a smirk.

"Pretty much. I swear the guys in the London Tower corporate offices are all rejects from big-name marketing and consumer product companies. They seem to forget that some guys are in here for 20 years, and earning a few days' or even 100 days' early release doesn't mean a thing to them."

"But if you're in your last year or so, it could seem more important, right?"

"I suppose. I don't think many of the inmates even look at this report, other than to play points poker. There are a couple of exceptions. You pick up extra points if you've gone a long time without any infractions, and you can pick up big points based on some tests they give you. I don't know all the details; they change the rules on a whim. At least they print the report and distribute it every month. I use the back to keep a journal."

"You can have mine." Mykola handed it to Alex.

"Thanks. Hey, speaking of points, we'd better get these collars on. Otherwise we're going to start today in the red."

Mykola and Alex put their collars on. A couple of minutes later, the cell gate opened. Walking out, Mykola asked, "One more thing: what happens if you die in here? What happens to the points?"

"They become part of your estate." Alex returned to his bellowing "official announcements" voice: "Each point is worth a dime. Your beneficiaries can buy some flowers for your gravestone with the proceeds."

"Cool. Better than frequent flyer miles."

Both laughed as they strolled down to the chow hall. It was a good way to start the day.

Monday, June 24, was Alex's parole hearing.
"Parole hearing" was the name of the process used to determine whether an inmate would be released from prison before completely finishing his sentence, but it was nothing like the process by that name used even 20 years earlier.

At that time, parole was a judgment made by a panel and based on several factors, some precise and readily verifiable, others entirely subjective. There was no formal weighting of the factors, and studies had shown that the panel's decisions could be predicted on the basis of how close they were to breaking for lunch and how many paroles they had already granted that day.

Even football game scores seemed to influence their decisions. If the hearing was on a Monday and the professional football team that everyone followed had won impressively on Sunday, parole was more likely to be granted. If the team lost to a team they were supposed to beat handily, inmates could look forward to at least another year in prison—if the panel members were football fans.

Naturally, panel members denied that lunch, football scores, and all the rest influenced their decisions, and probably they believed it was true, but the correlations were too high to call them coincidences.

In the past two decades that system had changed, supposedly for the better. A few states had eliminated the subjectivity of parole boards entirely, substituting "flat time" as the length of service, with no chance for early release. A federal prisoner could earn up to 54 days' credit annually for good behavior. However, there was still some subjectivity as to how much good behavior credit could be lost through bad behavior.

Now an algorithm approved by the New California Department of Corrections made the early release decisions. That algorithm used 90 percent factual, documented data and 10 percent expert opinion. The hard data came from prison records. In the case of the State Line Prison, it included the number of Level 1 and Level 2 violations, productivity in the industrial shop, completed online vocational courses, and higher-level yellow-shirt and red-shirt responsibilities.

Those were the factors the inmates were told about, but there were others as well, which inmates had a second sense about but could never confirm. These included disparaging comments made either vocally or in emails about the prison, the government, or the justice system. These measures were supposed to be indicators of whether the inmate would be a law-abiding citizen if released from prison.

In the past year a new type of measurement had been added, one that was supposed to better measure law-abiding intent: the dopamine-adrenaline-serotonin sensor, or DAS.

This would be Alex's first experience with the DAS, and

he made sure to be standing outside the DAS room a couple of minutes before his scheduled time. At the appointed time, a green light above the door came on. Alex opened the door and walked in. A red-shirt confirmed Alex's inmate number and walked him back toward a table at which a technician was seated.

The technician, a young woman wearing a starched full-length lab coat and wide dark-rimmed glasses, greeted Alex in the manner one might expect from a doctor's receptionist. She had explained the DAS process to him in her office a couple of days earlier. With her bright aquamarine eyes and delicate frame, she looked too girlish to be working in a prison, and the scent of baby powder that wafted from her only served to confirm that. She must have been aware of her impact on men in the prison, for she barely looked at Alex as she led him to the virtual reality chamber. Alex wasn't sure it was required, but he made sure to maintain at least two arms' lengths from her.

The virtual reality chamber was a room within another room. In sharp contrast to the walls throughout the prison, the outside wall of the spherical chamber was the darkest denim blue at its base, progressively becoming a lighter blue up the wall until at the top it was an arctic ice blue. There was no distinct separation of the colors as one might see on a color palette. They simply blended into one another.

Alex knew that blue was the most calming of colors. In fact, when he'd conducted therapy sessions with his patients years ago, it had been in a room in which the predominant color was sky blue.

The chamber door had no handles or hinges and was perfectly flush with the sphere. To open it, the technician entered a code on her tablet computer. Silently and mysteriously, the door slowly came straight out about three feet and then shifted up.

"Before we go in, you'll need to take off your shoes and socks and put these on," the technician said to Alex as she held out a pair of black, ankle-length socks that appeared to be knitted with some sort of microfilament wires woven into the soles.

"What are these for?" Alex asked, more out of curiosity than concern.

"They are part of the virtual reality experience. They will give you a sensation of walking, even though your feet won't be moving. It's nothing to be worried about," the technician replied.

The black socks fit perfectly. As soon as he put them on, the technician motioned for Alex to follow her into the chamber. Alex, more than six feet tall, had to duck slightly to walk under the raised door. Unlike the outside, the inside was azure, without any gloss or shine. It was illuminated by a series of small lights in a semicircle beginning directly above the chair and continuing to the floor. Without any seams in the walls and with no discernable shadows to provide perspective, Alex had no sense of how far the sphere walls were from where he stood. In fact, he couldn't be sure that he *was* in a sphere. The only thing that looked three-dimensional was the chair and the small, circular, flat floor around its base.

"Please step up and seat yourself comfortably in the chair, Alex," she said in a soft but firm voice. Alex nodded and then carefully stepped forward, turned, and lowered himself into the chair. Other than its gray color, which matched his uniform, the chair reminded him of the worn and stained leather recliner he had at home. Just the whoosh of air coming from the compressed cushions brought back memories of hours spent watching classic black and white movies.

His forearms lay on the wide, flat arms of the chair, which felt cool and slightly sticky.

"That's fine, Alex," the technician said as she used both of her delicate, perfectly manicured hands to turn Alex's left hand over and expose the scarred underside of his forearm. Oblivious to Alex's now questioning eyes, she wrapped rubber restraints around his left wrist and elbow.

"Now, as I explained the other day, I'm going to insert this probe into your vein. It's no more uncomfortable than giving blood."

Alex looked down as she pressed the tip of the four-inch silver probe against his skin. After an instant of resistance, it slid under the skin and punctured the vein.

"And now the headband." She stood behind him and placed a soft band around his forehead, then carefully positioned three bands from front to back over the top of his head. She made several small adjustments to the bands while looking at her tablet.

"How does that feel?" It was the first time Alex had noted a feminine, caring tone in her voice, and he savored the sound for a moment before replying.

He could feel the small metal sensors on his nearly shaven head, but they weren't in the least uncomfortable.

"Just fine; just what you told me to expect."

"Now I just need to position your feet." She bent down and positioned Alex's feet on the centers of two metal pads and secured them with the same type of bands used to secure his arms.

"Okay, Alex, we'll start in just a minute." She rested her hand gently on his shoulder as she spoke. "As I told you at our first meeting, you may find yourself to be very relaxed and tempted to close your eyes and doze off. Don't. Otherwise we'll have go through this process all over again, and I don't know when there's an opening on the schedule.

"Also, don't be surprised if any of the virtual characters refer to you by your name. If you are asked a question, answer it truthfully in a normal voice. If you try to guess what the system is looking for, it'll spot it and that'll count against you."

"Understood." Just being in her presence was soothing for Alex, and for a moment he considered not following her instructions so that he could go through her introduction to the DAS system again. That was only momentary; Alex had no assurance that he'd have the same technician next time. Furthermore, he reminded himself, the whole point of the next two hours was to convince the panel that he was worthy of early release.

"Last thing," she said as she slipped the 3D glasses over his eyes. "Now move your head back and forth and up and down; I just need to make sure the glasses don't slip and move around."

Alex did, and the technician made no further adjustments.

"We're ready," she said.

Alex heard her step back and out of the chamber. Simultaneously, the door closed and the chair back moved to a more upright position. Over about 15 seconds, the lights slowly faded and went completely out. Alex was in totally silent pitch-black darkness. Before Alex had time to react to this state of sensory deprivation, an image of an autumn day in the mountains surrounded him on the walls of the sphere.

It was as if Alex was transported to a day when he was a

child and he and his family would make their annual trip to the mountains to take in the blazing colors of fall foliage and breathe air that was perfectly clear and refreshingly cool, under a cloudless azure sky.

This was the first stage in the DAS system. It was designed to anticipate any inmate nervousness. For the first few minutes, this peaceful image was shown, soothing outdoor sounds of rustling leaves and birds chirping in the trees were played, and even a gentle breeze was produced.

It all made Alex forget where he was. It was no coincidence that it recreated a pleasurable experience of Alex's youth.

Unlike the home systems most people used to watch movies, the DAS system covered the entire visual field, the full inner surface of the sphere. Alex could look left, right, up, and even down and the perspective was real. After a few minutes, the scene shifted to create the illusion that he was riding in a car, with the wind blowing through his hair and the fresh smell of pine after a spring rain. He could feel the bumps in the road and the centripetal force as the car went around a corner.

Then the scene shifted again and Alex was back in the woods, walking through them this time. He had forgotten about the illusion of walking the technician had explained earlier: the sound and pressure of feet on a pavement and the slight oscillation of his head with each step convinced him he was in fact walking, though he hadn't moved from the chair.

When the sensors indicated that Alex had calmed to a normal state, the vignettes began to play and continued for the next two hours. Unknown to Alex, the scenes changed in response to the chemical, physical, and neurological measurements that were being taken. As the technician had explained, the system's virtual characters interacted with Alex in a manner indistinguishable from that of real people.

Alex is sitting at a kitchen table along with a young couple he somehow knows are husband and wife. It's strange: Alex thinks he recognizes the man sitting before him, but he can't place him. The table is clean but worn, and appliances in the background are from another generation. Alex hears the weak cry of a baby from another room.

The man has received a duplicate government tax refund check, which lies on the table between the two. He tells his wife that the second check is a mistake, a duplicate, and that he has already cashed the original.

When the wife doesn't respond, the man turns to Alex and asks what he should do. Should he attempt to cash it or should he return it?

Alex has the sense of someone "looking over his shoulder," and he's tempted to tell the virtual man to return the check to the IRS. He's still in the zone between reality and virtual reality, trying to maintain cognitive control of what he's experiencing. But the next instant he reminds himself of the technician's caution not to attempt to game the system.

"I can't tell you what to do," Alex says to the man, "but if you cash it and the IRS later finds out it was an error, you'll probably just have to return the money. Just make sure you don't spend it for a couple of months."

The man looks up at Alex, then at his wife, who smiles. He then endorses the check.

The scene faded into a new vignette.

Alex walks into an Asian "massage parlor" in the dead of night. He recognizes it; it's only a couple of blocks from where he had his medical practice. As soon as he hears the door close behind him, he smells the faint aroma of jasmine and lilac. Adjusting his eyes to the dark room, he feels himself step forward and is greeted by a friendly, mature Korean woman. She smiles in a way that shows Alex she recognizes him.

In the background Alex sees young women wearing loosely fitting full-length silk robes. They walk toward him one by one, smiling seductively at Alex and beckoning to him.

Alex nervously explains to the mature woman that he must have made a mistake and walked into the wrong building.

"Very well, perhaps another time. Mai Ling and the other girls will be disappointed. You are one of their favorites."

The image slowly dissolved and the next vignette appeared, one obviously intended to calm Alex. He felt his pulse racing and concentrated on taking slow, deep breaths. Was he reliving a repressed memory or was this a dream? There were too many details for him to be unemotional about what he'd just experienced, regardless of whether it was part of a memory or a dream. This was a genuine experience for him, and he would not be able to forget it. Worse, he would not be able to share it with anyone close to him for fear of losing their respect.

The vignettes continued. Alex became less and less aware that they were virtual. The sense of time faded, and he was very much in the moment.

Alex is walking down the aisles of a grocery store. He feels hungry, and the aroma of barbecued meat draws him to the back of the store.

He slows his pace as he sees a handsome young man helping a disabled woman of a like age with grocery shopping. The young woman catches Alex looking at her and returns a gentle smile.

Alex continues walking. There are many other shoppers, all rather nondescript in appearance. None of these virtual people look familiar to Alex.

As Alex is returning to the front of the store, he sees the young man using his card to pay for the young lady's items at checkout.

The vignette ends with Alex standing outside and seeing both of them getting into a van. They are holding hands.

Each vignette lasted three to ten minutes, with a brief pause between each. Some had no human interaction, such as a virtual drive through a forest or a lion running down a young antelope.

The last vignette begins to bring Alex back to reality.

He is alone in his prison cell, sitting on his bunk and looking at his small stack of books and the chess set. Outside the cell he hears other inmates talking. The collar is on his neck. With his free right hand he reaches up to feel its cold steel.

The images inside the sphere faded, the lights came on, and the technician came in. Not saying a word—perhaps she recognized Alex's need for a few moments of silence to readjust to reality—she removed the intravenous probe, the 3D glasses, and the bands around his arms, feet, and head.

"Take your time," she said when she was done. "Just sit here, and when you're ready, get up and leave. You have lots of time before dinner."

Like a doctor who had just sent blood to a lab for analysis, she gave no indication of whether the DAS results would be favorable or unfavorable. She simply said, "They'll have your parole decision tomorrow. Perhaps you'd like a glass of orange juice?"

Right. The parole decision. It took a moment for Alex to remember this was why he'd gone through these virtual reality experiences. It didn't seem all that important at that moment. He just sat there and reflected upon what he had seen and felt. At times he had enjoyed the scenes, and at other times he'd found them disturbing or agitating. Some scenes he'd found interesting and pleasantly stimulating; others had reminded him of embarrassing or humiliating things he had done. A couple, like the massage parlor scene, had been particularly intense.

In some way he knew the vignettes had changed him, and he didn't know if those changes were for better or worse. He also couldn't know if the memories he'd formed would be permanent, like those he had about traumatic real-life events.

That evening Alex made it a point to avoid Mykola, returning to the cell just minutes before 8:00 and making up a headache excuse so that he didn't have to tell him about his DAS experience. He needed time alone to think it through.

9

When Mykola returned to the cell the following evening, he could feel a simmering tension emanating from Alex. Alex was sitting on his bunk just staring at the floor, with fingers spread wide on his thighs in a position that looked as if he were ready to strangle someone. He didn't bother to look up when Mykola asked, "How'd it go?"

"Obviously I wasn't paroled, if that's what you mean," Alex replied with caustic sarcasm.

Mykola knew better than to press Alex for details. He just stood there and waited for Alex to explain when he was ready. A minute of quiet passed by, but the eerie stillness that seemed to spread from their cell down the hall made it feel as if time had slowed. Finally Alex spoke.

"I'm disgusted with myself for getting my hopes up. I knew being granted parole on the first hearing was unlikely. Hell, I haven't heard of one in ten being granted parole on the first hearing, and that was before they brought in that machine."

Mykola cocked his head. "Machine? What machine?"

"They call it the DAS. It's a virtual reality contraption that measures your reactions to various situations. I used a crude version of it in my practice when I was treating patients for debilitating phobias and PTSD. The difference is that the DAS isn't used in a therapeutic process; it is just used to determine whether you are fit to return to outside society." The words came out of Alex like sharpened knives, and Mykola took a half step back to avoid them.

"So, did they give you an explanation of why you weren't granted parole . . . ?"

"No, those London Tower admins just had me sit at a table across from them and they read the decision off a tablet. It was something like 'Based on the points you've accumulated in the last six years and the results of the tests you've taken, the Board of Corrections for the State of New California is unable to grant you parole at this time.' There was a bunch of legal and administrative mumbo jumbo, but I stopped listening when I heard that line."

"I thought there was supposed to be an interview too. Didn't you get a chance to answer questions and make your case?" Mykola asked, now thinking about his own future possibilities of early release.

Alex forced a laugh. "That's what I asked, but they told me that an interview with the board was granted only when the hard data didn't clearly point to either granting or denying parole. The implication was that the hard data in my case clearly pointed to denial, but they didn't take the time to explain it to me. I guess they figured I was just a stupid inmate."

Mykola had no response. Trying to console Alex, he knew,

would come off as condescending, and Alex's anger would then be directed at him.

The white noise and circulation of chilled air coming through a register in the hallway increased the sense of emotional distance between the two men.

Alex turned away and stood totally motionless, facing the cell gate. His arms were now folded across his chest and his hands were grabbing his shoulders; it was the body language of a man who had clearly lost hope and was intimately aware of it.

The four-faced clock suspended in the cellblock hallway showed 7:59:59 in bright green lights and then 8:00:00 in stop-sign red. At that precise moment the cell gate began to close. The tiny steel wheels on the bottom and top of the gate initially seemed to protest being forced to move, but then rolled steadily, and with each turn, a rhythm of squeaks came from them. A residue of rust probably accounted for the noise, but as long as they kept rolling, the prison staff wasn't concerned.

The clock continued to tick off the seconds. The gate rolled to the closed position and stopped. For a moment there was no sound from the gate, but Mykola could hear Alex drawing in a deep breath. Then the latch to the door came down with a sound as shuddering as two heavy iron hammers being swung against each other. An electronic beep, totally incongruous with the sound of the rolling gate or closing latch, signified the end of the process.

Alex let out his breath, dropped his arms, and cast his eyes upon those two inches of cell bar that separated the outside from the inside. From the hallway he could hear the other cell latches rapidly falling into place, sounding much like the teeth of giant zippers being closed. The last one, from the far end of the hall, left a faint echo.

A few minutes later the collars were off, and Mykola placed both of them on the shelf in the bars.

Alex started shuffling slowly back and forth in the cell, the soles of his shoes producing a sound like wire brush sticks sliding over a snare drum. His eyes still downcast, he began to think out loud.

"There was something strange about the video in that DAS machine . . . some of it reminded me of people and places I know, and others didn't remind me of anything I had ever experienced, except for things I'd seen in movies . . . the voices, the dialogue, the sirens . . . I couldn't consciously keep up with everything that was going on . . ."

Suddenly he stopped and stared directly at Mykola, who was now sitting on his bunk. Alex had a look that portended violent rage, and Mykola felt his muscles tighten.

"I know what they were doing!" Alex practically shouted. Just as quickly, he reminded himself that he might be heard by a passing guard. He sat next to Mykola on the bunk and continued in just above a whisper, "The machine wasn't just measuring indications of whether I'd be likely to commit more nonviolent crimes like fraud, tax evasion, and illegal sales. It was also being used to determine whether I was likely to be a pyromaniac, a sociopath, or a pedophile. The tech didn't explain it to me, but I'm now convinced that was what the DAS was doing. That's why I wasn't granted parole. It had nothing to do with points earned or remorse and shame for those crimes I did commit. It was all about keeping me in prison to prevent me from committing crimes I've never even considered."

"Well, *are* you a pyromaniac, a sociopath, or a pedophile?" Mykola asked, regretting his question as soon as his words spilled out.

Alex was seething now, not only at the system but also at the man sitting next to him, a man he had come to consider his best friend.

"No!" he said. "I know technology has advanced in the years I've been in prison, and perhaps it can measure someone's predilections, but I don't believe for a moment that it can predict my future actions. How would you like it if I spread the word that you're a necrophiliac?"

"I wouldn't like it—and I don't even know what it means," Mykola said in an apologetic tone.

"Necrophiliacs," Alex said, "like having sex with corpses."

Mykola blinked.

⊙

"Allen, look! We got an email from Dad," Sarah called out as she sat back on the couch in what they called their "playroom," a large bedroom crammed with all sorts of technology, some classic and primitive, but mostly the latest and most sophisticated available to the general public. Some of the tech, courtesy of ZG and used by Sarah when working from home, the general public wasn't even aware existed.

Emails from Alex had been infrequent ever since the time Allen had forwarded an email Alex had written him to Morris Brown, a longtime friend who had graduated from med school with Alex many years earlier. It was just friendly news, but someone was tracking the path and content of all emails that originated in the prison, and Dr. Morris Brown found himself being investigated, charged, and convicted of offenses similar to the ones that had landed Alex in prison.

People always hung around with like-minded people. So if you knew one crook, he'd likely lead you to other crooks. That was the conclusion Sarah had come to. She guessed that this "benefit" of allowing inmates to email family and friends had been sold to the Department of Corrections and the State Panel on Law Enforcement on just that basis.

"So, what does he have to say?" Allen asked without turning away from the game he was playing.

"It's kind of strange. I'll read it to you."

Hi guys. It has been a while. Same old stuff going on here, as you might expect. In fact it is really boring, and so I thought I would take an e-class in something I'd find challenging: integral calculus. Unfortunately, there aren't any available on the prison system.

"Are you sure that's what it says?" Allen pressed pause on the game and turned around to look at his sister. "Dad was never into advanced math of any sort. Heck, I remember he had trouble helping you with your math classes in high school."

"I know, I know. Let me continue."

I was hoping that you could make some calls and see if one could be uploaded, or if none exist, perhaps you know someone who could create such a class.

"Dad's either losing his mind or he's trying to tell us something," Sarah added. "He knows most everything is available online. Somebody doesn't have to create such a course."

"It is kind of peculiar that he wants to learn integral calculus. That was your favorite course and got you hooked on a career in science and math," Allen chimed in. "I remember Dad was so proud of you, beating out those boys in your class who thought they were math geniuses."

"My favorite course!" Sarah's eyes opened wide, and she felt she was reading her father's mind. "He wants *me* to put together the course and be the instructor."

"You've got me totally confused now. Why would he want you to do that? It seems like a lot of work for you and not much value for anyone. Wouldn't it be nice if we could just go visit him? Heck, the prison is only a 90-minute drive from here."

"Sure, seeing and talking to him in prison might make this easier, but you know that isn't allowed. It's either email or videoconference unless he's on his deathbed. Let's focus. Dad is up to something, and the course is just a cover. You know how paranoid he's been about talking to anyone about anything more personal than today's weather."

"Don't rub it in," Allen groaned. "I know: I shouldn't have forwarded that email to Dr. Brown. Sarah, could it be that Dad wants to use the instructor-student communication function in the course to talk to us? It probably isn't monitored like emails and video calls are. The assumption is probably that student and instructor don't know each other and that any chitchat will be about the course materials."

"I guess that's possible . . ."

Sarah paused for a moment. Allen knew not to interrupt her when she was solving a problem. He could see her eyes narrow and hands cup over her mouth as if she were trying to prevent any good ideas from escaping.

"I know somewhere I've got the outline for the course I took. And we have all the tech we need to put the course together without leaving this room. Allen, we can put it together in a week, but we need to give it a twist so that it really stands apart from the courses already out there."

"I'm all for it, but how are you going to get it uploaded?" Allen asked, beginning to feel the excitement of a new project, especially one that was intended to be deceptive.

"Let me worry about that. I've got a plan."

With that, Sarah and Allen began to put together the course. Working on it every night, they had it finished late the following Sunday.

Sarah's upload plan was simple and aboveboard. She quickly found the name of the company that hosted the online courses for the prison: NiNo Learning Services. She contacted the administrator and introduced herself in a videoconference as a ZG scientist. ZG had been in the news lately, showing off the new prosthetic heart valves they had produced in zero gravity, so the ZG name got his attention immediately.

The rest was easy. She asked if they had any special requirements for courses that could be taken by inmates. As Sarah had expected, there were restrictions about profanity, controversial topics, and projects that couldn't be completed in a prison environment.

The only question the administrator had for Sarah—one she had hoped he would ask—was, "Why are you doing this?" Sarah explained that ZG anticipated rapid growth in the coming years but didn't think they'd be able to find staff with the necessary skills. If they could train inmates now, those inmates might be able to walk right into a high-paying job the day they walked out of the prison. It would be a win for both ZG and the ex-cons, and naturally it would reflect positively on NiNo Learning Services and the prison as well.

She told the administrator that she had been asked by ZG to set up a pilot program to see if it had potential. She had produced a calculus course, reasoning that if some inmates could find the material interesting and master it, she and ZG would know they were on the right track.

That was all it took to make the sale. Sarah thanked him for the opportunity.

A week later she sent the course to him and, after a cursory review, it was uploaded to the London Tower server.

Neither Sarah nor Allen ever responded to Alex's original email.

10

"It's uploaded and ready," Sarah informed Allen.

It had been one of those days at work where people were at odds with one another, and they weren't making any progress on several key projects assigned to Sarah and her team. Coming home and seeing that the course was now available to the inmates renewed Sarah's flagging confidence in her ability to get things done.

"Lemme see," Allen said as he pushed an office chair next to Sarah and the computer monitor. The introductory page was open. It showed a photo of the instructor, but the photo wasn't of Sarah.

"Aren't you the instructor?" Allen asked, wondering if he'd misunderstood something when they had decided to embark on the project.

"Yes, of course I am. But if I used my real name, someone might make the connection between me and Dad. So when I talked to the admin about uploading the course, I asked if I could use a different name. I told him I was afraid an inmate might want to look me up after he completed his prison sentence—and not for purposes of learning more about calculus." Sarah cocked her head and gave Allen her "know what I mean?" look. Allen knew right away what she was implying.

"Anyway, he said I could use a different name, and there it is," Sarah said, pointing to the screen. The name beneath the photo was "Brenda Kołodziej."

"Brenda *what*? I can't even pronounce that name!" Allen said, thinking this was a joke of some sort.

"Exactly. I found it doing a search of Polish names. I figure if people can't pronounce it, that'll make it even harder to find me." Sarah grinned.

"And the picture? It kind of looks like you, but it's not you . . ." Allen mused.

Sarah began to speak, but Allen quickly interrupted her. "I know, I know—you did a digital combination of your face and someone else's!"

"Right. Actually, it's my face and those of two other women whose pictures I found on the net. It didn't take me more than five minutes. I like her, but she really needs to get those teeth polished."

Every day since Alex had sent the note to Sarah, he'd checked the London Tower online learning site to see whether a course on integral calculus had become available. Sure enough, ten days later it was there. Saying a prayer before he opened it up and read the introduction, he was pleased to see a photo of someone who looked somewhat like Sarah but wasn't the Sarah he knew.

Then he noticed she had a different name too. Had the online class already been compromised?

That depressing thought came and went in a flash. She clearly didn't want the system to identify a potential family relationship between an inmate and instructor. Still, the photo was disconcerting. He wanted so much to believe that this Brenda, the instructor for the course, was his daughter Sarah and not someone Sarah had found to be the instructor. Cognizant that wishful and hopeful thinking often led to rash decisions, Alex promised himself he'd be very cautious until he could confirm it was his Sarah.

Alex enrolled immediately, noting that no one else had enrolled in the course thus far. That wasn't surprising: this just wasn't the type of course an inmate would enroll in. Prison was punishment enough.

That first week Alex went through the first module slowly and thoughtfully, actually trying to learn the basics of integral calculus. The questions he asked of Sarah were all about the course material, and her responses were professional but with a style and wording distinctly Sarah's.

Not only did he need to confirm that Sarah was writing the messages, but he needed to be sure the messages weren't being monitored. At the end of his third message, Alex entered an eight-digit number: 20874205. If the instructor was in fact Sarah, she'd know what the code meant.

Sarah's response came the next day. Alex didn't bother to read it. He just scanned down to see whether there was an eight-digit code at the bottom of it. There was: 98971952.

"Yes!" he whispered to himself.

98971952 was one of the numbers that passed the authentication code system. It was a code they had worked out years before, when Sarah and Allen were just kids playing secret agent games. Alex never would have dreamed they'd be using it in a real-life situation.

Now confident that he was communicating directly with Sarah, Alex focused on whether their communication was being monitored. Gradually he became bolder and asked nonsense questions, then asked personal questions that were clearly inappropriate for a student to ask of an instructor.

Sarah understood the process completely. She knew you couldn't just hope that a security system wasn't at work: you needed to gradually push to find out exactly where the boundaries were.

⊙

Three weeks had passed since Alex's parole was denied, and neither Alex nor Mykola had brought up the subject since that day. Yet Mykola could see Alex's mind working. They didn't play chess as often, and Alex was spending most of his free, out-of-the-cell time taking online courses in the prison learning center. There was always a terminal available; most other inmates would rather simply go outside, perhaps work out, and wait for the next meal.

One evening Alex lost the chess game in just 24 moves. Mykola would have liked to think he was becoming Alex's equal, but he knew better. Alex had made some moves that were practically gifts; clearly he didn't have his head in the game. Now, with the lights turned off and both of them lying on top of the blankets of their bunks, Alex leaned over and said to Mykola, "There's something I want to talk to you about."

"Okay, what is it?"

Alex looked directly at Mykola and said in a hushed tone, "I want out."

"Everyone wants out," Mykola said, unsurprised, "but the calendar goes at its own speed."

"I've got a plan that will get me out much sooner than London Tower has on their calendar."

Mykola looked at him with questioning eyes. From what he had heard, there hadn't ever even been an attempt at escaping the State Line Prison. With all the technology used to control the inmates, including the collars, he couldn't imagine anyone being smart enough to figure out a viable method. Yet Alex was obviously very smart, and perhaps he had a good idea.

"Okay, I'm listening," Mykola said.

"Before I outline my plan, I want you to agree to help me execute it."

"I can't agree to something I don't know about. Whatever you're considering isn't just another game."

"Okay, understood. I'll find someone else."

Mykola rolled over in his bunk and stared at the wall, thinking about all he'd learned from Alex about the prison, how it operated below the surface, and its long-term impact on inmates. He then thought about his videoconference with Roberta and her desire to rein in any hope of his near-term release. He could feel his chest tighten as his hands gripped his pillow.

Long after Alex had fallen asleep, Mykola was still wrestling with his decision. Did he know enough about Alex to trust him on this? Finally, the memory of Roberta's somber reminder about the seven-year sentence he was serving sealed it.

In the morning, he heard the squeak from Alex's bunk as he

got up. Looking straight up at the ceiling, Mykola took a deep breath, exhaled, and quietly but distinctly said, "Okay, I'm in. I'm going to trust you and hope for a positive outcome."

Alex exhaled through his nostrils loudly enough that Mykola could hear him. He was relieved; perhaps another inmate would have been willing to help him, but right now Mykola was the only one he felt would be reliable. Because they were cellmates, Mykola was also the only inmate he could talk to without either of them wearing their collars. In addition, he knew that as Mykola's cellmate he'd be able to keep tabs on Mykola's emotional state and provide him with only as much information about the plan as he needed.

"Good," he said. "I'll be in the learning lab tomorrow at about 4:00. We'll get started then."

Tuesday afternoon Mykola walked into the learning lab. It was laid out in a manner similar to that of the communications room. However, instead of having small tables with monitors and a chair before each, the learning lab had ten long tables with monitors separated by partitions. The back of the spacious room was mostly bookshelves on which there were hundreds of books.

Before each monitor was a traditional keyboard, built into the table so that it was immobile. A set of wired headphones hung from a hook on each partition. Mykola noticed an absence of red lines on the floor; apparently more than one inmate could be standing or sitting near a screen.

The partitions made it difficult to see who was at each station, so Mykola walked up and down the aisles looking for

Alex, noting that very few of what he estimated to be 60 stations were in use.

He found Alex studying a formula onscreen, so immersed in it that he didn't notice that Mykola had walked in behind him. A quick "hey" and tap on his shoulder got Alex's attention.

"So, here I am," Mykola said expectantly.

"Hey." Alex typed a few characters into a text box and then turned to face Mykola. "You know, I think you're right: it is helpful for anyone to improve their math skills. I've found a course on integral calculus that I think you'll get a lot out of." Alex spoke as if this were the continuation of an earlier conversation.

"Integral calculus?" Mykola whispered, looking over his shoulder, expecting to see someone listening.

Because this was Mykola's first time in the learning lab, Alex showed him how to log in and sign up for the course. He then showed Mykola how to navigate through the different functions. Alex spent extra time on the student-instructor message feature, suggesting to Mykola that he send the instructor a brief note just to introduce himself.

Verifying that Mykola was enrolled in Sarah's course and had introduced himself through the student-instructor messaging system, Alex sent a final message to Sarah. In it he mentioned Mykola and described him as an inmate he'd convinced to take the course.

Alex also explained that he himself was going to drop the course, with the excuse that it had already advanced to a point where he could no longer understand the math. He knew it was best to break the father-daughter connection before anyone started to get suspicious. As much as he enjoyed communicating with Sarah, she was at more personal risk than was he. Alex had vowed to do everything possible to minimize her risk while still giving himself a chance to escape.

"Hey, before you go, tell me a little more about this lab," Mykola asked as Alex got up. "When Sly gave me the tour, he just opened the door and said this was the learning lab, and that was about it. I'm guessing he isn't into learning any more than is absolutely necessary."

"Well, I've shown you how to enroll in a course. What else do you want to know?"

Pointing to the back of the room, Mykola said, "How about those books?"

"Most of the books were donated by a nearby library. They were transitioning to all-digital and didn't have the space for printed books anymore. Anybody can take a book and read it wherever they want."

"Like back in the cell?"

"Sure. Most of the books are novels. A lot of them look brand new, but I like to read the ones that are well worn. I figure those are the best, because they've been read by the most people," Alex explained. "You can also read books onscreen. Here, let me show you something pretty neat."

Alex went back to the screen and selected a book at random from the catalog.

"On this screen you can select text or audio," Alex said as he held up the headphones.

"That's what all the regular libraries have gone to," Mykola observed.

"But you can also select the language. Every book is auto-matically translated. Here's the real kicker, and maybe they have this on the outside too: you can choose a male or female voice!" Alex sounded as if he were showing off something he'd personally developed.

"Yeah, I'm pretty sure I've seen that," Mykola said, a little puzzled.

"I like to come in here, select a book, and have a woman read it in French," Alex continued, letting out a sigh.

Mykola was puzzled. "You don't speak French, do you? Are you trying to learn it?"

"No, of course not; I'm too old to learn a new language. Just sitting back in the chair and listening for an hour or so is pure relaxation. The voice could be giving me a lecture on tax law; I wouldn't care."

"You are a weird dude," Mykola said in a joking yet complimentary tone.

"You just remember what I'm telling you. I bet a year from now this will be one of your favorite things to do."

Hopefully in a year we'll both be out of this place, Mykola thought. He couldn't say it out loud with his collar on, but from Alex's grin, he knew Alex was thinking the same thing.

Mykola spent about an hour most days learning integral calculus. It wasn't anything he thought he could put to practical use, especially inside the walls of the State Line Prison, but it was good brain exercise. Certainly it was much more challenging than his "day job."

As per Alex's instructions, he sent questions to the instructor most days, even if he already knew the answer. Still, he was at a loss for how this could be a part of Alex's plan to get out.

Two weeks went by, and though Mykola was dutifully working through the modules and doing the online assignments, Alex could sense his patience was wearing thin. Mykola didn't share with Alex what he was learning, and occasionally he would pound on the keyboard with much more force than necessary. Alex was concerned that Mykola could easily be provoked to say something that would hint at Alex's intentions. Alex had no choice: he would have to share another piece of the plan with Mykola.

That night, with their collars off and not a sound coming from the corridor or nearby cells, Alex explained to Mykola that the instructor for the calculus class was his ZG-employed daughter and that he was counting on her to help execute his plan. She didn't know what Alex had planned, but she knew something was afoot. She was being patient, much as Alex had expected of Mykola.

The next step, Alex explained, would be to get her commitment to help him escape. Alex wanted to begin by sharing his parole hearing experience with her. More importantly, he wanted her to understand the type of information the prison was collecting and how it was being used to unjustly deny parole. Though he had no proof, Alex was also beginning to see how this privately run, modern, state-of-the-art prison could also be engaging in some corrupt practices that the Arizona and New California departments of corrections were either a party to or were conveniently overlooking.

"For the past week you've been sending typical student messages to Sarah," Alex said. "I just wanted to get a sense of whether we're being tracked, and so far, it looks good. Have you seen or experienced anything that indicates you're being monitored?"

"No, but then all our messages have been exclusively about the course content. I haven't even mentioned your name."

"Excellent." Alex was pleased that Mykola was following his instructions to the letter and hadn't said anything that might raise a red flag if they were being closely scrutinized.

"Now," he said, "the next step is for you to send Sarah notes with everything I told you about the parole hearing process and my understanding of its potential for corruption. Leave out names entirely, of course. I want Sarah to get a sense of what it's like to be an inmate in this prison. You can embed this information in one of your assignments."

"Me? Why should I do that? She's your daughter, and this is part of your plan." Mykola was incensed that Alex was making him the point man and still wouldn't divulge the plan.

"I would communicate directly with Sarah if I were 100 percent sure no one knew she was my daughter. There's much less likelihood that your communication with Sarah will be tracked," Alex said as softly and calmly as he could. "I understand your annoyance, and—"

"*Annoyance*? You think this is like the chow line running out of lima beans? Get real, Alex. I want to trust you on this, but you're making it real hard. For all I know, I'll be the collateral damage and you'll be on the outside." Mykola could feel his blood pressure rising.

"Okay, sorry. 'Annoyance' was the wrong word." Alex was using his psychiatrist-sales-pitch voice, the one he used when a patient balked at his proposed course of therapy. "And you're right to be cautious. Up until now, if someone had suspected something fishy, you could honestly have claimed you had no knowledge of what was going on, that you were simply taking an online class. Sending this message to Sarah changes all that. If anyone gets wind of what you're doing, we'll both be toast.

"When I first told you I had a plan, I said you'd have to trust me, and you agreed. I can't tell you more of the plan, not yet. All I can say is, if you don't want to take the next step, I understand."

"I know what I agreed to, but trust goes both ways, Alex."

Alex didn't say a word, waiting patiently for Mykola to make the next move.

"Okay, I'll do it, but the next time we talk, I get the full plan or I'm done," Mykola stated bluntly.

"Understood. Oh, and don't rush through the course, even if you find the content too easy or boring. You need to be in the course until we execute the plan, and I can't be sure exactly when that will be."

"Too easy? Definitely not the case," Mykola said with a tired sigh. "In fact, I'm so lost I'm thinking of going back to the beginning."

"Good. There's one other thing I need to explain to you: the authentication code. To this point, all your communication with Sarah has been about the class, and it hasn't much mattered whether Sarah or someone else was responding to your questions. Now that we're pushing the envelope, we need to be sure that only you and Sarah are sending and reading the messages."

Alex proceeded to tell Mykola about the code system he and his children had worked out as part of a game they'd played years before.

"This code probably wouldn't pass a computer's cybersecurity system, but you can produce and check it without a computer if you know the rules. The quickest way to explain is to give you an example." Alex paused and looked at Mykola.

"Yes, yes, go on, I'm listening," Mykola said.

"Okay, first you subtract today's three- or four-digit month-day number from 1,000. For example, today is March 22, and so you'd subtract 322 from 1,000 and get 678. Next look for the first instance of those consecutive digits in pi. When you've found that, note the 3 digits before and after the 678."

"Pi? You mean, as in 3.14 pi?" Mykola asked.

"Right."

"So where do I get the list of digits that follow 3.14?"

"Right here." Alex took the pieces off the chessboard and turned the board over, revealing the list of the first 2,000 digits of pi.

"You mean I have to look through all these numbers to find 6-7-8 in order? Seems like a job a computer could do in an instant." Mykola was already getting annoyed with this system.

"Sure, I know it's cumbersome, but the fewer trails we leave on the computer, the less likely we are to be found out," Alex said. "I've already found 6-7-8, and you can see that the three digits before and after are 378 and 316. Now add another random digit to each of these numbers—say a 4 and a 9—and you have the eight-digit authentication code 37849316. Those random digits can be added anywhere before or after the three-digit pi numbers. See how it works, Mykola?"

"Yeah, I think so. But still, it seems like a tedious process. I have to add this kind of code to every message I send to Sarah?"

"Yes," Alex said in a tone that implied this was not open to discussion. "If she doesn't send a confirmation message with a valid code back to you, we may have a problem.

"I know there are holes in this system, but my impression is that the security on the online classes isn't nearly as robust as the security on the email and videoconference systems."

"What about when we get to October, November, and December? That'll produce a negative number," Mykola asked, thinking he'd found a flaw in this security system.

"I'll explain that to you in late September," Alex responded. "No need to fill up your memory bank with information you can't use right now."

A bit condescending, but practical, Mykola thought to himself. At least he has an answer for every question.

11

"What do you make of this message from this inmate Mykola Steinman?" Sarah asked Allen a few days later, referring to Mykola's description of a parole hearing.

"Well, Mykola is no English literature professor, but what he's describing sounds like something only Dad or another psychiatrist could possibly pick up. I have a hard time imagining he just dreamt this up," Allen replied.

"That's my thought as well, and if only half of what Mykola says in the note is true, Dad could be doing the full 12 years no matter what."

"But how do you know this wasn't sent by some parasite who is using Mykola's handle?"

"An important question, my dear brother," Sarah said. "The answer, I believe, is in the eight-digit number at the end of the message."

"You've got me now—wait, wait, are you telling me he included an identification code like Dad has been doing in his messages to you?"

Sarah grinned. "That's it. I checked the number, and it's a perfect match to the pi code identifier."

"So we know that Dad and Mykola are in this together."

"Right. My guess is that Dad hasn't shared this with anyone except this Mykola fellow. He's learned from past slipups to be extra cautious."

"Okay, so Dad's got a plan, and you know it involves us probably doing something that isn't entirely legal. I'm not sure what it might be, but short of driving a bulldozer into that place, I'm ready to go." Allen's voice was getting louder with each word.

Sarah could feel her pulse quicken. "Me too, but let's be patient. I'll simply respond to the assignment Mykola submitted and won't mention the parole hearing. The less either one of us says about this, the safer it will be for everyone. In the meantime, let's find out as much as we can about London Tower."

Over the next few days, Allen and Sarah found a lot of information about London Tower and their "prison without walls," as they and many reporters called it. Most of the articles were "puff" pieces, highlighting the freedom within the complex, its security, and most of all, the cost savings to the state over traditional prisons.

Yet there were indications of problems both inside and outside the facility. Some inmates reported sadistic guards, though that could have been said about any prison. Of greater concern were the high blood pressure, nervous tics, and weight loss among many inmates, symptoms that could not be attributed to any specific aspect of the prison. Inmates who had been released from the prison experienced periods of high stress and tension followed by periods of depression, making it difficult to transition to civilian life. These mental health issues were reported at a much higher rate and severity in former State Line Prison inmates than in those released from traditional prisons.

On the outside, London Tower was showing some financial difficulties with draining cash and an executive team that was gently trying to lower investor expectations. Some analysts pointed to the contract London Tower had signed with Arizona and New California, saying London Tower had given away too much in order to get the deal. Now, to save cash, they were laying off some of the people providing "non-essential" services to the prison population.

Perhaps the biggest issue was underutilization: the prison was authorized for 1,500 inmates, but currently there were only about 1,100. Contract payments were made exclusively on a per-prisoner-housed basis, and analysts calculated that a count of 1,100 inmates was near the break-even point for London Tower.

"This place needs to be closed," Allen proclaimed after reading one particularly critical article about the prison.

"With this information and the notes we're getting from Mykola and Dad, I'm ashamed that we didn't do some research when Dad was transferred to this prison a year ago," Sarah lamented. "Perhaps we should do some more research and then go to the Department of Corrections and our legislators to demand some changes."

"There you go, getting all professional again. Sure, Sarah, we could do that, but you know there are too many people who have financial or political stakes in seeing this prison as a new age in corrections." Allen gave air quotes to "new age in corrections." Once again he was talking himself into a state of rage. "It could take years to get some action. My guess is that

Dad and this Mykola fellow have something else in mind, that we're being recruited to help get them out. Let's see if we get any more hints in the next few days."

"I suppose that's possible." Sarah slowly exhaled and eyed Allen with the unspoken message that she was still the boss in this household. "Okay, if that is the case, would you be willing to do just that? I mean, helping someone escape from prison isn't a strawberry or chocolate ice cream kind of decision."

Sarah suspected Allen would be all for it, but she needed confirmation.

"Of course I would! Not sure of how we'd make it happen, but I think we should try, don't you?"

"Yes, I do," Sarah said calmly but with conviction. "Still, we need to be careful, and if at any time we think the risk is too great, we simply shut it down. I don't think Dad would be upset with us. A failed escape attempt is worse than no attempt at all. There could be serious consequences for him and for us."

"So that old axiom of 'no harm in trying' doesn't apply here?" Allen asked.

"Right. Instead we need to apply the axiom Dad learned in med school: 'First do no harm.'"

"Your game has definitely improved over the past few weeks," Alex sighed as Mykola moved his knight into position to take either Alex's queen or bishop.

"I suppose it's time for me to tell you about the plan," he added in a low voice while intently considering his next move on the board. "I'm not going to last another five years in this place. Sure, I'll survive, but I'll be a different person, and no one will recognize me. Sarah will get me, and you, out.""

Speaking so softly that Mykola could hear his every breath in the quiet of the cell, Alex explained his plan. There were no guards to bribe or tunnels to dig, the staples of old-time prison escape movies. To escape, they had to disable that which kept them in: the collar and the technology behind it. That couldn't be done from the inside; neither of them had the skills or access to do so. Sarah, however, with a couple of years of experience in maintaining the security of the ZG computer system, did.

Alex made his case for Sarah's cybersecurity skills, expounding the ZG Digital Security Department's annual "hackathon." Two teams in the department would work for 24 hours to see if they could hack into the ZG system, and Sarah's team was often the first to do so. From this exercise they devised enhanced security systems. So Sarah had knowledge and experience on both sides: maintaining security and breaking through it.

Alex didn't understand the details of computer systems, but he did understand the principles behind them. They were in many ways like human brains: very complex, with multiple inputs and outputs. But, as with human brains, with each expansion of thought or computer power, vulnerabilities increased. The protective covering, the security system, could be stretched just so far. Once you got through that covering, you could cause all sorts of havoc if that was your intention.

The latest expansion of the "brain" that ran the London Tower system was the learning lab. Alex found out that it had been installed just a couple of months before he got there and that it was designed and administered by another company, one that specialized in learning, not prison administration. That was why he had pointed Sarah in that direction and why Alex and Mykola had been probing the system's security over the past two weeks.

"I can't tell Sarah exactly how to get into the system that controls these collars or how best to disable them, but I can tell her what it does and how it works. I'm hoping she can figure out the rest."

"That's the plan? Hoping your daughter will figure it out?" Mykola asked with obvious disappointment. He had gotten the impression that Alex had a complete plan in mind and that it simply needed to be executed. If he'd known Alex's plan was so vague, he wouldn't have agreed to help him. Snickering to himself, Mykola now understood why Alex had demanded a commitment from him before he'd shared any details. It was a move worthy of a chess master.

"Sorry, but I have faith in her, and we'll just have to do what we can from our side," Alex said. "The next step is the riskiest yet: we need to get her all the details we can about how the collar works. She'll need to know how it's integrated with location tracking, how it delivers the jolt levels, and any other detail that might help spot a vulnerability in the system."

"But haven't you shared all that information with Sarah over the past year? You must have had some videoconferences. It seems natural to share things about your experience here."

"You're right, I did explain how the prison works, but only in general terms. I spent more time telling Sarah and Allen about my job here and how we have lots of free time than about how the collars worked. I didn't want them to get the impression that I couldn't handle it here; I wanted to maintain that traditional father-children relationship where I was the strong one. I asked about their well-being—I think about it every day—but I didn't share my own worries and fears with them. So they know the rudiments of this prison's operation but not the details."

Mykola ran his hand over his nearly shaven head.

"I think I understand. You want me to send that information through the calculus class assignments like I did before," he stated, just to confirm what he already suspected.

"Exactly. You'll need to send it, but I'll help put the list together. We've got to avoid using words that might be flagged, like 'escape' and 'hack' and even 'computer.'"

Alex was asking Mykola to send far more—and more detailed—information than they had since they'd set up this behind-the-scenes message system, and that made Mykola wary. Even he, with his limited knowledge of security systems, knew they'd been more lucky than clever so far. He wasn't ready to commit, and Alex could sense it.

"What is it? What's the problem?"

"I've trusted you to this point," Mykola said. "Now you're going to have to trust me. I have an idea for sending this information more securely. Don't know if it's perfect, and I'm going to have to work through the details, but it'll be better than we've been doing so far. And if Sarah is the magician of code you say she is, she'll figure it out."

"Okay, I'm listening. Tell me what it is," Alex demanded.

"There's nothing for you to listen to. You either trust me or you can send messages to Sarah yourself." Mykola was still whispering, but there could be no doubt of his resolve.

Alex paused for a long moment before he spoke.

"Do what you need to do."

The following evening, neither Alex nor Mykola was in the mood to play chess. Though neither was tired, they both lay back on their bunks, thinking about nothing and everything.

"Anything of note happening in your day job?" Alex had his hands clasped behind his head.

"You mean identifying what people are thinking from videos and then predicting their behaviors?"

"Yeah. You're still doing that, right?"

"Sure am, but it's been boring as hell. I've gotten to the point where I just don't care if I get it right or wrong. Today I watched a video with two other inmates. We had to agree on what the woman in the video was thinking when her car broke down on a desert highway and two guys in a beat-up pickup truck stopped to help her. I said she was happy to see the guys and get some help. My co-watchers said she was frightened and was getting ready to pull out a knife to protect herself. We went round and round, and I finally just gave in."

"Sometimes I wonder if there isn't a computer that's judging my emotional reactions," Mykola said, talking to himself, the ceiling, and Alex simultaneously.

"I'm not surprised. We continually make judgments about the people we interact with. It's a matter of survival in a few cases, but most of the time it's just to maintain good relationships. You've got to know, without them actually saying so, if someone is getting pissed off at something you said or is happily agreeing."

"Can't and don't want to argue with that," Mykola responded.

"But when you're looking at a monitor and have to evaluate people's facial expressions, body language, and vocal inflections, you don't have any skin in the game. Even if you're way off base, there's no harm to you. So after the novelty of the exercise wears off, you're going to be bored, and your own emotions have as much to do with the assessment as what you're seeing onscreen."

"I can see the gears in your psychiatrist brain working," Mykola commented with a lilt in his voice.

"And I can read the words unspoken," Alex said. "You'd like me to continue."

"Well, sure . . . I've got no place to go."

"Okay. Well, you're not going to like this—or maybe you don't care—but all this work you've been doing to identify people's thoughts and emotions is being used to educate the 'eyes' in the ceilings here. For years computer systems have been able to identify emotions from facial expressions, but they couldn't identify the source of those emotions except in the most obvious situations. So they're using you and lots of other guys to teach the computers how to think like a human."

"How do you know all this?" It all sounded a bit too much like a science fiction movie to Mykola.

"One day I was called from the infirmary up into the control room. That doesn't happen very often, but one of the guys there was complaining of consistent headaches and thought it might be from the glare of the monitors they were watching for hours each day. They had me come up to take a look, and we got to talking. It was all friendly-like, and I'm sure they didn't think they were sharing any company secrets.

"Anyway, they showed me one huge screen that was a layout of the whole prison, inside and outside, divided into squares. There were probably 300 squares, and each square was color-coded based on the emotions expressed by the inmates in that square. The colors ranged from bright green to white to bright red.

"White meant everything was fine. Everyone there was really rather unemotional, maybe a little bit bored or just daydreaming. Green meant the emotions were on the happy side. You might see green in the chow hall when something new was being served. Red was an indication of anger, intense frustration, or fear. The brighter the green or red, the more intense the emotion."

"The system could tell if someone was getting pissed off, even if nothing was said?" Mykola asked, now finding this quite fascinating.

"Oh, yeah. And that was if just one guy was showing intense emotion. If several guys were experiencing intense red or green emotions, the square would start flashing, but again, the system couldn't figure out what was causing the emotion because it didn't understand the context. So the guys in the control room would send a guard to the location that was flashing to find out what was going on and quell it before it got out of hand."

"Even if there was a flashing green?"

"Better believe it. Nobody wants prisoners to be too happy. If they are, there's something amiss."

"That, in a sad way, is kind of funny. But I guess it's supposed to be punishment, not a vacation resort," Mykola stated.

"The weird thing," Alex continued, "was that some inmates started to show signs of paranoia. It seemed every time they started to get angry or upset, a guard would show up."

"Yup, that is pretty spooky."

"When I learned about how the control room got its inmate emotional information from the computer, I thought there could be a simple solution for those guys who came into the infirmary complaining of being followed and constantly watched by guards. I simply told them to look down at the floor whenever they felt any intense emotion. The overhead cameras couldn't see their facial expressions and so couldn't identify the emotions."

"Meaning no flashing reds or greens in the control room."

"And, consequently, no guards hiding behind corners," Alex agreed with a grin.

"What about the guy with the headaches?" Mykola asked.

"I told him I didn't think the lighting was bright enough to cause headaches. It wasn't any worse than what kids get when playing video games all day. I told him to see a doctor. He did. Turned out to be a brain tumor."

"Alex, you seem to understand how the system works even better than the guards do. Now that I know some more about it, I'm not entirely disappointed about being transferred to another department tomorrow."

"And that would be . . . ?"

"Laundry."

"Good!" Alex said with feigned excitement. "Go easy on the starch in my shorts. I'm beginning to get some chafing." He glanced over at Mykola, expecting a reaction. There was none.

"One more thing," Mykola said. "I saw Sly today at lunch, and he told me there are plans to return the Level 2 and 3 jolts to full AI control, the way it was when they first opened this place. He couldn't confirm it, but he said when he asked a guard about it, the guard didn't deny it."

"That's decidedly more serious than chafing from my shorts. If they go to full AI control before Sarah has a chance to do her thing, there may be a major rewrite of code. We might have to start over or simply admit we're going to remain here for the full term." Alex sounded like someone who'd just been told he'd been diagnosed with cancer and that it was unclear as to whether it could be successfully treated.

He didn't sleep well that night.

12

"Why are you here? Did lunch produce nausea again, or did you just want to see a friendly face?"

Alex was surprised to see Mykola in the infirmary; it was the first time Mykola had been there.

"I figured you might be surprised to see me. Actually it's neither nausea nor a friendly face. And if I wanted a friendly face, this is the last place I'd expect to find one."

"If I smile, will that help?" Alex asked with a stern face, knowing Mykola wasn't taking him seriously.

"It might. I'm supposed to be here, according to my schedule, but I don't know why. Am I here for some kind of checkup?"

"No, I don't see you on our patient list. You must be here for that presentation by Alcort Pharma. You're a little early. You can go have a seat in the conference room," Alex said, pointing to a door where a guard stood.

As Mykola walked toward the door, the guard glanced at his inmate number and the computer tablet he held.

"Yup, this is the place. You're good." The guard took a

couple of steps to the side of the door so that Mykola could enter without getting a jolt.

Mykola took a seat toward the back of the room. During the next 15 minutes, about 60 other inmates entered. No one was sure what this was all about, but most speculated that it was a request for volunteers to test a new drug. Using inmates to test new drugs was fairly common, and if the number of points that could be earned was high enough, the companies would get their volunteers.

At the scheduled time, an older man wearing a lab coat with the Alcort logo embroidered over the left pocket showed up, followed by a guard.

Mykola nudged the inmate sitting next to him. "Look at this guy. Silk tie, dress slacks, polished black shoes; I wonder if anyone told him he'd be talking to a bunch of inmates who hadn't recently shopped for uniforms at Nordstrom."

"Yeah, and that lab coat looks like it was cleaned and pressed this morning by his mouse of a wife in preparation for this big day." In a falsetto voice the inmate continued, "Oh, you look so handsome!"

Mykola and the other inmate bent over, looked down at the floor and snickered, but immediately sat up straight and put on their serious, attentive faces when they saw the guard glaring at them.

The guard closed the door.

After a few words introducing himself as Mr. Ling, a company representative, and describing Alcort's business, the man in the lab coat reached into the briefcase he'd brought with him and pulled out a collar.

"Not what you expected, I gather," he said, looking at the

group, whose members had begun to squirm in their chairs and roll their shoulders.

"Alcort is partnering with a tech company to produce a comprehensive health data collection system that can be used to develop drug combinations specific to individual needs. Obviously we already have the basics, like height, weight, sex, age, and medical history, but we don't have real-time data on measures like blood pressure, heart rate, and respiration. There's lots of other measures too, like blood chemistry and neurological activity, but that's too involved to explain to you right now.

"We know that if we can get real-time data on a person's health, we can use that to produce a customized prescription that may change from day to day. This device could do that and also deliver the drugs automatically. It could also tell us if the drugs are working. Patients wouldn't have to wait until their next doctor's appointment to find out."

The Alcort representative could tell the inmates were getting bored already; this wasn't a group of private equity investors or physicians, the type of people he was more accustomed to speaking with.

"We're still a long way from a final product, but we've got something we think is workable," he said, holding up the collar. "This new device will collect all of the data I've mentioned. We're just looking for people who can help us test it and refine it."

"How many points?" came from the back of the room. The Alcort man looked over at the guard.

The guard took a couple of steps toward the center of the room before speaking. "7,500 if you complete the 30-day test."

That was substantially more than what inmates had typically

earned for participating in drug tests, and immediately the Alcort man could feel the mood in the room brighten. Still, he could see skepticism in the faces of a few inmates.

"Thank you, Mr. Berger. You've clearly gotten everyone's attention. Why don't you continue and explain the test?" Mr. Ling was more than happy to give up the spotlight to the guard, who clearly had command of the room.

Mykola noticed that the word "test" was used rather than "trial." On the outside, drugs were put through a series of trials, not tests. Of course, in a prison, "trial" had a different, usually negative connotation. Was the use of "test" a conscious decision?

The guard now turned to Mr. Ling and took the collar from him.

"This collar works just like the ones you wear," the guard said, "so don't think you're going to have it any easier. It'll collect the data Mr. Ling explained, and you won't notice a difference. If there are signs of a health problem, you'll be issued a command to report to the infirmary.

"Couple of other differences. You probably noticed this collar is a little bigger than the one you're currently sporting. It may be bigger, but it's lighter and more comfortable. It also has a new type of battery, and instead of taking it off every night, you'll take it off every third night."

That comment produced neither cheers nor smiles from the inmates.

"Alcort needs 40 guys to sign up for the test. If I were you—and I'm glad I'm not—I'd sign up. See, whether this test is successful or not, I'm pretty sure we'll be converting to this new style of collar in the next few months. You might as well pick up some points."

So much for the "benefit to humanity" appeal I was going to make, Mr. Ling thought. Comfort and points were much more enticing.

"Are there any more questions?" the guard asked, fully expecting there to be none.

From the back of the room came a meek voice. "How do the drugs get into you?"

Before the guard could respond, Mr. Ling stood up. "Good question. The collars have microneedles built into them. They go just below the epidermis to deliver the drugs. You'll feel them, but it is painless, I assure you."

"You mean we're going to be injected with drugs?" a burly inmate in the front row asked in a tone that expressed his displeasure with the idea. Several other inmates made comments to others seated near them.

"No, no, not in this test. I should have explained that right away," Mr. Ling said, suddenly feeling threatened. He was glad the guard was standing just a few feet away. "The collar has that functionality, but there will be no drugs in the collar during this phase. We're just going to be testing the accuracy of the data collection. You'll be asked to come to the infirmary every day for a five-minute traditional type of physical, and we'll compare those results to the data collected by the collar. If this goes well, we'll do a full test in the next phase."

Not everyone was convinced that needles were painless or that Mr. Ling was telling the truth about not injecting any drugs. However, there would be no argument, and the room was quiet.

"Okay, then," the guard said, "it's the first 40 who sign up. Signups start tomorrow, so you'll have time to think it over. If you decide to participate, see one of the yellow-shirts in the infirmary. We're done." He pressed a couple of buttons on his tablet and the conference room door clicked open.

As Mykola walked out, he made eye contact with Alex, who was talking to one of the other inmates who had just emerged. Mykola gave a discreet shrug of his shoulders. They'd have to talk that night.

⊙

"So, what do you think?"

The cell gate was closed and the lights were off. Mykola had already explained to Alex how the new collar was to be used to collect individual health data and, eventually, administer drugs.

"I think it was lucky that you were one of the inmates selected to participate in this test," Alex said. "I had no idea of what it was about; just figured it was a typical test of a new drug."

Alex put his hand to his face and rubbed the stubble of hair on his unshaven cheek.

"You definitely should not volunteer for this test," he continued. "I'd find it interesting to know what sort of data they'll be collecting, but we don't know how this changes the programming of the collars. I can't ask Sarah to research this."

"I understand, and that was my thinking too. I'll just decline tomorrow."

"You said everyone would probably be going to a prisoner version of the new collars in a few months, right?"

"That's what the guard said, but I'm not sure he was supposed to let that slip. You know that's going to spread like wildfire, and everyone is going to want to know the details."

"Right. When you first come here, you're irritated and de-pressed by the never-changing routine. After a couple of years, you get nervous when there's a rumor that the routine is going to change. My concern is that three-day battery life. If we can only take off the collars every third night, that means a lot less nights when we can have unmonitored conversations to work on our plan."

The escape plan implications were obvious to Mykola. He pursed his lips and nodded.

"Looking forward, you know what else bothers me?" Alex asked.

"Another level of privacy broken through?"

"Yes, certainly that, but there's more to it. You said the collars are bigger?"

"Yeah, they're about half again as big."

"They could put high concentrations of drugs into the collar, and the collar could deliver them on a regular basis or even continuously. With microneedle technology, you wouldn't even feel the injections."

"That's what the Alcort guy said, pretty much. Sounds like a benefit. I know my uncle had a terrible time following the prescription schedule for the eight different drugs he was taking. He was constantly under- or overmedicating."

"Sure, I can see that for older people and even people in hospitals or nursing facilities. Everything is automatic, and not even the nurses have to keep track of what drugs they need to give patients."

"So what's the problem?" Mykola asked, now intensely curious to hear Alex's vision of the future.

"The problem is that you don't know exactly what symptoms are being treated and what drugs are being used, especially in here. For all you know, the collar will be injecting a steady stream of haloperidol and promethazine into your bloodstream."

"Haloperidol and prometha . . . ?"

"Promethazine. Sorry, didn't mean to go all pharmaceutical on you. These are drugs used to treat aggression in psychotics, but who is to say they couldn't be used to control prisoners? And some drugs like that, used continuously, can cause serious and permanent damage."

Mykola sat back on his bunk and leaned against the wall. "Scary thought. We could be controlled by chemicals we didn't even know about."

"Worse, we could be controlled by drugs selected and ad-ministered by artificial intelligence."

"But not tonight." Mykola raised his arms and yawned. "I'm going to try to get some sleep. After this conversation, that'll be tough, though. Maybe when we do get the new collars—if we're still in here by then—they could inject a sleep aid if we wake up in the middle of the night. That part wouldn't be so bad."

13

"Any news from Dad or Mykola?" Allen asked, noticing that Sarah had the calculus course up on her screen.

"Yes, a bunch, or at least I think so. In the middle of the last assignment, Mykola sent along a bunch of text that I thought was just garbage, but then I thought it might be some foreign text, maybe Russian or Polish. On a hunch I checked Mykola's name, and it's Ukrainian. The Ukrainian alphabet has lots of characters that English doesn't have but that kind of look like our letters. So I checked a bunch of short words to see if I was right. I'm pretty sure that *komip* is collar."

"That's cool. I didn't know this guy Mykola was Ukrainian," Allen said.

"And we still don't, but he apparently knows the language. He was smart enough not to share this with us until he thought it necessary. Now I've got a project for you, Allen. I want you to translate what he's written. It's going to take some best guesses on the letters; it isn't just a matter of typing the text into a translation program."

For Allen this was becoming a real-life version of an online video game, but with much more at stake than a high point total. Winning, for Allen and Sarah, was defined as seeing their father out of prison.

"I can start right now," Allen said excitedly.

"I was hoping you'd say that. We just have to be extra careful. The further we get into this, the more exposure we have." Sarah looked directly at Allen and paused to see if he understood what she was implying.

"Got it," he said. "I'll take photos of the text off your screen and then run a Ukrainian dictionary off an old-fashioned CD on that pre-2K computer we have. You're right, it'll take some guessing to translate this, but I suppose that's part of the security, right?"

"Precisely, my dear brother." Sarah said. "One other thing before you get started. Here's something I'd like you to read."

Sarah handed Allen an 8½-by-11 hardbound book with a red cover.

"*People, Power, and Processes*," Allen read the title out loud. "This is your old master's thesis, isn't it? Is reading this some sort of punishment for leaving the lights on in the garage? Sorry, but forced boredom strikes me as cruel and unusual punishment."

"No, it isn't punishment, though you're right, I wish you'd remember to turn off the lights in the garage."

"Motion detectors are cheap. I'll even install it." Allen shifted himself in the chair, getting ready to get up and walk out.

"Allen, you're getting off the subject. Forget the lights in the garage." Sarah was exasperated with her brother, the young man who could go from near-genius technologist to sniveling little boy in an instant. "I think we're both anxious to come up with a plan, and since we're both pretty good with digital tech, that's the likely solution. That temptation to solve the problem quickly, though, may take us down the wrong path."

"Sorry, didn't mean to get hung up on the garage lights," Allen said. "But isn't Dad giving us all this information about their system so that we can break into it?"

"Yes, that's my assumption. However, every system that uses electronics has three basic components: the computer processes, the power to run them, and the people who control both. If we focus on just the processes, we may be missing some simpler power or people solutions. Worse, we may be overlooking the ability of one component to override another."

"You mean like someone taking manual control of a self-driving car?" Allen asked in a respectful tone.

"Yes, exactly. So, though I know my writing is boring, please read it and keep the principles in mind when we talk about what you've learned from Mykola's notes. We may have to send some questions to Mykola to fully understand the whole prison system."

"Okay. Now I'll go see if I left the lights on in the garage." Allen winked: the unofficial signature of a truce.

Over the next three days, Allen worked diligently at translating the English-alphabet Ukrainian text in Mykola's messages. Many times he had to use intuition to determine what Mykola was trying to say, and even then he couldn't be 100 percent sure. As he worked, he passed along each message translation to Sarah, and she used the information to get a much clearer picture of how the system was intended to operate.

As Sarah had expected, the messages were primarily about how the technology worked. In some cases there was more detail than needed; in others Sarah wished she could get Mykola on the phone to provide a more comprehensive explanation. The biggest miss was how the prison staff interacted with the system and how much control they could take over it. Did they have emergency procedures? Could they override system decisions before those decisions were carried out? What parts of the system could administrators control remotely?

Sarah also scribbled down a lot of power questions. If main power was cut, did the system have a battery backup? Could power be drained from the collars, making them ineffective in delivering jolts? Did the system ever go down for offline maintenance?

⊙

Sarah came down to the kitchen dressed in her casual but not too casual work clothes: comfortable jeans with a pressed crease that broke on the top of her mid-heeled shoes, a pale blue long sleeve blouse with two buttons open to show a modest woven-silver necklace, and a linen jacket that would spend most of the day hung up in her office.

Allen was already at the breakfast bar, enjoying his favorite breakfast of the previous night's leftover pizza with an extra splash of hot sauce. In his hand he held Mykola's translated notes, which he was reviewing intently.

Allen didn't bother to look up when Sarah observed, "You're going to be late for school if you don't hurry . . . and you're not wearing those." She was pointing to the dusty sandals on his bare feet.

"Classes have been canceled."

"Oh? Some sort of air quality advisory?" Sarah asked, quite

aware that recent days had been hotter than usual and that there had been virtually no wind to push in fresh air from the ocean.

"No, nothing like that. I just decided that my classes would be canceled. I'm not going to school today."

"Allen . . . ?" Sarah was frustrated with Allen's growing disrespect and defiance.

"It's just lectures today on stuff I already know or stuff I don't care about, like health science and ancient history. Besides, I'm going through all these messages Mykola sent us. I really think we need to start making some decisions."

This wasn't worth getting into an argument. One day of classes missed wasn't going to change anything for Allen. In fact, his teachers would probably be happy to see that his seat in class was vacant for at least one day, Sarah rationalized.

"Can't you call in sick?" Allen now turned and looked at Sarah with imploring eyes. "We could go through all these notes. Besides, I read your thesis and I think it's the basis for making the best possible decisions."

A compliment from Allen? Maybe he was making some progress in becoming a more sociable young man, or maybe it was just a well-rehearsed negotiating tactic.

"I'm not calling in sick." Sarah pulled out her phone and checked her schedule. There was nothing that couldn't be pushed off a couple of days or done over the phone. "But just this once I'll call in and tell my assistant that I'll be working from home today."

"Good."

"Any pizza left?"

"I saved a slice for you." Allen pointed to the pizza box on the counter.

"You mean I got here before you had a chance to finish it. Let's see what we've got." Unlike Allen, Sarah decided the slice needed to be warmed; she put it in the microwave.

All that morning Allen and Sarah reviewed Mykola's notes and got a better picture of how the London Tower system worked. For what they didn't know specifically, they made reasonable and logical estimates, listing the confidence levels of each estimate and the downside cost if they were wrong. Everything was fed into a decision support software package originally marketed to help people make decisions about major purchases like a new home or postsecondary education. The designers of the software surely had never anticipated it would be used to help engineer a prison escape, but overall both Allen and Sarah were happy with how it guided their decision-making process.

"I think we can cross off everything having to do with the power supply. We can't be sure, but they must have a battery backup system in case there's a routine power failure." Sarah drew a heavy line across everything listed in the power component page.

"And, based on those satellite photos, we know they have a rooftop solar system," Allen added. "Plus we'd have a devil of a time cutting off power only to Dad's and Mykola's collars."

"Great point. One of the things we want to do is make the escape as invisible as possible. The less London Tower knows about how it was engineered, the better for us and Dad. I'll add that to the list of sub-objectives.

"We've got lots of information about the processes, but I'm still concerned that we don't fully understand how the administrators and guards interact with the system and the extent to which they can control it at all levels. For instance, can the guards deliver a Level 2 jolt anytime they deem it necessary?" Sarah rested her chin in her cupped hands.

Allen waited for moment to see if Sarah could answer her own question before he suggested, "Should we send Mykola a note and ask?"

"I thought about that, but perhaps neither he nor Dad know. Just asking that question might raise a flag in the system, even though we know learning communication isn't monitored nearly as closely as email. It's not worth the risk. Our plan may have to just assume the worst: that the guards have that capability."

"Already added to the decision model."

"Because we don't know much about the people-system interaction and control, that basically eliminates an entire class of solutions." Sarah's face brightened with that revelation.

"Which ones?"

"We aren't going to be able to bribe or blackmail anyone on the inside to help us! Even the warden might not be able to help—even if he wanted to."

"And that leaves us with process," Allen commented. "That's where we were when we first started talking about this. We wasted a bunch of time."

"No, don't look at it like that, Allen. We eliminated the worst approaches, and now I'm more confident that our time and energy will be focused on something that has the best chance of working. You wouldn't want to be thinking about power and people solutions while we're digging into the software, would you?"

"No. I suppose you're right. Thinking you've made the right decision often *makes* it the right decision."

"Whoa, where did that bit of philosophy come from? Maybe you learned more in that philosophy class than you're willing to admit." Sarah leaned back in her chair and looked at her brother, the young man she'd been given the responsibility for raising when their father was sentenced to prison. The look on his face told her that he couldn't help but be pleased with himself.

"Let's go on to process. Here it gets more complicated because there are countless options. You've been studying Mykola's notes. Any insights?" Sarah asked more as a courtesy than with the expectation that Allen would have something worthwhile to say.

"Yeah, in fact I do." Allen could see the surprise in his sister's face, and he felt he had just bested her in the little verbal game she likely played at work. "There are two ways to get out of that prison before serving your full sentence: the old-fashioned climb-over-the-wall approach and expedited parole."

"Expedited parole? What are you talking about?" Sarah thought this might be some term Allen had picked up from one of the games he was always playing.

"Mykola explained that they use a points system to track inmate behavior."

"I read about that, but Mykola didn't provide many details as to how points were gained or lost."

"That's true, but he said points were used to determine whether to grant parole. If Dad or Mykola had lots of points, they'd be granted parole."

"I'm with you now. If we knew what the threshold was, perhaps we could alter the records so that they'd have the necessary points." Sarah made a note on her tablet.

"Uh-huh, sort of like when you doctored the grade you got on your course project back in college. Well, that's the rumor, at least." Allen teased his sister with an exaggerated look of shocked horror.

Sarah pretended she hadn't heard that comment. "You want some apple juice or something?" she asked as she got up and opened the refrigerator.

"A Coke would be good. I feel my caffeine levels dropping precipitously."

"The points system could be a good approach," Sarah said as she placed a bottle of water and a large can of Coke on the table. "Unfortunately, you're overlooking a couple of things: one, Dad just had his parole hearing and won't have another one for a year, and two, Mykola is a new inmate. He probably won't have a parole hearing for three years at least. And even if everyone agreed to be patient, we have no assurance the thresholds won't change."

"Speaking of points, that's two for you, I suppose." Allen looked as if he'd just lost a round in a video game. "That leaves us with the over-the-wall approach, though there's no physical wall."

"Yup, and I see a three-story wall in the form of a collar. If we could somehow disable the collar, that might do it. There would be little in the form of a physical barrier to prevent escape," Sarah noted.

"Except for, as you highlighted in your thesis, the people and power components. If the guards saw them walking out, you'd think they would use a backup system, like an eight-pound baton, to prevent it." Allen held up his fist as if he were holding a baton and then brought it down as if hitting someone with it.

"Okay, let's not let our imaginations get too glum. Let's go back to that decision support app and add everything we know so far."

For the next couple of hours that's just what they did, but even before the app was able to provide some guidance, they realized they'd need much more information about the inner workings of the London Tower system. They knew neither Mykola nor Alex would be able to help them with that.

"I've got to hack into the system to learn how it operates. There's no other way," Sarah said out loud, as if confessing to a crime. In fact, she knew that was exactly what she was about to do. She and Allen were going to cross a line, and it was unlikely their path across that line would ever be completely erased.

"You don't sound particularly happy or confident about it," Allen observed. For him, this was an expedition into a strange and dangerous territory without having to bring backpacks full of gear and high-caliber rifles. They could do this from their playroom, with an ample supply of Cokes and frozen pizzas just a short hike away.

"I guess I'm not. All this time, I guess, I was doing this work as if it were a simulation. That's something we do at work all the time to figure out system vulnerabilities. But the reality is hitting me now: we're at an inflection point, and I suspect we'll both remember this afternoon for years to come. I hope we'll remember it with a glass of wine in hand rather than a paper cup of water out of a prison faucet."

"It's not too late to back out . . ." Allen said, hoping Sarah would not take that as a suggestion.

"I know, but when I think about how that prison operates, how it seems to slowly eat away at the humanity of every inmate,

I know I'd be disappointed in myself if I didn't do something to get our dad out of there." With that last phrase, Sarah's face brightened, and she now looked confidently at Allen. "I've got a good idea of how we can do it."

14

A day later, Allen walked by the playroom and saw Sarah sitting before the monitor. Instead of having her hands on the keyboard as she had for the past several hours, she had both hands on the table, with her fingers tapping away as if playing a sprightly tune on a piano.

"Okay, I see something's up," Allen said as he walked in behind Sarah and glanced at the screen.

"We're in." Sarah turned to Allen with a confident smile. "I sent a note to Bill at NiNo Learning telling him I'd found an error in module 8 and asking that he upload my correction. I'm sure he put it through virus checking, but I put in a line that effectively disabled the virus reporting temporarily."

"Genius!"

"Uh-huh, that's a piece of code I lifted from our last hack-athon at work. Not surprising it worked," Sarah explained. "We're constantly being attacked by foreign companies and governments, so we've got protections to guard against anyone trying to disable our first-line protection systems, but I can't imagine many folks wanting to hack into a prison computer system."

"Sounds like you're almost disappointed it wasn't more challenging," Allen observed.

"Yeah, sort of, I guess. Anyway, since the NiNo programs are linked to the prison's inmate course tracking system and that subsystem is linked to a master inmate tracking system, I got high-level access to most of the system's functionality. Too early to tell, but it appears there are only a few things I can't access," Sarah explained.

"Such as?"

"The GPS system that tracks the location of the inmates and the nightly system scan-and-restore function. I'm not too worried about the GPS, but not being able to access the nightly scan-and-restore process will likely limit what we can do."

"Any obvious holes in the system?" Allen asked, pleased with himself for being able to talk to his sister almost as if he were a fellow employee at ZG. At the same time, he wasn't really expecting anything so soon after Sarah had hacked into the system.

"Yes. Come take a look at this piece of code," Sarah said, pointing to a subroutine. "See anything strange?"

"Hmm . . . looks like a patch to fix some sort of problem. The style and logic of the code isn't anything like what comes before or after," Allen noted.

"Exactly. What this does is send a shock command from the guard control room to the offending inmate's collar. I'll have to check it, but my guess right now is that the inmate who's committed whatever infraction has his number fed to the control room screen from the GPS and the artificial intelligence system. The guard sees the inmate's number on the screen—and perhaps real-time video of the infraction—and just presses the 'yes' button to send the shock command to the collar."

"Wow! That means we can put in another line of code to have that command sent to some other inmate or to a nonexistent inmate. It can't be that simple, can it?" Allen asked theatrically.

"Don't know, but I want to be sure I thoroughly understand this code before we do anything. From Mykola's note, I already know that Level 2 is debilitating and Level 3 is potentially deadly, especially if the inmate has a heart condition or is just in overall poor health. We're not messing around with code to destroy space aliens in a game."

⊙

The next day was Sunday. Sarah was up early and began to systematically examine the "patch code" and all it was connected to. Fearful of leaving a trail, she made no changes to any of the code, though she had to fight the urge to simplify some of the unnecessarily complex logic in parts of it.

She could find nothing in the code that prevented her from simply adding a line that would transfer the shock command from one inmate to another. The implication was clear: if she made that change, her father could be doing something to get out of the prison, like walking out the front door, and some other inmate would get the painful consequences.

"I think we're onto something here," she explained to Allen with a tone of satisfaction. "As you noted, it could be as easy as modifying or adding a line of code. I could simply put in a formula that sends the jolt command from the inmate ID identified in the control room to another inmate."

"Could you enter an inmate code that doesn't exist? That would be the perfect 'get out of jail free' card."

"I could definitely do that, but there's added risk. I don't know if there's any real-time checking of the codes. Putting in an invalid inmate code might send a flag somewhere, maybe to the control room, when the instruction is executed. I haven't been able to track the entire sequence of actions. No, I think the best approach is just to substitute a real, validated inmate code."

"Super. That makes sense." Allen was delighted with the progress they were making. "Say, did you notice this line in Mykola's note about the collars? 'The fence is fully automated.'"

A shiver went down Sarah's spine. She had made a freshman's IT security mistake. She'd looked for all the parts of the program that used the patch, but she hadn't checked for any that didn't. With millions of lines of code, that kind of checking wouldn't be easy to do manually; it would take days, maybe weeks.

On a hunch, Sarah decided to copy the code before and after the patch and then do a system search to see if it appeared anywhere else.

It did. She found a complete duplicate of the entire code she'd been looking at, without the patch that required guard control room confirmation. This portion of the code controlled the virtual fence security. What a waste of computer processing power, but it was consistent with the sloppy work she'd found throughout the program.

Sarah's mind went through the progression of what would have happened if Allen hadn't reminded her of that line in Mykola's note. The modification she'd intended to make to the patch would have had no impact on the fence security programming. That would have continued to work as it did right now, with no control room confirmation. She might have killed her father and Mykola while wishing them the best of luck.

Tears started to swell in her eyes, and her hands trembled. That was enough hacking for this day.

⊙

The next day, Sarah's resolve to get her father out of the prison was stronger than ever. Just knowing that a computer program could "decide" to kill someone was all it took. The fact that the program had apparently been written by a bunch of coders who wouldn't get a second interview at ZG only served to add a sense of urgency.

At breakfast with Allen, Sarah laid out her plan. "There are probably a half dozen ways we could recode the system to give Dad and Mykola a chance for escape, but we don't have time to check it all out. I say we go with redirecting the Level 2 and 3 shocks to other inmates. That's the simplest hack and would be easy to explain to Dad and Mykola. Since Level 3 could be deadly, they could pick out inmates who are big enough, strong enough, and healthy enough to withstand it. We'd keep the hack off-line until they decide when they're ready to take advantage of our handiwork."

"Wow, that's kind of like running on the edge of a cliff, isn't it?" Allen asked. "What if there's some part of the code that we didn't find and our hack is either overridden or traced back to us? *We* could end up in prison."

"I've thought of that, and that's why Dad will have to do a

live test. It's the most expeditious way to find out if our hack works, and it reduces our risk of exposure. We ask them to do a Level 2 test; 3 is too risky, but since they're part of the same code, they should work the same."

"Okay, I'm with you on that. Now, how do you explain this to Dad or Mykola without actually talking to them?"

"Pretty simple. In the replies I send to Mykola's notes, I'll include one line that starts with a keyword. Hopefully Mykola will be able to figure it out. It may take several notes, but the information we give them on each note won't mean anything unless they are all put together."

The keywords and the explanation of what Alex and Mykola were to do were sent over the course of eight days. Sarah was confident that she was getting through when after the fourth message Mykola wrote back, "Now I understand. Thanks." Clearly that was in reference to the single-line directions; Mykola obviously didn't understand calculus any better than he had a few weeks ago when he'd started the course.

⊙

With both Mykola and Alex hunched over the chessboard and the faint light coming in from the hallway, Mykola said in a whisper, "I've read Sarah's messages several times. Putting all the lines together, my understanding is that Sarah is going to change the program so that when one of us does something in the course of our escape that triggers a Level 2 or 3 jolt, another inmate will get the jolt. That sounds like a good approach, but if I'm reading this right, she wants us to test it before we make our break."

"Mykola, that makes sense. This is risky; we've got one

chance to make it, and she wants to be sure it works like she expects. She's always been very thorough in testing software before making it go live."

"Well, then, why doesn't she try with a couple of other inmates? Why should you or I get the jolt?"

"C'mon, Mykola. Sometimes I think this place is putting too much pressure on your noggin. If she uses this with some other inmates, the guys upstairs will know there's something wrong with the system when they jolt a guy and he doesn't collapse. Then they're going to check the whole system, and everything Sarah has done will be a waste."

Embarrassed that he hadn't thought it through, Mykola hung his head. "Sorry. You're right. I guess the tension of sending these notes back and forth is getting to me. I keep worrying that one day a couple of red-shirts are going to haul us upstairs."

"That's okay; we're 90 percent of the way there. We've just got to focus and get this test right."

Alex paused, looked at Mykola, and waited. For a few moments there was absolute silence. Then Mykola looked up and gently nodded.

"Here's what we'll do." Alex explained in detail how they'd conduct the test, and Mykola appeared to understand. "Any questions?"

"No, I've got the plan down. But I guess I do have one question. Why do I get the jolt and not you?"

Alex put his hands to his face and pressed hard, trying to hide his initial frustration with Mykola's question. He took a moment to remind himself that Mykola hadn't had the length and intensity of prison experience he himself had. This was no time to belittle Mykola. The only way they could pull this off was if Mykola fully understood what they were doing and why.

Putting his hand on Mykola's shoulder and speaking as calmly as he could, he said, "Mykola, they're going to think I'm the offender and got the jolt. After I 'recover,' they're going to put me in detention for a week, maybe more. I know what that's like, and I know how to keep my mouth shut. You'll get the pain of the jolt, but you'll be able to come back to this cell. I'll be in detention, simply hoping that the test worked and we weren't found out."

"Okay, I suppose that makes sense."

"Mykola, tomorrow you send a note to Sarah saying you need an extra day to study and asking if you can take the test on Friday. She'll know what you mean. Until after the real test—and after I get out of detention—let's not talk about this anymore. We can't afford a slipup."

On Friday at 3:00, Mykola was in the yard walking around the perimeter for exercise and to settle his nerves. He had seen one of the other inmates get a Level 2 jolt, and it looked painful and disturbing. Mykola's breathing was forced. He was just hoping he could hold up his end of the test. Seeing Alex come out, lift his head up to the sky, then look at him, was the signal to begin. A quick nod back to confirm, and Mykola started to walk back inside the complex.

Alex had identified a corner just outside one of the janitorial supply rooms that was hidden from the ceiling cameras. Perhaps it had been a last-minute design change when they were building the prison, but it was exactly what they needed for this test. The GPS would know where Mykola was, but there was no corresponding camera visual. In addition, there was little reason for any inmate to be in this part of the prison. Mykola looked around to make sure no yellow- or red-shirts were paying attention to him and then stood quietly in the corner. He hoped Alex would be quick on his end and get this over with. Thinking about it a bit more, Mykola realized that if he *didn't* get the jolt, that would actually be worse. It would mean the hack Sarah had put in didn't work.

Meanwhile, Alex went to the big room and looked for a potential victim. Alex was going to try to start a fight, but he knew the inmates who had been there for some time would quickly walk away if they sensed any aggressiveness on his part. It had to be a guy who was new to the prison and had something to prove.

There he was: a self-confident guy in his 20s who outweighed Alex by 30 pounds and had tattoos on his face, hands, and grotesquely muscled forearms. Alex had not seen him in the prison before and was hoping he hadn't read all the rules. I doubt he can even read, Alex thought.

Knowing that Mykola couldn't be counted on to wait much longer in his corner by the utility closet, Alex didn't hesitate. He walked over to the tattooed inmate and tapped his shoulder from behind. As Tattoo-Man turned around, Alex yelled "Asshole!" and with all his might took a right-armed swing to Tattoo-Man's face.

It was just a glancing blow to his chin, but Tattoo-Man fell back for a moment. Then, before Alex could swing his left arm, he felt Tattoo-Man's fist in the pit of his stomach. It knocked the wind out of him, causing him to fall back on the floor. It was all that Alex could do to get up and lunge at Tattoo-Man, but he knew he had to. He had to keep fighting until he could see that the other man was being jolted.

Other inmates immediately crowded around, being careful not to get too close and become involved in the fight. Most wondered how long this would go on before one or the other or both would be jolted.

Up in the control room, a flashing red light appeared on the panel, and the image on one of the small screens was copied onto the larger screen in the center. Tim, one of the two guards on duty in the control room, hadn't seen such a fight in quite a while, but he knew what to do. Glancing quickly at the inmates' numbers on the screen and confirming that they were the same as the numbers on the prison uniforms the inmates were wearing, he pressed the flashing Level 2 button next to each of the inmate numbers.

The jolt hit Tattoo-Man like being hit in the temple by someone with brass knuckles. He felt a charge of electricity go down his back and radiate toward his fingers and toes, curling them like the claws of a lion. His arms and legs shook, his head felt hot, and his eyes watered. Try as he might, he couldn't produce a sound. For an instant he thought: so this is what it feels like to die.

The jolt lasted only three seconds, but Tattoo-Man couldn't know that. As soon as it ended, he fell to the floor, crumpling like an imploded building. His head hit the concrete and he lost consciousness.

Alex knew what to expect, and as soon as he could see that Tattoo-Man was being jolted, he mimicked the expressions he saw. Fortunately, Alex was just beginning to get up from the floor and so didn't have far to fall. Nevertheless, he gave an all-star performance and hoped that the guys in the control room believed his act. The other inmates now crowding around him unknowingly helped with the subterfuge: they made it difficult for the overhead camera and the guys in the control room to get a complete view of Alex.

At the same time, standing in his corner, Mykola had the same experience as Tattoo-Man. Alex had told him to avoid trying to fight the spasms he would experience and get on the floor as quickly as he could. Falling and hitting his head on the concrete could produce a concussion or bleeding head injury he wouldn't be able to explain.

It was over pretty quickly, and Mykola just lay there for a few minutes trying to compose himself and restore feeling and strength to his legs. Just as he was getting up, another inmate saw him and asked, "Are you all right? Your face is pure white and you don't look very steady."

"Yeah, yeah, I'm okay. I must have slipped on that puddle of water," Mykola said, pointing to a puddle near his feet. "I guess I bumped my head too, but I'll be okay in a minute or two." Funny, Mykola thought. That puddle wasn't there when I got here. Then he noticed his trousers were damp. The other inmate had since walked away.

Back in the big room, two yellow-shirts pushing gurneys were out in moments. They loaded Alex and Tattoo-Man onto the gurneys and rolled them back to the infirmary. Alex had to continue his deception, and it took some effort to remain limp and ignore everything that was going on around him.

In the infirmary Alex was moved to a bed, but his collar remained in place. When he was lying down, it pressed uncomfortably into his neck, but he couldn't move or say anything. He knew from having seen other inmates come into the infirmary after a Level 2 jolt that it took five or ten minutes before they became coherent and fully aware of their surroundings. So for what Alex thought was at least ten minutes, he just lay there with his mouth slightly open and drooling onto the sheets.

He could hear Manuel, the nurse on duty, and the yellow-shirts talking about what had happened. From that he was fairly confident they believed he had gotten the Level 2 jolt. That was the logical conclusion, of course; what common sense explanation could there be for faking it?

When Manuel walked over to check on him, Alex finally decided it was safe to open his eyes.

"Alex, how are you feeling?"

"Like a truck hit me. Did you get the plate number?" Alex replied in slow, slurred, barely audible speech.

"What the hell were you thinking? You've seen enough guys get Level 2; you knew fighting that guy would get you a jolt before you had time to do any damage to him. He must have pissed you off about something." Manuel didn't seem to expect a response from Alex, and Alex simply nodded.

Manuel then reached over and took a closer look at where the collar touched Alex's neck.

"Wow, you got really lucky. I only see some redness here. I've seen a couple of guys in here with Level 2 jolts; their necks had blisters and the skin looked like someone had taken a file to it. Yours doesn't look much worse than a sunburn." Alex had roughly rubbed his neck with a short piece of cord that morning to produce what he hoped looked like the result of a Level 2 jolt, but it had already started to heal.

Manuel looked at Alex and was about to ask another question, but the expression on Alex's face told him not to. This was one of those times, Manuel decided, when you don't want to know the answer to your question.

"I'll let you rest here for another couple of hours, but then I have to send you down to detention," Manuel said as he walked away from Alex's bed.

15

Alex didn't need a couple of hours of rest, of course, but he was glad to have the time to mentally prepare himself for detention. His first experience had been bewildering. In his university studies he had read about isolation and solitary confinement in prisons, but the descriptions of inmate reactions were just words, and professional words at that. Hallucinations, panic attacks, paranoia, and diminished impulse control were all terms he used professionally and with unemotional objectivity. Actually experiencing detention and its isolation was a new experience for him.

Initially he found it intellectually interesting as he introspectively examined his feelings. That inward examination lasted about 24 hours, and then he became and acted like any other inmate in detention.

Studies had shown that solitary confinement could cause brain damage. Those inmates who experienced 30 or more days of continuous solitary confinement often could not regain their social functions. Anger, depression, and suicidal thoughts stayed with them even when they were released from prison.

Detention was London Tower's version of isolation. They felt it was a much more humane way to punish prisoners than solitary confinement; while detention had prisoners in individual cells, they shared a common room throughout the day. They could walk or lie down in their cells. Yes, it was better than solitary confinement, but inmates who had experienced detention said they now had sympathy for horses that spent much of their lives in stables and corrals.

Alex knew he had to exercise his mind regularly throughout the seven days he was to remain in detention. He was determined to come out of detention just as mentally and physically healthy as he went in. Otherwise, all the work his son, daughter, and cellmate had been doing would surely be wasted.

A guard walked Alex to detention. It was just a hundred yards from the infirmary. Alex made sure to listen closely to the words spoken by passing inmates. He wasn't interested in what they were saying; he just savored the sound of human voices. He knew that in minutes, a memory of human voices was all he'd have for the next week.

There were two detention rooms, and Alex was assigned to Room A. He assumed Tattoo-Man had been assigned to Room B to eliminate the possibility of a rematch. The guard put in a code which opened the door. With a gentle shove on his shoulder, the guard pushed Alex into an empty room about six feet square with another door on the facing wall.

"Take off your shoes," the guard demanded, "and put these on." He held out a pair of black foam booties. Alex had forgotten about these booties. They were very soft and comfortable but were also virtually soundless. There would be no clopping or the sound of shuffling when in the detention room.

The guard called out Alex's prisoner ID. The door they had just entered closed behind them and the second door opened. Alex didn't wait for a push; he just walked in.

A red-shirt was waiting for him. Without saying a word, he pointed to the detention room rules posted on the wall at the far end of the room. He then pointed to the numbers painted on the ceiling above each of the cells and held up six fingers. Alex nodded to show he understood that Cell 6 would be his.

Unlike the rest of the prison, the detention room walls and ceiling were a flat black, with only the slightest bit of light reflected from them. The floor, however, was platinum gray, and that was the only way anyone could see they were approaching a wall.

The red-shirt went back to his chair. It too was black but had a faint red stripe painted across the back of it, indicating it was only to be used by the red-shirt on duty.

Room A was a long room with 20 cells along the left side and 20 chairs and a table that ran the length of the wall bolted on the right side. Vertical partitions that rose above the height of a seated inmate were attached to the table. They also extended about 12 inches to the side of the seated inmate, creating virtual isolation when meals were served.

As in the general population area, the individual cell gates were left open during the day. The gates weren't actually gates: they were solid, heavy sliding doors that when closed were flush with the walls, both inside and out.

Alex looked around and was surprised to see only eight other inmates. The first time he was in detention, there had been 14 or 15. Either prisoners had learned to follow the rules and stay out of detention or enforcement of the rules was becoming more lax. Alex was quite sure it was the former.

All of the inmates were doing "laps": walking from one end of the detention room to the other in an oval pattern, always turning left. Maybe that was another component of detention that reminded inmates of the horse farm.

Alex ambled over to his cell and sat on the bunk. Cell 6 was painted in the same black and platinum gray scheme as the common area; however, the material used for all horizontal and vertical surfaces, including the floor, was a sound-absorbing dense foam. There were no clocks in detention, nor windows, but based on the time when he'd been released from the infirmary and sent to detention, Alex figured it must be near 6:00. Sure enough, a few minutes later the door through which Alex had entered opened once again and a red-shirt pushed in a cart of dinner trays, then turned and left immediately.

The inmates walking the oval continued to do so until they came to the cart. One by one each picked up a tray, went over to the long table on the wall, took a seat, and began to eat. Alex noticed one of the inmates, standing just outside the table partition, holding his hands in prayer with his lips moving, but there wasn't so much as a whisper of sound.

Alex waited for all the other inmates to take a tray and then got up and picked up the last one for himself. He wasn't particularly hungry, and the sight of food that looked like lumpy oatmeal in various colors did nothing to stimulate his appetite. Yet he knew this would be the last meal for the next 12 hours at least, and he promised himself he'd do everything he could to keep up his strength.

174

In detention for only an hour and he was already tempted to splatter the black wall in front of him with the pale mold green, muddy parchment, and dirty brown food on his plate. The pale green stuff tasted like broccoli or perhaps green beans, but since all green vegetables tasted pretty much the same to him, without any distinctive shape or texture he couldn't be sure. It didn't really matter.

The muddy parchment stuff was sort of tasty, however. He'd eat that. It had the taste and texture, if not really the appearance, of vanilla pudding. It must have been a mistake, Alex decided. He didn't remember having dessert of any sort during his first detention.

A few minutes later dinner was over. Alex couldn't remember if he was to put the tray back on the cart or just leave it. Looking over his shoulder, he saw several other trays with half-eaten food on the cart and figured he should put his tray there too. One of the other inmates had mixed all the food on his tray together and shaped it into a rough cylinder. Alex had to repress a laugh: it looked like food that had been eaten, digested, and expelled. He hoped he wouldn't have that image in his mind every time he sat down for a meal.

As he set his tray down, Alex looked up and recognized the inmate walking up to the other side of the cart. Impulsively he began to call out "Bill!" but caught himself just as the B sound left his lips. He paused for a moment, holding his breath and remaining perfectly still. There was no jolt.

Alex was surprised by his instinctive "deer in the headlights" reaction. Being a human statue wasn't going to fool the system.

Bill heard the B sound and turned to face Alex. Initially he didn't know who this new addition to detention was, but as soon as Alex put up his hand and gave a little wave, Bill recognized him as an inmate who worked in the infirmary. He was surprised to see Alex here. Most of the detainees were in their 20s and early 30s, and Alex was old enough to be a father to most every one of them.

Alex took a couple of steps and extended his hand to Bill. Expecting a smile and a handshake, Alex was confused by Bill's look of alarm. Bill waved his arms across each other to give the universal "no" sign and then pointed to the rules posted on the wall. Alex had forgotten: besides no talking, there was also no touching of other inmates. Alex put his hands up and gave a gentle nod to indicate he was sorry.

Still, Alex wanted to connect with Bill. They couldn't talk, but perhaps with lipreading and some hand gestures they could communicate.

Alex mouthed, "How long are you in for?"

Bill didn't understand.

Alex tried a different approach. He pointed to Bill and then to the closed door and made a walking motion with two fingers. Then he mouthed, "How many more days?"

Bill now understood the question and put up a thumb to signal that. Then he shrugged his shoulders and mouthed, "What day is it?"

"Friday," came the silent reply.

Bill pulled at his chin and held up three fingers. He quickly changed to four fingers and nodded his head quickly to emphasize he was in for four more days.

Alex pointed to himself and held up seven fingers.

This was going to be a tiresome and frustrating way to talk, and both men knew it. There was no real possibility of conversation. They just stared at each other for a painfully awkward moment. Then Bill shrugged and walked away.

The balance of the day in detention was similar to the process on the "outside." Inmates had to be in their cells at 8:00, but without a clock the only indication was a countdown timer that started at 15 minutes. Alex was in his cell long before that. The collars came off shortly afterward, but still no talking was allowed. The rules posted on the wall said that a microphone in the ceiling of the cell captured all sound and that any inmate who talked even to himself would serve additional detention time. How much additional time wasn't stated, but the mere threat was enough to keep everyone quiet. Alex wondered if the talking prohibition also applied to talking in one's sleep.

When the sliding door closed, Alex felt himself to be totally alone in a way that was decidedly distressing. In the common area of detention, he at least saw other inmates and they could exchange looks of acknowledgment. There was motion. Inside the cell there were the black walls and ceiling to look at and nothing more.

At 9:00 the light in the cell gradually faded until there was total darkness. Alex felt like an animatronic doll that had been placed in a box and put on a shelf. He could only hope that in the morning someone would take the cover off the box and let him see the light again.

Hours later, Alex woke up. It was still pitch black. There was no sound, not even that of air coming through the ventilation system. With neither windows to let in sunlight nor clocks, Alex could only guess at the time. Was it 4:00? His collar had not yet been returned to the tray, so he knew it had to be sometime before 6:00. Getting some additional sleep seemed impossible, so Alex just lay on his bunk listening to the silence.

The concept of silence was an intellectual exercise, and thoughts of past soundless experiences came to mind. How can I listen to silence? he thought. It's like feeling the texture of air or seeing this total darkness I'm in. Still, silence isn't always the same.

Alex thought back to grade school, when the teacher had asked him a simple math question in front of the whole class. Alex knew the answer but decided not to speak, just to see how long the teacher would wait for any response from him. He could see classmates becoming embarrassed for him, even though he was grinning. The teacher was also uncomfortable, and it wasn't more than 30 seconds before she demanded he at least try to answer the question. But gee, those 30 seconds were wonderfully quiet.

Then there was the time when he was at a professional conference in upstate New York. He'd had dinner with colleagues but declined to join them afterward in the bar. Instead he'd decided to go for a walk in the wooded area around the resort. It had been snowing much of that day, and the snow was continuing to fall steadily into the evening. Large flakes were falling quietly and softly to the snow-covered ground. Alex remembered sitting on a bench as the snow became a sound insulator. There were no voices, no wind rustling the branches of the pines, no distant sounds of trucks rolling on the highway. It was wonderfully quiet. He could feel the individual snowflakes melting on his tongue, and his bare hands felt the cold as if it were a new experience.

And there were the nights when he was at home and everyone else had gone to bed. The TV was off by then, and the only sound was the hum of the refrigerator. Just the quiet time to himself, to reflect on the day and the family he loved safely sleeping upstairs, was a pleasure he never tired of.

But the silence of detention was different. It was forced and lonely. A sensation had been taken away, and there was nothing to replace it. It wasn't like the snow or the quiet of home late at night. There he knew he could bring back sound with the flip of a switch or his own voice and there would be no punishment. Perhaps worse, Alex and everyone else knew that sounds and voices were just outside the door of the detention room but would not be heard for days.

With thoughts of a gentle snowfall, Alex drifted off to sleep again until the morning wake-up alarm came. This was sound, but unlike the alarm he heard in the cell he shared with Mykola, this one was a loud, scratchy, high-pitched sound that was painful to everyone's increasingly sensitive hearing.

After a tasteless, noiseless breakfast, Alex started walking laps. To keep his mind active, he began counting steps. After a long hour of counting, he switched to doing math problems in his head. He tried multiplying consecutive prime numbers, wondering how many he would have to multiply to get to a million. Then he tried working out how many days he'd been alive. If Sarah and Allen could read his mind right now, Alex was sure they'd be impressed with his mathematical efforts.

Just thinking about his children was a refreshment for the mind. Alex made a commitment to himself to do that for at least five minutes—or what he guessed would be five minutes—twice each day.

He couldn't help but think about how this minimalist sensory environment was affecting him. He'd been in detention once before, but that was different. That time he'd been angry because he'd thought detention was not deserved, and he had made a commitment to fight it. That fight wasn't physical; it was a fight to show everyone he could handle it. He'd smile at the red-shirts and the occasional guard who came in. He'd make wild gestures and act like a chimpanzee, bringing a smile to those few inmates who were paying attention to him.

This time Alex was not in the mood to fight; fighting in any form might be perceived as threatening to other inmates or the system. His pressing objective was to complete detention and come out with the same resolve that had brought him into detention: to escape this prison. At the same time, his professional psychiatrist brain was thinking about the other inmates. Were some of them here for more than seven days? He couldn't recall ever seeing guidelines for the length of detention based on a particular violation. Were some violations deemed more serious and assigned more days in detention? Did second offenses result in longer stays? In talking to inmates who'd been in detention previously, Alex had understood that seven days was typical. Occasionally that would be extended to eight to ten days because an inmate didn't follow the rules of detention.

For serious or continuing infractions in detention, inmates were confined to their cells with the sliding door closed. Meals came through the tray used to pass collars out. That and the weak light coming on in the morning and off at night were the only ways inmates confined to their cells had any way of marking time.

What Alex found remarkable was an absence of violence and

hostile emotion. The inmates in detention had all committed some sort of offense, like Alex's fight with Tattoo-Man. These were typically men who never cared much for following someone else's rules. Yet in here everyone did. There was no fighting, no screaming, and no pounding of walls. If there were conflicts between the inmates, one couldn't readily identify them. Certainly just being here for days should cause someone to lash out, if nothing more than in weariness. Yet somehow everyone had managed to maintain self-control. Some were walking the circuit and others were in their cells, just lying in their bunks, staring at a ceiling that was no different from the walls.

Could it be the threat of additional days in detention or a blotch on their record that would deny them parole? That might be part of it, Alex thought. More likely, however, these men had been broken. Again the horse farm analogy came to mind. Wild or young horses had to be broken so that they would allow themselves to be ridden or to pull a wagon. The breaking was accomplished with a combination of rewards and restraints, until the horse submitted to the control of the rider. Tying a horse to a post was a first step. The horse would fight the rope and try to flee but would eventually tire.

Men weren't tied up here, but the minimal sensory experience for humans was much like what a tied-up wild horse was experiencing. For those who had never experienced detention, it seemed like minimal and justified punishment. It was thought to be a good first step to bringing these men back to a civilized and cooperative society. The reality was much different—and much darker.

Time dragged on. On Sunday, a rare desert thunderstorm came directly over the prison. Despite the sound-deadening walls, all the inmates in detention could hear the crashing, rumbling sounds of thunder. They stopped walking and looked up at the ceiling, almost believing they'd see lightning. They imagined the rain coming down, washing the dust out of the desert air and leaving a clean fresh scent that confirmed the sensation of freedom and independence. Even the red-shirt who was taking a nap woke up. Seeing the inmates standing there, some looking as if they were about to cry, made Alex think something was desperately wrong. He quickly realized the rapture of the storm and stopped to enjoy it as well.

For Alex, the sound of thunder produced a mixture of emotions. The initial sound was invigorating, and he stood motionless so that he might focus on it and savor it. Then a memory of a time in his former life began to form, and he knew he had to sit down or he'd fall down. His cell was only steps away, and without hesitation he quietly moved to it and sat on the edge of his bunk. No one was paying any attention to him, and for this he was thankful. He imagined his face had turned pale. He could see his hands shaking. Surely anyone who saw him in this condition would think he was having a heart attack or stroke.

Alex turned away from the other inmates and then hung his head and closed his eyes. The last time he'd heard a storm so loud and powerful had been seven years earlier. That was a night he'd never forget, and painful as it was, he was sure he'd never want to forget it. The memory came to him in a torrent.

His wife Valerie. Sparkling blue eyes. Shining copper hair. Flawless cream skin. Gentle smile. A discussion about money. Her need for respect. His obsession with control. Escalation. Harsh words. Cruel words. Loud voices. Dramatic gestures. An argument. Her demands. His unwillingness to compromise. Her unwavering stance. Her tears. "Going to spend the night with my sister." Door slams. Left alone. Thunderstorm. Cracking lightning. Vibrations through the house. Power failure. Lights off. A message from God? Sitting in the dark. What has he done? His love not enough. She deserves respect. A call to apologize. No answer. Worry. Call again. Still no answer. What to do? Phone rings. Not Valerie. Unrecognized voice. Highway patrol. Serious accident. Drive to the hospital. Too fast. Not fast enough. Somber doctor. Valerie has died.

Alex clenched his fists and pounded them against his temples, and it felt like the thunder. It was an attempt to replace the emotional pain with physical pain, but it didn't work. He then realized he'd been breathing rapidly, as if he'd just run a sprint. A long, deep breath brought him back to the here and now.

A new revelation formed: that night was the beginning of a downward slide for Alex.

The storm had knocked out power to street lights, and that had probably contributed to Valerie's accident. A cursory investigation found paint of another color on a fender, indicating that Valerie was the victim of a hit-and-run. There were many accidents that night, and the police never found out who the driver of the other car was. Alex was sure they hadn't tried hard enough. The pain of Valerie's death, helping their children cope with it, and a sense of helpless emotional isolation and guilt were too much for Alex to bear.

That unpunished hit-and-run driver produced a second victim: Alex. When the driver wasn't caught, nobody outside Alex's family seemed to care. That put Alex into a mindset that doing wrong was okay just as long as you didn't get caught.

So Alex started overbilling his patients small amounts and then started billing National Health Insurance for services that were never rendered. It was easy, and in a small way, Alex felt he was protesting against the system and the people who didn't care. Previously always vigilant and attuned to details, he was emboldened by his criminal success, and he threw caution to the wind. That led to his arrest and conviction and to where he was now: in a detention room in a desert prison, thinking what might have been had he just listened more thoughtfully and lovingly to Valerie's simple request that night 12 years before.

It couldn't have been more than five minutes until the storm moved on and the thunder with it. Then detention was as quiet as an empty cathedral late at night, as no one moved and of course no one spoke. The stillness reminded everyone of the isolation they were experiencing even in sight of one another.

Then one inmate started to slowly clap his hands with wide powerful swings of his arms. In seconds all of them, including Alex, were enthusiastically clapping in a slow, steady, synchronized rhythm, creating their own version of thunder. Alex could feel the hair on his arms bristling, and it felt good. It felt human, and he regained a long-forgotten sense of awe in the simple sounds and tactile sensations of hands coming together. He looked around and could see in the eyes of the other inmates that they shared his feelings.

The red-shirt knew this noise would be picked up by the system and would reflect poorly upon him. He quickly walked over to the inmate who had started clapping, extended both arms, and held them across each other in the shape of an X. His face became an angry red, but all the inmates ignored him. They continued to clap. Moments later a guard walked into detention and, without saying a word, began to enter inmate IDs in his pad. One by one, inmates began to receive a Level 1 jolt. The others made the connection between the guard and the jolts and quickly brought their hands down to their sides. Most moved back into their cells.

16

"I got a note from Mykola. Without exactly saying it, he made it clear to me that the test was successful. I feel bad that he had to experience that high-voltage pulse, though, especially since he didn't do anything to deserve it," Sarah said as if she were consoling Mykola right there in their home.

"Yes, but don't forget about Dad. If I understand it right, he's in detention for at least a week, and that actually sounds worse. At least with the jolt it's over and done with; you start getting better as soon as it's over. With detention, it gets worse every day until you finally get out.

"I went over the notes again from Mykola, the notes he sent about how the prison operates. There was something strangely familiar about what he was describing . . ." Allen trailed off.

"And what was that?"

"Do you remember Becky?"

"Becky? You mean Becky, the Border collie we used to have when we were kids? Sure, I remember her, but what does she have to do with the prison?" Sarah asked, now wondering where Allen's sometimes convoluted logic was taking him.

"Well, when we got Becky, we were living in the old house, with a fence around the backyard. We'd just let Becky out, and we knew the fence would prevent her from running away. Then we moved to that new house, where the neighborhood rules said you couldn't build a fence. So Dad had that company come in and install an electric fence for dogs."

"Yes, that worked great. We could let Becky out the front door and she never left the yard."

"See what I mean? Collar, electric fence, never left the yard," Allen said, looking for acknowledgement from Sarah. "And where did Becky sleep at night?"

"In her crate, which she couldn't get out of." Sarah saw it clearly now.

"They're treating Dad and everyone else in that prison like a bunch of dogs," Allen said with an anger in his voice that Sarah had never before seen in her younger brother. "We've got to shut that place down!"

"Allen, I understand you're angry, but let's not get ahead of ourselves. We're so close to getting Dad out now; let's not do anything that'll dash his and our hopes. Okay?"

"Okay, I won't."

Sarah wasn't entirely sure she believed him.

In the morning, a week later, Alex was released from detention. He returned to his job in the infirmary and the old routine. Nothing had changed in the prison, but Mykola could see a change in Alex when he came back to the cell that night. The lines in his face were deeper, his arms hung loosely and seemingly no longer in his control, and his posture had slumped. He walked with his head down as if he were looking for something he had dropped on the floor.

One week? I thought this guy was tough, Mykola thought. But he kept it to himself. Mykola had recovered from the jolt in a couple of days, and the only comment he'd gotten from others was that he seemed to be distracted and had no energy as he worked in the laundry.

"Glad to see you back, Alex," Mykola said in an effort to lift Alex's spirits. "Game of chess tonight? I've been working on a new opening."

"No, not tonight. After we get these off"—he pointed to his neck—"and after the cell locks, though, we need to talk."

Alex looked up with steely eyes focused on his cellmate.

For the next hour Alex just lay on his bunk, and that surprised Mykola. He thought for sure that after a week of not talking to anyone, Alex would be anxious to chatter up a storm about most anything.

Even after they'd taken off the collars and the cell gate was locked, Alex didn't say anything. It was only after the lights went out that he moved closer to Mykola and said, "We've got to get out . . . now."

"*Now*? I sent a message to Sarah letting her know the test was successful, but I didn't tell her when we'd be ready, and she didn't confirm that all was a go on her end. Hell, I didn't even know you were out of detention until I saw you an hour ago."

"Okay, not now, but just as soon as we can. The longer we wait, the more likely someone or something is going to give us away," Alex said.

Mykola got the implication that he was the "someone." It wasn't fair, but Mykola was in no mood to get into that discussion right now.

"Send a message to Sarah tomorrow and let her know we plan on making our break Thursday. You'll also have to send her a couple of inmate numbers. From what we know, we can't be sure Sarah's hack will work unless there are active inmates who will receive the jolts meant for us."

"Thursday?" It suddenly struck Mykola that the patient, methodical, and cautious Alex was now being impulsive and reckless as they were approaching the finish line. "Alex, I think we're going too fast. I need to know the rest of the plan before I'm ready to go over the berm."

"Rest of the plan? There *is* no rest of the plan. This is it. This is exactly what we've been working toward all this time." Alex's exasperation at having to explain the obvious to his cellmate was wearing on him.

"And you know I've been following your lead all along," Mykola said. "You've thought this through, and I've trusted you to make the right decisions, even when you weren't sharing the full plan with me. But now you're missing a step."

"What do you mean, 'missing a step'?" Alex tried to think of what he might have overlooked.

"Getting that Level 2 jolt last week was an experience I don't want to repeat. I'm not ashamed to admit it: for a moment I thought I was dying. You explained how it would feel and how my body would react, but until I experienced it I didn't really understand it."

"What's that got to do with me missing a step?"

"Pretty simple. I now know I can recover from a Level 2, and

I'm going to assume most everyone here can too. But what about Level 3? The only thing I know is that it's potentially deadly. Sly told me that, it's in the handbook, and you know it too. But what is 'potentially deadly'? Is it a 5 percent chance? 25 percent? 80 percent? Is it almost 100 percent for some inmates and next to zero for others?"

Mykola kept his voice just above a whisper and as unemotional as he could manage. He was amazed at what he was saying; he was expressing his concerns in the same sort of logical, factual manner he had come to expect from Alex.

"Sure, Mykola, it could be deadly, but I understand how this place operates. As long as all the inmates believe a Level 3 is potentially deadly, that's all that counts. London Tower doesn't want to use Level 3; they just want inmates to believe they will. It's like the old-time prison, when they had armed guards on the walls. The assumption was that all the rifles had bullets in them, but did they?

"Mykola, I'm not even sure there *is* a Level 3. In all the time I've been here, I haven't heard of or seen an inmate getting a Level 3. For all we know, Level 3 is just a Level 2 that lasts a bit longer.

"Early on, there were a couple of guys who tried to walk out over the berm, and they were stopped by the Level 2. A minute or so later, guards came out, hauled them back inside, and dumped them in the infirmary. If a Level 2 incapacitates an inmate for long enough that the guards can get to him and subdue him, why would London Tower ever risk using a Level 3?"

Mykola was relieved that some of the tension in their conversation had dissipated, but he wasn't yet convinced. "Still, just like the old-time inmates didn't know if there were bullets in the rifles, we don't know if Level 3 is actually deadly. There's only one way to find out, and that's by committing a Level 3 violation."

"So what do you want to do? You want to try to choke a guard, just to see what happens when you do get a Level 3?"

"No, of course not," Mykola replied. "But it's not right to subject another inmate to a Level 3 when we bolt out of here."

"Dammit, Mykola, you knew this was the plan when you agreed to do the Level 2 test. What the hell did you expect me or Sarah to do?"

"I don't know, but like I said, I thought you had this all worked out. Maybe Sarah could figure out a way to turn off Level 3 in the whole system for the minutes it takes us to cross the berm."

"Sure, there might be a better way to handle this, but like I told you, with every day that goes by, the likelihood of us being found out or of the Tower making some changes to the security system increases, and then we're back to square one . . . or worse. There comes a time when you have to make a decision based on what you know and what your gut tells you, and that time is now!"

The cell was quiet for a couple of minutes as Mykola thought through Alex's argument for executing the plan as it currently stood. Alex knew that anything more he might say would only create more doubt and confusion for Mykola. He waited patiently for Mykola's response.

Finally Mykola let out a long, slow breath, almost a whistle.

"Alex, I'm not going to do it. You may be right that Level 3 is a phantom, but I won't take the chance of my escape being the cause of some other inmate's permanent injury or death. I simply won't be an executioner."

"Fine. Then I'll pick the guys who'll get the jolts. I'll pick the biggest, toughest inmates in this hole, and while they'll feel it, they'll be able to withstand the jolts better than some scrawny punks. You won't have any responsibility other than communicating the information to Sarah."

"But you don't know for sure if a guy you pick will survive a Level 3. He could have a heart condition he doesn't even know about." Mykola stared at Alex to see whether he was convincing him that this was the wrong thing to do, but Alex's chiseled look of determination was still there. "Alex, I'm going to be brutally honest with you. I think your obsession with getting out is overriding your moral judgment. If you're going to continue with the plan as it now stands, I'm done; this partnership is over as far as I'm concerned."

"Okay, be stupid. That's your right. Then I'm going out on my own," Alex snarled.

"And then after you're out, how do you think Sarah is going to feel if her code hack *did* kill an inmate? Maybe a guy up for parole pretty soon, with his own family waiting for his release? How would you explain that to her and to Allen?"

Alex was silent for a few moments and then said, "I'm going to sleep."

Mykola also went to sleep, but he woke up during the night when he heard Alex tossing restlessly and punching his pillow.

Several days passed, and Alex and Mykola had few discussions about anything more substantial than what was being served for dinner. The chess pieces remained in a box on the shelf. One night after the cell gate had been locked and the only light in the cell came from the weak corridor light, Alex turned over in his bunk and looked at Mykola.

"You asleep?"

"No."

"I thought some more about the selection of other inmate numbers. You're right; it wouldn't be fair, especially if it was some guy who was scheduled for release pretty soon. I don't know why I didn't see this before. Maybe I got so focused on the details that I didn't see the big picture."

If it killed him, it wouldn't be fair no matter who got the jolt in our place, Mykola thought, but he waited to see if Alex might express that conclusion on his own.

"I don't know what the solution is, and I'm concerned about asking Sarah to do any more work on this," Alex said. "She and Allen are already taking a huge risk, and I'd never forgive myself if it caused either of them to be arrested and charged."

"We've been careful . . . and lucky," Mykola said.

Alex nodded. "We'll have to be aware of an opportunity from our side."

"Like what?" Mykola asked, glad to see Alex being more cognizant of how their actions could have disastrous consequences for others.

"No idea right now. We just have to be aware and explore anything that might work."

Alex shifted, put his feet on the floor, and sat up on his bunk.

"There's more?" Mykola asked.

"You know that in detention there's no talking. That's one

of the worst things about it. In all that silence, I began to think about how we might talk without our voices."

"You mean like sign language?"

"Sort of, but I don't know sign language, and I assume you don't . . ."

"Right."

"And we couldn't have a private conversation if someone did see us sign. See, we may not ever need to talk with our collars on, but I think we'd be better off if we could."

"Makes sense. You have anything in mind?" Mykola wasn't sure this was relevant when they basically had everything on hold, but at least there would be no harm in talking about it, and it was good to hear Alex speak once again in a composed, rational tone of voice.

"Yes, in fact I do. It's not perfect and it's probably slow, but I think it's easy to learn. Most importantly, it doesn't involve materials like pencils and paper, nor does it involve any big arm motions that could attract attention."

Mykola still laid on his bunk but now folded his pillow so his head was more upright.

"You use your fingers for letters of the alphabet. Consonants are in your left hand and vowels are in your right. Starting with your thumb as letter *B* and going on in alphabetical order to your pinkie, you divide your left hand fingers into top, middle and bottom. You touch the letter on your left hand with a finger on your right hand. It's sort of like typing." Alex touched the top of each left hand finger as he said, "*B, D, F, G, H*."

"Seems simple enough so far."

"And then vowels are expressed by forming a semi-circle with your right thumb and another finger. So *A* would be touching your thumb to your forefinger, *E* is your thumb to your middle finger, and so on"—Alex demonstrated—"and *U* is a fist."

"That's only 20 letters by my count."

"I'm glad you're paying attention." Alex gave Mykola an exaggerated wink. "Z, X, Q, J, V, and Y we won't use. Oh, and a space is a gentle clap of the hands."

"And numbers?"

"Remember how on old-fashioned keyboards there was a 'number lock' key? Putting the tips of your fingers together on both hands signifies turning the number lock on or off." Alex put his fingers together and gave Mykola a look that made it appear he was thinking carefully about something.

Mykola couldn't suppress a grin. "Okay, let me try this." Mykola pointed to the tip of his little finger.

"I think you're going to have to sit beside me; I don't think I can read your fingers backwards."

Mykola got up and bounced down on Alex's bunk, where he slowly spelled out GOOD NIGHT with his fingers. Someone who didn't know what Mykola was doing might have thought it looked like someone making an argument and counting off the points on his hands.

Alex replied with two thumbs up.

17

Throughout his imprisonment, Mykola checked his email about once a week. There were only four people who could send messages to him and to whom he could send messages. He had never bothered to figure out the process for replacing Janice as one of his requested contacts. If anyone else on the outside wanted to stay in touch with him, surely they would have contacted his father, younger sister, or business partner to get a message to him. But no one had.

Email relied exclusively on text; no attachments were permitted. And, of course, everyone involved knew the emails would be read by prison staff, which didn't encourage anyone to pour out their heart. Thus the information that went back and forth was just a series of unemotional, non-sensory facts. We went here, we did that, our neighbor got a cute puppy, business is good, and the doctor says I have to lose some weight. It all became a wastebasket of information that Mykola forgot almost as soon as he read it.

His emails to them were probably worse, in that his days

varied so little from one to the next. The extent of the excitement he could share with them was something new in the lunch or dinner trough. So checking and sending email became a once-a-week experience of low expectations.

Particularly disappointing was the absence of progress being reported by his attorney, Roberta. After that initial videoconference a couple of months ago, there was no purpose in setting up another one. Mykola didn't use all his allowed minutes that month or the next.

Last month, however, he'd gotten an email from his father asking him to set up a videoconference for the next day. He had something important he needed to share. Mykola set a time, fearing his father was going to have some news about his steadily declining health. Instead it turned out to be a video birthday greeting. Mykola had forgotten all about his own 27th birthday. He was serenaded by his father, his sister, and a couple of his father's neighbors with a sour, out-of-tune rendition of "Happy Birthday" that had everyone laughing before they got to the end. That was a pick-me-up Mykola needed, and he'd recalled it many times since then to remind him there was still something to look forward to even if he did spend the full seven years here.

Mykola didn't expect any messages this week and wasn't of a mind to send any either. He'd been careful not to mention his conversations with Alex, reporting only the results of recent chess games and what they called the "season standings." Prepared to shut down email as soon as he opened it, Mykola was astonished to see a message from Roberta with the subject line "May have a breakthrough—need to talk." The message was curt: "Set up videoconference for tomorrow at 3:30 p.m."

Mykola checked the date on the message and was relieved to see it had been sent earlier that day. "Tomorrow" really did mean tomorrow, not some day in the past week.

This was the kind of hopeful news Mykola wanted to share with Alex, but given their squabble the other day, he decided not to. Alex would likely reflexively try to tear down his optimism, much as Mykola had quashed Alex's enthusiasm for the escape plan when he'd found out about the risk to other inmates. No, he'd wait until he'd gotten more information from Roberta before he shared it with Alex. Even then, it might be difficult to tell Alex that there was a possibility of his leaving through the front door while Alex's only near-term hope was a risky backdoor escape.

Mykola called Roberta promptly at 3:30 the following day. He still had the full hour of allowed videoconference time available and did not anticipate a need to rush through this meeting. Still, he was anxious to hear what Roberta had found out and if and when it might lead to a new trial or outright release.

"Hello, Roberta, glad to see you again."

Roberta was at her desk as before, but this time she was flanked by a younger man.

"Mykola, I want to introduce you to Byron Mead. He's been with our firm for about a year and has been helping me with your case ever since the verdict. He's been researching legal precedents that might apply to your case, the sort of academic work that lays the groundwork for a successful appeal."

"Pleased to meet you, Mr. Steinman," Byron said in a tone and posture he hoped would show confidence but fell well short. This was his first time actually talking to a convict, and he wasn't exactly sure what to expect. His shaggy, sun-bleached blond hair looked as if he'd just washed it and forgotten where he'd left his comb. A complexion free of any moles, creases, or wrinkles, along with perfectly white straight teeth, gave him an appearance of innocence. His lawyer "regulation" blue suit hung loosely on his shoulders, and a burgundy tie completed the look of a recent law school graduate.

"Likewise," Mykola replied, his eyes remaining focused on Roberta.

"As I hope you gathered from my short email, I think we may have a breakthrough here. However, I don't want you to get the impression that we just have to tie up some loose ends; we're just starting, and ultimately it might be a dead end. Nevertheless, I thought it appropriate to share what we've learned and our way forward." Roberta spoke in a controlled, measured voice consistent with the caution of her words.

"I understand; I have hope, but I also have enough experience with disappointment not to plan too far ahead."

"Good. You recall that the linchpin to the prosecution's case was identifying you as the attacker using facial recognition software. It connected all the other information, including your heated discussion in the bar with the officer and past encounters with his wife, all of which ultimately made it easy for the jury to find you guilty."

"Yup, that's what it is." Mykola had gone over the trial so many times in his mind that he'd developed emotional calluses.

"Well, Byron did some research on a case in Oklahoma City that also had electronic facial recognition as a key evidentiary component. Byron, go ahead and explain what you've learned."

This was Byron's chance to be the star onstage, with his supervisor Roberta the theatre critic. He'd practiced what he was going to say, and now confidence did come through. Mykola looked at him expectantly.

"In the Oklahoma City case, a man was convicted of burglary of a high-end art gallery. None of the vases and porcelain figures that allegedly were stolen were ever recovered. Like most stores, the gallery had several security cameras. The lighting was weak, and the burglar was wearing a nylon face covering and couldn't be identified visually from the security tapes. So the police ran the tape through their new facial recognition software, which is supposed to be able to adjust for most anything a person might do to distort his appearance, such as wearing a fake beard or in this case a sheer nylon head covering. It identified the burglar as an employee who had been fired a year earlier for sexual harassment of another employee."

"You can see where this is going," Roberta cut in.

"The lawyer for the ex-employee saw it as well and made the unusual request to have his experts examine the facial recognition software. 'Unusual' because such software used by law enforcement has to go through a two-stage certification process before the results from the program can be used as evidence. Of course they don't certify every copy of the program, just a master copy. Most judges deny such a request on the basis of the certification and the unwarranted time it would take to check the integrity of the software, but this judge granted the motion. He apparently has a reputation for distrusting technology.

"Now, here is where it gets real interesting and where this Oklahoma City case might be a starting point for your appeal, Mr. Steinman." Byron was getting excited, and Roberta reached over and rested her hand on his forearm. He got the signal and brought himself back to an objective, composed state.

"Two weeks later, the defense presented to the judge two images very similar to the one taken from the security tape, from the standpoint of lighting and facial detail, but from different perspectives. The judge acknowledged that they could be the same person but might not be. However, the facial recognition software had identified them as the same person. Now, remember, these weren't the actual security tape images; this was something the defense had produced as a demonstration."

"Okay, I understand . . . but . . ." Mykola was beginning to get impatient.

"But they were images of *two different people*," Byron said. "The defense then showed the judge full-light, multiple-angle photos of the actual two men who had posed for the security tape photographs. One was Latino, and the other's primary ethnicity was Native American. Ironically, the defense had been able to find two men who looked alike by doing a facial recognition review of prisoners throughout the United States.

"Bottom line: the defense provided solid evidence that facial recognition software was not infallible," Roberta declared. "Mykola, that case is still continuing, but you can see how it might apply to your appeal. It was a dark night, with only one overhead light on the far side of the officer's car and only one angle of the attacker's face on the security camera."

"That's just amazing. You know, none of us would be here now if that guy had turned around so the camera could pick up the right side of his face. I doubt he had a scar like mine," Mykola said, pointing to the scar that ran just over his right jawbone, the result of driving too fast on a rain-slick road and crashing his first car. "What's next?"

Roberta continued, "As I said, that case in Oklahoma is still in progress. But we've contacted the defense attorney to get more information. We're going to file the notice of appeal in the next week and just make it under the 180-day deadline. I think we've got one chance at this, and I want to be sure to get it right. It's particularly challenging because state laws vary somewhat about evidence admissibility, and in the age of technology, they are still being fine-tuned. We've got a lot of work to do, and I'm going to be conservative here and suggest it might be another year until this is resolved." Roberta said this last in a tone she might have used to tell her son that he might not get everything he wanted for Christmas.

"Still, it is progress and something upon which to build hope. Thanks to both of you." Mykola looked intently at Roberta and then at Byron.

"I almost forgot to mention one other thing: gait analysis." Roberta looked at Mykola to make sure he was still paying attention.

"What's that? I don't remember a gate at the bar," Mykola said, wondering if this was a legal term he hadn't heard before.

"Gait," Roberta explained. "Not gate like you have on your cell, but gait as in how you walk. There was a recent case in which the defense showed a video of an attacker walking away and compared it to a video of the defendant walking some time before the attack. They were clearly different, and that was all it took to get the case dismissed. People don't think about how they walk because they don't think it can be used to identify them. That's the legal standard, but in this case gait wasn't used to help convict someone; it was used to exonerate someone."

"So I'm guessing you have to find some video of the attacker walking?"

"Yes. That's a bit of a long shot, since the security camera didn't record the attacker walking into or out of the frame, but perhaps some other camera in the parking lot did."

Mykola leaned back and tried to process what he'd just been told. He looked away for a few moments. Roberta and Byron remained silent, cognizant that Mykola was thinking.

"Roberta, like I said, you've given me some hope," he said at last. "But now you're telling me about this 'gait analysis' and I can't help but wonder why you didn't talk to the parking lot owner about looking at other videos before my trial began. Maybe that would have provided evidence that I wasn't even there at the time."

Mykola was aware that he was suggesting Roberta had failed him; he tried to ask his question in a detached, unemotional tone.

"You're right, Mykola. We were so focused on the tape from which the facial recognition was made that we didn't consider other tapes that might have brought into question whether you were even in the parking lot at that time." Roberta was scrambling to provide an answer that Mykola could accept, but she wasn't even sure she was being honest with herself. She paused and then confessed: "I guess I was also afraid that it might show that a person who fit your description was in the parking lot shortly before the assault. That wouldn't have been enough to convict you, I know that, but it wouldn't have helped our defense either. We—no, I—made a mistake." Roberta looked at Mykola and waited for his reaction.

"I understand," Mykola said, almost feeling sorry for Roberta. At least she was being forthright and candid with him.

"Mykola, please understand that gait analysis is just another piece of evidence, and while it may be helpful in identifying the person who committed the assault, it wasn't brought up in the trial and so can't be used as part of your appeal. It might, however, be used in a retrial. I just want you to know we're doing all we can to have your conviction set aside, and we hope we still have your trust."

"You do." The videoconference that had started out so professional and objective had evolved into a recommitment to trust. That wasn't bad as far as Mykola was concerned. Trust was the basis of any enduring relationship: legal, professional, or personal.

"We'll keep you posted. Bye for now." Roberta ended the call.

Mykola let out a deep breath, now aware that he'd been unconsciously taking long, deep breaths during much of the call. Sitting back in the chair, he allowed himself the luxury of imagining himself back home, standing in front of an open freezer door and trying to decide between chocolate mint and natural Madagascar vanilla ice cream. His skin prickled at the thought of the cold freezer air, and his mouth watered in anticipation of the flavors he'd loved since childhood.

"Hey you, are you done?" The coarse voice of another inmate brought his fantasy to a hasty close.

"Yup, all yours," Mykola responded as he got out of the chair. He was sure the other inmate was wondering why he had the look of a child who had just been told an extra special secret.

18

Roberta thanked Byron for his participation in the call and then cleaned up the notes she'd entered on her tablet. Glancing up at the oak-trimmed antique analog clock on the conference room wall, Roberta suddenly realized she was already late for her next meeting. Damn, must have muted the reminder on my phone, she told herself. Sometimes human memory serves as a good back-up for the electronics.

"Sorry I'm late," she said as she entered the conference room. "The conference I had with a client went a little longer than I'd anticipated." Roberta sat down in a plush executive chair at the end of the conference table. Already seated at the table were the three other senior partners of the small law firm.

"Not to worry; we were just chatting about some new legislation that will redefine culpability for accidents caused by self-driving long-haul trucks. I think you remember Mr. Reed of AI Methodologies?" John Winthrop, the founder of the law firm, asked Roberta.

"Yes, of course. Good to see you again." Lawrence Reed

and Roberta walked toward each other and shook hands in the middle of the room, then returned to their seats.

"Four weeks ago I gave you a presentation on the background, services, and products that AIM offers. Unless you have some follow-up questions, I'll get right into the substance of our proposal."

Lawrence waited for a moment. The partners looked at one another and subtly shook their heads. Lawrence continued.

"At that time we agreed to use AIM technology to analyze one of the cases your firm had recently lost. I understand you haven't lost many, but if we can't help you be even more successful, there's no point in us being here."

Such a smooth-talking salesman. He sees losing as an opportunity to get better, Roberta thought to herself.

"John gave us the transcripts for the Steinman case."

Roberta froze. This was her case, and the thought that some outside company had come in and evaluated her work made her angry and fearful at the same time.

John saw Roberta's reaction and tried to calm her. "Roberta, Lawrence and I decided on using this case as the test of AIM after everyone had left the meeting. I didn't tell you or anyone else because I didn't want you fretting about what AIM might have to say." John looked around the table. "You're all top-tier attorneys, and nothing said today is going to change my opinion of you in the least."

"As we agreed to in the signed contract," Lawrence said, "no direct references to your firm or your client can be made by AIM in any material that could be exposed to individuals outside either of our organizations. We set up code names for your firm and client before we started work on the project." He was fully aware that Roberta was likely to maintain a focus on defending her reputation and her work on the Steinman case.

"First thing we did," Lawrence continued, "was to get transcripts of all the prosecutor's recent trials. We had 23 of them. We then analyzed them using the Legal version of our AIM system. All our versions are legal, of course; the name is misleading. Perhaps we should refer to it as the Legal AIM Legal system."

Lawrence hoped the attorneys would see the humor, but no one even broke a smile.

"Whether you know it or not, everyone has patterns and preferences in the way they analyze and present evidence. It's a little bit like knowing the mannerisms of a baseball pitcher or a poker player. If you figure out the pattern, you might have a good idea he's going to throw a curveball . . . or has jack squat in his hand and his bet is nothing but a bluff."

"We *do* know that," Roberta piped up. "We already have a pretty good idea of how other attorneys work and of their courtroom styles. We get that through experience, and I can tell you that's more than 23 trials." The other attorneys nodded in agreement. "So I'm not sure this is going to be much help."

"This is just the first step," Lawrence said in a soft, unchallenging voice. "May I go on?"

"Go ahead." John motioned with his hands.

"I don't want to offend you with this analogy, but we see a trial as being a bit like a game. You can have great talent on your team, but if you don't have a good strategy for using that talent and the evidence you have, you may not win. As in a game, you have to be able to adjust to the actions of the team you're playing against and to do that in real time."

"I think we all agree with that. Especially when you're

presenting a case to a jury, the facts are important, but so is how and when they're presented." John spoke to Lawrence and the other attorneys.

"There's a small industry built around this," Lawrence continued. "On the big cases you've got consultants who tell you how to dress, what words to avoid using, what unconscious biases the jury may have, and a lot more. Our Legal AIM system does all of that and more, and it does it in something approaching real time."

"What do you mean by 'real time'?" one of the other partners asked.

"Simply this: each bit of data you feed into the AIM system is used to update the strategy almost instantly. Besides all the background data you have and the facts you have, it will include the questions the other attorney asks, the witness responses, and even the confused expressions on the jurors' faces. It takes a bit of time to enter the data into the AIM system, but once that's done, the system responds in real time."

"Sounds like your machine is a licensed attorney and is applying for a job," Roberta said without any attempt to hide her disgust.

"No, not at all. It simply provides you with suggestions, much as a second chair would give you if you were the lead in the trial."

"But we'd have to accept those suggestions, I assume," Roberta continued.

"Roberta, I think what Lawrence is saying is that you could accept or reject any suggestion or part of a suggestion, or you could move the strategy in an entirely different direction," John said, his voice demanding attention. "Is that right, Lawrence?"

"Exactly."

"This all sounds well and good," one of the other partners said, "but as I see it, this whole meeting is a bit of a trial, and you're the attorney who has to prove your product works. Where's your evidence?" Roberta looked over at him and gave him a look of "You got him now."

"Good point, and exactly what I hoped you'd ask for. We conducted a mock trial of the Steinman case. We employed two experienced attorneys, one for the defense and one for the prosecution. We then gave them all the evidence you made available to us and asked each of them to build their case. The defense had the benefit of the AIM Legal system; the prosecution did not. We then paid some people to be jurors on the mock jury and hear the case. The defense followed the AIM suggestions. It wasn't exactly like a real trial, of course. We had to cut some corners because of cost and time constraints, but—"

"—but, as we all now expect, the jury found Mr. Steinman not guilty, right?" Roberta was becoming more belligerent with every word out of the salesman's mouth.

"Correct."

"We suspect your machine of conspiring with your sales department to defraud customers," said the partner who had not yet spoken. The other attorneys chuckled and gave one another knowing looks, but Lawrence maintained his composure and waited for a moment until he had everyone's attention again.

"We're aware of appearances. So we conducted the mock trial again, with two new attorneys and a different panel of jurors. The only change we made was to put the services of AIM Legal in the hands of the prosecuting attorney. In this second mock trial, the defendant was found guilty." Lawrence was beginning to feel a bit like an attorney himself, having just discredited the opposition's star witness.

The room fell quiet. Finally Roberta spoke. "So you're saying that your legal AI will enable us to win all of our cases?"

"No, certainly not," Lawrence responded as he took a step toward Roberta. "However, it does have predictive capability that is updated every time new data is collected, either from your input or from its periodic search of online information contained in 20 of the top legal libraries. It then produces a probability of winning."

"You mean like a weather forecast probability of rain?" Roberta asked derisively.

"That's not a fair analogy." Lawrence was beginning to get frustrated with what he perceived as sniping from Roberta and its growing acceptance from the other attorneys. "The difference between a weather forecast and an AIM Legal probability calculation is that you have no control over the weather, but you do have control of your legal strategy and how it is executed. With AIM Legal, you enter different 'what if' factors to see how they would increase or decrease your likelihood of winning. Wouldn't you like to know that? Wouldn't your clients appreciate you having that edge?"

John could sense the rising tension in the room. "Could we use AIM Legal before we took on a case?"

"Yes, you most certainly can and should," Lawrence said, thankful that John was encouraging him to present some of the other benefits of using AIM Legal. "For those cases you consider taking on a contingency basis, AIM can not only help you decide if the case is winnable, but it can also help you set a fair contingency percentage. You're a small law firm, and you can't afford to have too many cases in which you don't get paid. Furthermore, when you take on cases you don't win, your reputation declines and you have trouble attracting new clients. I'm telling you something you already know, but AIM Legal will simply help you make better decisions before and after you've made a commitment to a client." Lawrence was relieved that he hadn't lost the support of the founder of the firm.

"I know you have other commitments this afternoon and that you'll want to talk about our proposal privately. I've given it to Mr. Winthrop. Please call me with any follow-up questions you may have. Thank you." Lawrence looked at each partner in the room for a moment. Seeing that there were no questions, he got up and prepared to leave. John shook his hand, but the other attorneys simply got up and left.

⊙

The door to John's office was open, and Roberta walked in. John waved a hand toward one of the two hard-backed chairs opposite the desk, and she sat there.

John's office was no bigger than the other attorneys' offices, but it had pictures on the wall and mementoes on his desk that reflected his professional success, the important people he knew, and his passion for baseball. Roberta saw herself as the visiting team, with John having home field advantage, besides the fact that he was her boss.

John put down his pen and set his notes aside. "So, Roberta, what did you think?"

This was a loaded question. Roberta knew that John, the founder of the law firm, had a favorable impression of AIM.

Given his age and experience as an attorney, this was unusual. Most successful and seasoned attorneys were hesitant about bringing in more technology and having to change their routines. The standard line was "Why fix it if it works?"

Yet John liked technology. He'd been one of the first people Roberta knew who'd bought a self-driving car. When interns were interviewed, John spent as much time asking about their ability to use technology as he did on their knowledge of the type of law they focused upon.

Roberta was still peeved about his decision to share the Steinman case information without telling her. That was her case, and she had a right to know who was looking at the files. She certainly wouldn't have approved of AIM getting copies, especially in light of the fact that Mykola Steinman was still a client.

She knew she would have to use all her skills to walk a narrow line that balanced John's position and authority, her need for control, and the interests of her client.

"I can't say I particularly care for Lawrence," she said. "However, their system could help us, especially since we're small and don't have the resources to take on really big cases."

"I'm glad to hear you say that. We have to grow if we want to take on bigger clients, but I don't want to lose the personalized relationship we have with our clients as a small firm. So if we don't want to simply build the firm the old-fashioned way by adding staff, we've got to work smarter and more efficiently. AIM is one of three companies I know of that provide AI-based legal support services. What makes them different is that legal is their primary focus. Like us, they're still trying to build their client base. We could actually benefit each other."

"What are they proposing, John?"

"Two things. First, a three-month, single-case trial period in which they would teach us how to use the system and demonstrate that it does what they say it does. This would cost us $15,000. Second, a full-year license to use the system on any and all cases for $150,000."

"That's a substantial expense."

"I prefer to think of it as an investment," John countered.

"Okay, investment. Which case would we apply it to during the three-month trial period?"

"The Steinman case." John sat back in his chair as if in a defensive position and ready to take on any attacker.

"I guess I should have seen this coming," Roberta said in a tone of resignation. "But I'm in the appeal stage; the work they've done so far and the mock trial example they showed us don't really apply."

"Good point, but that whole case rested on facial recognition, and to this point, facial recognition hasn't been successfully challenged."

"I know that; I've got Byron doing some research on an Oklahoma case that involved a defendant who was misidentified through computer-based facial recognition." Roberta felt herself becoming defensive but didn't want to come off as being overly protective of what she saw as her territory.

"You've been working diligently on this, but how long is it going to take before you're ready to file the appeal? Isn't the deadline fast approaching? Meanwhile Mr. Steinman waits impatiently in the new prison. The AIM system could cut the research time in half and give you and Mr. Steinman a better chance of winning."

"I think we're just about ready to file the appeal, and that's what I told Mykola—I mean Mr. Steinman."

"Wonderful. But what if your request is denied? You said yourself that the basis of your appeal is a stretch and that there's no backup plan. If your appeal is denied, do you want to tell Mr. Steinman it might have been granted if you hadn't been so self-righteous and had been willing to use the state-of-the-art technology that was offered to you?" John put his hands on the arms of his chair, raised himself just off the seat, and leaned forward.

Roberta knew she wasn't going to win this argument. In good conscience she couldn't argue against something that might benefit her client.

"Okay, you've made your point, John. But I still make the decisions. I'm not going to be second chair to a machine."

John leaned back in his chair just a bit and calmly replied, "I never suggested that, nor has anyone at AIM. The system is a source of information, strategies, and suggestions. Plus, it works anytime you need it. Nothing to put on your calendar."

"There is that. I won't have to take it out to lunch once in a while either."

"Good," John said with a satisfied smile. "I'll call Lawrence, let him know we're ready to proceed, and have them here on Monday to begin work."

"As I mentioned in our meeting with AIM," Roberta said, "I was on a video call with Mykola just a couple of hours ago. He seemed more upbeat when I told him about the Oklahoma facial recognition case. Should I tell him there's a new addition to the team?"

"I'd hold off for now. It'll take time to learn how to use the system, and we don't specifically know what to expect from it. If he's feeling better, that's great. But you don't want him planning a going-away party just yet."

"Agreed. I will tell Byron about the AIM system. He likes technology; he was excited to learn about facial recognition, and I'm confident he'll embrace AIM Legal."

19

Over the past three days, Alex and Mykola had had little to talk about, and Mykola hadn't sent a single message to Sarah. The escape plan had come to a stalemate, much like the chess game Mykola and Alex had played the night before they did the test. With the lights out, both lay on their bunks, hearing the white noise of the ventilation system and an occasional indiscernible voice from the far end of the corridor.

Alex could tell Mykola was still awake from the rhythm and sound of his breathing. When he was asleep he took long, slow breaths; when awake, his breathing was much less deliberate and almost soundless.

Still staring at the ceiling, Alex asked, "Mykola, when we get out of here, how are you going to celebrate your freedom?"

"What do you mean? Have a party or something?"

"Sure, that might be a nice way to celebrate."

"I haven't given it much thought, but I gather you have," Mykola replied softly.

"I have. I know that whatever happens, freedom isn't on the

other side of the virtual fence. It's a state of mind, and I'm sure that a lot of the habits I've developed here will stay with me for months or maybe even years to come. Still, I can envision the night when I'll celebrate freedom." Alex paused, waiting for the image in his mind to come into focus.

"I'll have a sailboat, moored in a small ocean harbor somewhere north of here, perhaps in Canada or Alaska. It'll be big enough that I can live on it but small enough that I can sail it by myself. One night when the skies are perfectly clear, the wind is gentle and steady, and there's a new moon, I'll sail out by myself about ten miles so that I'm out of sight of the shore lights . . . and then drop a sea anchor. Then I'll lie down on a cushion in the cockpit, sort of like I'm doing right now, and talk to my friends."

"Your friends?" Mykola asked, thinking he'd misunderstood something.

"Yes, my friends Orion, Sagittarius, Cassiopeia, and others. I'll reach out and wave to them, and they'll twinkle in response. Then I'll talk to them about whatever's on my mind, shouting if I want to, knowing my secrets are safe with them. I'll be happy to see them, and they'll be pleased to see me once again. Do you know how long it's been since I've seen these friends?"

"I guess I never thought about it, but you're right," Mykola said. "With the bright lights in the yard, we never see the stars here. That will be a satisfying way to celebrate freedom."

"So, are you going to have a party?" Alex asked.

"I suppose so."

"Tell me about it. Who's going to be there, where will it be, what will you do?"

"Let me think for a minute." Mykola felt he was going to

be making a public commitment and had to be careful in what he said. A minute or two passed with neither Alex nor Mykola speaking.

"I'm going to have a small house out in the country, some-place where there's four real seasons," Mykola said. "It'll be on a nice piece of property, with trees the only thing obstructing my view of my neighbors' homes. In the backyard I'll have a big garden in which I'll grow my own fruits and vegetables. There'll be raspberry bushes, three colors of tomatoes, green beans, cauliflower, sweet corn, and ten different herbs. An apple tree—a Golden Delicious apple tree, in honor of Sly—and an apricot tree, both filled with fruit."

"Sounds nice. I can taste those raspberries," Alex said with a sigh.

"And I'm going to learn to cook. Not just things from a cookbook, but dishes I create on my own. I want everything I make to have a distinct flavor. Then one night I'll invite the neighbors over for dinner and together we'll enjoy the aroma, taste, color, and crunch of fresh food. I'll eat the food I've grown, experiencing every bite as if it were the first one.

"Oh, and one more thing: dinner will start sometime after 8:00. That's when I'll know I'm really free."

"Touché. Save a seat for me." Alex could feel a tear rolling down his cheek.

On Friday at 2:15, just as Alex was ending his shift in the infirmary, a call came in to send gurneys to the manufacturing workshop. There had been a small explosion in one of the machines, and three inmates had been burned, two of them severely. Most minor injuries were handled by the inmate nurses with a guard looking on, but these blistered and charred burns to the inmates' upper torsos and faces obviously needed treatment far beyond what the infirmary could provide.

The shift warden was called down from the control room. On his way down, he called for ambulances to take the inmates to the public hospital nearly ten miles away. Alex and Manuel did what they could to bandage the wounds and ease the inmates' pain. Morphine brought their screams to an end.

"Get out of my way," the warden yelled at Alex and Manuel. Neither of them had met him before, but they figured he was tracked like a guard and it was best to step at least six feet away from him. Alex saw the warden take a dongle chained to his wrist and put the tiny pins in sockets in the injured inmates' collars. The collars opened automatically. The warden flipped the latch on each collar and took them off, setting them on a counter. Moments later the ambulances arrived, and within minutes the three inmates were taken out.

Inmates from the shop who had witnessed the explosion had gathered in the infirmary and were talking among themselves, many expressing relief that they weren't closer when it happened. The warden, clearly upset by seeing the inmates' injuries and their faces twisted in pain, demanded to know who was responsible for the explosion. Several inmates who had witnessed the event gave conflicting stories of what had happened in the minutes before, but no one was identified as having caused the explosion. "It just happened" was the consensus.

The warden could sense that speculation as to what had happened could lead to rumors of faulty and dangerous equipment and inmates refusing to work in the shop. To gain control and quash such rumors, he asked a couple of the inmates who appeared to be the most objective regarding what they had seen and heard to join him in a private room to discuss it further.

"We've got this. Go back to your workstations," the warden demanded of the other inmates, and they did so, still talking among themselves as they walked down the hall.

Everyone was out of the infirmary, and Alex noticed the injured inmates' collars still lying on a counter. He began to wonder. What if . . . ?

He walked over to the counter, glancing about to make sure he was alone. At one end of the counter were several large, heavy, clear plastic medicine jars in which cotton swabs and other supplies were stored.

The jars approximated the diameter of a man's neck.

Alex put on a pair of latex gloves from the dispenser mounted to the wall above the counter. The collars and counter had blood on them, and Alex dutifully cleaned them. This was standard procedure and wouldn't bring any attention to him from the guards in the control room watching his image from the overhead camera. Surely they had put camera images from the infirmary on the main screen when the injured inmates had been brought in, but now it was just Alex cleaning up. After a couple of minutes, the guards would be bored and shift to another area of the prison on their monitors.

Still acting as casual as he could, he picked up the collars and took them to the end of the counter, where the medicine jars were. Positioning himself so that his body blocked the camera view of what he was doing, Alex held one of the collars over a plastic jar. It looked to be a bit tight, but it would still fit. He could just slip the collars over the jars and close the latches.

Could the system be confused into "thinking" that the jars were inmate necks? It couldn't possibly be that easy.

He couldn't stand there much longer; there was no telling how long it would be before another inmate or a guard noticed him holding the collars. At the same time, a mistake, something he overlooked, could land him in detention once again.

If it were simply a matter of putting the collars around something circular, why hadn't an inmate just put his collar around a rolled-up pillow in the morning? The cell gate would open, and he could practically walk out the front door. Perhaps no one had ever thought to do that. What if he and Mykola were to try it tomorrow morning?

Alex was about to walk away from the collars on the counter when it suddenly became clear to him: temperature. The entire prison was kept at a comfortable 72 degrees, and there must be a sensor in the collar that was activated by an inmate's 92-to-98-degree skin temperature. Nothing else in the cell approximated that temperature. The water was unheated, so you couldn't even wet the pillow to bring it up to at least 92 degrees.

Fortunately, there was hot water in the infirmary, and thermometers too. Reasoning that the outsides of the jars would be cooler than the water in them, Alex ran the water until it was 102 degrees and then filled both jars. He felt the outside of the jars: they were warm, but not warm enough. He poured out the water and again filled the jars with hot water, this time at 106 degrees. If anyone saw him on a monitor in the control room, he hoped the assumption would be that he was simply washing out the jars.

Alex waited for a minute and then measured the jars' outside temperature. It was 99 degrees; close enough, he figured. Again using his body to shield the collars and jars from the overhead cameras, he slipped the collars onto the jars and closed the latches, his pulse quickening. Seconds later the collars tightened until they fit snugly around the jars.

Alex wrote down the engraved numbers of the collars on his palm.

Alex knew the jars wouldn't hold 92-plus degrees for long, and he didn't know how the system would react when they began to cool. Logically, though, a skin temperature below 92 would send an alert to someone in the control room: either an inmate was dying or he had somehow managed to get his collar off.

One alternative would be to take the jars outside, where it had to be over 90 degrees. Sure, he could walk down the long corridors holding two jars with collars attached without anyone asking any questions. Alex had to laugh at that image.

The only thing to do was to put some insulation around the jars. Alex's initial thought was to put some warm towels around them, but it seemed doubtful they'd be able to retain heat for more than an hour or so. Then it came to him. Probably by mistake, the infirmary had been shipped some Mylar blankets. These blankets were standard survival gear in cold weather climates, but in a desert prison, it was unlikely they'd ever be used.

Alex last remembered seeing them at the back of the top shelf of a supply cabinet. He reached up and closed his eyes in hope he'd feel the plastic packages. Yes! Alex brought down two packages of never-opened Mylar sheets. He could wrap the sheets several times around the jars. Not only would they retain the heat of the water, but they'd also cover the collars.

Alex slid the Mylar-covered jars onto the shelf where he'd found the sheets. Up high and at the back, they were unlikely to be seen unless someone was looking for them. How long they'd hold temperature was anyone's guess, but this was the best he could do. Someone might open the cabinet and find the collared jars, or the temperature might drop to a point where an alert would be triggered. Either scenario would doom their escape.

It was just after 3:00. For the next three hours, Alex's time was his own. Mykola could be anywhere, but given his habit of walking around the yard perimeter a few times after his work shift, most likely he'd be there now. Sure enough, that's where Alex found him. He really wanted to run across the yard to him, but that would likely draw too much attention. He walked the perimeter in the opposite direction of Mykola and met him.

Mykola could see that Alex was excited about something, more excited than he had seen him in quite a while. "Hey, what's up?"

"Why don't we go sit down over in the shade," Alex said, pointing to the prison wall shaded by the roof overhang. They both walked over and sat down side by side on the concrete with their backs against the prison wall. Several other inmates, some by themselves, others in pairs, could be seen along the wall, and Alex was confident he and Mykola wouldn't attract any attention.

They had to get this right: there would be no second chance. And while there was time pressure, Alex knew they couldn't afford to abandon the caution that had gotten them this far. The microphones would pick up anything he told Mykola; just the word "escape" might bring out a red-shirt or a guard who would escort them inside for a discussion with the shift warden.

Alex began by explaining the injuries sustained in the workshop explosion and then shifted to the finger code they'd been practicing late at night in their cell. When they sat side by side with their knees pulled up, only Mykola could see Alex's hand and finger motions. Still, the finger code was slow, and Alex used as few words as possible, thinking quickly to avoid words with letters not included in the code:

2 COLARS OFF

ON WARM CANS

LOCKED ON

After each phrase, Alex looked over at Mykola to see if he understood and Mykola gave a subtle thumbs-up with one hand. Alex signed again:

OUT TONIGHT

Alex wasn't seeing the reaction from Mykola that he'd expected. Certainly he was sharing positive and exciting information, and yet Mykola's facial expression didn't change. If anything, he seemed to be concerned about something. This was what they'd been working toward for months, *and* nobody needed to get hurt. Didn't he understand?

NOBODY GETS HURT, Alex responded.

GOOD PLAN BUT, Mykola began, but before he could continue, Alex nudged his shoulder to get his attention and tapped TALK.

After a moment, Mykola understood: they needed to try to make it sound as if they were continuing the conversation about the explosion and injuries.

"That's really too bad. They're doing some remarkable things in treating burns these days. I sure hope they'll be okay. Alex, on a more uplifting note, did I tell you about the video call

I had with my attorney? She thinks they've got a way to prove I didn't club that ex-cop in the parking lot. It has to do with a flaw in the facial recognition program."

"A flaw in the facial recognition? I don't want to quash your hope, but you have to be realistic. I don't know much about how facial recognition software works, but I do know that overturning convictions takes a couple of years at best. Hell, you might serve the full seven years before they get this sorted out."

"I know," Mykola said as he tapped out CONFUSED.

2 HOURS I GO, Alex tapped back.

Alex wished that Mykola could read his mind at that moment. He couldn't say what he was thinking: Dammit, then you've got about two hours to get yourself unconfused. I'm going, with or without you. Oh, and while you're trying to figure it all out, remember that you've been part of this from the beginning and likely have left a trail of evidence that'll make you an accomplice even if you decide to stay here. You might do even more than seven years.

All of this was too much for Mykola at this moment. Images of freedom and being in the cell or detention flashed before his mind's eye. Hope, fear, panic, and elation were all mixed into a steamy broth of emotion.

"I can't decide," he said, barely audible to Alex and with his eyes downcast.

Alex had a sense that Mykola was losing it and might blurt out something that would trigger the AI system. It was time to bring this conversation to a close. Alex set his emotions aside and refocused on his objective of obtaining his freedom. He tapped two more messages:

STIL NEED UR HELP

EMAIL SARAH

WILL DO, Mykola tapped back. He realized the worst thing he could do now would be to derail Alex's escape. Alex had done much to help him adjust, as best as possible, to prison life, and surely Mykola owed him something for that. They had already agreed upon the format for such an email.

Quickly, and with as little visible motion as possible, Alex produced a scrap of paper from the waistband of his pants. Mykola took it from him while staring straight ahead and then glanced down at it before bringing his hands together to cover it.

On the scrap was written:

93865011

1800

C246555

L612690

GOT IT, Mykola tapped.

Alex had decided to make his break just before they were expected to be in the chow hall.

"Sounds like you have a good attorney. Maybe she can work a miracle," Alex said. Mykola didn't hear him as he concentrated on what Alex was tapping out:

540 IF U DECIDE 2 GO

Alex stood up, rubbing the small of his back. "Going back to the cell and lie down for a bit. I had a pretty rough shift in the infirmary and need some rest. See you later, okay?" Alex gave Mykola a quarter nod of his head in the direction of the communications room.

Until 5:40, the only thing to do was wait and hope. That didn't sit well with Alex. You could always tell when someone was just waiting for something to happen. Shifting their weight from side to side, talking but not listening, and a questioning, guilty look of expectation on their faces could be enough to cause suspicion. In fact, identifying unusual behavior was what Mykola was working on in the lab. If the computer eye had learned enough from Mykola and others feeding it data, there was no telling what it might pick up.

"Fine. See you later," Mykola replied. As he said it, he wondered whether it was his subconscious mind making a decision or just a conversational goodbye. Mykola told himself it was just a goodbye, but he wasn't at all sure.

He walked to the learning lab and 15 minutes later had sent the message to Sarah. Alex sent an email from the communications room and then, just as he'd told Mykola, went back to his cell.

Walking down the corridor to his cell, Alex made it a point to see if there were other inmates in their cells. Keeping his head straight, he shifted his eyes to see who might be in the cells. Right now he didn't want to talk to anyone. He was relieved that only a couple of inmates were in their cells and none paid any attention to him.

Guards were seldom seen in the inmate cell wings at this time of day, but Alex saw one walking his way. Could it be that their plan had been exposed? Before they passed one another, Alex came to his cell, turned, and went in. With a stretch of his back and a noisy exhalation of breath, he fell face-first onto his bunk. He could hear the hard leather soles of the guard's boots pounding on the concrete. He dared not look up and wished that the guard would continue past his cell.

The sound of the boots came nearer and then stopped. Seconds passed.

"Alberto, if you're still feeling sick in the morning, get yourself to the infirmary. You got that?"

"Will do."

The guard had stopped and talked to the inmate in the next cell. The clomping of boots continued down the corridor.

I've treated so many people with paranoia, Alex thought to himself. I guess this is what it's like to experience it.

In the quiet of what now seemed like a concrete vault, Alex went to work. First he took all the books and periodicals he had and placed them under the bunk, back against the wall. They couldn't be seen unless someone bent down. The chessboard he placed under the blanket, and the chess pieces were placed inside the pillowcase. Then he made his bunk as neat as it could be: hospital corners, not a wrinkle in the sheet or blanket, and the pillow fluffed and perfectly centered. He did the same with Mykola's bunk, though he assumed Mykola would be returning to his cell.

He placed his two additional prison uniforms on the bunk, again making sure they were neatly folded and centered on the bunk. All the while, Alex was listening for anyone approaching the cell and at the same time working as quietly as he could to avoid the attention and questions of nearby inmates.

Last Alex reached under the mattress and took out the 12 pages of notes he'd made on the backs of the monthly points reports. This was his record of what he'd seen and experienced in the prison. It included his professional observations of the mental health of inmates, especially those who had received multiple jolts or had spent time in detention. His intent was to write a paper critical of the prison and have it published in a professional journal, under a pseudonym, of course.

There were still a few blank sheets, but he saw no reason to take them. Folding the two sets of six pages of notes into quarters, he slipped them under his shirt and then under the elastic waistband of the pants: one set of six on each hip. With his shirt over the pants, it wasn't likely that anyone would notice the bulges.

The floor of the cell was still somewhat smudged and certainly could use a washing, but Alex figured he'd been lucky not to draw any attention so far. Best to leave well enough alone and get out of the cell. Alex stepped out of the cell and looked back into it. Everything was in its place. It looked like it had on the first day he was assigned there.

Shortly after 8:00, a guard would be coming by to pick up the collars. When he noticed Alex was not there, perhaps when he saw Alex's apparently vacated area of the cell he'd assume Alex had been transferred out. That was Alex's thinking. The guard might assume he forgot to check the updated inmate list for this wing. The electronic tracking system was relied upon so heavily that the few guards in the prison didn't pay much attention to who was or was not in a cell.

Even if this gave Alex just 15 extra minutes before anyone noticed he was not accounted for, that might be the 15 minutes he needed for a successful escape.

The phone rang with his sister's identifying tone. Allen pressed the speaker button.

"Allen, it's Sarah. You're home, right?"

"Yup, just walked in."

"Listen, I just got an email from Dad, but it doesn't say a thing. It's just a blank message; there's not even a subject. I'm wondering if he's trying to tell us something."

"Tell you something by telling you nothing . . . is that like reading between the lines when there aren't any lines?" Allen replied, pleased with his linguistic logic.

"Allen, this isn't a joke. Get serious, will you?" Sarah's voice was loud, loud enough that she thought someone might hear her outside of her office.

"Okay, okay, don't get all bent out of shape."

"I'm wondering if he's ready to execute the plan. I set up a code with Mykola to send a message through the learning center, but I don't want to access it from here."

"So you want me to open the instructor portal from here and see if there's a message?"

"Right. The log-in and password are taped to the bottom of the keyboard."

"Gotta go to the playroom . . ." A moment later Allen entered Sarah's log-in code.

"Sorry, but the last recorded activity was three days ago," Allen said with disappointment.

"Damn. What am I missing?"

"Maybe he hasn't entered the information yet. Let's wait a couple of minutes and see if there's an update." Allen now saw himself as the one to be logical and patient.

"Good. Good thinking. Let's give it five minutes. I'm going to get some coffee."

"I doubt that caffeine is what you need now," Allen responded as Sarah walked away.

A couple of minutes later Sarah was back at her desk. Looking down at the coffee cup she was holding, she noted the ripples on the surface. She set it down without taking a sip.

"Anything now?" Sarah asked with hope that was all too obvious to Allen.

"Not really, but he did post his exam."

"No, no, that's excellent. Now scroll down to the final question on the exam and see what he entered."

"Okay, scrolling now . . . he got it wrong."

"Never mind, Allen! Just tell me what he entered."

Allen read it back to Sarah: "93865011, 1800, C246555, L612690, 93865011."

"It's on," Sarah said confidently. "First number is the date, and since it is the same as the authentication code, that means they're planning to make their break today. Today at 1800! The next two are the other inmate numbers." Sarah reached out with her right hand, seemingly grabbing the numbers from the air, and clenched her fist as tightly as she could.

"Now," she continued, "the problem is that I'm still at work, and the only access I have to the London Tower hack is through that system we have at home. They want us there at 6:00 for the pickup, but they might be crossing over at any time between now and then. We need to run the hack now. You remember the process for changing the inmate codes, don't you?"

"Of course. I wrote it down just in case something like this happened."

"Great."

After a moment, Allen said, "Got it. I'll do it right now."

"You're a lifesaver, Allen. I'll leave work now and be there in about 30 minutes. Now for part two: I need you to rent a car." Sarah began straightening up her desk as she spoke and then turned away from the door so she wouldn't be overheard.

"Rent a car? Why don't we just use yours?"

"Can't explain it to you right now; just do what I tell you, okay?"

"Okay. Okay."

"Take Dad's old phone out of the desk and make sure it's turned off—completely off. Then leave your phone on the kitchen table or somewhere in the house. You can leave it on. I don't know if you have any other tracking devices on you, but if you do, be sure to take them off before you leave the house."

"No problem. Then what?"

"Ride your bike to that auto e-rental place just off the freeway— I think it's called Drive Now—and take along Dad's phone."

"That's got to be five miles!"

"I'm sure you can make it in 15 or 20 minutes."

"Sure, after I put air in the tires," Allen replied with an air of disgust.

"When you get there, rent a car using Dad's phone. Get one big enough so that you can put your bike in the trunk."

"You want me to pay for it through Dad's cryptocurrency account? I've got the private code."

"Good thinking. Do it." Sarah's anxiousness to get out of the office was causing her to skip over important points, but Allen remained calm.

"Got it. Where should I pick you up?"

"Let's see." Sarah thought for a moment. "I'll be under the big sign of the grocery store we always shop at. We'll drive to the prison and, with any luck, pick up Dad and Mykola. Anything else?"

"Nope, that covers it."

"Okay, bye." Sarah didn't bother to shut down her computer or explain to her assistant where she was going. She just rushed out the door as if late for an appointment.

"Lifesaver . . . isn't that rich?" Allen laughed out loud as he entered inmate codes into the patch Sarah had developed and then uploaded the patch to the London Tower site. There was still time before he had to leave to get the rental car.

"Better make sure Dad's phone still has battery left. Sarah would be plenty PO'd if I couldn't rent the car. Hmmm . . . so would I." Allen spoke out loud as he attached the phone to a charger. It was, not surprisingly, completely dead. He selected rapid charging mode. This wouldn't provide a full charge, but it would last the few minutes he'd need to make the call.

While the phone was charging, Allen figured he'd upload another patch he'd been working on for the past week. He hadn't told Sarah about it, in part because he wasn't sure it would work and in part because she was so cautious about everything.

Allen's patch wouldn't have any impact on the code Sarah had entered, so if it worked, great, and if it didn't, he assumed no one would know. All upside and no downside, Allen figured as he was exiting the London Tower program.

Allen made sure he had his father's phone in his pocket—now partially charged but totally powered down—and left everything in his bedroom that might identify him electronically. Surprisingly, the tires on his bike held the air he pumped into them, and 15 minutes after speaking to Sarah he was on his way to pick up the rental car.

These self-service lots are great, Allen thought. They'd never rent a car to me if this was one of the old-fashioned rental car companies. Still, his father's phone hadn't been used in a couple of years, though Sarah had paid the monthly charges. Would the rental system still recognize it?

When he'd pedaled to within a mile of the rental lot, Allen pulled over, turned on the smartphone, found the website, and prepaid for a full-size hatchback SUV. The confirmation told him specifically where he'd find the car on the lot. A couple of minutes later he was there.

This is the real test, he thought. Though he hadn't done anything obviously illegal, Allen was still nervous and looked around him to see if anyone was watching. Certainly a 16-year-old riding a dirty bicycle was not the typical rental car customer. A police vehicle was parked across the street, but it appeared to be unoccupied. Hesitancy would probably bring out suspicion, and so Allen rode as confidently as he could through the short aisle of cars until he found the inconspicuous gray hatchback he'd reserved. Again, he couldn't help but look around to see if anyone was watching him. He saw no one. Allen held the smartphone up to the micro-scanner just below the door handle. After an agonizing five seconds, three melodious tones told Allen the car door was unlocked.

Practically throwing the bike into the back, Allen was quickly on his way to the grocery store to pick up Sarah.

In the meantime Sarah had arrived at home, parked her car in the garage, and run inside the house. Her business attire was quickly exchanged for running shoes, shorts, and a nylon jersey. She forgot she was wearing her sapphire earrings, obviously inconsistent with her outdoor athletic apparel.

Her phone on the kitchen counter and no watch or purse on her, Sarah closed the door and began her run to the grocery store where she was to meet Allen. The afternoon heat had her sweating before she'd run to the end of the street, but her long legs covered ground at a brisk pace. It was almost relaxing, she thought. Certainly the run brought down her anxiety. Ten minutes later, she was under the grocery store sign. Allen honked at her from a SUV parked nearby.

"Been here long?" Sarah asked as she came up to the driver's side.

"Naw, just a couple minutes."

"I'm going to drive; move over," Sarah said as she put her hand on Allen's shoulder. "And I don't want any arguments. Now move."

"Okay."

"Sorry, I don't mean to be harsh. I'm just a bit frazzled."

"I understand; happens to the best of us," was Allen's sarcastic response.

"Now, did you upload the file like we discussed?"

"Locked and loaded."

"And you left everything that could be used to track your location at home?"

"Only piece of electronics I have is Dad's phone. I turned it off as soon as I got the car. I've got 30 dollars in cash in case we need to buy something."

"Good thinking. I forgot about that; we might need to get a recharge on the car before we're done."

Looking into the back seat, Sarah asked, "Did you bring the change of clothes for Dad and Mykola?"

"Change of clothes? You didn't tell me about any change of clothes!"

"I'm sure I did . . . Maybe I didn't. We're going to have to go back and get it."

"You know this car is tracked. The whole purpose of me riding my bike and you running here was to avoid tracking." Allen was getting exasperated with his sister.

"Ride your bike and pick it up. The backpack with the clothes is in the playroom. I'll wait for you here." Sarah popped the hatchback.

"Okay, but if this is any sign of how this extraction is going to go, it's a bad sign." Allen's displeasure with his sister's directions was at the point of boiling over.

Ten minutes later Allen was back. He loaded the bike back into the trunk, and a few minutes later they were driving on the freeway, headed to the state border. In self-driving mode, the car would go no faster than the posted speed limit. After traffic had thinned, Sarah put it in manual mode and drove over the limit, but not so fast that she'd have to change lanes to pass other cars.

In their rush, neither Allen nor Sarah had thought to confirm receipt of the messages from Alex or Mykola until they were in the rental car. At that point they decided it wasn't worth the risk to try to do it on Alex's phone.

Regardless of whether Alex and Mykola made the break tonight, the programming Allen had uploaded would automatically be removed at 8:00, and there would then be no evidence of their hack. They could try again some other time.

⊙

Alex was outside standing near the back wall at 5:30. In the heat of the late afternoon, few other inmates were out. Those who were out were clustered in pairs or small groups, standing in what little shade the overhang provided at this time of day. There were a few red-shirts and yellow-shirts too, but they were in isolated groups and talked only amongst themselves, as if they were distinct species.

Alex figured most of them didn't know their conversations were being monitored and recorded through the microphones in their collars. What they thought were private conversations were actually anything but private. Fortunately, what they were talking about was usually innocuous enough that the control room didn't send guards to investigate.

But just then the door opened and a blue-shirt walked out. One of the inmates near the door called out "Guard!" and everyone, including Alex, turned to look. The guard surveyed the yard and made eye contact with many of the inmates; Alex turned away as soon at the guard's eyes focused on him, fearing that his facial expression and carriage would raise suspicion.

The guard stared at Alex; he was one of only a few who was standing by himself. Alex couldn't decide if he should make a casual comment to the guard or walk away, so he just stood there and hoped the guard wouldn't begin walking toward him.

High above the yard a vulture was riding an updraft, and that caught the guard's attention. As soon as the guard looked up, Alex started walking toward a group of inmates. The guard, apparently now satisfied that there was no reason to be out in this heat, quickly returned to the cool comfort of indoors.

Alex couldn't believe how nervous he was. It would be calming if he could talk to Mykola right now, but he was doubtful that Mykola would join him. Mykola was probably standing in the corridor outside the chow hall along with hundreds of other inmates, waiting for the gate to open and dinner to be served. Rumor had it that meatloaf was on the menu that evening, and even in soy form, it was pretty good.

"I'm here." The words startled Alex. He turned to his right and faced Mykola.

"I'm surprised . . . and pleased," Alex said, studying Mykola to get a sense of whether he intended to join him in the escape attempt or simply watch it.

"I'm sort of surprised too, but here I am."

"Good. We've got 15 minutes before we have to be in the chow hall. Let's start moving." He tilted his head toward the perimeter.

At this point, Alex could no longer afford to be overly concerned about the system listening to him and understanding his intentions. Although he still maintained the habit of avoiding keywords that might send an alert to the control room and guards, there was no time to use the finger code he and Mykola had used earlier. If he and Mykola didn't make it, well, they'd just have to hope no one had heard or recorded their plans.

"Okay, but I never got confirmation from . . ." Mykola hesitated, not wanting to use Sarah's name.

Alex understood. "Neither did I, but she knows we're looking for the right time, and I trust that she's checking messages frequently. At this point, I'm committed and hoping for the best."

Already many of the other inmates were heading inside, and Mykola and Alex found themselves 20 yards from the warning track with nobody near them.

"Tell you what," Mykola said. "I'm feeling lucky today. I'll go first, and if I make it, you'll know it's safe for you to go. No sense in both of us frying in the desert."

Alex simply nodded.

After a quick look back at the prison structure, Mykola started to run and then stopped. The sun was already low on the western horizon, and it had given Mykola an idea.

"Alex," he said, "if we cross another 100 yards down, in a line directly between the sun and the door, it'll make it harder to see us. If a guard or anyone comes out that door and looks in our direction, they'll be blinded by the sun."

"Fine, let's do it, but we've got to hurry now."

When they were about in line with the sun, Mykola ran as fast as he could toward the limestone warning track. It probably wouldn't make any difference how fast he ran, but he figured speed would give him less time to have second thoughts and back out of his commitment.

Alex's heart was beating as fast and hard as Mykola's as he watched him run toward the limestone berm. He glanced over his shoulder to see if anyone else was watching and then turned to see Mykola trying to leap over the track but coming up just short.

Before Mykola even came down on the track, he felt a jolt of electricity go through his body, and for a moment none of his muscles responded. He landed awkwardly on one of the rocks, then fell facedown just beyond the limestone. The fall knocked the wind out of him, and he just lay there for a moment. He quickly realized he'd just gotten a Level 1 "warning jolt." He was already on the other side and should now be getting Level 2 or 3 shocks if the hack wasn't working.

No further jolts came.

Looking back at Alex, Mykola put up one finger, and Alex instantly remembered with a sigh of relief that Level 1 had never been turned off. The plan was still on track. Still, there was no time to waste. It couldn't be more than five minutes before the dinner deadline.

Mykola got up and sprinted toward the four-foot fence that kept visitors out, then threw himself down into a shallow depression. This was what they'd both agreed to: there was always the possibility that someone, even another inmate, would see them and report them. By falling into the depression of sand, Mykola would at least appear to have been knocked down by a Level 2 or Level 3 jolt.

Alex kept up a slow walk, looking back toward the door to see whether anyone had noticed Mykola's escape. A last few inmates were filing in and so had their backs to the perimeter. With a final glance, Alex turned, ran toward the limestone track, then took three long steps to get over it, feeling the Level 1 jolt before the first step touched a stone. Perhaps because he'd anticipated it, or perhaps because of the surge of adrenaline, the jolt did not knock him off his feet. It was painful, but a reasonable tradeoff for getting closer to freedom. On the other side, he ran and fell down a few feet from Mykola. Both positioned themselves so they could see the entire prison yard.

Hot, gritty sand got into the sleeves of Alex's shirt and stuck to his sweaty skin. He brushed sand from his chin and cheek. Still breathing hard, he looked up at Mykola and whispered just loudly enough to be heard over the gently gusting wind, "Worst part is over, and so far, so good. You didn't turn your shirt inside out, though."

Wearing the shirt inside out would hide the reflective orange of the inmate numbers, and if anyone did spot Mykola or Alex, they couldn't readily identify them as inmates. The pants also were numbered, but those digits were smaller and harder to see from a distance.

"I'm not going," Mykola whispered back. Alex couldn't hear him, but he could clearly read his lips. The look of consternation on Alex's face made it clear he'd heard.

Now speaking louder, Mykola explained. "I just wanted to make sure you got out. I knew I could withstand a Level 2 better than you could, maybe even a Level 3. But you don't need me anymore . . . and I need to stay. I don't want to live on the run. I want to prove that I was wrongly convicted."

Alex understood his cellmate, and at that moment he realized he should have seen Mykola as one who stuck to his principles. There was no time to convince him to continue the escape. Alex just nodded and mouthed, "Thanks."

By now only a couple of inmates were still in the yard, none near the perimeter, and Mykola gestured that it was safe to go over the fence. Alex quickly pulled off his shirt, careful not to lose the notes still held onto his hips with the elastic from the pants. In seconds he turned the shirt inside out and slipped it back over his head. The sand that adhered to the shirt's outside now scrubbed his skin like sandpaper as he yanked it down.

Mykola again gestured, this time more frantically, for Alex to go over the fence.

Even at his age, getting over the four-foot fence wasn't a problem for Alex. Soon he was jumping down on the other side, and both he and Mykola saw that the fence would provide some cover if Alex ran with his head down.

Alex paused for a moment to look toward the desert. No one was in sight, but there was a car parked on the road that ran parallel to the prison perhaps a mile away. In between were cacti of various shapes and forms and rolling tumbleweed that would make Alex's gray prison uniform harder to see.

"I hope that's Sarah," Alex said, pointing to the glint of light flashing off the hood and windows of the car. "Good luck to you, my dear friend."

But with the blowing wind, Mykola was no longer within earshot.

21

Earlier, in the prison induction room, Sly had been summoned to conduct another new prisoner orientation. There was only one new inmate, Joey, a fresh-faced 19-year-old who looked even younger. Sly could see a bit of himself in this young man. He was about Sly's height but weighed 30 pounds less, and he tried to display an attitude of bravado. But Sly knew that inside, this new inmate was shaking like shutters on an abandoned house in a desert windstorm. As they walked through the prison and Sly explained the rules and what Joey could expect in the next few days, "abandoned" seemed to be the perfect description of this new inmate.

Joey had joined a gang while still in high school, looking for the support and sense of family he never got at home. Even in the gang, however, he was abandoned. He and a couple of the older gang members broke into a pharmacy late one night, but they hadn't thought to first disable the alarm system. Police were there within minutes, and the gang members all ran. Joey tripped and fell over a box in the dark store. He severely sprained his ankle, but none of the other gang members stopped to help him. Joey was the only one arrested.

Sly and Joey were now outside. Despite the intimidating stares directed at both Sly and Joey from older inmates, Joey seemed more relaxed here. Perhaps it was the virtual freedom of being outside. He could look up and see blue sky and the contrail of a jet miles above him. With his back to the prison, he could see mountains in the distance as they met the sky and could feel the wind as it ruffled his hair. It was so much different from the sensation-starved feeling he got in the all-white rectangular corridors inside the prison.

Sly and Joey were running late, as usual for the talkative Sly, and so instead of walking out to the limestone berm, Sly just pointed to it as he explained the warning track and the invisible wall beyond it. In the course of the past couple of hours the conversation between the two had become more amiable, and Sly felt he was gaining Joey's trust. He was aware that his explanation had to convince Joey to control his emotional urge just to keep walking west toward the sun and leave the prison behind. In fact, Sly was tempted to suggest that Joey walk onto the berm after dinner and get the Level 1 jolt just to confirm what he was saying, but he thought better of it. Doing so would alert the control room and generate a demerit on Joey's prison record, and it would probably cost Sly some points as well.

They turned around and walked back to the prison door, now talking about the weather and other harmless, inoffensive topics. As they opened the door, they heard a commotion down the long hallway and Sly put out his arm to hold Joey back. Several inmates rushed past them, out the door and into the yard.

"Don't know what's going on, but this can't be good," Sly said.

"You think it's a fight, Sly?" Joey asked with a mix of curiosity and trepidation.

"Could be, but this isn't something you want to get too close to. You never know if someone is going to include you in it. Even if you have nothing to do with it, if you end up in it you're gonna get a jolt. That's not the way to begin your first day."

⊙

In the control room, Bill and Jake were multitasking: talking about the previous night's last-second winning goal scored by their favorite team in a World Cup soccer game and keeping an eye on prisoners through the bank of screens. Their shift had been uneventful, though when they'd come on, the outgoing shift had told them about an explosion that injured three inmates in the workshop. There'd been nothing of any note for the past couple of hours, though, and Bill and Jake willed the clock to move faster to the end of their shift.

They were shaken out of their lethargy by a flashing red light on the screen and a wailing sound they hadn't heard since they'd gone through their training on the control system. The clock showed 5:55 p.m.

"We've got an attempted break!" Jake said in a loud but steady and controlled tone, sounding much like the captain of a navy ship under attack. "Going to main screen." With a push of a flashing red button, a new image appeared on the main screen.

"What the hell is that?" Bill asked, his head cocked in a questioning expression.

Both Bill and Jake had expected to see an image of the induction room, the loading dock, or the yard, but instead an image of a long white cabinet appeared.

"That looks like the kitchen. No, wait, that's the infirmary. There's not even an inmate on the screen!" Bill looked at all the other screens to see if there was any unusual activity, but everything appeared normal. The first shift of inmates were either in the chow hall or standing just outside it. Others were in various other parts of the prison, but there was nothing to indicate that a prisoner was attempting an escape.

"This has to be a glitch in the system," Jake said dismissively. "We'll just have to report it in our log."

"Hold on. Before we do that, let's do a 360 scan from the central camera. Maybe there's already someone outside the prison."

"Okay, but I'm telling you, this is a big nothing."

Just as he was getting ready to shift to a 360 view of the grounds outside the prison, a flashing red light alerted Jake to another of the small screens. An inmate was lying on the floor outside the chow hall, his limbs flailing as if in some sort of seizure.

"Bill, look at screen 14. What's going on?"

Jake brought the image to the larger center screen, which automatically turned on the audio of the stricken inmate. They could barely understand him, but he seemed to be saying, "What'd I do? What'd I do?"

"I'll call the infirmary and tell them to send down a couple of yellows with a gurney," Bill said. "Looks like some sort of seizure or maybe a drug reaction. He might even be faking it, though I don't know for what possible purpose."

Bill stepped over to the intercom to call the infirmary, but before he could, Jake saw another inmate go down in another part of the prison.

"Bill, we've got another one on screen 48. He's too young for a heart attack, and there's a bunch of other inmates standing around him, looking afraid to get close to him. It looks more like he got a Level 2."

"C'mon, Jake. We haven't gotten any L2 alerts all day, and we sure as hell haven't approved any."

Jake hoped these two inmates in obvious pain were just an unfortunate coincidence, but he feared there might be something amiss in the system, beyond the false escape attempt report. His plans for finishing his shift as scheduled and enjoying a pleasant evening with his girlfriend were quickly falling apart. "I'm calling the boss."

Moments later, the shift warden rushed into the control room, clearly irritated and ready to jump all over Bill and Jake for their apathetic approach to their responsibilities.

"What the hell is going on?" he demanded. "I got the escape attempt alert, and now we've got a couple of L2s. What caused you to authorize L2s in two different parts of the prison at the same time?"

Jake tried to keep his cool and explain what they had just seen, but the warden wasn't particularly interested. He had already made up his mind that this was a story Jake and Bill were concocting to cover up their incompetence or failure to pay attention to the screens.

Then it happened: A third inmate was seen staggering out of his cell and collapsing on the floor. There were no other inmates within 50 feet of him, and he had nothing on him that looked like it could be a weapon. On the big screen, it was clear he had a hand on his collar, trying to get a couple of fingers under it.

The 300-square emotion monitoring screen then caught the warden's attention. When he'd come in, there had only been a couple of flashing red squares, and they'd corresponded with the locations of the inmates who appeared to have received Level 2 jolts. Now the flashing red squares were spreading. The warden could only assume they represented inmates who had witnessed the jolts of fellow inmates and were now either frightened or angry. They were likely sharing what they saw with other inmates, thus spreading the fear and anger.

"Jake. Send guards to all the hot spots," the warden demanded as he pointed to the emotion monitoring screen.

"I don't think we have enough guards on the clock right now," Jake responded, his voice reflecting the tension that had enveloped the control room.

"Start with locations 12-15 and 22-6. Those squares seem to be the centers of the turbulence. We've got to get this under control while we still have a chance. Do it!" the warden screamed, glaring at Bill and Jake to make it clear he wanted no further discussion.

⊙

Sly and Joey were standing there waiting for something that could tell them what they should do next when a scream came from one of the open cells perhaps 50 feet from where they stood. They were seeing what Jake and Bill were seeing on the big screen in the control room. A yellow-shirted inmate staggered out of the cell and collapsed in the hallway, his left hand grabbing his collar. He glanced up, and Sly recognized him as one of the lifers who had befriended him when he was first transferred to this facility. There was no one else around and no indication of a weapon. What was clearly a Level 2 jolt had no explanation.

Joey's face went white at the appearance of this inmate's pain, and his demeanor changed from anxious curiosity to outright panic. Yet he stood there frozen.

Sly ran to the prone inmate, bent down, and shouted harshly, "What did you do?"

"Nothing, Sly," the man moaned. "I was just lying on my bunk. I've had jolts before, and I know what'll get you one. I wasn't doing a thing. It just hit me."

Both men expected to see yellow-shirts pushing a gurney toward them, but none appeared. Some of the men at the far end of the hallway were now running toward them and the door. Sly stood up and put his hands with splayed fingers before him to prevent them from trampling the traumatized inmate. His back was turned to Joey, and he had forgotten all about him and the orientation.

The sight of the men running down the hall toward Joey reminded him of times in school when a bunch of older students would pursue and assault him. Far too small to fight them off, he would run as fast as he could toward anything that promised some safety. That was his instinct now: to get out of that narrow hallway and run outside.

It was only a few steps to the door. Joey yanked it open, and the oven heat of the desert blew over him. The glare of the sun, now half covered by the western mountains, flashed in his eyes, disorienting him for a split second. The sound of the yelling men brought his focus back to his objective. He ran toward the center of the yard, the area where Sly had explained the berm and the invisible fence to him just minutes before.

Now, with the yelling fading and in the full shadow of the mountains, he looked up to see what appeared to be an inmate running far beyond the other side of the four-foot "visitor fence." Did Sly lie to me about the invisible fence? he asked himself. Perhaps the system wasn't working, and that's what had allowed that inmate to escape.

Whatever the case, Joey didn't take the time to think through the logic and the risks. This was an opportunity he wouldn't pass up. He sprinted across the yard toward the nearest part of the berm, his speed hindered only by his small feet pushing into the soft sand. He was going to get out of here, he was sure. Within inches of the berm's forward edge, he launched himself and cleared it with ease. He felt the warning jolt Sly had told him about, but the adrenaline rushing through his arteries was more than enough to compensate. He ran another couple of yards, and a second, more powerful jolt coursed through his body. He stumbled and put his hand down into the hot sand to maintain his balance. The pain as his muscles seized took over his cognitive function. His actions were animalistic now. He was the bear with his leg caught in a steel-clawed trap, stronger than he'd ever been, fighting desperately to free himself. Another couple of steps and the virtual gun blast of Level 3 hit him in the neck and spine.

Within seconds his heart stopped. Joey fell forward, and a lifetime of pain and disappointment ended.

The inmates who had seen the first two stricken inmates responded immediately to someone's shout of "Level 2 without any reason!" Panic swept through them with the thought that any one of them might be the next victim of someone's sadistic prank. Their fear and anger were irrationally directed to anyone standing near them. Then one inmate noticed a guard standing off to the side, urgently and forcefully pressing the screen on his tablet. "It's him!" he cried, and three inmates rushed the guard, fists raised. One of them had a plastic fork from the chow hall clenched in his hand.

The system automatically identified the Level 2 violation, and the center screen showed it. On the control panel were three inmate numbers and flashing Level 2 lights. Neither Bill nor Jake had the time to confirm the inmate numbers; before they could even react, the warden shoved them aside and pressed the three L2 approval buttons in rapid succession.

He was a second too late. The inmate had plunged the plastic fork into the guard's carotid artery, and blood sprayed on the attackers and guard. A fourth inmate, a slender doctor in his late 60s, ran up to the guard and put his hands around his neck. Was he trying to stop the bleeding, or was he choking the guard? The system couldn't distinguish between the two actions, and a Level 3 light flashed on the control panel. Again the warden's emotional need to regain control over the imploding prison took over, and he pressed the confirmation button that delivered a Level 3 jolt. Within seconds the inmate was still.

No one came forward to help any of the five men now lying on the floor in a crimson pool. A guard and an inmate were dead.

Level 2 alerts were now constantly flashing on the control panel as fights broke out throughout the prison. Inmates were grabbing anything they could to defend themselves or to damage the ceiling cameras. There was no way for any of the three in the control room to react in a sensible manner. The flashing lights and rapidly changing screens were overloading them with information.

"You've got to shut the system down!" Jake shouted to the warden. Jake was as muscled and intimidating as any of the red-shirt inmates, and up here in the control room there was no automated protection for anyone, including the warden. Control over the inmates had been lost, and the look of anger in Jake's face told the warden he was about to lose control over his staff as well.

"Dammit, the control system is on a separate circuit, and I can't turn it off," he said. "If I try, it'll go to full auto."

This was part of the security London Tower had built into the prison. The authority to shut down the inmate collar system was randomly assigned to five corporate executives; any one of them could give the order. This dramatically reduced the possibility of a riot and of anyone holding the warden hostage until he turned off the system.

"But you can switch off main power! Maybe that'll calm things down!" Bill screamed.

The warden stood frozen for a moment, then realized there wasn't anything else to do. He quickly went back to his office. Moments later, main power was off to the prison. All was dark for perhaps 20 seconds, and screams of angry inmates died down to faint cries. The control panel and the monitors in the control room, however, on a separate power circuit, remained on.

Breathing hard, Warden Gray waited another minute before deciding to call in a request to shut down the control system.

If it was on full auto, it might continue to deliver L2 jolts and possibly even L3s. There was risk in turning it off but greater risk in leaving it on.

The call went through on the emergency line, and voice recognition immediately identified him as a shift warden of the facility. Explaining the situation to the London Tower executive as calmly as he could, Warden Gray was unwavering in his demand, and his explanation that at least one inmate and one guard were already likely dead was a convincing argument. The executive knew he'd be held accountable for any additional injuries and deaths caused by the system.

"It's off," the executive said, and simultaneously the glow from the three monitors in the warden's office faded. The time was 6:06 p.m.

In all parts of the prison, soft, ashen emergency lighting progressively came on. It was as if a supernatural being had suddenly intervened, and everyone felt they'd been saved. Even the L1 jolts delivered to prisoners who were not in the chow hall for the 6:00 shift ended. Adding to the otherworldly atmosphere, a voice from the loudspeakers came on.

"This is Warden Gray. I have a special announcement." The warden paused so that everyone could quiet down before he continued. "We've had a minor malfunction in the security system, and it is being repaired. All inmates will return to their cells immediately and remain there until further notice. Inmates who are outside of their cells exactly ten minutes from now will automatically receive a Level 2 shock."

Most of the inmates walked quickly back to their cells. A couple dozen inmates decided this was their chance to attempt an escape, and they headed for one of the three doors to the prison yard. A guard at each door let prisoners who had run outside during the riot come back in, but none were allowed to go out. The guards couldn't be bothered with those few inmates who were already outside and had "run for the hills."

"Warden, I didn't know you could initiate Level 2 shocks en masse," Jake questioned.

"You're right, we can't. It's just a bluff, but it seems to be working. Right now I've got to talk to London Tower and the state departments of corrections and tell them what's happened and what we've done. I'll ask London Tower headquarters to temporarily repower the control system in ten minutes. Then we'll advance the clock to the cell gates' closing time, and that'll give us some time to figure out what to do next.

"In the meantime, Jake, get emergency services in here and tell them we've got severely injured inmates and staff. Bill, I need you to call in all the off-shift guards and get them in here. Better call local police too and alert them to the possibility that there are some prison escapees in the area."

"What about the collars?" Jake asked the warden.

"What about them? They're staying on the inmates; since power to the control system is off, there's no way to automatically remove them for now. And I've got to find out if there's a way to disable their release when the control system power is turned back on.

"It's going to be a long night, for everyone up here and down there."

22

Mykola remained in the shallow depression of sand while Alex crouched down and quick-walked maybe 50 yards toward the far road. In the quiet of the early evening, both heard a scream coming from the prison structure. Sure that someone had seen them get out of the yard, they both turned and were amazed to see nobody in the yard and the door to the structure wide open.

I'd better pick up my pace, Alex thought nervously. He began to jog toward the car, avoiding sharp rocks and prickly cacti as best he could.

Then there was another scream. Moments later he heard a third scream, but with the increasing distance and a freshening wind, it was fainter.

Mykola saw that some inmates were coming into the yard, but rather than looking out to the west, they turned and looked back inside the door. Were some inmates fighting, or were they violating some rule that resulted in Level 2 jolts? From this distance Mykola couldn't tell. However, with everyone's attention focused on the inside, he figured this was the best time to cross back into the yard. A few quick steps and he was on the limestone rock berm. As expected, he received the Level 1 jolt, but for some reason it wasn't as strong as the one he'd gotten just a few minutes earlier when going in the opposite direction. Perhaps, he thought, he'd just built up some tolerance.

As soon as he was back inside the virtual wall, he walked slowly toward the gathering of inmates. As he did, another inmate broke out of the group, grabbing his collar and groaning in agony. He staggered a few steps and fell to the ground. The other inmates stepped back as if the fallen inmate were cursed or the carrier of some terrible communicable disease.

"What's going on?" Mykola feverishly asked the nearest inmate. The inmate's face was strained with fear, and Mykola could see his hands shaking.

"Don't know. Couple of guys were jolted inside. They weren't doing anything; just standing around and talking. They weren't loud or pushing anyone or breaking any rules, but suddenly one got a big jolt, and then about a minute later another guy got a jolt, and he wasn't even near the first guy. We looked around to see if there was some mean-ass guard around but didn't see anyone."

"So why did you come outside?"

"I don't know. Probably same reason you did. Some guy yells out that it's safer outside and we just follow him out here."

Mykola was relieved that this inmate hadn't noticed he'd been outside all this time.

The inmate's breath was becoming less labored. "But clearly it isn't any safer," he said, nodding in the direction of an inmate lying motionless in the sand. "I'm about ready to run for it.

Don't care what happens. Gotta be better than just standing here and waiting for the damn collar to fry my brains."

Mykola could sense the mood of the group of inmates gradually shifting from fear to anger, ready to strike out at anyone associated with authority in the prison. Four red-shirts stood apart from the group, obviously aware that they might be the closest targets.

⊙

Alex continued to move as quickly as he could, glancing over his shoulder frequently to see if there was any evidence that someone had spotted him. Nothing; it seemed Mykola's idea of walking directly toward the sun might have helped him avoid detection. But as the sun continued to go down, it now blinded him. Bringing his right hand to his forehead blocked the sun, and his focus now was simply on the next five yards in front of him. He had been headed toward the car, but a couple of minutes later, when he looked up, it was gone. Panic set in.

He was sure he and Mykola had seen a car from the prison yard, and there was no reason to think it was anyone but his son or daughter. Who else would have stopped their car in such a desolate place? Yet it was gone. Just off to the left, he saw a hazy cloud of dust from a car moving farther and farther away from him.

Maybe they're just late. Maybe they're on their way, Alex said to himself, trying to be optimistic. In any case, there was nothing he could do but continue to move as quickly as he could toward the road. Some large rocks on a rise about 200 yards ahead and to the right of him would be a good place to hide and wait a few minutes.

The wind was gusting and starting to pick up sand from the parched ground. As he neared the rocks he heard a voice, a faint but familiar voice.

"Dad, Dad, over here."

There, peering around the edge of the largest rock, was Sarah.

Alex sprinted as best he could toward her. As he did, she motioned for him to get down. Going behind the rock, he fell to his knees and looked at Sarah squatting there before him. Even with the dry wind blowing in his face, Alex could feel his eyes moisten. For a moment neither knew what to do. Then Alex put out his arms and hugged her in relief. Alex realized he hadn't felt he had escaped the prison until this moment, and he wished to savor it. But Sarah, to his surprise and disappointment, quickly pulled away.

"Don't have much time," she explained in just above a whisper. She reached for a folded sheet of paper in her pocket, took it out, and gave it to Alex, putting her index finger to her lips. Then she pointed to the sheet of paper. Alex unfolded it and read it.

Did lots of research on the collar but can't be exactly sure how it works. Know it tracks your movements in the prison; can't be sure it isn't tracking your location even here, perhaps using GPS. It may be recording your voice and the voices of people nearby. Need to disable that capacity if it exists. Here's what you must do:

Continue on your path and cross the road. Head toward the mountains on the western horizon. About 500 yards past the road, find a spot where you are not likely to be seen and stop there.

Wrap the silver foil around the collar. Cover as much as you can on all sides. Crumple it as necessary. This will block the GPS electromagnetic signals.

Come back to the road as quickly as you can. The car will be there to pick you up.

Say nothing more. Go NOW.

Alex looked up to see Sarah holding out a sheet of thick foil. He paused, then gave her a smiling nod. At the moment it was the only way he could express the pride he felt for his daughter. She was covering all the possibilities, no matter how remote they might be. Technology was no match for Sarah.

He touched her hand as he took the foil.

Alex followed the instructions precisely, and just as he came back to the road, a car pulled up. Allen was driving, and as soon as he stopped, both he and Sarah got out. Still nothing was said. Alex put out his hand to Allen. Allen grasped it and they shook hands in the manner of two executives who had just signed a merger agreement.

"We spotted you just as you got over that short fence. But where's Mykola? Wasn't he supposed to be with you, or did something happen?" Sarah asked with touching concern for a man she'd never met.

"He decided not to go, but I'll have to give you the story later. Right now we have to go," Alex said.

Allen stood quietly to the side, recognizing that with those words his father had resumed command and responsibility for the family.

"We've got some clothes in the back for you," Sarah said with a big smile. "You're no longer a number."

Quickly Alex changed, happy to see a bulky sweatshirt included in his new wardrobe. It would cover his collar. Sarah helped him put it on, inspecting the foil around the collar to make sure there were no gaps. They were all confident the collar was no longer functional, but there was no way to get it off right now. Allen noticed his father zipping the sweatshirt all the way up even in this hot, dry weather and pointed to the collar. "I've got a way to get that off."

"Does it involve an acetylene torch?" Alex asked, hoping his question would be taken as a joke.

"No, it's something techy I found on the dark web. It's a dongle the manufacturer issues to prison administrators to use in an emergency. I didn't order one; they cost a bunch of cryptocurrency. I can show you the site where you can buy one, though."

"I'm familiar with those dongles," Alex replied curtly.

If Alex had turned and looked at his son, he would have seen the disappointment in his face. Allen had been sure his father would be impressed with his foresight and initiative, and not even getting a "thanks" from him was simply deflating.

Allen was about to get into the driver's seat when Alex reached out and held his arm. Allen turned back and looked at his father. Had he now done something wrong?

"Allen, I know you did as much as your sister did to help me get out of the prison. I want you to know I'm thankful."

Allen turned and looked at his father to see just the slightest upturn of a smile. In an instant Allen's disappointment was replaced by elation as he heard his father's expression of gratitude.

"And now I need you to do one more thing," Alex told Allen. "Let your sister sit in the driver's seat. I know you know how to operate the car, probably better than the autonomous function can. However, when they find out I've escaped—if they haven't already—they'll be looking for a guy behind the wheel."

Sarah took over the driver's seat. Before Allen got back into the car, he grabbed the prison uniform, tied it in a loose bundle, and covered it with sand alongside the road.

"Good thinking, son," Alex said from the back seat as he reached over and patted his son on the shoulder.

Sarah put the car in autonomous drive mode. She then set the GPS for a small, out-of-the-way motel as they headed back toward the city. For the first couple of miles theirs was the only vehicle on this narrow and isolated road. All three were quiet, not even shifting in their seats, perhaps subconsciously assuming that any sound would draw attention to them. The radio was off, and the only sound came from the tires as they rolled over the patches of gravel and windblown sand that covered much of the road.

Surely by now the warden had been informed that someone had escaped. When another car passed going in the other direction, they all held their breath and couldn't bear to look behind them to see if it had made a U-turn and was now following them. On this straight piece of road, there was nowhere to turn off. Sarah shifted her eyes and checked the rearview mirror to confirm the passing car was continuing in the opposite direction.

After perhaps five minutes, the tension in the car began to dissipate. They knew they were now outlaws on the run, and they couldn't be sure if their sweat and pounding hearts were the manifestations of fear or excitement. The prison was now almost out of sight.

Allen spotted the lights first. "Look, red lights coming toward us!" he shouted. Alex leaned forward and shifted to the center so that he could better see the road ahead of them. The cars were all in a line, so they couldn't tell how many there were, but it appeared to be two or three.

"What do we do now?" Sarah asked as she reached to turn off the autonomous mode.

"No, don't do that; leave it in autonomous mode," Alex commanded. "We don't want to do anything that might raise suspicion. Auto mode doesn't know we're escapees; it will operate the car as if we're out for a Sunday drive. Allen, you and I need to get out of sight now."

Alex scrunched down in the back seat, doing all he could to get himself below the window line of the car. Sarah understood the need to appear calm and sat upright, looking straight ahead. She didn't dare look over at Allen, who was now huddled on the floor of the passenger side. The red lights were still coming toward them, and Sarah could now see it was several vehicles. It looked like three police cars and three ambulances. With Alex and Allen crouched down, only Sarah could see the vehicles, and she didn't want to convert alarm into panic, so she said nothing.

With flashing red lights now less than a half mile ahead of them, their car began to slow. "What's going on? Why are we slowing?" Allen asked; he couldn't see they were slowing, but he felt momentum pushing him forward. Then they all heard the sound of tires on gravel and the car rolled to a stop.

Allen could only think that the police had somehow taken remote control of their car. Now he was sure what he was feeling wasn't excitement but rather adrenaline-generated fear. Everyone heard it in his voice.

Then Alex's voice came from the back seat, steady and calm.

"Don't panic. The autonomous sensors picked up the flashing red lights, recognized them as emergency vehicles, and pulled the car to the side of the road to let them pass, just as the law requires."

Moments later, Alex and Allen—still scrunched down—could only hear the vehicles pass, their sirens screaming. Quickly the sounds faded into the distance. Just when the three began to wonder whether something was wrong with the car, it began to move again. The tires were no longer on the gravel shoulder, and the comforting sound of rubber on asphalt returned.

"They're gone," Sarah announced with a long exhale. Allen and Alex raised up, got back into their seats, and looked behind them to confirm it.

Finally they reached an intersection and turned onto a state highway that had much more traffic. They could blend in. With that, everyone relaxed and began talking about how they had engineered this incredible escape. Allen was particularly boastful, and Alex and Sarah let him enjoy this moment in the spotlight.

When he finally paused to take a breath, Sarah interjected, "Allen, I know you know this, but I just want to remind you: we're not saying a single word about our little project outside of this car. We don't know who might be listening. Just as soon as we can, we need to get back into our routine. That means you are going to school every day."

As Sarah said this, it occurred to her that she was saying it to herself as much as she was to Allen. Everything had worked according to plan, and that was exciting, even exhilarating—but they had committed a felony. The stakes were high. They now had to put as much thought and effort into protecting themselves as they had put into planning and executing the escape. There could be no letdown.

"You're right, Sarah," Alex said. "When they figure out I'm no longer at the prison, there are sure to be investigators knocking at your door. I know you've been careful to hide your trail, but the slightest verbal slip could start an avalanche of questions. So getting back to your routine, beginning just as soon as you get home tonight, is important."

Alex knew he'd be worrying about his son and daughter for the next several days at least.

"What about Mykola?" Sarah asked. "You said you were going to explain why he changed his mind."

"Mykola is sort of the ballast in a ship that keeps it from capsizing in rough seas," Alex began. "He's the one who recognized that innocent inmates might be severely injured if we acted rashly. I didn't appreciate it at the time, but he was right. I'm out, and nobody has had to pay the price. That's mostly thanks to Mykola."

"But he's still there. He could have been in the back seat with you right now, Dad." Allen turned and looked over his shoulder at his father.

"He got some promising news from his attorney, and he wants to prove he's innocent of the crime he was convicted of, even if it takes a couple of years. He got all the way to the fence with me before he turned back; I hope he got back in without being noticed.

"You know, his going back in helps all of us. I know he's going to continue with that online course, and Sarah, you need to respond to his questions as you have been. He's going to help you get back into the routine."

Traffic had become congested, and their speed had dropped to 30 mph. All three were engrossed in the conversation, and with the self-driving function keeping a safe distance from the car in front of them, they could have been sitting around a coffee table having this discussion.

"One thing bothers me," Alex said. "Mykola and I heard some screams after we'd gotten over the warning track and lay down in the dirt near the fence. Then some inmates came running out, all yelling and screaming about something. I know it wasn't connected to the code patch you entered, Sarah; we'd already been out for about five minutes. There must have been some other sort of crisis; maybe another explosion in the workshop."

"That prison is a terrible place, even for people who have committed serious crimes," Sarah said. "Allen and I read the notes Mykola sent out about the technology they are using and then did some more research on our own. I assume the science is well intended, but it seems they haven't done the follow-up to verify that it's working as planned. It's a wonder screaming isn't part of the daily soundtrack. Will anyone have the courage to speak up and acknowledge the system's shortcomings?"

"That place needs to be closed!" Allen bellowed as he punched the air above him with his fist.

"And it will, or at least they're going to have to make some dramatic changes. That's one of the things I hope I can facilitate after I've established a new identity," Alex added in a somber, reflective tone. "I won't be able to show my face, but I can submit articles to professional journals."

"That could take years, Dad. You know how hard it is to make changes, especially when so many people have a vested interest in keeping things the way they are." Sarah had shifted in her seat so that she could look at both Allen and her father in the back seat. She could see the same caring in Alex's face that she remembered from when she was a little girl and told him of the typical childhood problems she faced and thought could never be solved.

Allen grinned. "Sarah's right. To make changes, you've got to have a major event that gets everyone's attention. You know, like that 9/11 thing we learned about in grade school or the lithium poisoning at that battery plant last year."

Allen made eye contact with Sarah. The look on his face, Sarah thought, was that "I'm the master of the universe" look Allen would get when winning an electronic game. It sent a shiver through Sarah's entire body.

"Allen, what did you do?" Her voice trembled.

"Well, when you called today and told me to make the inmate ID changes to the program, I also uploaded a patch I've been working on for the past week. Didn't know if it would work, but from what you're saying, Dad, it sounds like it did."

Alex leaned forward in his seat. With all the control he could possibly muster to hide his dread he asked, "Exactly what sort of patch?"

Now ready to explain and be applauded for what he thought was his own unique combination of social engineering and computer technology, Allen continued.

"Well, I thought the plan was a good one, but we might have overlooked something, like a guard who was outside smoking a butt. You needed some distraction so that you wouldn't be missed, at least until cell-closing time."

Sarah nodded and extended her hand if receiving something. "Go on."

"It wasn't all that hard for me to figure something out. First I linked the perimeter GPS to the shock-controlling function. I wanted to be sure you guys got out before anything happened. Then I programmed the shock controller to deliver Level 2s to inmate IDs I found on another file, one every minute or so for 15 minutes. That would have everyone trying to figure out what was going on and would give you time to get to the car. It worked, but the added benefit is that it exposed the shortcomings of their whole AI system. If I can hack the system, what would someone who had *real* computer smarts be able to do?"

If pride were a suit to be worn, Allen was now wearing the most gaudy, ostentatious one in the closet.

"Allen, you fucking idiot!" Alex screamed so loud he felt his lungs burning. Sarah was shocked by her father's choice of words and the sheer power in his booming voice. Her breathing quickened, and she put her hands over her mouth and nose to keep from hyperventilating.

"Allen, what you did might have resulted in men dying or being seriously injured," Alex went on. "Maybe 15 or 20 of them, maybe many more. And we're all going to pay for it."

"But—but, Dad—the shocks were just Level 2, and Mykola told us Level 2s weren't deadly. He said only Level 3s might be deadly. Was Mykola lying?"

"It's not a game of logic," Alex said, grabbing Allen's shirt and spitting the words into his face. "You've likely caused a riot. Level 2 shocks aren't going to be the killers. It'll be inmates venting their rage against other inmates and guards. It was a stupid thing to do. You should have checked with Sarah before you decided to become a guerrilla technologist."

"I'll see if there's any news." Sarah reached for the radio in the dash and began searching through the various pop music and talk radio stations. Finally she found a 24-hour news station. They all listened intently for a couple of minutes, but there were no special alerts. Perhaps it wasn't as bad as Alex had feared.

Alex took a deep breath to regain his calm and now spoke in a more controlled, measured voice.

"Allen, I'm sorry, but this is the worst thing you could have done. You may know science and programming, but you're woefully behind in understanding *people*. When you punish people without telling them why they're being punished, you confuse them and cause them to panic. They become distrusting of one another and lash out at anything or anyone they think might be the source of the undeserved, unexplainable punishment. What we heard wasn't like anything we've heard before in the prison. It could only have been the sounds of many men in pain and anger. I doubt that anyone, much less the warden and his understaffed cadre of guards, was in control."

Everyone in the car became quiet. The pride Allen had felt just moments ago had vanished. The multiple emergency vehicles that had passed them earlier now made sense to Sarah.

Alex broke the silence. "They probably wouldn't even have reported our escape to the police for at least a day or two; they want to keep up their image of a perfectly secure prison. They would have done everything they could to hide any shortcomings in the software. Now every US law enforcement agency is going to look for the guys who hacked that computer system, and they'll pretty quickly link it to the escape."

"What do we do now?" Sarah asked, fearing even her father wouldn't be able to come up with a good response.

"I'm not sure. I need to stay on plan. We'll drop off the car at the rental place and I'll go to that fleabag motel where you set up the reservations for me. You need to go home. You've got to make it look like you're not linked to this in any way and go about your routine. At the same time, you'll need to be prepared to leave at any time if you think the investigation is getting too close."

Alex could hardly believe what he was telling his children. In the course of ten miles in the car, he'd discovered that everything that had appeared to be perfectly executed had been turned on its head.

"I've escaped, all right. From prison. Now I'm in a new prison, without walls, and I've brought you in with me. I'm very sorry, to both of you." Alex reached up to his neck and fingered the silver foil on the stainless steel collar.

23

When he heard the announcement that all inmates should return to their cells, Mykola was relieved. At least the warden was trying to reestablish control, and hopefully the group panic and anger would come to an end. If nothing else, his cell was probably the safest place to be. Surrounded by three walls and a gate, it was the easiest place in which he could defend himself.

Two guards in the yard began motioning to the nearly 100 inmates to go inside. They stood at either side of the door, each six feet from his respective edge. Quickly inmates began filing in, careful not to get too close to either of the guards. Mykola, standing farthest from the door, figured to be among the last to go in. Yet there were a number of inmates still standing and talking, not making any move toward the door.

The guards were focused on getting inmates back inside as well as preventing others from coming out. The group of inmates still milling about obstructed their view of an inmate slowly walking to the berm. When he got close, he broke into a run. Mykola saw him and involuntarily tensed his entire body in anticipation of the pain the fleeing inmate would feel. He fully expected to see the inmate experience the full series of Level 1, Level 2, and—if he made it that far—Level 3 jolts.

But he didn't. The inmate ran over the berm and through the Level 2 and 3 zones and apparently did not receive a jolt.

From Mykola's perspective, it was impossible to tell if this inmate's collar wasn't working or if there was some temporary breakdown in the overall security system. Was it possible that Sarah's hack had done this? There was no way to know. However, the group of inmates who were slow to move to the door saw it and, like a small herd of spooked gazelle, began running in all directions toward the berm and freedom.

Among them were three red-shirts. Although the red color was intimidating inside the prison, the red-shirts were now easy to spot against the tan sand and brown-green desert vegetation.

The guards saw the running inmates and also assumed they'd be stopped by the virtual fence. When they crossed and nothing happened, one guard began pressing numbers into his tablet to deliver jolts to the escaping inmates, but again nothing happened.

Mykola continued to walk toward the open door; he had no thought of reversing course.

"Get inside now. Go to your cells!" the guards yelled as the last of the inmates were filing in. The guards realized that the longer the door remained open, the greater the chance things would come to a boil once again. There was nothing they could do about the 20 or so inmates who were now outside the prison bounds; they had to get the last of the compliant inmates inside immediately and close the door. That they did, closing the door behind them. Then they stood before it to discourage any other inmates from going outside.

Mykola went to his cell and found Alex's uniforms on his bunk and everything in the cell clean and neatly organized. As far as he could tell, there was no evidence of any escape attempt having been engineered from this cell. Three minutes later the cell gate rolled slowly on its tracks and closed. The clank was a familiar sound, but it symbolized an exceptional day. Mykola couldn't imagine that Alex was going to miss this sound after hearing it hundreds of times in days past.

There was now a new sound: the rumble of his stomach. He had missed dinner, and even the dreary brown taste-minimized soy meatloaf would have been welcome right now.

⊙

"Allen, you said you know where I can get a device to remove this collar?"

"That's what I said, Dad."

"Write it down for me; I'm going to have to order it and have it sent to that motel where I'll be hiding."

"I already have." Allen reached over the seat and handed a piece of paper to Alex. Alex glanced at it to make sure he could read all the characters and then shifted his position so he could look out the front window. By this time they were driving through one of the distant eastern suburb cities of the Los Angeles-San Diego metropolis.

"Look for a metro transit stop," Alex said. "There's got to be one around here someplace. We've got to split up. If anyone puts two and two together, we could be stopped at any time. I'll catch the next metro headed west and then figure out how to get to that motel. You guys get this car back to the rental lot and then get yourselves back home. Remember, you've got to get back to normal routine as quickly as possible."

A couple of miles later Sarah spotted a metro stop, pulled over, and let Alex out. There were no emotional goodbyes; just a quick "thanks" as Alex took the bag of clothes and supplies Sarah had assembled for him and slipped out the back door.

"How do we contact you?" Sarah asked through the rolled-down window.

"You don't. I'll contact you when I'm ready," Alex hastily replied. "Don't know when; might be a week, maybe more."

Sarah returned the car to the lot, leaving it in the same spot from which they had taken it several hours earlier. Allen rode his bike home, and Sarah decided that walking the five miles would be the safest thing for her to do. It would give her some alone time to think as well.

It was approaching 11:00 as Sarah reached the intersection where she'd be able to see their house in the middle of the block. She'd already made up her mind to continue walking straight if there were any evidence of police nearby. A glance to the left revealed everything to be normal. There were a couple of parked cars that looked familiar, though she couldn't be sure. At the very least, they didn't look like official cars. The light on their front porch was on, and Sarah could see a faint light coming from the lower floor playroom of the triplex. That's where she expected Allen to be.

"Allen, I'm home," Sarah called out as she unlocked the front door using the keypad and walked in.

"Down here," in Allen's "I'm doing something" voice from the playroom.

Sarah stepped down the eight worn wooden steps, her rubber-soled shoes squeaking in rhythm. "You're playing a war game?" she asked with a mix of surprise and reproach.

"Dad said we should get back to our routines, and this is my routine," Allen said, neither taking his eyes off the big screen that dominated the room nor taking his hands off the controllers.

"Pause, please?"

Allen brought up a voice recognition prompt on the screen and said, "Signing off." The screen went blank before Allen could turn and face Sarah.

"Anything happen since you got home?"

"No, everything was as I left it, and there haven't been any calls on either of our phones. Remarkably quiet, I think."

"Any news?"

"Oh yeah, a bunch." Allen became much more serious. "The State Line Prison riot is all over cable news and scrolling across every news webpage. They are reporting that there were three deaths, including one guard, and 24 injured inmates, some as a result of fighting among inmates but most from the electronic security system."

"Any news about Dad?"

"Sort of. The reports aren't consistent, but at least 18 prisoners escaped. All but one have been recaptured. We know who that one is." Allen smiled with pride.

"They give any names, Allen?"

"Not a one."

"So one of the injured could be Dad's cellmate Mykola.

Or Mykola could be one of those who died," Sarah said with downcast eyes. "I wish we had found some other way to get Dad out. This is going to haunt me forever."

"But we did get Dad out," Allen said victoriously, "and we did shut down the prison."

"What do you mean, we 'shut down the prison'?"

"Well, you remember the report we heard that they'd gone to full lockdown?"

"Sure."

"The latest report is that they also shut down the state-of-the-art electronic security system and all prisoners are confined to their cells for now. They interviewed the warden, and he said they suspected a security system malfunction was the cause of the riot. They're going to have their geeks and the state geeks look at it."

"Allen, did they say when the system was shut down?"

"Sometime before 7:00, I think."

In the dim light of the playroom Allen couldn't see Sarah's face lose color, but he heard her cracking voice distinctly: "That means the reset we'd programmed into our hack didn't go off. They'll likely see the code changes we made."

"I suppose, but they'll have a tough time tracking it back to us when we trash that box." Allen calmly pointed to the unit on which they'd entered all their uploads.

"We need to do that now."

"Okay. Smash, burn, bury: what's it going to be?"

"All three," was Sarah's terse response.

"That's cool. Oh, before we get started, there are a couple of other things you should know. First, the NiNo site is down. I'm guessing they shut down everything electronic in the prison.

With all the prisoners in their cells, it couldn't be used anyway. The other thing is that I sent Dad an email."

"An email? You mean to his prison account? Why in the world would you do that?" Sarah once again was ready to explode at her brother's taking the initiative without sound judgment.

"Don't have a coronary, sis. Dad said we need to go back to normal. Think about what normal would be. We heard there was a riot at the prison and inmates were hurt, but we don't know who. The normal thing to do would be to try to contact the prison and find out if Dad was one of the injured. I sent him an email saying you and I were hoping he was okay. I know it didn't go through, but the investigators are going to be checking everything in that prison."

"And they'd suspect we knew something about the escape if we didn't try to find out what had happened to him," Sarah said. "I'm sorry for barking at you, Allen. You did the right thing. I'm going to call the prison in the morning to see if they have any more information about those who perished or were injured."

"Okay. Now let's go smash, burn, and bury." Allen was as gleeful as a five-year-old finding out what kind of damage he could do with a hammer he'd found in his father's workshop.

24

This was the longest and loneliest night Mykola had ever experienced. He estimated that the cell gates had closed at about 6:30, but he couldn't be sure, since the schedule board had been shut down and there was no other clock in sight of his cell. With the entire prison on emergency power, the corridor and cell lights were at half brightness, which gave a feeling of never-ending dusk. The cell lights, normally turned off at 9:00, were left on all night, so even that reliable marker of time was unavailable.

Mykola could hear inmates in nearby cells talking with one another, trying to find out what had happened and what they could expect the next day and the days to follow. A guard walked through the corridor periodically and was peppered with questions, but other than to say "They'll have it sorted out in the morning," he did not respond.

Eventually the inmate chatter died down and the loudest sound was the clomping of the guard's boots on the concrete floor as he passed Mykola's cell. Mykola tried to sleep but did so only for short stretches, waking up and thinking through the events of the past 24 hours. Sleep was made more difficult by the collar he still wore, which pressed into his neck even though he used Alex's pillow to cushion it.

He wondered whether Alex had made it out and met up with his son and daughter. Was he now free and safe? Or was he caught and now spending the night in another cell, in some jail miles from the prison?

Overriding all his thoughts, however, was the sense that the riot, with its injuries and deaths, had been related somehow to the escape.

Mykola's gut told him that he was at least partially responsible. This couldn't have been a coincidence. At the same time, others should share responsibility: Alex for masterminding the entire plan, Sarah and Allen for their computer system hack, the computer science engineers who had made it too easy to break into the system. Perhaps even the guards working in the control room were to blame for not taking immediate action to end what appeared to have been randomly delivered jolts.

Or perhaps this was intentional. Maybe some disgruntled guard had wanted to create a disturbance so that there would be a greater need for guards. Anything was possible.

Whoever shared responsibility, the investigation would surely lead through Mykola's cell, and he assumed that would begin in the morning. Even in the dim light, Mykola kept looking around the cell to see if there was any evidence that either he or Alex had had anything to do with that day's events.

Other inmates had attempted escape when it appeared that the virtual wall didn't deliver Level 2 and 3 jolts. Surely they'd be investigated as well. Did that first inmate who ran know something the others didn't, or was he just designated to be the first to test what they thought was a system shutdown? After all, that's what he and Alex had done. Mykola had tested the system, and when it was clear it would not deliver the incapacitating jolts, Alex had followed.

The more Mykola thought about it, the more unanswered questions came to mind. Certainly the London Tower staff had the same types of questions, and it could be some time before they had answers.

Mykola finally fell into a deep sleep in the early morning hours, only to be awakened by the wake-up alarm. Apparently power had been restored: lights in the corridor were at full brightness. Since Mykola had slept in his prison uniform, he saw no reason to do anything more than complete his bodily functions, splash some water on his face, and then just sit down and wait. Moments later he looked up as a scratchy noise came over the loudspeakers, followed by:

"Attention. This is Warden Liebermann speaking. All inmates will remain in their cells until further notice. Inmates will now remove their collars and place them in the tray for pickup. You have ten minutes to do so."

Mykola heard a faint click as the inside lock of his collar disengaged. He reached around for the latch and jerked it open, not sure if his action was an expression of anger at himself or at the prison that made him wear the collar. Whatever; the collar was off, and Mykola was quietly thankful for that. The familiar clang of stainless steel being dropped on the tray rang up and down the cellblock, but for the first time since Mykola had been imprisoned, the collars were coming off in the morning rather than in the evening.

The collars were picked up a short time later and replaced by what was supposed to be breakfast: a couple of slices of pillow-soft bread going stale. Mykola was in no position to complain; he ate the bread and washed it down with handfuls of water from the sink.

This was a change in the morning prison routine, and Mykola was surprised at his reaction to it. The routine was something he abhorred, but now that it was broken, he didn't know what to do or think. No "good morning" from Alex, no squeaking opening of the cell gate, no checking of duty assignments; Mykola realized he'd become accustomed to it all and now missed it. The routine had filled the time, but now Mykola was made intensely aware of the slow passage of each minute. He lay back down on his bunk, closed his eyes, and just let his mind wander.

His introspection was interrupted perhaps 30 minutes later when a short but powerfully built man in his mid-40s came up to the gate on Mykola's cell. Mykola recognized him as the man who had made the announcement earlier, Warden Liebermann, the most senior staff member in the prison. Two guards were with him, standing a foot behind him and obviously on alert to anything threatening or simply out of place. Mykola quickly stood up and turned toward them but remained by his bunk. This was no time to do anything that might be perceived as a prelude to an assault.

"Open cell 731." The warden spoke loudly and clearly, and for an instant Mykola thought *he* was being told to open the gate. The guards then repeated the instructions, also in loud, clear voices. Whether this was voice recognition that automatically opened the gate or a command sent to another guard actually controlling the gate wasn't clear, but as soon as the second guard repeated the warden's instruction, the gate began to open.

The warden walked in and, without any acknowledgment of Mykola, brusquely asked him, "What happened to you?"

Panic set in immediately as Mykola didn't know what the warden was referring to. The warden saw Mykola's eyes widen and his lips tense. He lifted one finger and pointed to Mykola's uniform. With everything that had happened, Mykola had forgotten that his uniform shirt and pants were dirty from when he had fallen in the dirt and sand on the far side of the berm.

"I got into a scuffle in the yard last night."

"Big guy like you? I'd figure you for someone who could take care of himself."

Now Mykola was unsure if he should act submissive or proud and defiant. He decided proud and defiant was what the warden expected of him, and so he straightened up and looked the warden in the eye.

"I can. Somebody slammed into me from behind. I was going to get up and make him regret it, but I've had a big jolt before. Figured it wasn't worth it."

As the words came out, Mykola remembered that the Level 2 jolt he had received had been intended for Alex; the only jolts he'd received that were on record were a couple of Level 1s. Too late; he could only hope no one was verifying everything he said.

"Okay, turn around." The warden reacted to Mykola's proud stance with an even firmer and more challenging voice. He motioned to the guards and Mykola was patted down, but it was a formality: there were no pockets in the prison uniforms.

Next the guards searched the cell. They found nothing of any note except for the chessboard and pieces hidden in Alex's bunk. The uniforms were shaken out, the mattresses turned over and then pressed and squeezed to find anything that shouldn't be there.

"Your cellmate is gone, but we'll find him soon enough," the warden said, glowering at Mykola. "You and the investigators will talk."

"When will that be?" Mykola asked politely but without expression of concern.

"Whenever they are ready."

"And until then?"

"Until then you stay here. Meals will be delivered through the collar tray."

"Warden, whadda we do with this game board, the pieces, and these paperbacks?" a guard asked.

"Did you check the books for any notes or papers jammed into them?" The warden asked as he eyed each guard in turn.

"Yes, sir, didn't find nothin'."

"You can leave the books here, but take the chessboard and pieces."

They were preparing to leave the cell when the guard holding the chessboard turned it over. "Sir, this might be of interest. Look at all these numbers on the back of this board." He handed it to the warden. Mykola flinched; Alex had forgotten to destroy the paper with the pi digits taped to the back of the board.

"What the hell is this?" The warden glared at Mykola. "And don't tell me you don't know."

A lie is much more believable when it is mixed with honesty, Mykola quickly thought to himself. "Those are the digits of pi. You know, the number that is used to calculate the area of a circle."

"I know what pi is; I want to know why these are taped to the back of the board!"

Now for the lie; it came from Mykola's lips without any effort. "Alex and I challenged each other to improve our memories. Somewhere Alex read that there were contests to see who could remember the most digits of pi, and we thought we'd see how many we could memorize." Mykola looked directly at the warden to both express his self-confidence and judge whether the warden was accepting his impromptu fabrication.

"That so? Then you wouldn't mind reciting the first 50 to me."

"I don't know if I can remember 50, but I'll try." Mykola had never studied the sequence of digits but had looked at them enough times that he could at least remember the first few. He took a deep breath and began: "3, 1, 4, 1, 5, 9, 2, 6, 5, 3, 5, 8, 9, 7 . . ." He paused for a moment between each number, pretending to concentrate when in fact he remembered the digits as a series of three-digit numbers.

The slow pace at which he recited the numbers had the desired effect. "I don't have time for this; I'll just pass this board along to the investigators," the warden grumbled. All three men walked out, and the warden, using the same tone of voice he'd used to open the gate, said, "Close cell 731."

As the gate rolled slowly across the track, Mykola asked impatiently, "How long before we go back to our normal routine?"

"Don't know, but you should have time to read all those books, maybe even twice." The warden winked and chuckled.

At least the collar was off, and even if it was a week in this cell, Mykola figured he could handle that. But if anyone found evidence of his involvement in the escape, a week in a cell by himself would be the least of his concerns.

25

An unseasonably cold wind was blowing in from the northwest, bringing with it a flat layer of gray clouds. It won't rain today, Roberta thought as she was heading out the door of her home in Del Mar. Yet years of practice as an attorney had taught her to prepare for the unexpected and improbable. She went back inside, threw a raincoat over her arm, and took an umbrella out of the cast-iron stand by the front door.

The drive to her office was uneventful except that her self-driving car took a route she was unfamiliar with. At first she thought she might have entered the wrong destination, but no, she had touched the correct one on the screen. Home and work were numbers 1 and 2 on the list, and she had touched 2.

Roberta decided she wasn't going to second-guess the technology. After all, it had never gotten her lost or driven her to the wrong destination. Anyway, she had to review her notes for the meeting she was going to have that morning on the Steinman appeal; she really didn't have the time to drive the car herself.

She arrived at the office a few minutes later than expected, but as she walked in, she overheard someone talking about a terrible accident on the freeway she usually took to work. Up the elevator to the fifth floor, hellos to staff members already at their desks, and Roberta was ready to begin her workday. Picking up a couple of folders set on her desk by her assistant, Roberta glanced out the big window facing the west. A few raindrops were slowly running down the glass in a sort of broken-field run.

"Hmmph. Good call on the raincoat and umbrella, and missed the traffic jam. I'm two for two so far," Roberta said to herself as she walked into the small conference room.

"Two for two? What's that all about?" Byron had heard Roberta. Absorbed in her thoughts, she'd spoken loud enough that others could hear her.

"Nothing at all; let's get started."

This smaller conference room had a round table with six evenly spaced identical chairs set around it. There were no windows, and none of the chairs was deemed to be a power chair. This was part of the culture in the law firm. There was a larger office for bigger meetings where someone had to be in control, but this smaller office was used when it was important for everyone to share their thoughts on an equal basis.

Roberta sat down and looked around the table. Joe Montane, a private investigator the firm used on a regular basis, was to her left, Byron sat next to him, and Chris from AIM sat next to Byron. Luis, an attorney new to the case who had been asked to provide a fresh perspective, sat to Roberta's right. Everyone had a tablet set before them. Roberta was the only one to use old-fashioned paper and pen in addition to her tablet.

Roberta cleared her throat and began. "Joe, Luis, I don't believe you've met Chris. She is our point of contact with

Applied Intelligence Methodologies and is working with Byron and showing him how to use their software in the course of our work on the Steinman case. Welcome to our little group, Chris."

Luis smiled and nodded in Chris's direction.

"Purpose of this meeting is to update everyone else on the work we've done individually and decide upon next steps," Roberta continued. "I've allotted two hours so that we don't have to rush, but I'm hoping we won't need that long. I've asked Luis to join us simply because he hasn't worked on the case and with his fresh perspective may see something we've overlooked.

"Before we get started: I assume everyone heard about the riot at the State Line Prison on Friday." Everyone nodded in the affirmative and twisted their facial expressions to indicate concern. "I tried to find out if Mykola—Mr. Steinman—was all right, but they are not releasing any information. They simply said he was not one of the three men who died in the riot."

"That's good to hear," Chris commented with a pronounced sigh of relief that caused everyone to look at her. Roberta wasn't sure if that was a personal view or a business perspective. After all, if Mykola had died, there would be no reason to appeal his conviction and no need right now for the AIM services. Roberta gave Chris the benefit of the doubt; she didn't think Chris was one who could fake compassion.

"The riot doesn't change anything for us. I wanted to update Mykola on what we're doing, but that can wait. Joe, what have you found out?"

"I went to the scene of the assault and checked everything from the positioning of the security cameras to the time stamps on the video to the weather that evening. Everything was consistent with what you already knew and presented at trial.

"I then had a couple of beers in the bar where Mack Beranger and Mr. Steinman had their argument. I was hoping to learn a bit more about Mr. Beranger, just to see if he might have some reason for not correctly identifying his attacker. I did more listening than asking; I didn't want anyone to get the impression that I had an express interest in Mack."

"Luis, at the trial Mr. Beranger said he never saw his attacker other than to get an impression of his height and weight," Roberta said to provide context to Joe's report.

"I went there and spent about an hour on a barstool each late afternoon for the next week," Joe said. "I wasn't making any progress and was about to give up on learning anything new that might help you. On what I'd decided would be my final visit, I saw Mack Beranger at the bar having a few beers with another man. Their conversation was about old times in the police department, and they seemed to have a good time telling stories. Later I did a bit of digging and found out that this guy was Beranger's partner up until Beranger retired. Or, I should say, until Beranger was forced to retire."

"Did this guy look anything like Mr. Steinman?" Byron asked.

"No," Joe said. "He's probably a native Haitian. Very dark brown skin and the characteristic Caribbean accent. You'd never confuse the two. He's also about 20 years older than Mr. Steinman."

Roberta looked askance at Joe. "But you're implying something more. What is it?"

"I'm a good listener, and while I was nursing my beer, I listened not only to what they talked about but for hints about their relationship."

"You mean that perhaps they were in a homosexual relationship?" Roberta asked.

"No, no, nothing like that. It was just that the Haitian seemed a little too subservient to Mack Beranger. He was laughing at his unfunny jokes and paying for his drinks, all top-shelf stuff. At one point they got kind of quiet, and I looked over at Beranger with one eye and could read his lips: 'You still owe me,' he was saying to the Haitian."

"Anything else?" Roberta asked.

"No. By that time I thought it best to go before Beranger got suspicious. I looked at my watch, quickly paid, and left as if I was late for something.

"I know some guys on the force; maybe I can get more information about these guys' partnering and what the Haitian owes Beranger. Might lead to something; might not."

Chris was taking notes on Joe's report and entering them into the AIM system. They were rough, but she could clean them up later. Just as Joe said, it might lead to something. Chris was about to share her update when Byron held up one finger.

"Joe, one more question," he said. "What sort of body type is the Haitian?"

"He's about six-one, 230 pounds, and pretty much all muscle."

"That's a pretty good description of Mr. Steinman, isn't it, Roberta?" Byron didn't need a response; he knew the answer, having seen Mykola during the videoconference.

Roberta pointed to Chris and said, "You're up."

Chris provided an AIM system update. Given the fact that they were still in the data collection stage, AIM didn't have specific recommendations for action. However, it had organized the data it had collected from the internet and the information entered by Chris and Byron as well as Roberta's limited entries.

One of the documents it had produced was a diagram of all individuals directly and indirectly associated with the case, now including the Haitian just discussed by Joe. Chris asked everyone to look at this on their tablets and also projected it on the large wall-mounted monitor. Only the key information, as selected by AIM, was presented next to each name, but a click on the name would open another page with the raw data.

"If you have any additional information on any of these individuals, please update it as soon as you can. Likewise, if you note an error, please make the correction," Chris asked the group. "Once each day, or whatever time period you specified in your personal preferences, you should be receiving an auto-mated report of additions and corrections. You'll note that any information you've entered that contradicts previously entered information will result in the old information being lined through. Nothing is lost. If you don't want to wade through old, outdated information, you have the option of seeing only the most current content with just a single click."

"Thank you, Chris. I've gotten the AIM updates and typ-ically read them on my way into the office." Roberta had to admit this was a convenient way to stay up to date on their progress, but it didn't replace the face-to-face meetings such as they were having today. Sometimes body language said more than words on a page.

Luis spoke up. "I agree, this is pretty impressive. It can be a big time-saver. One thing I am a bit confused about, however. What I'm hearing is pointing to a possible alternative theory of the crime. I don't have to tell you that the time to present an alternative theory has come and gone with the conviction."

"You're right, Luis. We're pursuing a possible alternative theory for two reasons," Roberta responded. "First, Mr. Steinman has made it clear to us that he doesn't want his conviction overturned on what he calls 'a legal technicality,' though at this point that is our best hope. He wants everyone to know that he did not assault Mack Beranger in that parking lot. When he says 'everyone,' he means everyone who knows him. He's very protective of his reputation and honor.

"The second reason is that we just haven't yet found a cause to appeal the case that has a good chance of success. Perhaps we can find a significant and intentional misstatement by one of the prosecution's witnesses. I know: it's a shot in the dark."

"And, if I might add, this is a chance to show how AIM can be an asset on the most complex and challenging cases." Chris hadn't forgotten that her job was as much to sell the AIM product as it was to train attorneys on how to use it.

"Let's go on," Roberta said. "Byron, do you have anything to add?"

"I do." This was Byron's opportunity to once again impress Roberta and take the next step to a full attorney position with the firm. "I've done some more research on that Oklahoma City case. It turns out the video security system used in that case is the same brand and model as the one used in the bar parking lot, the one that produced the tape that became the linchpin of the prosecution's case against Mykola Steinman. In the Oklahoma City case, they've already shown that the identification software can be fooled by videos recorded by this particular system."

"C'mon, Byron. No system is 100 percent correct in identifying people, but we rely on them because humans are even less reliable. A week doesn't go by without some convict being released because of false identification at the crime scene. You know that." Roberta was disappointed: from Byron's confident manner, she'd expected him to announce a real breakthrough.

"I'm aware of that." Byron was taken aback for a moment by Roberta's dismissive tone. "But my thinking is that there's a flaw in either the video recording system or the identification system, a flaw specific to certain types of situations. In both the Oklahoma City case and ours, the lighting wasn't perfect. I'd like to continue to pursue this, perhaps with the help of AIM." Byron turned to Chris and they exchanged smiles.

"Okay, you've got a week to show some progress, Byron. In the meantime, Joe, continue your background investigation on the relationship between Mack Beranger and his Haitian partner in the police force."

Roberta was almost glad she wasn't able to talk to Mykola right now. The last video call had gotten his hopes up; sharing what limited progress they'd made since then would surely dash those hopes.

26

Mykola was surprised he hadn't yet been questioned about his possible role in the escape and riot. It had been nearly 18 hours since the warden had made the announcement that all inmates were to return to their cells and about four hours since the warden and the guards had inspected his cell. He could only assume that since other prisoners had also attempted to escape, Alex was simply being thought of as another who had taken advantage of the confusion. There was no indication that the authorities had seen him as the first one to cross the berm. With as many inmates as had attempted escape, they likely hadn't known that Alex was successful in his attempt until the guards had walked by each cell and noted any prisoners who weren't in their assigned cells.

Sitting on his bunk, Mykola thought through the events of the past day and tried to look at them all from the perspective of the warden, corrections officers, and London Tower administrators. Certainly they had to consider every possibility, including the guards in the control room working with prisoners to create a crisis of opportunity. Would they think the system had been hacked from someone on the outside? Mykola suspected that was the last thing they wanted to find. It would reflect badly on London Tower and their artificial semi-intelligent design. Their relationship with the New California and Arizona corrections departments might be irrevocably damaged. The best the London Tower administrators could hope for was that the event had been an inside job. It would be easy to replace "corrupt" employees and call this a one-time incident. In fact, corrupt employees would strengthen the case for an AI-controlled prison.

Mykola also thought about his interrogation experience when he'd been arrested for the assault in the parking lot. If there was any benefit to that experience, it was that Mykola had a better understanding of what to expect when he was interrogated this time. The difference between that first interrogation and the one he now expected was that he had been completely innocent of the assault, but he was guilty of having taken an active role in Alex's escape. Back then he could tell the truth, but now he couldn't.

Unfortunately, as Mykola had learned, the truth wasn't always believed. He recalled that the more he had professed his innocence, the more aggressive the questioning had become. Just thinking about it made Mykola's pulse race, and he could feel perspiration on his forehead. He recalled the verbal push and pull of the two detectives who had questioned him. Normally well in control of his emotions and quite reserved, he'd found himself taking offense to the accusations of both assaulting Mack Beranger and lying to the detectives about things he thought were inconsequential. I never lied, Mykola thought, but when I rephrased my answers to the same question asked over and over again, they saw that as a lie. I won't do that again.

Mykola wished he could talk to Alex right now. Alex could be gruff and emotional in his responses when it came to his personal interests, but he was also remarkably knowledgeable and insightful about how things worked in the prison. More importantly, he knew how people thought.

Mykola leaned back on his bunk, his shoulders resting on the wall. He could picture Alex sitting across from him, leaning forward with his hands in a praying position. It was his way of showing he was listening and thinking. Suddenly a thought came to Mykola, and he couldn't help but chuckle: Never thought I'd admit this, but I sure could use the help of a psychiatrist right about now.

"On your feet," called one of the two guards now standing outside Mykola's cell gate. They went through the verbal command and confirmation process to open the gate, the process Mykola had seen for the first time just a few hours before. Neither of the guards entered the cell.

"Come with us," the other guard said.

Mykola stepped slowly and quietly out of the cell, his arms hanging loosely at his sides. He could tell the guards were still tense, and the sharp tones of their voices, their furrowed brows, and their forceful hand gestures told him that passive cooperation was his best course of action.

It was a long walk down the corridor, and as they passed the cells, some inmates made comments that would have earned them a jolt had they been made a day earlier. Both prisoners and guards recognized that the cell bars served to limit inmate movement but also served to protect the inmates from the guards.

They continued to the big room in the center of the prison, climbed the stairs to the second floor, and walked down a short hall. Mykola noted the "Warden" sign above a door at the end of the hall, but before they reached it, one of the guards opened a door to a small, six-chair meeting room. He motioned Mykola inside and pointed to a seat with its back facing the door.

The walls in the room were a soothing light beige. Hanging there were a couple of photos of mountain ranges from the Pacific Northwest, capped with snow. Mykola assumed this meeting room was normally used by the warden, shift wardens, and staff. Today, he was sure, it was an interrogation room.

Mykola sat down slowly, rather enjoying the soft padding of the upholstered chair. Before he had a chance to turn around, he heard a click as the guards exited and closed the door behind them. Could this room be on video? Mykola didn't see any of the ceiling-mounted glass half spheres that were in the rest of the prison, but he felt it best to assume someone was watching him. He sat and waited quietly for what seemed like ten minutes, though he couldn't be sure. They're probably just trying to rattle me by making me wait, he thought, promising himself he'd remain calm and then tell the truth when possible. Then he started counting slowly to himself. As he neared 300, the door opened.

Two men entered, one wearing a light blue long sleeve dress shirt with the London Tower logo embroidered on the pocket and the other wearing a navy blue shirt typical of state administrative employees. Both were middle-aged men, clean-shaven, with short-cropped hair.

Mykola glanced at their name tags. The London Tower guy was Marvin Kleib; he wore glasses and had a receding hairline that made him look like a stereotypical accountant. Dominick Kasali, the state representative, was more muscular; Mykola imagined he'd at one time been a guard and had come up the ranks in the New California Department of Corrections.

Kleib put a folder on the table, took out a sheet of paper, studied it for a moment, then simply said "Mykola Steinman" as if he were reading it from the sheet. Terrible actor, Mykola thought. He obviously knew before he came into the room who he was going to be talking to.

"We've got a few questions for you," Kasali said. "This shouldn't take long."

"We assume you are aware that your cellmate, Alex Rodgers, was one of the inmates who attempted an escape yesterday," Kleib began.

The temptation to offer a snappy retort was almost overpowering for Mykola, but he pressed his lips together to prevent himself from doing so. It was as if his emotional side, protecting his self-image now, was battling his logical side, protecting his future self. In this first joust, the logic side won.

"That was what I assumed, since I had seen several inmates attempting to escape and Alex had never returned to the cell. But I couldn't identify any of the inmates I saw running away."

"You saw inmates attempting to escape?"

"Uh-huh. I was in the yard when I heard the announcement that we were to go back to our cells. I was heading back in when a few inmates made a run for the berm."

"Why didn't you join them?"

"I haven't been here all that long, but Sly, the guy who did my orientation, told me the collars we were wearing would deliver a shock that would likely kill us if we crossed the berm. I'm out in seven years, maybe less. It didn't seem like a reasonable risk."

"We have strong evidence that the system malfunction that led to the rioting and escape attempts was not accidental; it was planned," Kasali said.

He paused and studied Mykola for any reaction. Mykola didn't respond, sat still, and gave the impression that he was waiting for an explanation. Waiting too long to say something would be a mistake as well, though; it wasn't normal. Perhaps five seconds had elapsed when Mykola asked, "And why are you telling me this?" His tone was conversational.

"We have transcripts of all your conversations with Alex Rodgers," Kleib continued. "You two appear to have struck up a friendship. You've played chess, he introduced you to the learning lab, and you've been to the infirmary when he was on shift."

"Sure, Alex was a good guy. I was glad to have someone here that I could call a friend. He told me lots about this place that wasn't in the orientation or that booklet we get."

Mykola caught himself talking about Alex in the past tense, implying that he'd only known him in the past, that he didn't expect to see him again. He could only hope neither of the agents had caught that slip. Mykola continued. "He told me about his son and daughter and about some of his experiences here."

"Did he ever mention a desire to break out?"

"I don't know. He might have. Who in any prison doesn't have that fantasy?" Mykola asked, hoping to turn the tables.

"Any specifics about how someone might make that fantasy a reality?" Kasali asked, ignoring Mykola's rhetorical question.

"I don't recall anything. Besides, you've got the transcripts;

if he did say something, you'd already know about it." Mykola let a bit of his emotional side seep through, but that was okay. It was likely what the two agents expected.

"I mean after the gate closed."

"After the gate closed, we'd play chess or Alex would read a book until the lights went out."

This sort of back-and-forth questioning went on for the next hour, with the agents asking for the same information but through different lines of questioning. Mykola knew they were trying to trip him up, to catch him in some inconsistency that would cause him to create a complex web of lies to cover it up. The conversation was a mental strain, but in some ways it reminded Mykola of some of the longest chess games he and Alex had played, classic battles of trying to figure out what the other player's next moves would be. Mykola was determined to win this game with the agents.

At last Kasali said to Kleib, "I think we've got enough information from Steinman to proceed with our investigation."

Kleib nodded, and both got up from the table.

Mykola felt he had won. He hadn't told them anything that would incriminate himself or Alex. The "proceed with the investigation" line was likely a standard way they kept suspects wondering what was next. Mykola's emotional self was ready to have a quiet little internal celebration, but his logic side said no, it wasn't time for that yet.

As Kleib was putting his papers into the folder, he didn't look up as he asked, "Just curious, Steinman: I see you're taking a calculus course through the learning center. What interest does a finish carpenter and furniture maker have in learning calculus?"

"Just something to exercise my brain. They don't let you work with power tools here." It seemed an innocuous question, and Mykola's guard went down a bit more.

"Makes sense. I understand the instructor, Sarah, does a good job of explaining the concepts." Kleib continued his paper shuffle. However, Kasali, standing to the side, kept his eye on Mykola, looking for any sort of physical reaction.

This was it, the final surprise move in this game. Mykola didn't flinch. Turning toward Kasali, he said, "Yup, she does, and I'm learning more than I thought I would. But her name isn't Sarah; it's Brenda."

"Right, right," Kleib said. "I got the names of Rodgers's daughter and the instructor confused. Okay, that's all I've got." He closed his folder and got up from his chair.

Mykola could feel the tension in his shoulders melt. It felt as if a storm had passed and blue skies were on the horizon—even if, for now, the horizon didn't go beyond his prison cell.

A knock on the door of the conference room instantly brought that vision to an end. Kasali opened the door and was given a half sheet of paper by a guard.

"Well, well, this changes everything," Kasali said with a broad smile as he glanced at the paper. He handed it to Kleib.

"How about that!" Kleib exclaimed as he read the message and then looked up at Mykola with a look that reminded Mykola of the look on Alex's face when he announced "checkmate" in a game Mykola was sure he would win. "It says here that the LAPD has apprehended Alex Rodgers, escaped convict from the State Line Prison. He's being held at the county jail and will be transferred here tomorrow."

"He's going to do serious time just for the attempted escape,"

Kasali added, "but as we've already told you, we think he had something to do with the system failure that allowed the escape. If we can tie that to him, he's looking at life in prison, because three men died in all that commotion." He eyed Mykola, again obviously looking for a panicked expression.

It was all Mykola could do to remain calm. A torrent of questions went through his mind. How could this have happened? Had someone turned Alex in? Did the police have any knowledge of Sarah and Allen's roles? Would Alex implicate him?

"We're also pretty sure your cellmate didn't engineer this all by himself. He had help, and it's only logical to assume you were the one to provide the help. When we get him here tomorrow, I figure it'll take about ten minutes of questioning and explaining his alternatives before he cracks and tells us everything.

"Of course, you can help yourself now by coming clean. We don't think you were the mastermind behind this; otherwise you would have tried to escape. Still, anything you did that contributed to Rodgers's escape is going to add to your seven-year sentence. If you tell us what you and Rodgers did—and tell us now—we're sure we can get the prosecutor to go easy on you. If we have to wait for Rodgers to tell us, that's a whole other long—and I mean *very* long—story for you."

Mykola was about to respond when it suddenly occurred to him that he was living the "prisoner's dilemma" Alex had explained to him shortly after they'd become cellmates. So many thoughts were going through his mind, emotions tangled with logic. It was Mykola's turn to speak, and the two other men quietly and motionlessly waited. The quiet made time seem to come to a standstill, but finally Mykola spoke.

"I'm sorry you don't believe me, but I've told you all that I know." With that, he crossed his arms over his chest and leaned back in his chair.

"You made a big mistake, and that's what put you in prison," Kasali said. "Now you're making another big mistake, but maybe you'll come to realize that in the next few hours. Think about it."

Kasali opened the door, motioned to the guard, and asked him to escort Mykola back to his cell.

Back in his cell, Mykola sat on his bunk and took several long, deep breaths. Being told that Alex had been recaptured had been unnerving, and Mykola could still feel his heart pounding. Yet he knew his emotions were focused on the immediate distress he was feeling. They would subside. The simple decision to deny any further knowledge of the plot might at least have bought him some time, just as the agent had told him: "a few hours."

He tried to remember what Alex had told him about the prisoner's dilemma model, thinking that could provide the logic to help him make the best decision. The key was the interaction of both his and Alex's decisions, and the model said that the best outcome, though not an ideal, would come from telling the investigators the truth.

Yet this was more complicated than just two prisoners trying to help themselves. There were other people involved, specifically Alex's daughter Sarah and perhaps his son Allen. The investigators obviously suspected that Sarah was involved; would Alex "give it up" in exchange for a guarantee that no charges would be filed against his children? What about Sarah?

When she found out her father had been recaptured, would she break under the strain and explain exactly what everyone had done, trying to avoid having her father serve the life sentence Kasali had threatened?

Mykola felt an obligation to make the best decision not only for himself but also for Alex and his family. Again his emotional and logical self were having a tussle. Even if there were a simple, logical way to avoid any responsibility for the riot, the thought of achieving this outcome at Alex's expense, or at the expense of Sarah and Allen, would leave a long-term emotional scar.

Then suddenly Mykola thought: That's it! That's it!

For the past half hour he'd been thinking about what Alex and Sarah might say, but he hadn't considered what the investigators were saying. When Alex had explained game theory and the prisoner's dilemma, he hadn't emphasized what the investigators stood to lose or gain based on their decisions. Clearly, a loss for them would be not finding anyone responsible for the riot, injuries, and deaths. A total win would be to convict everyone who had responsibility for this crime. Were they going for the total win, or did they simply intend to avoid a complete loss?

Mykola thought back to the conference room interrogation with the investigators. They had questioned him intensely for an hour, trying to catch him in some inconsistency. But he hadn't fallen for that trap. All those games of chess had had some real-life payoff, Mykola thought. At that moment, he wished Alex could see the smug smile on his face.

Just as the interrogation ended, they got that note that Alex had been recaptured, Mykola thought. How convenient! They knew I didn't have any way of confirming his recapture. They could have waited until Alex was returned to the prison and let me see him, but they didn't. They were lying; he wasn't in custody.

Mykola couldn't be sure he was right, but as thorough as Alex had been in all stages of planning the escape, it seemed unlikely he'd be recaptured so soon.

With that, Mykola made his decision and lay back on his bunk. Minutes later he was asleep.

After a couple of hours, Mykola was awakened by Officer Kasali banging his hand on the cell bars. "You have anything else you want to tell us? This is your last chance."

Mykola slowly put his feet on the floor and pulled himself into a sitting position. With a tone he hoped sounded as if he were tired of giving the same answer again and again, he said, "I wish I did, but I told you everything I know. Now leave me alone."

He looked up to see Kasali standing with his hands clutching his hips and a scowl on his face. They stared at each other for a few seconds as Mykola remained as calm and expressionless as he could.

Kasali walked away.

27

"This certainly isn't what I expected."

Byron was meeting Chris at the AIM headquarters located in a former industrial park in the eastern part of Los Angeles County.

"Isaac, the guy who started this company, did it on a shoe-string," Chris explained. "Though it has steadily grown and we've now got about 20 employees, Isaac is still pinching the pennies. There's usually just an admin and maybe a couple of programmers here; everyone else works from home. If it's a small meeting, we do it here. If it is a big meeting or we've got to impress someone, we meet in a hotel."

"Chris, are you saying I'm not someone you feel a need to impress?" Byron asked in a mocking tone of insult.

"You know that's not the case, Byron," Chris said, looking for a tiny smile from Byron to confirm he was just kidding. "I just thought meeting at our office would enable us to concentrate on the project without interruption. I've turned my phone off; how about you?"

"Done."

Picking a comfortable chair from the eight mismatched chairs around the conference table, Byron sat down and brought up the note file of the Steinman case. Chris did likewise, syncing her tablet to the screen at the back of the room to display her notes there.

"Let me begin with an update as to what the AIM system did," Chris began. "I've entered all the information we got at the meeting the other day as well as the notes you gave me."

"I see that. What are those color bars next to each item?" Byron asked, pointing to the screen.

"That's a confidence level. Whenever we enter information, we have to assign it a confidence level. It's a 20-point color coded scale. If you're very confident it is reliable information, you'll give it a rating of 15 or higher. If you don't have a lot of confidence in it—perhaps it's just a wild idea—you give it a confidence level of five or lower."

"I see you've given some of the notes I've given you a confidence level of 12 or 14," Byron noted with disappointment.

"Don't take it personally. If your confidence in the accuracy of the information is higher, I can change it right now."

"What happens then?"

"It may change the system's recommendations. Even if you don't change it, the AIM system recommendation may be to validate the information you've entered so that you can increase your confidence level. Sometimes the system will do its own validation and automatically increase the confidence level. You'll see a star next to it then, as on point number eight."

"I'm beginning to understand," Byron said almost reverently.

"You've got to leave your ego at the door and be as honest as you can be."

"Exactly, but that also means you shouldn't lower your confidence level just to appear humble. That doesn't help either. I suspect that isn't one of your shortcomings, though, is it?" Chris teased.

"Got me there."

"Let's go on," Chris said. She proceeded to explain that AIM's artificial intelligence system had already begun researching a basis of appeal. She knew Byron had much more legal training than she did, but she needed to earn his confidence, so she verified with him the six most frequent grounds for appeal: violation of privacy; a recent amendment to the US Constitution; a ruling error as to admissible or inadmissible evidence; an illegal search or unlawfully obtained confession; the prosecution's failure to disclose evidence favorable to the defense; incomplete or incorrect jury instructions; and ineffectiveness of defense counsel. Two others, material and undisclosed conflict of interest of the judge or jury and perjury, were far less likely to be used as grounds for appeal.

Because they hadn't added much more information to what was in the trial transcript, system confidence of success in pursuing any of these grounds was under 30 percent.

Chris also showed Byron a summary report of all the trials that had used computer-based facial recognition as a key element in the prosecution's case, as well as a few where the defense had used facial recognition to support the claim of innocence. AIM had searched cases not only in New California but throughout the nation. In 92 percent of these cases, the prosecution had prevailed.

The percentage was even higher in New California. This trend was up as well, climbing steadily over the past five years.

The percentages, Chris explained, would be even higher if the AIM system analyzed cases in which the defendant had pled guilty. Since Mr. Steinman had pled innocent, that percentage was irrelevant.

"I'm sorry Aimee isn't more optimistic, but you don't *want* her to be optimistic. The best advice is always to be realistic, and sometimes that means accepting that you won't win," Chris concluded. "That can all change, of course, if you have new information."

"Aimee?" Byron cocked his head and asked.

"Sorry; I should have explained. My boss doesn't like it, but I get tired of referring to it as our artificial intelligence system or AIM system. 'Aimee' is just my nickname for the system."

"Cute." In the short time he'd been exposed to the system, Byron could see how people could anthropomorphize this mass of silicon chips and lines of code.

"So, you were asking about new information. I've got lots, and I think Aimee will be impressed," Byron said. "Since facial recognition is an 800-pound gorilla, we've got to look for its weak points before attacking it."

He paused. He knew this wasn't lawyer-like talk; he'd have to work on that if he expected people at the firm to take him seriously.

"There are two soft spots: the programming that enables the software to recognize human faces and the representation of what is a unique human face," he continued.

"You've got my attention. Go on. I'm taking notes." Chris looked up from her tablet.

"You've heard of flexible rubber 3D printing, right? It's been fairly crude thus far, mainly used to make high-end Halloween masks of politicians and celebrities. But now the technology has advanced to the point where such masks are given to facial burn victims so that they can go out in public with confidence."

"Yes, I've heard about that; they use the masks until their skin grafting is complete," Chris noted.

"Well, suppose somebody had access to such a high-end 3D printer and made a mask of Mykola Steinman's face? It'd be easy enough to get a picture of him off the web or from his shop's pamphlets."

"You're suggesting someone would present themselves as Mr. Steinman? Whatever for?" Chris asked.

"I don't know what the motivation might be, but isn't it possible?"

"I suppose . . ."

Byron was getting more excited as he built his case before a jury of one. "Now let's take a look at the software side. In this case, the facial recognition software was used to identify Mr. Steinman from a recorded video, not a live feed. It really shouldn't make any difference, and usually it doesn't. However, I asked our private investigator to find out how old that system from the parking lot is. Turns out it's over five years old."

"So? It still works, doesn't it?"

"Yes, it does, but it's old technology. It doesn't include infrared light recording."

"Byron, I'm taking notes, but you're starting to lose me."

"Infrared light is a measure of temperature," Byron explained. "If you use infrared sensing at night, you should be able to see warmer objects like dogs, cats, and people. If whoever slammed Mr. Beranger was wearing a 3D mask that looked like Mr. Steinman, it might have prevented the heat of his face from being registered by even the latest videotape technology. Since in this case the FR software couldn't register any infrared light from the videotape, the entire recognition process was based exclusively on visible light. The attacker might have been a cyborg, for all we know."

Chris could see that Byron was loving this. He spoke with such conviction that he could have convinced her it was possible to raise beef cattle on the moon.

"There's one other thing. Facial recognition focuses on the face. That only makes sense. Now look at this frame capture." Byron displayed a frame of the attack from the video. "The attacker is wearing a long sleeve shirt, long pants, a cap, and gloves. The only skin showing is his face. This is the frame they showed the jury at the trial, zooming in on the face. It was obviously Mr. Steinman or an exact lookalike."

Byron advanced to another image. "This is an image from later in the video. See how he has his head turned away from the camera? You're not seeing his eyes, and from this angle neither you nor the facial recognition software can make out with any confidence who this is."

"I assume the prosecution didn't show this," Chris observed. "No point in it."

"Right," said Byron. "We didn't pay much, if any, attention to it either. I looked at it more carefully yesterday, though, and there's one thing that is different in this image. See how he's got his arm extended? A little bit of his wrist is now exposed."

"Sure I see that, but there's no tattoo or scar or anything that would identify this as someone other than Mr. Steinman,"

Chris responded, now beginning to wish Byron would get to the point a little faster.

"Just look at the color of his skin!" Byron said. "I know there's a shadow and the lighting isn't very good, but the skin appears too dark to be that of a Caucasian."

"Byron, I think you're trying too hard to find something. But I'm going to give this information to Aimee. Now, what confidence do you have that it is the skin of a non-Caucasian man?"

"I can't be sure, but on the 20-point scale, my confidence is 16."

"I think you're being optimistic, but that's what I'll enter."

"Optimistic would be 18 or 19. I think 16 is realistic optimism." Byron smiled broadly, but Chris didn't notice. She was too focused on getting everything entered into the AIM system.

"Anything else?" Chris looked up from her tablet.

"No, that's it. We've got the meeting with Roberta day after tomorrow. Will the AIM system be able to provide some new direction and guidance by then?"

"Most definitely," Chris assured Byron. "I'll just want to double-check my entries and also give my boss an update on what we're doing. I'll be there, and so will Aimee."

"Will I be able to get a preview?" Byron asked with the assumption that it wouldn't be an issue.

"I'm sorry, I can't do that. You've got a lot of yourself invested in this case, and I'm afraid that if I show you the output before we talk to Roberta at the meeting, you're either going to fight it if you don't like it or become overly confident if you do."

"There's that confidence thing again . . ." Byron quipped.

"I think it's important for Roberta to see what you've done

and understand your reasoning but to keep that separate from what Aimee produces. I'm no career counselor, but this could be your moment to shine."

"Okay, I guess I understand. I'll just plan on presenting the information to Roberta the same way I presented it to you, but maybe take it down an octave."

"I like that." Chris smiled and held her look at Byron for just a bit longer than was appropriate for a business meeting.

The group handling the Steinman appeal was scheduled to meet on Friday afternoon at 3:00. Roberta was well aware that this was one of the worst times to schedule an important meeting. It had been a long week, and everyone, including Roberta, was looking forward to getting the weekend started. Yet they were quickly running up against the deadline for filing an appeal, and they had to make some decisions. She would demand that everyone stay focused and not use expedience as an excuse for settling on less than thoroughly reasoned conclusions. If they had to come back Saturday and Sunday, so be it.

It was the same group as last time, but Byron's research and the work done with Chris and the AIM system would occupy most of their time and attention. Roberta couldn't decide whether she hoped the AIM system would show its value or whether she wanted to show she could do anything and everything just as well or better without AIM's help.

Chris began by explaining how she'd entered all of the data she'd been given in the prior meeting. She then shared the AIM system's predictions for success based on data she'd entered prior to her meeting with Byron.

The group today reacted as had Byron a couple of days before: very disappointed. Chris had anticipated that, and before she was asked to defend the system, she explained that she'd entered much more information during the course of her meeting with Byron. She would provide an update from the AIM system after Byron spoke.

Roberta liked Byron and his youthful enthusiasm, but this was the legal world, and sometimes Byron's enthusiasm clouded the hard facts. She was already thinking about how she might have to tell Mykola that they wouldn't be filing an appeal or that it had little to no chance of success if they did file.

Byron presented his findings, emphasizing the possibility of someone wearing a 3D-printed mask to look exactly like Mykola and telling about the outdated security system videotape that was analyzed by facial recognition software. He ended with the video frames that showed a darker skin tone on the wrist and downplayed the possibility that it could be due to the poor lighting or even a deep tan.

"Byron, you've obviously put a lot of effort into your analysis," Roberta said. "I think I speak for everyone here in saying I respect your out-of-the-box thinking and willingness to explore every possibility no matter how improbable it might be."

Everyone nodded, and Joe, the private investigator, gave Byron a subtle "thumbs up" gesture.

"Unfortunately, this isn't going to help us right now. We have to first file and then win an appeal. All the work you've done would come into play after a new trial was granted, but it will not be accepted as the basis for an appeal." Roberta felt she shouldn't have to explain such basics to someone who had graduated from law school and would be taking the bar exam soon, but she did so, in part to keep everyone focused and explain her thinking to the two non-lawyers in the room.

The room was quiet. Finally Chris spoke up. "I think Aimee can help you move forward."

"Aimee? Is that what you're now calling your artificial intelligence system?" Using a girl's name to refer to a complex technological system for which they were paying thousands of dollars just didn't sit well with Roberta. "I thought you said the AIM system reviewed all the avenues of appeal and none had a good chance of success."

Chris was taken aback by Roberta's harsh tone. She took a deep breath and tried to remain in control of herself. She clasped her hands together in a begging gesture but quickly realized that was the wrong message. She then quickly brought her arms out into a welcoming position and spoke clearly and confidently, making eye contact with each person around the table.

"That is correct, as far as traditional appeals are concerned. However, the AIM system—yes, I've gotten into the habit of calling it Aimee—is suggesting that you file an appeal on the basis of the judge's rejection of your request to cross-examine an eyewitness."

"Perhaps I've misunderstood something or your artificial intelligence Aimee isn't as smart as you think," Roberta countered. "The judge never denied us the right to cross-examine any witness. If he had, we wouldn't even be having this meeting."

The tension in the room continued to rise, and Byron felt a need to come to Chris's defense. As he was about to interrupt, Chris looked him square in the eye, shook her head to one side and mouthed "no."

"At one point you asked for an opportunity to examine the

software and hardware used to make the facial identification. The judge denied your request, saying that you had opportunity to cross-examine the AI expert brought in by the prosecution." Chris paused. "I'm paraphrasing what Aimee produced in the report."

"Yes, that's true. We made that request simply because Mr. Steinman demanded it. I was glad it was denied; facial recognition software has been shown to be more than 99 percent accurate, much more accurate and reliable than humans. We likely would have wound up making the prosecution's case for them."

"Again paraphrasing Aimee: the AI expert was representing the facial recognition software," Chris said. "We don't allow representatives to testify for human eyewitnesses. The eyewitnesses have to appear in court. Why shouldn't that be required when the facial recognition is done by AI?"

Byron looked over at Roberta. He couldn't tell if she was confused, outraged, or a little of both. The emotions seemed to cancel one another out, for now she spoke calmly and in perfect control. "So Aimee wants the facial recognition program to be treated as a person? I never heard of such a thing, even in a sci-fi movie."

"This isn't unprecedented. There have been two such cases where judges allowed it. Granted, they were in small communities that didn't have much faith in modern technology, and one judge was 85 years old."

Byron looked around the room. From the postures and concentration shown on everyone's faces, he sensed Chris was starting to make some progress. Ironically, Aimee, the legal artificial intelligence system, was being defended by Chris, with her "limited legal training."

You go, girl, Byron thought, looking at Chris.

"Okay, suppose we take this approach. What is Aimee's estimated probability that we'll be successful?" Roberta posed the question as a dare.

"Let me call that up." Chris tapped a couple of times on her tablet. "Aimee provides two estimates of success: 35 percent and 45 percent."

"What's the difference?" Luis asked.

"I don't think you're going to like this, but here goes: 45 percent if you use Aimee to help write your appeal and accept her coaching and 35 percent if you go it alone." Chris winced and brought up her shoulders in a defensive posture.

Silence. Then Byron couldn't control himself anymore and started to giggle. It spread around the room, and in the seconds that followed, even Roberta was laughing.

"I like confident attorneys, and by any measure, Aimee seems very self-confident." It was Roberta's way of saying she hadn't ruled out the AIM system recommendation.

When things had settled down, Chris began again. "Here's another projection I think you'll find interesting. The other day I entered all the information Byron presented to you today. Before this meeting I entered a query: What is the probability of acquittal for Mr. Steinman, assuming that a new trial is granted on appeal and we make judicious use of the information Byron has supplied?

"The probability is 80 percent."

Byron felt his chest expand. He felt he'd just received a major award. Chris's prophetic words, "You'll have a chance to shine," came back to him.

"Roberta, given this information, I don't think you have any choice but to follow Aimee's advice," Luis suggested.

Roberta brought her hand to her neck and fingered the gold chain around it as she looked up at a painting of a 19th-century courtroom on the far wall. Everyone waited pensively for her response.

She realized she felt threatened by the AIM system. She'd been subconsciously looking for reasons to discount its value. Still, the system's recommendation was all they had. All the work they'd done up until now hadn't produced anything on which to base an appeal. If she said no, she'd have to prepare to give Mr. Steinman some very disheartening news.

"I agree," she said.

The tension in the room melted as everyone sat back in their chairs. Byron glanced at Chris and gave her a satisfied nod.

"Just one more question for you, Chris," Roberta said. "What would the probability of a successful appeal be if Aimee did all the work herself?"

"You mean actually going before the appellate court and making the oral argument in addition to writing the appeal?"

"Right."

Chris tapped a few characters on her tablet. "Funny you should ask that. On a lark, I put in that query this morning. It came back as—here it is—five percent, with the explanation that nobody in power wants to be told by a machine what to do."

"So Aimee even knows what people think of her? She sounds like my ex-wife," Joe blurted out, then was suddenly embarrassed when everyone turned to look at him.

"You could put it that way." Chris looked at Joe and grinned.

"Furthermore, Aimee still isn't smart enough to pick up non-verbal cues on the fly, such as when you're making the verbal argument to the justices. That's something only people can do."

"Aimee certainly sent you a detailed explanation explaining the five percent success estimate. She seems quite modest. Perhaps there's hope for this relationship." Roberta winked at Chris.

"Those weren't the exact words. I rephrased it; Aimee tends to be insensitive in her word choice and, quite frankly, just too honest. It takes time to get used to her; even I have to remind myself that this is an unfeeling machine."

28

It had been a week since the prison riot, and both Sarah and Allen were surprised that they hadn't been contacted by the Department of Corrections or federal investigators. Contacting relatives of escapees just seemed like a logical first step. To Sarah and Allen's knowledge, their father was the only one who hadn't been captured and returned to the prison within six hours of the mass escape attempt. Wouldn't the authorities want to know whether he had tried to contact his family?

The day after the riot, Allen destroyed the computer from which he had uploaded the files to the London Tower system. Instead of bashing, burning, and burying it as they had talked about, Allen simply bleached the hard drive and then took it to an electronics recycling center. That was what Sarah wanted, because she believed in recycling everything that could be recycled and, as her father had told her, it was important to continue the normal patterns of daily living. Allen pointed out that with the computer in their playroom gone, there was a spot on the table that wasn't faded by the sun. Sarah agreed that Allen could buy a replacement computer, again because that was the normal thing to do.

Alex hadn't called. That made sense; everyone these days assumed their phones were bugged and were careful of what they said, even if they weren't trying to protect a prison escapee. Sarah and Allen took it one step further and limited their personal conversations about their father and the escape to those times when there was loud background music or a TV program with plenty of dialogue. Listening devices were becoming increasingly sensitive, and the longer they waited for an investigator to knock on their door, the more they suspected information about their participation was being collected through other means.

Initially Sarah had been concerned that the email communication between Mykola and "Brenda" was still on the NiNo servers, but that second concern had been ameliorated when she'd gotten a call from her contact at NiNo. He'd explained that all the NiNo programs at the prison had been taken off-line because of the riot and that he didn't know when they'd be back online. Sarah took the opportunity to ask him to erase the program and all the associated files, telling him she'd had only two prisoners sign up for the course and one had dropped out a week into it. She and ZG Manufacturing had decided that prisoners weren't going to be a good source of future employees for her company.

He agreed, and while Sarah hadn't gotten confirmation that the files had been erased, she thought it best not to follow up and make sure. That might have led to more questions.

Mykola himself was still an open issue. There was no way to

communicate with him. For all Sarah and Allen knew, Mykola's role in the escape might have been discovered. He might even now be working a deal to reduce his sentence.

Sarah confided her worries to Allen one night while they were watching a TV news talk program.

"What if Mykola gives us up? The investigators can talk to him any time they want, and after a while, the pressure will get to him," Sarah began.

Allen was surprised by the apprehension he heard from Sarah. They'd both known from the beginning that Mykola was the outsider invited to join this escape plan and that they didn't know anything about him other than that he was the trusted cellmate of their father.

"Sis, I'm not going to worry about it. If he was going to rat us out, he could have done that days or even weeks ago."

"I know that," Sarah replied, "but if they find out he had a part in the escape plan, his loyalty to Dad and us will be tossed aside in exchange for special consideration."

"Look, the fact that he didn't try to escape that night is probably a good thing for us."

"What do you mean?" Sarah was once again preparing to argue with Allen's alternative system of logic.

"If the investigators had any notion that Mykola was involved in Dad's escape, they'd expect that he would have tried to escape as well. And that was the original plan. The fact that he didn't try to escape, when Dad and several others *did* escape, gives him credibility when he says he didn't know anything about it."

"You're assuming that's what he's saying, Allen."

"That right, but you're assuming he's going to fall over in the next gust of wind coming out of some investigator's mouth.

You'd have a real right to worry if Mykola had escaped and they'd caught him, but he didn't escape. So stop worrying. If an investigator comes knocking and senses that you're worried about something, you may be the one who brings down this tower of deception we've built."

Sarah was amazed at what she was hearing. Allen's logic was spot-on, and his counsel to avoid worry was what she might have offered him if he'd been the anxious one.

"Thanks, Allen. I needed that."

"Anytime, sis. You can always count on me to provide exemplary service with a sneer."

Allen is maturing, Sarah thought, but he's still Allen.

⊙

The expected knock came the following Monday. Allen had already left for school, and Sarah was just checking the kitchen to be sure the stove had been turned off and anything that belonged in the refrigerator hadn't been left on the counter. That was her routine before heading off to work.

When she heard the knock, Sarah jumped a bit, then took two deep breaths, walked over, and opened the door. Two strangers stood there.

"Ms. Rodgers, I'm Dominick Kasali with the New California Department of Corrections, and this is Marvin Kleib, a representative of London Tower. We'd like to talk to you about your father. We assume you're aware that he has escaped from the State Line Prison."

Each of them handed her a business card. Marvin Kleib's card said he was VP of security systems.

"Yes, I heard about the riot and that several prisoners had

escaped, including my father. I was just heading off to work now, though," Sarah said respectfully. "Can we do this some other time?"

"Ms. Rodgers, this shouldn't take long," Kleib said.

Sarah could read between the lines: either it was now or they'd find some other time and location that would be less comfortable for her. Already she could sense that Kasali was the one in charge. He'd done the introductions, standing a step forward of Kleib, and he looked Sarah in the eye. Kleib looked a bit unsure of himself, happy to have Kasali take the lead. As with many people Sarah knew in the IT field, Marvin Kleib's extroverted characteristics were clearly learned and practiced, not instinctive.

"All right, come in. I just need to call my office and let them know I'll be late." Sarah swung the door wide open and pointed them to the living room as she took out her phone and walked into the kitchen.

The agents made a point of looking at the framed photos and pictures in the hallway and living room. There were the usual family photos, showing a young Alex Rodgers and his wife, Sarah and Allen at various ages, and the family dog, many taken in front of a home where they presumably had lived.

This house was neat, clean, and well organized. The furniture in the living room was of a modern design and in complementary colors, but dated. Everything in this room indicated it wasn't lived in; there had to be another room in which Sarah and her brother spent most of their time.

Sarah wished she hadn't had that second cup of coffee this morning. The caffeine normally got her into work mode, but now it was just making her anxious. Be calm, she told herself— but she feared her self wasn't listening.

Calling her office helped, however. She provided some instructions to her assistant, rescheduled a morning meeting, and replied to a voice mail. She was in charge. She decided she'd maintain that same "in charge" attitude in talking to the agents.

"Please have a seat," she said to the agents as she walked into the living room. The men sat on the sofa while she perched on a nearby armchair. "Now, how can I help you?"

"When did you last speak with your father?" Kasali asked.

"I'm not sure. It has been some time." Sarah assumed that all of her phone and email records had already been reviewed by the agents. To move this conversation along, there was no sense in trying to hide anything—or at least anything that wasn't going to expand their investigation. "Mostly we communicate via email, and even that isn't often."

"We're aware of that; seems rather strange, since the prison is pretty liberal with email and videoconference privileges. Just looking at the photos in the hall, it appears you've had a happy family life. Seems you would want to stay in close contact with your father."

Sarah looked down with a sad expression to give herself time to think about how to respond to the question. Would it be the truth or some fabrication? She decided the truth would be easier to remember.

"We were a happy family, but when my father was convicted of defrauding the National Health Care System, among other things, I felt that was a bad reflection on me."

"How so?"

"I was applying for an IT job with NASA, and as you probably know, they do a thorough background check. They never came out and said it, but I'm pretty sure his criminal activity had something to do with my application rejection. I've harbored resentment ever since, and he knows it." This was the first time Sarah had said this to anyone, and in doing so, she realized it was the truth.

Sarah now turned to Marvin Kleib. "As for the liberal email and videoconference policies, I'm fairly sure none of that communication is private. You've got programs scanning every word, looking for something that could imply illegal activity. Isn't that right, Mr. Kleib?"

"We inform prisoners on day one that all communication is subject to monitoring and censorship." Kleib could feel the tables turning. He just as quickly turned them around once again. "Are you suggesting that your father wasn't writing emails because he was engaged in something illegal and wanted to hide it?"

"I don't know what he was thinking or doing. I just know we didn't have much to talk about. Now, are there some other questions I can answer for you?"

"Ms. Rodgers, you work in the cybersecurity department of ZG Manufacturing, isn't that correct?"

"Yes, I've been there for nearly four years."

Sarah had suspected this would be coming, but at this point she had no idea how much the agents knew. Best to simply respond to the questions directly, without supplying more information than was asked for.

"We are convinced that the prison riot was caused by operational failure of the security system."

Sarah was tempted to play dumb and ask what "operational failure" meant, but that might lead down a path where she had to pretend even more ignorance. She simply listened.

"It might be a programming error that slipped through our

beta testing, or it might be something else. We have hired a company that investigates cybersecurity breaches to help us determine what happened," Kleib explained.

"We'd like to bring them in to review your personal technology," Kasali added. "It would be much more efficient than an extended face-to-face review. We're making this request of everyone associated with prisoners who attempted escape."

Sarah noted Kasali's careful phrasing that it was a request rather than a demand.

Both Kasali and Kleib saw the wary look on Sarah's face. In this day and age, everyone was concerned about protecting their privacy, even if they weren't part of a criminal investigation.

"Ms. Rodgers," Kleib said, "you know that when there is a security issue in a computer system, the best course of action is to quickly eliminate the simple causes. No sense engaging in an international expedition before you look around your own neighborhood. That's what we want to do, and we fully expect to cross you off the list just as quickly as this process is completed."

"That makes sense, Mr. Kleib." Sarah paused and Kleib smiled, expecting that the next words from Sarah would be "I agree." That would also please Kasali. Instead Sarah continued, "However, I don't know exactly what you're looking for, and I suspect you don't either. I certainly wouldn't allow another company to go into the ZG files in my office, and I won't agree to have your hired contractor going into my personal files. For all I know they're going to extract data that'll be used to steal my identity or plant spyware on my computer. Also, if my supervisor at ZG finds out you're reviewing my files, I'm fairly sure my security clearance there will be suspended."

"We certainly don't want to create any problems for you with your employer," Kleib said in an almost apologetic tone.

"However, if necessary, we'll get a warrant for an electronic search." Kasali was back in charge, and he pronounced each word in this threat slowly and carefully. "Think it over. In the meantime, could I use your bathroom? I'm afraid the greasy breakfast I had isn't agreeing with me."

"Certainly. Down the hall; first door on the left." Sarah had seen enough crime dramas on TV to know that this was probably an excuse to look in any open doors, but she also saw it as an opportunity to talk to Kleib one on one. She waited until Kasali got up and was out of earshot before returning her attention to Kleib.

"Mr. Kleib, I've followed the news reports on the riot quite closely, and everything I've heard so far indicates that it was precipitated by an inmate who attacked a guard. Both the guard and inmate died as a result—"

"Actually, there was a second inmate who died in the riot, a young man," Kleib interrupted.

"Oh, that's right. I was sorry to hear it." Sarah paused as if in a moment of prayer, then continued, "But, as I understand it, he wasn't the cause of the riot. Now you're telling me you think it might have been the result of a programming failure and that the failure might have been intentional?" Sarah didn't wait for a response. "Seems to me that you've hired a company to investigate you and your department. The best result for you is that they don't find anything."

Kleib shifted out of his investigator role and listened to Sarah as a fellow respected IT administrator. "Exactly what do you mean, that it would be best to find nothing?"

"Well, is it possible that your code is bad and the flaw should have been caught in beta testing, yet you rushed it through to get it online in accordance with your state contract? Maybe you already know that. Another possibility is that your cybersecurity had so many holes in it that a 16-year-old could break through."

Sarah was aware she was making a veiled reference to Allen, but the image of a lonely, ostracized 16-year-old working alone at night on his computer was too strong to pass up. She hesitated as she watched Kleib taking it all in.

"It might also have been operator error," she went on. "Maybe the guards on duty weren't properly trained on how to use the system, one error led to another, and you had a riot. If the company you hired comes to any of these conclusions, you're going to see lawsuits from every relative of the men who died or were seriously injured in the riot. Still, I know you want to get to the truth, Mr. Kleib."

Kleib tried to maintain his composure but realized Sarah had made a good argument for not opening the proverbial can of worms. Sarah knew she'd delivered her message as she saw Kleib's face turn pale. Still, she couldn't resist the temptation to pile on.

"Finally, I read in a financial report about London Tower that a number of employees had been laid off recently with the intention of reducing cash burn. I assume that includes some people in your department."

Dominick Kasali walked back into the living room and remained standing. "Have you decided, Ms. Rodgers? Can we bring in our experts, or do we have to get a warrant?" As he spoke, he could see that Kleib had slouched down just a bit on the couch and didn't look up at him.

"I'm sorry, you'll have to get that warrant," Sarah said. "Just as soon as you leave, I'm going to call my attorney and see what rights I have. Good day, gentlemen. I think we're done."

⊙

It was about 4:00 that afternoon when Allen came home. Walking into the kitchen, he found his sister sitting at the island counter with a nearly empty bottle of Scotch and a glass with melting ice cubes before her. Everything in the kitchen was clean; in fact, Allen had never seen the stainless surfaces shine so brightly or every canister and countertop appliance perfectly arranged. Even the grout in the tile floor was so clean that it looked new.

"Sis, what's going on? Are you drunk?" He knew that Sarah seldom drank alcohol and that when she did, it was among friends. A glass of rosé was her preference, not Scotch on the rocks. He also knew that cleaning the kitchen—or any room in the house—was her way of calming herself and thinking through a problem. A perfectly clean kitchen and his sister drinking were an incongruous image.

Sarah hadn't turned to look at him when he'd come in, but now, in response to his question, she lifted her head and faced him. Her puffy, reddened eyes told Allen that the midday Scotch was not part of a private celebration.

"No, I'm not drunk. I found the bottle in the back of a cabinet with just a bit left in it. I thought it might help. It tastes terrible, and it didn't help."

"Then what is it? What happened?" Allen's tone was intense and demanding.

"Some investigators from the prison came by, just as we

thought they might," Sarah replied as she once again turned her head away from Allen.

"What, Dad's back in prison?" Allen was impatient with his sister, and his voice become louder with every word. "Did they find out about our hack?"

"No, and please keep your voice down," Sarah implored, still sensitive to the possibility of their conversations being electronically monitored. "It seems Dad is still on the run. They suspect a bug in the system was the catalyst for the prison riot, but right now they're not sure whether it was a bit of bad code or whether someone planted it."

"Do they suspect us?" Allen came closer and softly asked, afraid of the answer Sarah would give him.

"They might, but I think I convinced at least the London Tower guy to look elsewhere. I can't be sure, but I think we're okay."

Allen realized his tone of voice had been harsh and only contributed to Sarah's downcast affect. Now he spoke with calm concern. "Then what is it, Sarah? You're obviously upset about something."

"Well, you and I heard on the news that a guard and two inmates had died in the riot. Mr. Kleib, the guy from London Tower, brought that up during the interview as well. I didn't ask him for any details; I just assumed all three died in fights between inmates and guards."

Sarah looked up at Allen, her eyes once again glistening with tears.

"After they left I started to wonder why Mr. Kleib would share that with me. So I went online and got the whole story.

One of the inmates wasn't killed by a guard or another inmate. He died as a result of the collar—a shock from the collar he was wearing."

"I'm sorry to hear that," was the only response Allen could think of at that moment.

"Allen, he was 19 years old, just three years older than you, and this . . ." Sarah had to pause to catch her trembling breath. "This was his first day in the prison. He was in prison for theft, and we turned it into a death sentence."

"No, no," Allen argued. "I switched those codes, and it couldn't have been to someone there on their first day. He must have done something that triggered that—what do they call it?—that Level 3. We didn't kill him; it was the system that killed him. It was the system Dad told us about. It has too much power and control."

Allen was fighting the temptation to share in Sarah's self-doubt.

"No, Sarah. This was just an example of the system going terribly wrong. Maybe it'll get everyone to rethink this idea of a prison run by some crude artificial intelligence."

"Perhaps you're right. Still, I have to wonder if this would have happened if we hadn't hacked the system." Sarah was aware that Allen's extra bit of code change could well have been the cause of the riot, but trying to allocate blame at this point wasn't going to help. "I just wish we could do something for that young man's family. They must be grieving terribly."

"I do too, but you have to know that would just put us under the spotlight again. Please don't say anything to anyone about this," Allen asked hopefully.

"Yes, I know you're right. It wouldn't change anything; it would just give me a temporary feeling of peace. You know, I can almost hear Dad's words in your voice. That's exactly what he would say if he were here."

The full lockdown of the State Line prison remained in effect for eight days. During that time, all but those who had less than one year of their prison sentences to serve remained in their cells. The short-timers were assigned to laundry and kitchen duties as well as general cleanup. Email, videoconferencing, and learning lab privileges were suspended for everyone. Additional guards were brought in from other prisons, and all guards worked a 52-hour week. That meant 16 hours of overtime.

The additional guards were needed to provide security because the collar-based system was still being updated, and there was no word as to when it would be reinstituted. London Tower was, however, pressuring the Arizona and New California correction departments to approve the updated software as quickly as possible. The additional guards, especially with the overtime pay, were costing London Tower much more than they had anticipated. Furthermore, they argued that keeping

80 percent of the prisoners in lockdown was cruel: they had attorneys help them make that case.

It was finally agreed that one wing of the prison would reinstitute the collars as a test. Prisoners with less than four years remaining of their sentences would be assigned to that wing and their routines, with some exceptions, returned to pre-riot standards. The big exception was access to the outdoors. Guards were now stationed by the three doors that led to the yard. Outside, a 12-foot barbed wire fence was being built just outside the Level 1 warning berms. The Arizona and New California agencies had not decided if this was to be temporary. The electronic collars and updated system software first had to be proven to be reliable.

For Mykola the days dragged. He was glad to have a couple of paperback books to read in the cell, and he occupied a good portion of the day doing sit-ups, push-ups, and leg presses against the concrete wall. Meals, which had been served to prisoners in the cells for the first couple of days, were now served in the chow hall. Prisoners from one wing at a time were released and escorted to the chow hall for lunch and dinner; breakfast was still served in the cell and consisted of a cold breakfast sandwich, some raisins or a banana, and bottled tea.

"You've got a call from your attorney," the guard said one day as he handed Mykola a phone through the bars. This was the first contact Mykola had had with anyone outside the prison since the riot.

"Great, but do I have to talk to her from my cell? Can't I get some privacy?" Mykola asked before the guard had a chance to step away.

"That is your right." The guard motioned to another guard down the corridor and, using confirmed voice commands, the cell gate was opened. At least that component of the electronic security system was still functional, Mykola observed. The guards led him to another cell closed on all four sides. Inside was a small table and two bolted-down chairs. Mykola was told to press the "end" button when the call was complete: that would signal the guards, and they'd come and escort him back to his regular cell.

"Press 'hold'; she should still be there," the guard said as he exited the room.

"Mykola Steinman, is that you?" The familiar voice on the phone sounded sweet and melodious, at least to someone who hadn't heard a female voice in about a month.

"It is, Roberta. I was starting to wonder if you'd forgotten about me."

"I'm very sorry. I was going to call you and give you an update a couple of weeks ago, but after the riot they said only urgent calls would be accepted. I could have said it was urgent, but I figured it best not to push the system when it really wasn't necessary."

"So you're saying there's nothing new?" Mykola asked as his shoulders slumped and he looked down at the floor.

"No, quite the contrary. In fact, I have excellent news, better than I would have been able to report a couple of weeks ago."

"And that is . . . ?" Mykola now stood up straight and pressed the phone harder against his ear.

"We filed an appeal, and I was surprised at how quickly the appellate court issued a ruling. Perhaps the riot at the prison got their attention and they felt that prisoners in the State Line prison deserved to have their appeals reviewed and ruled upon promptly. The bottom line is this: you've been granted a new trial." Roberta paused, expecting some sort of jubilant response from Mykola, but he was quiet. "In addition, we've uncovered some new evidence, and based on that evidence we have a new strategy we believe will give us a greater likelihood of getting your conviction overturned."

Roberta explained how they had convinced the court of appeals that the facial recognition software should be treated as an eyewitness and therefore should be subject to cross-examination, something that hadn't been allowed in Mykola's first trial. Roberta didn't mention the AIM program's part in the process; Mykola didn't need to know that.

"I can explain the strategy to you in person after the bail hearing."

"Roberta, that's wonderful news. After everything that's happened here since I last talked to you, it's especially welcome. There may be a problem, however; I don't know for sure."

"What is it?" Roberta suddenly felt that the balloon of optimism aboard which she was riding was about to burst.

"I don't know if you've followed the news on the riot and the escapes, but the only prisoner who escaped and wasn't recaptured was my cellmate, Alex Rodgers. There's an investigation as to what precipitated the riot, and some believe either a prisoner or outside associate hacked the system and caused its malfunction. I've never seen so many guys get Level 2 shocks. Anyway, since my cellmate was one of the prisoners who attempted escape, I've been questioned as to my knowledge of any plans he may have had."

"And what did you tell the investigators?"

"I told them I didn't know anything about what he was thinking or doing."

"Mykola, the bail hearing is set for tomorrow, and the Department of Corrections has already been informed. If they have evidence that you were part of an escape plan, I'm sure they've told the prosecutor, and he'll use that to either request that the judge deny bail or increase it dramatically. You haven't been charged with anything to this point. The only thing for me to do is focus on the assault for which you've been wrongly convicted."

"Roberta, you know I don't have a lot of assets. If the bail amount is substantial, I'm not likely to be able to post it, and I don't know of anyone who would post it for me."

Roberta had dealt with a number of prison inmates over the years. They were all anxious to be granted parole or have their convictions overturned, but when it appeared they'd actually be walking out of the prison, there was still a lingering doubt, a nagging sense that something would suddenly and unexpectedly derail their plans. Mykola, it seemed, was no different. That hesitancy was what Roberta heard in his concern about posting bail, but it surprised her in that Mykola had been in prison for less than a year.

"Let's not get ahead of ourselves," she said. "We'll find out tomorrow where you stand, and then we'll decide what to do next. Regardless of the outcome of the bail hearing, we're going to continue preparing for the new trial. We've asked for a short date and hope it'll be calendared within six weeks."

"Thank you. I'd certainly like to be able to go outside one night and not worry about being in my cell by 8:00."

With less than six weeks before the trial, Roberta knew she'd have to begin pulling in new evidence to support their case for Mykola's innocence. It wouldn't be enough to simply prove that the facial recognition software could be wrong; they had to show that it was wrong in identifying Mykola as the attacker. Anything short of that would send Mykola back to prison to serve the full term of his sentence.

Joe had been assigned to find out what Beranger's Haitian partner might know about the attack and to learn about the 3D-mask-making industry. Joe was scheduled to meet with Roberta and Byron to provide an update, but he postponed the meeting twice, once because he said he was having trouble linking different elements of his investigation and the second time because of a dental emergency.

Roberta suspected the dental emergency was just a convenient excuse to get a bit more time. Joe had other clients in addition to the law firm, and perhaps their work took priority. Regardless of how much or how little Joe had found out, Roberta couldn't wait any longer. She demanded he come in and provide an update. He sat with Roberta and Byron now.

"Sorry about canceling our meeting the other day, Roberta. I had an abscess that was giving me so much pain I could hardly think."

"But you're better now?" Roberta asked out of politeness, not waiting to hear the answer. "Let's hear what you've got."

"Yes, much better now, thanks." The air-conditioning in Roberta's office was set so low that Joe was tempted to get up and walk around to generate some body heat. Roberta's impatience added to that frosty feeling, and he quickly decided to address that first. "I think I have some good news for you. I met Oliver Franklin, Beranger's former partner on the police force. I tracked him down in a café eating breakfast and invited myself to join him. He recognized me from the bar and, like any good cop, knew that I knew something about him before I even gave him my name."

"Okay, we've got the scene. What did he tell you?"

"I told him I knew Beranger was holding something over him. I didn't know what, but I was sure to find out soon enough. I told him it would be better for him to explain it to me now.

"Turns out a couple years ago Franklin shot a man in the line of duty, and an internal investigation was pointing to him not showing appropriate restraint in accordance with police procedures and training. Beranger was there and made up some story that put much of the blame of the bad shooting on himself. Beranger was given the option of early retirement, and Oliver Franklin kept his job."

Joe slid forward on his chair and ran his hand through his hair.

"Well, ever since then, Beranger has been taking advantage of Franklin. The attack that was caught on video was, according to Franklin, staged. Franklin agreed to participate but said this would be the last time he'd do a favor for Beranger. The debt was paid off."

"Participate? How did he participate?" Roberta hoped it was more than incidental support of the staged attack.

"Byron, it was you who pointed out the exposed dark skin of the wrist on the video. When I mentioned that to Oliver, he came clean. He was the one who hit Beranger with that bat."

"Am I understanding this correctly? Beranger staged a physical assault upon *himself*? Why on earth would he do that?"

"For a woman, of course," Joe said. "Well, I don't mean 'of course' . . ." Joe was embarrassed by his choice of words.

"I get your drift; don't worry. What woman?"

"Here's what Franklin told me. Beranger was convinced that Steinman was making unwanted advances toward his wife. His wife claimed she'd done all she could to discourage Steinman and that she was afraid of him. Beranger, in turn, convinced his old partner Franklin that his wife was a victim and that Steinman deserved a couple years in prison for disrupting his happy marriage."

"You're kidding, right? That's the most preposterous story I've ever heard," Roberta asked incredulously.

"I'm not kidding. Franklin seems too gullible and naive to be a good cop. I have no doubt that Beranger took advantage of Franklin's trusting nature.

"I have to confess: I should have seen there was something amiss in the video the first time I saw it, before Steinman's first trial." Joe looked at Roberta and paused. "A civilian who hit someone with a bat in that way would likely have broken his victim's back. Cops, on the other hand, are trained in how to use billy clubs so that they can disable someone temporarily without causing permanent injury. And the hit probably looked harder than it was; I'm sure Beranger added to the drama by falling down on the asphalt and remaining there."

"Okay. That by itself didn't make or break our defense. Now, did Franklin say he wore a mask?" Roberta was intent on staying focused, and self-pitying confessions weren't of much interest at this point.

"Yes, he did. But he said he took it off and threw it away just as soon as he was out of the parking lot and was sure he wasn't on camera anymore."

"So Mykola really is innocent," Byron said.

A quiet, uncomfortable stillness dropped down into the room.

Finally Roberta shifted her chair so that she could face both Joe and Byron. "He told me that again and again, and I wanted to believe him. But the facial recognition was a piece of evidence that was virtually impossible to argue against—either with a jury or in my own mind. I thought he must have committed the attack, but I did believe him when he said he hadn't had designs on Beranger's wife. The only explanation I could come up with was that Mykola was simply defending his honor, that he wouldn't tolerate Beranger accusing him of something he didn't do, especially in a public place. Of course I couldn't present that to the jury, but it's what I thought.

"And then when Mykola wouldn't consider any avenue of appeal that didn't completely exonerate him of the assault . . . well, that only served to reinforce my impression of him as a man who demanded respect at any cost."

"I know as defense attorneys it's our job to defend our client whether he's guilty or innocent," Byron said. "But I have to say, I like Mykola, and I'm glad to hear he really is innocent."

"So am I, and thanks to your work"—Roberta pointed first to Byron and then to Joe—"I think we've now got a way to prove that Mykola's honor and pride are justified."

Roberta brought her hand to her chin and looked upward, as if the plan were written on a board behind Joe and Byron.

"This is important, Joe. Did you find out who made the mask and if they can make another one?"

"I figured you might want to know that. Oliver didn't know who had created it, but there are three companies in the area that make them. They produce lots of masks for the entertainment industry, like for stunt doubles. A lot of their clients are foreign politicians, too."

"Foreign politicians . . . ?" Roberta asked, perplexed.

"Third world politicians sometimes use body doubles when they're making public speeches or want to be seen among the people: lots of good press without the risk of assassination. It's really quite remarkable what they'll do to protect themselves and their public image—"

Roberta twirled her right index finger in a "hurry it up" signal. Joe got the point.

"Anyway, I got lucky. The first one I went to, 3D Expressions, recognized the picture of Mykola I brought in and said they could produce a duplicate in about 24 hours. If we need it in less time, there'll be an extra charge."

"Did they ask why we wanted another copy of the mask?"

"They didn't, but I explained that we had damaged the first one in a movie we were shooting. I said Mykola was an up-and-coming star in Eastern Europe."

"How's the mask applied?" Byron asked, leaning in closer.

"It's pretty interesting," Joe said. "They start with—"

Joe was a big fan of action movies and loved to talk about how they were made, but Roberta stopped him in mid-sentence.

"Byron. Joe. You can talk about this some other time. Please."

"Sorry," Joe replied sheepishly.

"Order an exact duplicate of the mask Oliver Franklin was wearing that night. Make it a rush order, even if it costs twice as much. I think we're almost there." Roberta reached up and repositioned her glasses.

"Consider it done."

"Good. Next step: can you get Franklin to come into our office? He's potentially in a lot of trouble, and he's going to need a lawyer."

"I think so, but what if he says no? The conversation we had was private, and he can deny it."

"Joe, we want him on our side, so threatening him isn't the best approach. Simply tell him we can work together for our mutual benefit. I can explain it to him when he comes into our office . . . not later than the day after tomorrow."

"Okay, I can do that . . ." Joe paused.

"What is it, Joe? Speak up!" Roberta's impatience with Joe was boiling over.

"Roberta, though I don't know what you're planning to do, isn't there a potential ethical issue here? I mean, I'm no lawyer, but if you're thinking about representing two clients with potentially opposing interests, isn't that going to get you in hot water?"

Roberta sat back and collected her thoughts. Calmly, and in a much softer voice, she replied, "Joe, you always seem to find the problems and inconsistencies in anyone's story. That's what makes you a good investigator. And you are right about the potential conflicting interests. I don't think I have a conflict, but appearances matter. Tell Franklin he must bring his own attorney with him to this meeting. His attorney will be able to tell him if what I'm going to propose is in his best interest."

Joe met with Oliver Franklin later that afternoon. Though

Franklin was initially hesitant to come in and see Roberta, Joe made a convincing case. The truth was going to come out sooner or later, and it was better to act now and help himself. Meeting with Roberta was his best choice if he hoped to avoid serious prison time.

To further assuage Franklin's concerns, Joe strongly suggested that he bring his attorney to the meeting. He reminded Franklin that he only had to listen to Roberta. He would not be under any obligation or expectation to talk about his part in the staged attack. Oliver agreed. Joe called the office and set up a time for Roberta and Oliver to meet privately.

Oliver and his attorney met Roberta at the appointed time. While Oliver quietly listened, his attorney had several questions for Roberta. They were all answered to his satisfaction, and he recommended that Oliver go along with Roberta's plan. It was agreed that Roberta would contact Oliver's attorney if anything changed and before asking Oliver to commit to anything beyond what they had agreed to in the meeting. Sixty minutes later they left.

Mykola's bail hearing was much ado about nothing. He was brought to the courtroom in ample time to update Roberta on things that had transpired since their phone call, but there was nothing. Mykola had experienced no further interrogation from the officers investigating the riot and escape. Furthermore, none of the other prisoners had been interrogated in the past couple of days, or at least that was the scuttlebutt. Perhaps the investigation had concluded.

Mykola pleaded not guilty in a firm and confident voice.

The prosecutor was asked for a bail recommendation, and both Roberta and Mykola were surprised to hear him suggest $100,000. That was within Mykola's means: he could get his partner in the furniture and finish carpentry shop to arrange posting that amount on his behalf.

The prosecutor did not mention the fact that Mykola was being investigated in connection with the prison riot and escape attempts, though surely he would have been informed by prison administration when Mykola's appeal for a new trial was granted. Roberta knew enough not to turn over rocks to see what was under them.

When Mykola nodded upon hearing the $100,000 recommendation, Roberta did not object. By the end of the day the bond had been posted through a bail bondsman, and Mykola was free to go home and keep the lights on until the early morning hours.

"Mr. Eisen, this is Roberta Marshall, Mykola Steinman's attorney." A day after the bail hearing, Roberta was on the phone to the prosecutor.

"What can I do for you?"

"My client would like to discuss a plea deal."

"So soon? I must say I'm surprised. With all the work you put into the appeal, I would have thought you'd be working hard and preparing for the retrial."

"I can't say it's my idea. I'm confident we have enough evidence to convince a jury that Mr. Steinman did not assault Mr. Beranger. However, my client is risk-averse and would like to get this settled without a trial if possible."

"I'm willing to listen, but we got a conviction once, and I see no reason why we shouldn't get a conviction again."

"Can we meet in our offices?" Roberta asked. Knowing that such meetings were usually held in the prosecutor's office, she explained, "You see, I'm having cataract surgery tomorrow, and for the next week the ophthalmologist wants me to stay inside and avoid bright lights. Just walking through your brightly lit hallways would be unpleasant."

Stuart Eisen agreed to meet with Roberta in her office that Friday at 1:00.

When Eisen arrived, Byron met him in the lobby and walked him into Roberta's office. As Eisen had expected, the office lighting was subdued. The shades had been drawn and the rheostat turned down so that the lighting in the office approximated that of an old-fashioned cocktail lounge. It took a few seconds for Eisen's eyes to adjust.

"Thanks for meeting us here," Roberta said. "My client will be here in just a moment. Let's sit at my conference table."

Almost as soon as Roberta said this, the office door opened and Mykola walked in, his hands in his pockets. "Oh, there you are; please sit here next to me. Mr. Steinman, this is Stuart Eisen; I think you remember him from the bail hearing."

Mykola looked over at Eisen and nodded but said nothing.

There was something odd about Steinman, Eisen thought. At the bail hearing he'd been alert and displayed an air of confidence, but today he seemed withdrawn and decidedly uncomfortable.

"Let's get right to the point," Roberta said. "We're here to propose a plea deal. As we agreed, Mr. Steinman"—here she looked directly at Mykola—"I'll do the talking."

Stuart Eisen looked over at Mykola, but his head was bowed and Eisen could not make eye contact with him.

"My client wishes to plead guilty to a lesser charge in exchange for a reduced sentence," Roberta continued.

"As I mentioned to you on the phone," Eisen said, "I don't see my office as having a weak case here, but let's hear it. What specifically do you have in mind?"

"Criminal facilitation, with a three-year suspended sentence," was Roberta's immediate reply.

"I'm sorry, but I thought you'd have a serious proposal. This is a waste of my time and yours." Eisen pushed back his chair, got up, and took a step toward the door.

"Wait," Roberta said, motioning for him to sit back down. "Before you go, my client would like to share some information about the assault that didn't come out in the original trial."

Satisfying his curiosity was worth another minute or two. Eisen sat back down. "Go ahead, Mr. Steinman," he said.

"Mr. Steinman did not hit Mack with the baseball bat," said the man he was addressing. "I did."

With that, the man Eisen had thought was Mykola Steinman brought his hands up out of his lap and rested them on the table.

Eisen was stunned, first by the deep voice with an English Caribbean accent and then by the hands. Even in this dim light, he could see they were of a darker tone than the most suntanned Caucasian might have—even a California surfer.

"What sort of joke is this supposed to be?" Eisen said disdainfully. It was the only thing he could think to say.

"It's not a joke," Roberta said. "This is Mr. Oliver Franklin. Both he and Mr. Steinman are my clients. Mr. Franklin is wearing a mask, a perfectly crafted 3D printed mask which, I'm sure you will agree, makes him look exactly like Mr. Steinman."

"Well, in this low light, sure he looks like Steinman, but I could sense there was something amiss the moment he walked in, though I couldn't put my finger on it."

"The lighting here is set at the same illumination level as that in the parking lot on the night of the assault. You were fooled by the mask, and so was the facial recognition program, the cornerstone of your prosecution."

Roberta had Eisen cornered; it was now just a matter of letting him escape gracefully.

"But I knew this man wasn't Steinman," Eisen objected.

"Perhaps so, but only because you've previously met him and were familiar with his mannerisms. The computer recognition system didn't use sound, gait, mannerisms, or any other unique human measures to confirm the visual match."

Eisen sat stunned. A case he'd won easily the first time had been overturned, and now there was a good possibility he'd lose the retrial.

"It takes about twenty minutes to put the mask and makeup on and another five to ten minutes to remove it. Mr. Franklin, why don't you go take off the mask and get cleaned up, and in the meantime I'll explain everything to Mr. Eisen."

Oliver got up from his chair and stood behind it for a moment until Stuart Eisen looked up and made eye contact. Oliver smiled broadly. Eisen shuddered. He was still spooked by seeing a near duplicate of the man he'd seen in a courtroom just days before, and the odd warping of the mask as Oliver smiled added to the uncanny feeling.

Roberta then shared with Eisen everything she knew about

the staged assault. She still hadn't confirmed Mack Beranger's motivation in staging something so elaborate, but with Oliver as a witness and all of the technical research Roberta was willing to put at his disposal, Eisen shouldn't have difficulty in making a criminal case against Mack Beranger.

Oliver came back into Roberta's office, showing his own face and shiny black scalp. He was obviously much more at ease.

"Okay, Oliver, I think we have a deal," Roberta announced. "You plead guilty to criminal facilitation and Mr. Eisen will ask the judge for no more than a three-year suspended sentence."

"That means I'll lose my job with the police department," Oliver said.

"That is likely the case, but isn't that better than serving time in prison for assault, a crime which you admitted to before we ever met?" Roberta looked at Oliver intently, hoping he wasn't having a change of heart.

"No, no, you're absolutely correct. I'll lose my job, but I'll also lose that chain around my neck that Mack was always pulling on. This is good."

"You'll also have to be a witness for the prosecution against Mack Beranger," Eisen said.

Roberta interjected, "Stuart, I assume you're going to charge Beranger with staging a crime for personal benefit and defrauding the justice system."

"Yes, that's what it will likely come down to. I'm going to have to do a lot of work on this one; I doubt there's much case law I can use as a starting point," Eisen responded. Then, turning back to Oliver, he asked, "Mr. Franklin, do you agree to be a witness for the prosecution of your old partner?"

"With pleasure. By the way, what's going to happen to Mr.

Steinman?" Oliver asked. "I sort of know what it's like to be him; I could feel your judgment when you thought I was him. It would be terrible to feel that way, especially if you hadn't done the thing you were being accused of doing."

Eisen explained, "Ms. Marshall is going to give me all the technical information and other evidence she has amassed, and I'm going to ask the judge to dismiss all charges against Mr. Steinman. That reminds me; I'd like to get that mask from you."

With a more calm and relaxed Oliver Franklin sitting across from him, Stuart Eisen felt he'd made the right decision for all concerned.

30

"You know anybody in Canada?" Allen asked as he put a stack of mailed advertisements on the kitchen table.

"Not that I can think of. Why do you ask?" Sarah replied, taking dishes out of the dishwasher.

"Well, there's an envelope here without a return address, but it's postmarked British Columbia and your name and address are handwritten on it."

"Well, go ahead and open it; it's probably some tourism ad."

Allen tore open the envelope and pulled out a folded piece of beige lined notepaper. "Nope, it's just a short note. Sis, you better get a grip on that counter; it looks like it's from Dad."

It had been more than six months since the escape, and after all the initial anxiety brought on by the subsequent investigation, all was quiet and had returned to normal. No warrant had been issued to search the computers and phones in their home, and Sarah could only guess that her comment to Kleib about the potential liability for London Tower had made an impact. There really was a risk that London Tower would be found negligent if they dug too deep into their software design and firewall protections.

No one except Sarah, Allen, Alex, and Mykola knew what had happened, and they'd covered their trail as thoroughly as possible. And, with all the other prisoners who'd attempted to escape, guards who might have had an incentive to cause the riot, and London Tower executives who had more interest in corporate profits than an impenetrable AI system, there were countless avenues of investigation. Yet no one had identified any one individual or group responsible. The New California and Arizona Departments of Correction had ultimately issued a joint statement that said the computer system had been hacked but that they could not identify the source; it could well have originated offshore.

Neither Sarah nor Allen knew this, but Allen's hack that had produced random Level 2 jolts to 15 inmates had probably saved the day. Without it the focus of the investigation would have centered on Alex's escape, and given enough time, a crack in their cover-up would likely have been found.

Since the escape, though, they had not heard from their father, and because there was still a possibility that someone was tracking them and any efforts they might make to contact him, they had agreed not to do so much as an online name search.

"Well, don't keep me in suspense. Read it!"

"Okay, here goes: 'Hi, it's been a while since I've heard from you. Hope you're doing well. I certainly am. I'm now living on a ketch moored in the harbor town not far from where my grandparents grew up nearly 100 years ago. It would be great to see you. Why don't you come up sometime?' It's signed 'Valerie.'"

"Valerie? That's Mom's name. You're sure it's from Dad?"

"Handwriting sure looks like Dad's."

"Why would he sign Mom's name, then?" Sarah was wary; was this some sort of government agency's low-tech effort to entrap them?

"Well, he says he's living on a sailboat, but he doesn't give its exact location or its name. My guess is that he named it after Mom."

"More secret agent stuff from our childhood," Sarah sighed.

"Sure, but we don't have to leave the house to check out my hunch. What was the name of that small town Dad told us about, where his grandparents grew up?"

"Nanaimo, I'm pretty sure."

Allen scampered into the playroom and ran the system security scan package Sarah had borrowed from ZG. When it found no threats, he called up a map of British Columbia. "Found it. Better yet, Nanaimo has a harbor cam. You can see all the boats that go in and out of the harbor."

Sarah walked into the playroom and looked at the image projected on the big screen. "That might be it," she said, pointing to a two-masted boat. "But I can't make out the name."

Allen looked at the boat Sarah was pointing to and immediately corrected her. "No, that can't be Dad's boat. He said he had a ketch, and that's a yawl. All those years of college and you didn't learn the difference? What a waste."

Sarah knew Allen was just teasing, but there was a bit of his typical one-upmanship in the comment too.

"Okay, just let this run and perhaps we'll see his boat. I've got to go to work."

Allen kept the link to the Nanaimo harbor cam running for the next couple of days and finally saw a ketch heading out of the harbor. The boat's name was *Carmine*, not *Valerie*, and yet the gray-bearded man at the helm looked quite a bit like his father. No harm in printing a screen capture, he figured. He put the color print on the kitchen counter and continued to watch the harbor cam feed.

"I haven't seen a lot of ketches going into or out of the harbor," Allen said to Sarah as soon as she walked into the kitchen later that day, "but take a look at this picture. It kind of looks like Dad steering the boat."

Sarah looked at the photo and immediately broke into a broad smile.

"The only problem is the name of the boat. I thought it would be *Valerie* or something else we might recognize." Allen couldn't understand why his sister seemed so happy.

"It is," Sarah said. "You probably don't remember this, but Dad would affectionately call Mom 'Carmine,' especially if he wanted something from her. It was a reference to her red hair."

Allen and Sarah were on their way to see their father the next day.

⊙

Roberta's morning had been brutal, beginning with a panicked call from a client she was representing in a contested divorce. The client had discovered that the assets held in a joint account weren't nearly as much as her husband had led her to believe in all the years they'd been married. After nearly an hour of trying to calm the client down, Roberta had to end the conversation so that she could attend the deposition of another client, who was contesting a civil case of plagiarism. A snarl of traffic on the way—and her self-driving car, which seemed to be in the mood for an out-of-the-way, leisurely joyride along the beach—made her a half hour late.

When she'd finally concluded the deposition and was ready to return to her office, a message on her car's communications screen had said she'd been issued a parking violation. Apparently when her car had stopped to let her off at the other attorney's office, it had assumed she'd be right back out . . . and hadn't moved out of the loading and unloading zone.

It was near noon when Roberta opened the door to the law firm offices. The receptionist, who could see she was frazzled, courteously told her a large package for her had arrived and been placed in her office. Roberta had no idea what it might be; she seldom ordered anything delivered to the office. Hopefully it wasn't another crisis that would throw her afternoon schedule into the wastebasket.

The box, weighing about 15 pounds, was marked "Rush— Perishable." Roberta noted it had been sent from Wyoming. The only person she knew there was Mykola Steinman.

It had been several months since the prosecuting attorney had decided to withdraw the aggravated assault charges against Mykola. Roberta had helped Mykola sell his portion of the furniture refinishing and repair business to his partner, but other than a lunch before he'd moved to Wyoming, there had been little more than some email updates.

Roberta opened the box, and immediately a mix of fresh fruit and vegetable aromas wafted up. For an instant Roberta had a feeling of being in a garden. In the box were Granny Smith and McIntosh apples, a couple of Bosc pears, zucchini and yellow squash, an orange bell pepper, radicchio, blue pearl onions, and a container of what appeared to be salad dressing. A couple of sealed plastic bags had fresh dill, thyme, and oregano in them.

Roberta opened the envelope and took out the card. Holding it up to her nose, she inhaled the fragrance of fresh, unwashed chocolate mint. "Perfume for a farmer," she said quietly and smiled. She read the note:

Dear Roberta,

I've settled in, and though I got a late start on the growing season, I still got a nice crop of vegetables. Perhaps you recall that I intended to celebrate freedom with a meal among friends, made from the freshest foods I could grow or find locally. The celebration of freedom is going to happen this Sunday evening. Since you and your firm made my freedom a reality, I'd love to have you join me. However, I also realize that flying a thousand miles for a dinner isn't logical. So I am sending this box of fruits and vegetables, fresh from my garden, so that you might enjoy the meal in the comfort of your home. I've enclosed my recipes and underlined all of the other ingredients needed to prepare them.

Thanks again for making this possible,
Mykola

Roberta set the card down, reached into the box, and took out the biggest and shiniest McIntosh apple. Biting into it and relishing its sweet crispness, she thought, "Why not?" A trail of juice running down one side of her chin, she checked her calendar for the next three days: no work that couldn't be pushed off a day or two, no social commitments. A couple of clicks on her cell phone and she had booked a trip to Casper, Wyoming, that afternoon.

ACKNOWLEDGMENTS

Collared went through several versions before it was deemed publication-worthy. Along the way, many people provided encouragement and suggestions to make it a better story.

Les Abramson, a law professor at the University of Louisville, gave suggestions that connected future legal issues with current legal practice.

Kathy Eigelbach, a retired police officer, provided insight into correctional practices.

Others, including Trina Dorwart, Michele Hubler, Bob and Peggy Meyer, Mary Klemp, Art Hoffman, Fran Sapienza, Ken and Nancy Martin, Carl and Ruth Kline, and Eileen Perry Steenberg, provided helpful feedback on specific chapters or overall flow.

Sarah Jane Herbener added much-needed polish to the story with a detailed edit of every line, noting inconsistencies and providing an understanding of how readers might react to key elements in the plot.

Thanks to all.

Made in the USA
Las Vegas, NV
31 October 2021